GH

OF THE

ABBEY

GHOSTS

OF THE

ABBEY

ASHLEY
WELLMAN & PATRICK
KINKADE

A NOVEL

atmosphere press

Published by Atmosphere Press

Cover design by Matthew Fielder

Atmospherepress.com

For my brother, Gerrad, who shared my first adventures, is always good for a laugh, and was so busy getting into mischief it allowed me to get away with everything.

For my sister, Kate, who has always been there for me with a hug, word of encouragement, and cover story to keep me out of trouble.

TABLE OF CONTENTS

PROLOGUE

(Present Day – London, Westminster Abbey)

IT WAS A cold winter's day as the wind blew hard against the grey stone of the old abbey. The magnificent edifice solidly stood as silent sentinel seeming to be untouched by time or the elements. It is known by mortal man that Westminster had its beginnings over a thousand years earlier, but the truth is it was destined to be long before that. The old church sat atop hallowed ground, a point of transition between the here and now and the afterworlds beyond. In a universe of gods and fates, Westminster Abbey was always meant to be. But many now feared that what had been so steadfast was weakening, that the fabric in reality was changing. The ghosts of the abbey were perhaps the most keenly aware of the undeniable shift, and thus, they felt a call to act.

The dim glow of a candelabra barely illuminated the ominous chamber. In the faint light, the head of a man could be seen carefully folded over his journal. He scanned its pages methodically, pausing at moments to scribble a quick note before he'd turn the next page. The quiet air was palpable with an intense worry that swirled around him.

The silence was interrupted by a winded exclamation. "We are running out of time! Please tell me you've found something, Dickens!"

Charles Dickens barely looked up from the pages before him. "I am afraid I have not."

"And I am afraid you are lost to the urgency that we are facing," Charles Darwin barked with disdain.

"I am lost to nothing, Darwin. Do not come into this room with such foolishness and disrespect." Dickens was now fully attentive and shaken by the tone in the scientist's voice. He paused as not to engage in Darwin's hostility. "I have done as you asked and will continue to do so until we find our answer, but I cannot simply concoct a solution. I have hunted feverishly through my notes and agonized over the details of my intimate conversation with Nostradamus, and, still, I have no more clarity. There is nothing new to know."

"He is an old fool...We both know Nostradamus was useless as was the information he left behind."

"Not useless," replied Dickens. "He gave us what he could, and while not specific, there is much insight and guidance in what he shared. He, himself, did not often understand his own visions. But, because of Nostradamus, we know that horror and disaster is coming."

"Indeed..." scoffed the naturalist.

"Yet," the author raised an eyebrow at this companion and drew out his opening word to silence any more of Darwin's acrimonious concern. "The seer also noted that there is a way to counteract the damage."

"The vessels?" Darwin muttered questioningly.

"Correct, dear friend, 'the vessels.' Before crossing over, Nostradamus predicted that as catastrophic damage looms, human vessels will be made apparent to aid in the fight against evil. These vessels will be able to help us define our own responsibility in the cataclysm to come and deliver us to where we must be to combat the darkness. I am haunted by his warning, Charles."

"Dickens, please." Darwin held up his hand as if to silence his companion.

"No. Let me speak," the author pushed on. "It is heavy on my heart and shall always be. Nostradamus warned that the vessels will be at grave risk when they arrive. Rarely has he been clearer. He saw in his vision that while these vessels carry with them unmatched hope, they will also be targets of whatever evil there is to come. The goal of darkness will be to decimate them."

Darwin shook his head less out of disappointment than of frustration. "I have not the time to concern myself with the fragility of the vessels. We are not even sure what they will carry. And in any event, if Nostradamus is right, the cost to the vessels will be far less than the damage they prevent. Even unto their deaths."

"That is not the issue," Dickens rebutted. "I am not comfortable asking our fellow spirits to unknowingly aid in a plan with such consequence. They have a right to know the full scope of the danger to all and the consequence of failure."

"Do you think they aren't aware there are risks? We are all concerned, but I will not have them distracted by potential dangers that are as of yet simply a fiction suggested by a witcher to his acolyte. Nostradamus did not say the vessels would be destroyed. He said that they were at risk. So, we create the best plan of attack to minimize costs to both ourselves and our allies, but the priority will be to prevent evil's spread, no matter the sacrifice. We have no choice but to use the vessels if and when they come to try and halt the wave of devastation that is sure to follow. So, let me repeat, you will not tell the others of this ominous prediction. Are we clear on that?"

Dickens did not respond. Instead, he stared off as if contemplating his reaction.

Darwin lowered his voice and said, "Need I remind you of what has already happened in our time here in the abbey? Perhaps I should recount the great plague, the great smog, the great fire, or the floods. Or better yet, if natural disasters don't justify our work to you, let us reflect on the unprecedented havoc of terrorist attacks and the heinous murders of mortal leaders. Maybe I could count for you the souls that have crossed our path as a result of our inability—or, is it our unwillingness—to act? We sit here doddering while evil grows. With or without the vessels, if we do nothing, we become complicit in the dark tide that is rising."

"Enough, Darwin. I need not be told of current events nor be reminded of the history we are trying to halt. I am very well aware of what is happening. Your constant, domineering pressure will not expedite my progress. I've been nothing but relentless in my search. I am confident that what we have already learned will prove fruitful." The author took a deep breath to regain his composure. "I just need more time, and we will find out more."

"We do not have time. That is the point, Dickens!" Darwin shouted in frustration. He softened the tone of his voice as he almost whispered a warning to himself. "There is no more time."

Dickens placed his head into his hands, resting his palms against his temples. He slowly slid his hands together, having them meet as they covered his mouth and nose. His eyes were closed as he contemplated the magnitude of the situation. Gently shaking his head back and forth with a sense of vulnerability, he sat still and silent. After a few deep breaths to calm his thoughts, he lowered his hands to his lap, composed his ever-racing mind, and raised his face towards Darwin. "We have little to do but wait and pray that the vessels arrive before it is too late."

"Well then, you better start praying, Dickens," mocked Darwin. "You better start begging your God to give you a sign of where we go from here. I fear that if these vessels do not make themselves known soon, we will be defenseless, and our time here will have been for naught. I did not stay behind to sit back and watch horror unfold and the earthly plane of mortals end."

Without another word, the ghost of Charles Darwin

stormed out of the chamber. The spirit of Charles Dickens grimily turned to the next page of his journal.

+ + +

In a small fishing village located on the northernmost coast of the Isle of Man in England, a community elder looked down into his augury bowl and gasped.

A young man rushed into the room and broke the silence of the day. "It is happening. We can wait no longer."

The old man looked up at the intruder and closed his eyes, hoping for one last moment of peace.

CHAPTER 1 | A Haunted Tour

(Present Day – London)

THE BOYS OF the Westminster Choir School boarded a red double-decker bus and headed from the abbey towards the Tower of London. Each looked like a carbon copy of the other, dressed from head to toe in their uniforms, which consisted of a burgundy blazer adorned with the Westminster seal, a grey dress shirt, black dress shorts, and shiny black wing-tipped shoes, only made comfortable by the thick knee-high grey and burgundy socks that hugged their legs and feet. Their clothes were so perfectly pressed and their shoes so sparkling you would think they were heading to the queen's palace for an afternoon tea.

For the past month, the students had been learning about the old fortress, which at one time housed royalty before it turned into a prison so infamous that it was often referred to as the "bloody tower." Today, the historical landmark stands as a tourist attraction, supposedly haunted by the specters of the prisoners and notorious villains somehow still held captive by its cold stonewalls even after death. Indeed, prior to the field trip, the boys filled the quiet of their abbey dormitory with terrifying ghost stories, tall tales, and secret wishes to see an ethereal being as they toured the tower.

William Darlington, just turning eight, and his older

brother, Thomas, now fully twelve, had paid particular attention to the stories of spirits that haunt the tower. For them, it was not at all a far stretch of the imagination that a ghost world existed just beyond their own. As young boys, they had both seen and interacted with ghosts that lived near their home. Their earliest encounter was with the shade of a young boy who had died in their house many decades before. The child ghost became a regular visitor, talking, playing, and teasing with Thomas and William before and after school. Originally, chalking it up to an imaginary friend, their parents didn't seem to pay any attention to the boys as they shouted out to no one, shadowboxed the air, or ran from nothing. It wasn't until the spirit became a normal fixture in everyday activities that the Darlington adults were concerned at all. When asked about their "imaginary friend," the boys were quick to correct their mother. "He's not imaginary. He is a ghost, mama," William would argue.

"There is no such thing as ghosts," their mother would reply, and their father would chime in, "You know we don't like it when you boys fib." Insistent that they were not lying and set on the fact that they talked to, could see, and cared for a ghost, the boys found themselves in front of a psychiatrist who chalked their behavior up to vivid imaginations and a priest who told the parents if the outbursts continued to consider a spiritual cleansing of the house. To protect their ghostly friend and avoid more "appointments" to evaluate their mental health, the boys learned to distance themselves from the spirit that they so easily saw and with whom they bonded. In time, the lad's ghostly visits became less and less, and the clarity of all spirits began to fade. It had been so long since either boy had been visited by an otherworldly guest that they had nearly forgotten what it was like to be connected to that separate reality. In fact, Thomas and William had spent the past few years wishing their ability to communicate with spirits would return. It would allow them another chance to be with their parents, who had died tragically in a car crash several years before. It was nearly a year later, after their loss and some time in foster care, that a local priest had recognized their pitch-perfect voices, and thus provided them a home as students at the choir school.

The bus pulled into the iron gates decorated with the tower emblem. A once dominating structure of royalty, war, and imprisonment, it now appeared less daunting given the signage and tourist markings that hung from its walls. Parking alongside a guard shack, the students eagerly peered out the left side of the bus, looking at the worn granite walls that created the historic fortress. The scheduled tours attracted thousands of people daily, and a long line had already formed as tickets were checked and visitors were permitted into the tower. Luckily, the students were granted group access when they arrived, thus avoiding the dreaded wait.

As the brakes screeched the bus to a stop, its folding door opened, and the boys flooded out of the vehicle like soldiers storming the beaches of Normandy. Headmaster Rattlebag raised his voice as he shouted reminders to the boys, "No running. No pushing. No fighting. Remember to stay with your partners. You will have exactly three hours to explore the tower before meeting me in the courtyard. Please remember, you represent the abbey." Thankfully, he had recited these rules prior to and during the bus ride as well because he may as well have been invisible given the students' eager entrance into the tower yards.

Once inside, the boys ran through the halls, their dress shoes clapping against the stone floors. They would only slow their sprints to a stroll and pause their boisterous noise as they passed one of the guards. As soon as they were out of the sightline of those stoic rule followers, however, they would resume their play. One group of older boys decided to try to scare younger students with ghostly cries and startling screams. Soon, almost all were attempting to reenact the stories of the tower haunts they had shared at the abbey. James, always the class clown, seemed to particularly relish the role of instigator. Burt, the most mature of the group, tried to redirect the energy of the older boys, but Nigel, the school's biggest blabbermouth, had already run off to find Headmaster Rattlebag to tell on the boys who were misbehaving and hopefully gain his professor's favor.

William and Thomas had agreed before their arrival that it would truly be a better use of their time to avoid all the horseplay and study the tower. Both were fascinated with the history, the monarchy, and the architecture of the castle and the mystery and horror it contained as it turned into a prison. To maximize the limited time they had there, they obtained an old guidebook and carefully planned which rooms and sites they wanted to see, leaving little time to waste on the pranks and games of hide-and-seek that many of their classmates were enjoying. Beyond that, both knew that spirits were no laughing matter and that mocking the dead would only lead to problems. As the other choirboys roamed the tower, breaking every rule that the headmaster had forcefully defined, the two brothers learned the layout of the castle. From the tattered map in his pocket, William directed Thomas towards the ravens which lived at the tower. The brothers had agreed this would be the first stop of their whirlwind tour.

Arriving at the bird keep, Thomas read aloud from the tour book. "Once viewed as a nuisance, the ravens have now become a staple at the Tower of London. Folklore has it that the resident birds were a distraction to an astronomer who was attempting to study the stars, only to then have the ravens obstruct the view from his telescope. Others claimed the king could not sleep when the ravens would squawk and scream. Regardless of the story to which one subscribes, when there was a plea to remove all ravens from the castle because of the problems they caused, there also came an ominous warning: if the tower ravens fall, so would the Kingdom of England. No one knew exactly where that notion had come from, but with it, the ravens had evolved from hated birds to a veritable tower staple. Eight ravens currently serve at the castle and an entire graveyard is dedicated to the black creatures."

Standing at the avian burial site, William and Thomas studied the ravens' tombstones, reading off the names and exploring the dates each bird met its dreadful fate. Several of the names made them laugh, and, in their amusement, they did not attend to the imposing shadow being cast over them. The tower's Ravenmaster and keeper of the birds snuck up behind the boys while they talked. "Did you know that our ravens eat bird biscuits soaked in blood? It's likely the 'red' of little boys who mock them," he scolded. The boys stood upright, embarrassed and shaken. The man now standing before them was a character fit for the role he held. He was a large fellow and dressed in a traditional guard uniform that somehow looked ominous as opposed to regal in his wearing. He had wild grey hair that slipped from under his hat and one cocked-eye that stared off at an unnatural angle. His nose was rounded to a bulb and his hands were thick and calloused enough to break chestnuts with a single squeeze. He looked the boys up and down. "The raven will snatch your soul if you find yourself doing wrongly, young masters, and take your spirit straight here." The odd man laughed to himself softly. He looked back down at the boys as if he were seeing them for the first time. He scoffed. "Be careful and be gone, less I loose the birds on you." The Ravenmaster's voice took on an ominous tone.

William needed no further prompting and pulled at Thomas' sleeve. "Hurry up. I want to see the Crown Jewels." The two turned from the odd keeper and briskly walked away. William glanced back only once to check on the strange fellow, in fear that he would be following. Both the man and all the birds he tended remained eerily still, but William would have sworn that all were staring directly at him. A chill ran down his back and he walked faster to keep up with his older brother.

From what Thomas and William had learned, the Jewel House was home to the English crowns and various other artifacts of the monarchy, ranging from robes and swords to jewelry and powerful, royal symbols, all encrusted with precious stones. On arrival at their destination, the two found the displays heavily watched to protect the valuable collection inside. They were almost intimidated by how many guards were present upon their approach. But even beyond the opulence and the security, as they walked into the main vault through its entrance archway, they both could feel a unique energy in the room. Experiencing the history and tradition represented there was almost electric. Its contents seemed to take viewers on a tour through time. Clothing and personal items from each lineage of English rulers and their families were displayed. It all emanated mystery and mystique. Being there made the boys daydream about who wore these clothes, how heavy the crown must have been on its wearers' heads, and how the English queens must have had a field day selecting which massive piece of jewelry they would use to accessorize their strolls through the royal gardens.

As time and their musings passed, Thomas and William eventually found themselves standing in front of a cross adorned with rubies, sapphires, and emeralds. It was then that it happened. While reading the plaque that detailed the purpose of the encased object before them, out of nowhere and yet seemingly from everywhere, an intense bolt of energy surged through William, who had his arm draped over Thomas' shoulder. As his brother's body fully stiffened, Thomas jerked as the almost kinetic shock traveled from William's arm into his own body. "Bloody hell!" screamed Thomas.

"Quiet!" instructed the guard closest to him.

"Sorry," William noted sheepishly, looking at the official's face. "You ok?" he asked Thomas while shaking off his own jolting experience.

It took Thomas a second to regain his composure. He shook his arms and legs and looked at William. "Cool," he said as if he was impressed with the event but intending to affirm his well-being. "That was so weird. Do you think it was a short in the power system?"

"If that's what you want to call it," replied William. "Whatever it was, let's get out of here before the guard turns us into Headmaster Rattlebag for noise violations or we get shocked unconscious." The brothers exited the jewel vault and headed towards the anteroom. They were surprised to find it empty, as the tower was buzzing with tourists. Still, there was not much to see in there, except for some furniture, though it was far fancier and bigger than that which they had back in the abbey. Standing still while glancing about room, William startled as he spotted two other boys emerge from a corner where there had clearly been no one just seconds earlier. He only first saw them in his peripheral vison, but it did not seem like they came in from behind him. Rather, it appeared to Will that the two new visitors had just appeared and walked straight through a blank stonewall. William blinked his eyes to clear his vision. He looked again, and the two boys were still there, only closer. Their relative size and ages seemed to match him and his brother. But, after those initial observations, the similarities stopped. They were translucent and their coloring took on muted hues. Their clothes were elaborate, from a period that looked far from the present. Their hair was cut long, and William noted the loose fit of the billowing shirts that adorned their chests. Their pants were fitted tightly and carefully slid into riding boots fastened with what appeared to be metal buckles. But most apparently, they both seemed incredibly curious about William and his brother.

"Do you suppose they are the ones that caused the tower to surge?" asked the smaller figure to the other while William stood looking.

"What did you say?" asked Thomas as he closed the tour book and turned towards the voice. He assumed his brother was asking him about some classmates approaching the room. With Thomas' complete and focused attention, all four boys froze. William shot his brother a perplexed look and quietly asked, "You can hear them? Can you see them, too?" Thomas and William looked at each other and then simply stared at the two other boys.

"Can you see us?" asked the taller of the boys staring back at Thomas and almost echoing William. All four stood silent as apprehension grew. William and Thomas both independently recalled their parents warning about engaging with spirits, which these two standing before them most assuredly were. William was further certain that if he and his brother were to admit to anyone that they could once again hear and see ghosts, they would be taken from school immediately and sent away to the looney bin.

"Our parents always told us not to talk to ghosts," mused Thomas. He remembered the trouble they had when they were younger. "But then again, they aren't here anymore." The cold in his voice as he blankly stated that fact and sad reality suggested the trauma he felt at the loss of his mother and father had not yet fully dissipated.

The ghost boys' shoulders dropped, and the tension seemed to fade as the smaller spirit said in a most quizzical manner, "Edward, I think they can see us."

"Quiet, Rake," said Edward.

William's voice cracked as he immediately responded, "We can see you. We can hear you, too."

The spirits seemed surprised and hesitant. After a moment, the smaller of the two excitedly exclaimed, "We've been waiting for centuries to find mortals who will help us. You will help us, won't you? Are you Templars? You seem so young? Has the Order come back? Will we be able to leave?"

Rake reached forward to try and touch William.

"Help with what? What is a Templar? And you can leave right now as far as I am concerned!" piped up William, stepping back. There was a hesitance in his voice. He wasn't sure he wanted a ghost touching him just yet.

Thomas shook his head at his brother's dismissal. He wasn't ready for this conversation to end nor for the ghosts to go. Offering what he felt might be assurance, he cleared his throat. "Ahem. Yeah, you don't want his help. Will barely knows how to tie his own shoes," Thomas cracked as he pointed his thumb at his younger brother.

"Shut up!" William said as he punched his older brother in the arm.

The taller ghost boy seemed less than impressed with the two mortals who were acting decidedly un-regal in comparison to how he felt he and Rake were comporting themselves. Through his mild disdain, however, Edward knew the importance of this sudden meeting and needed to intently talk with these two, no matter their behavior. He stared the mortal boys into quiet. Leaning forward, he whispered, "Evil resides here. We've been stuck in the tower for more years than I can recall, hiding and trying to escape the darkness that haunts this place." William and Thomas looked at each other with concern and the beginnings of fear. "You see," the ghost continued, "Since our father and king died, the good souls of the tower have been trapped here with the evil."

"Wait! Are you the tower's two ghost princes?" asked William excitedly, almost disregarding what else had just been said.

With William's words, Rake's head immediately dropped. The idea of being a ghost was still hard for him to accept even after all these years. Edward appeared to try to touch his brother in consolation.

William recognized that what he had said upset the two ghosts and so quickly added, "I just mean you are royalty, and it is an honor to meet you. You are the sons of Edward IV, correct?"

"Why yes. I am Prince Edward, and this is my younger brother, Prince Richard. I call him Rake." Edward nodded to William, recognizing the boy's attempt to make up for his earlier stated indiscretion.

Thomas looked at William in surprise. "I read about them in the tour book," William offered.

Edward raised an eyebrow at both but continued to talk with a sense of urgency. "We are unable to cross through the outside walls into the mortal realm beyond this place or find our way to Arcadia in the afterworld. We cannot locate the key to get out and have long hoped the Templars would return to help us find it."

"Key? What key?" asked Thomas, who had now composed himself and taken on a more serious demeanor. He left the issue of "Arcadia and Templars" for later conversation and attempted to focus on what he could understand and recognize.

"The key that will open the tower!" said the smaller of the ghosts. Then he added with a tone of remorse, "But we aren't even sure what it really is."

"Well, that's a problem. How are we supposed to help you find something you don't know anything about?" asked Thomas with a note of incredulity in his voice.

"Our father told us that the key was hidden here and that it was more powerful than the kingdom itself. None of the good souls trapped here have any information to offer about it," said Edward. "And those here who are bad would certainly not share anything with us. What they know, they would only reveal to him."

"Him?" asked Thomas. He did not like the sound of that.

"An evil presence who has grown more violent of late," said Rake, hoping to inspire understanding after seeing the confusion on the mortal boys' faces. "No ghost can leave without the key. We need to find it or we are doomed to stay with him." Then he added emphatically, "Please help us. You are special, you can see us, and you may be the only ones who can." The statement of the smaller ghost had turned into a plea.

"Westminster Boys' Choir School: This is your final call for boarding the bus. Again, final call." The announcement gave both Thomas and William a start. If they were not back on the bus immediately, they would not only be confined to the dormitory and have a late dinner, but they would also lose free time for an entire month. "There are plenty of chores around the abbey to be done by tardy boys!" Headmaster Rattlebag had huffed during his warning. This was a stiff penalty for Thomas because food was his life, but more important for William, who went near mad when he couldn't get outdoors and escape the rigor of the boarding school's strict schedule.

"We have to go!" exclaimed Thomas. "I can't face a 'dorm' dinner."

Slight panic came across the ghost boys' faces, who looked to William, noting his hesitancy to leave and hoping he would prove to be an ally. "You don't understand. No one has seen us in hundreds of years. If you leave, we lose the chance to find the key. We need you."

"You don't understand. If we are late, we are going to starve and will miss out on an entire month of kickball and exploring the city." Thomas forcibly turned William to rush to the bus but stopped in further thought after seeing the desperation on the ghosts' faces. "But I promise we will come back. I PROMISE. Just give us a few days to figure out how to do it," he offered.

The two ghost boys looked defeated but nodded their acknowledgment. The larger encouraged, "Go, but don't forget us! I don't know how much longer we can go on. The evil here is strengthening."

"We will be back. Promise," concurred William. As he

pushed Thomas, the brothers rushed towards the exit. They had to run back down corridors, through the yards, and beyond the gates to get to out to where the bus was waiting.

As they passed through the tower, there seemed to be whispers flowing up from behind them. "Do they know?" "They can see." "Oh, he is going to have fun with these little ones." "One step closer to crossing over." "Hush, these mortals won't help us." Different voices called out.

As the boys glanced over their shoulders, a small gathering of new ghosts had formed behind them and seemed to be floating in their direction. Unnerved, the boys focused on the light that surrounded the door marking their last exit. Still, and even while attempting to ignore the sounds, William couldn't help but see what was unfolding. Translucent figures with strong radiant glows were coming out of doorways, gliding through walls, and descending from the ceiling. The small gathering at the start of the boys' run had grown into a parade of spirits and each had something to say about or to the mortals. "Help us!" "Save our souls." "Don't leave," some cried as others warned them of the dark realities that loomed. "He will kill you." "Run, boys!" "You cannot help us!" "Hell awaits."

Their quick pace became a full-on sprint as the cacophony of ghostly voices became an overwhelming, haunting howl, pushing them forward while pulling them back at the same time. As the door grew closer, the boys shielded their ears from the chaotic din and darted out of the building, directly onto the bus. Running up the narrow aisle, they dove into their seats.

"What's wrong with you two? See a ghost or something?" asked Nigel, smirking as he did when he told on the group to Rattlebag earlier in the day. Thomas and William's classmates erupted in laughter. "Enough," called the headmaster, waving his hand at the boys while motioning to the driver to start back toward the abbey. The late arrivers sank down in their seat, hoping for a quiet ride home and an opportunity to digest what they had just seen.

"Thomas, did you hear that?" asked William in a near panic. "The ghosts warned that 'he' would kill us!"

"And," asked Thomas softly, "what was that whistle?"

William sat wide-eyed almost tearing, and quietly nodded. "I heard that too, it seemed to want me to stay."

"I know," whispered Thomas, hoping to soothe his younger brother. "I felt it."

"And Thomas?" William's voice became almost inaudible. "I felt myself wanting to."

CHAPTER 2 | The Ghosts of the Abbey

AS THE BUS pulled into the abbey, the boys were instructed to make their way to the dormitory to freshen up. Still perplexed by what they had just experienced at the tower, Thomas and William waited for their classmates to file off the bus before they made a beeline straight for the church. They both wanted a moment alone to talk about what they had seen and heard before they said anything to anyone.

As they opened the ornate wooden doors that led to the sanctuary and walked in, they felt small in the massive room. The High Altar's appearance matched its name; it was a large structure towards the back of the church, intricately carved into a host of golden figures and symbols, surrounded by the archways that comprised the backdrop to all church services. Chandeliers and candles carefully lit the podium. Behind it, a massive dome loomed high over the inlaid marble of the floor and stonework that adorned the walls up to its peak. Careful inspection of the rotunda revealed the delicate ivory carvings that covered the ceiling rose from both sides to meet in the middle and form into beams of gold. The marble floor was of a simpler design and provided a blank canvas on which all other ornamental accents could dance. Decorated screens and the tombs of history's renowned were thoughtfully placed around the sanctuary, adding both life to its feel and a recognition of its sense of the eternal. Colorful flags hung alongside hundreds of pipes overlaid with gold, which comprised the church organ that came alive during services and provided a background for the boys' choir. A confessional booth sat off to the side of the sanctuary, standing like a gothic cave. Dark wood formed the walls of the box and its hand-carved mantle ledge was decorated with delicate designs. A cross sat upon the top, serving as a beacon to those looking to cleanse their sins.

Just as the boys fully entered the building and began to pick a place for quiet conversation, they were again hit with a bolt of energy. It was the same as they had felt in the tower, except this time it was prolonged and almost seemed to lift them from the floor of the abbey. The brothers would have screamed if they had the capacity, but whatever held them strangled their voices inside. Then it left them, just as suddenly and without warning or reason. Their minds reeled and their senses heightened. It felt like an awakening.

"Thomas," stated William hesitantly, still trying to regain his bearings, "Something is happening. Look!" He was pointing out to the abbey in no particular direction. A cold rush came over the boys, and then their world changed. The abbey they knew still existed, but it was also new, different, and wonderful. Where a vast space had simply existed between the pews and the expanse to the ceiling, an intricate series of walkways suddenly appeared. An eerie overlay of sidewalks, passages, and trails were illuminated like a maze above the pews. Blue lights lined the paths and created a three-dimensional world with access points, tunnels, and seating for souls needing to rest. The benches seemed little used, however, as a bustle of thousands of spirits were rushing along the promenades fully engaged with each other and seemingly also where they needed to go. They moved with purpose when entering the church and dispersed in assorted directions. The ghosts moved both through and around the mortals who also occupied the space but who took no notice of the ethereal world around them. A large number of spirits made their way straight for the confessional booth by William and Thomas and abruptly disappeared though its door, each nodding to a uniformed man who stood by it and seemed to be a keeper for the egress. Martlets flew about the opening chirping their approval for each soul who walked in and on to whatever lay beyond. A grand station had opened in the abbey apparently for the exclusive use of ghosts, and the booth was seemingly one of its major exits and attractions.

The boys stood and stared, their eyes wide and their mouths open.

"It's amazing," Thomas said, even if only to himself. "Not even the shopping arcade at Kings Cross Train Station is as grand."

"Thomas?" William was trying to get his older brother's attention. "Is this real? Are you seeing what I'm seeing?"

"I am not sure what you're seeing, Will, but if it is half of what I am looking at, you can be assured we've both gone daft!" Thomas replied.

Yet, in all the hustle and chaos of this newly opened world, the boys both noted one spirit that did not seem to be in any hurry to navigate the crowds that were roaming about the abbey or even to take much notice that they were there. Instead, he sat upon the confessional's ledge, with one leg propped up, allowing him to lean against it with his elbow and another leg dangling over the edge to steady himself. He wore a velvety sage green robe with a white billowing shirt and scarf at his neck. His hair was a tightly curled powdered wig that was perfectly parted down the middle with significant volume of the quaff framing his face. His nose was long and thin and almost seemed to touch his delicately puckered lips. He appeared distracted as he threw what seemed a translucent red apple up and down in rhythm, watching as it rose and fell into the palm of his hand. A sign below his perch oddly read 'Highway to Heaven,' and, even stranger, there seemed to be the sound of motorcars coming from inside. Still, unlike all the others who the boys were seeing, he seemed utterly disengaged from purpose and idling without direction.

"Sir?" The boys called in unison to the top of the confessional. "Sir, can you help us?"

The ghost continued to toss his apple, and as they got closer, they noticed he was seeming to converse with himself to pass the time. Perhaps he hadn't heard them. "Sir?" they asked again, this time standing in direct view of the figure. As the apple flew from his hand, he snatched it in midair and froze. Careful to still himself like a statue, the figure looked down at the boys. He made eye contact and seemed startled when they both asked again, "Can you help us?"

Very quietly, the ghost, still frozen, barely moved his lips as he muttered, "Can you see me?"

At this point, it seemed like an obvious reality to both Thomas and William. They could not only see the odd fellow in front of them, but they were fully aware that the sanctuary was buzzing with ghosts all around them. "Yes, sir. We can see you." Thomas took the lead to answer.

The ghost leaped to the top of the confessional, sucked in his stomach, and stood as erect as possible. "Can you see you me now?" he grunted, trying not to breathe.

"Yep," the boys again replied together.

He collapsed to the top of the confessional, lying on his belly, and sank slightly into the wood. "What about now?"

"Still see you," they repeated.

He floated above the boys and twisted his body into a pretzel-like shape. "Can you see me now?"

The boys looked at each other and grinned. "Yes, we see you."

In a final attempt to allude the boys, he drifted down to the floor, covered his eyes with one hand, and threw his robe around his body, mimicking Dracula. "Surely, I have disappeared."

"No, sir. We still see you just fine, and we need your help!"

For several moments, the three stared at each other not speaking, the ghost tapping his finger against his chin. "Hmmmm," he eventually intoned while looking puzzled and continuing to tap. Then suddenly, as if pushing aside all consideration, his figure popped straight up as if to point toward the sky. "Euuuuureka!! It's happening!" shouted the spectral man. He approached the boys and began walking in very fast circles around them. "What to do? What to do? What to do?" he muttered to himself. His gait was frenetic until he pulled up quickly and stood stiffly again with a single finger pointed up in the air as an idea struck him. "Why! I need to wake them all. Come along, you two!" And with that pronouncement and a tone of expectation, the man began to walk away from the boys with speed.

William and Thomas looked at each other and then at the rapidly disappearing ghost. "Excuse me, sir!" Thomas called after the fleeting spirit, "Who are you?"

The ghost again halted. "My boys," said the ghost, turning back to William and Thomas abruptly while almost sashaying toward them. He continued, "Do the schools of today teach you nothing?" The ghost stopped before them and cleared his throat. "I am Sir Isaac Newton," he offered with a foppish bow. "And despite what that exercising maladroit numerist Stephen Hawking suggests, I am the greatest mathematician the world has ever known!" Newton had popped back up from his curtsey and his voice got higher and louder in aggravation. "Of course, I am best remembered for discovering gravity which ironically now plays an insignificant role in my life as a ghost since what goes up doesn't have to come down in my world. Even with that, it was really my wonderful facility with numbers that earned me my full renown." Sir Isaac's voice was now fading as he seemed to consider that last point for a moment, and then he burst out, "Ha! Gravity! Let Hawking claim that!" Newton, it appeared, was now talking to everyone at once. The ghost clutched his chest as if he were wearing a necklace he didn't wish to lose and composed himself. "You two. I can't believe it. We've been waiting for centuries to reveal ourselves to mortals."

"Pleased to meet you, Mr. Newton," chimed the boys in tandem. "I am Thomas," "and I am William." The boys offered their names to the ghost in a manner they had rehearsed across many previous introductions. They stuck their hands out to shake.

The ghost raised an eyebrow at the mortals. "Sir Newton, please, and, if you would, kindly take a seat." He gestured to what appeared to be a bench. Retracting their hands, the boys followed the directive of their newfound host and walked toward the seat he had indicated. They turned to sit, promptly bent at the knees, and fell to the floor on the backside of their pressed trousers. "Hey!" they both cried with the sudden thump to the floor. They immediately scrambled to their feet.

"Gadzooks!" exclaimed Newton, in an expression of sincere surprise. Then, with a bit of humor in his voice, "The mortal body can be so cumbersome! Here now, boys. Sit there!" Newton led them to a church pew and pointed for them to take a seat.

As the boys sat, Newton continued excitedly, "We've long attempted to communicate with the mortal world. So few have the ability to sense us, and those who do often refuse to completely allow their hearts and minds to be open to our existence. We learned long ago that communication with mortals is near impossible. We speak but are not heard and anything we scribe most miraculously turns to gibberish for the living. Until you two arrived, I was sure I would never speak to a mortal again." He had started to pace back and forth, muttering under his breath as if he was again contemplating what to do with the boys and this newfound connection.

For their part, Thomas and William felt an urgency to tell

the ghost about the princes in the tower and their rather odd pleas for help to find a mysterious key. In sitting, however, they also had another opportunity to look around. In truth, the view melted the immediacy of that first concern. The scene in front of them fully opened their minds and sent their heads spinning. The jolts of energy that had shocked their bodies earlier had settled into a low tingle, but one that was constant and becoming a part of them.

The abbey did indeed look like some sort of grand ghost station, complete with eateries, shops, and offices of various sorts. Still, it also all felt very familiar, and through the translucent additions, it even looked the same with many recognizable features. But there was no denying that some things in the old church were wildly different. Its size seemed to have expanded, and large rooms appeared where none existed before. It was like one was looking at the historic building through some type of funhouse mirror. What appeared to be a diner on the left of the abbey's main sanctuary had a sign above it that identified the eatery as 'Phantasmal Foods' serving 'Bogy Burgers.' A line of ghosts stood outside, apparently awaiting a seat to eat at before moving on to whatever destination may await them. Oddly, the food they were eating had the same ethereal quality of the ghosts themselves: a bit translucent but with the same general look of what might exist in the mortal realm. On the other side of the abbey was a pub that was simply called 'Spirits.' There, as with the restaurant, was a line of ethereals waiting to get in though they were far more jovial in demeanor than those waiting for the diner. Thomas assumed it might be because of the featured drink, 'The Gravedigger,' that was advertised as "on special" on the outside wall. From the display of boisterous behavior, it may have been that the ghosts left outside had already had a few of those libations during their long wait to enter. However, of most interest, and sitting directly in front of them, was a singular signpost pointing to a large number of businesses and very important sounding bureaus, offices, and administrations. It gave sense to the size and nature of this great ghostly doppelganger of the physical abbey. One sign pointed to the 'Administration of Avalon,' and another to the 'Office of Elysium,' and yet a third to the 'Division of Valhalla.' Directional indicators to the 'Border Crossing of Jannah' and the 'Depot to Nirvana' finished off the top of the signpost while yet other more colorful pointers beneath mentioned a variety of businesses further inside the parish. A coffee store called 'Ghostly Grinds,' a clothier named 'RIP Robes,' and a convenience store named 'Seven to Heaven' all apparently were a short walk away. There was also the 'Happy Hunting Ground Armory' that offered 'The Largest Selection of Ghost Blades in the Station' and a certain 'Holmes Detective Agency,' with a slogan boasting 'Let us find who killed you! It's elementary.' William and Thomas sat transfixed in the moment.

"Boys. Boys. Boys." Newton clapped his hands, drawing their attention back to him. Both Thomas and William were a bit surprised they could hear a ghost clap, but they also clearly realized they had much to learn about this new world. "We really have no time to dawdle here!" continued the mathematician. To punctuate the pronouncement, Newton bit a piece of his apple he was still holding and threw the rest into a trashcan by the sign.

Thomas was confused. "But Mister Newto..." he began to ask.

The ghost cut Thomas short, "Sirrrrrrr!!!???" Isaac again implored that the older of the two mortal brothers use his given title.

"Sir," Thomas corrected himself as he pushed forward with his thought, trying to assert himself as leader of the little troop and protector of William. "Before we go any further, I have another question. Where are we now? What is this place?"

"Ah-ha!" exclaimed the ghost. "That was precisely *two* questions, not *one* as implied! Did you think the world's greatest mathematician would miscount questions?"

"Well," continued Thomas patiently, "No, I guess not. Two then, but, still, I want to know."

Newton seemed to calm himself and smiled a bit at Thomas, "My fine young lad, you may ask me two more questions as you wish, but after I give you your answers, we are off. All your interests will be met quickly when we are all together with those others who have been waiting, and who we shan't wish to keep waiting any longer." Newton stopped in front of the pew where the boys sat and hopped up on the back of the one placed directly before it.

"Thomas and William," Newton looked directly at each boy individually as he addressed them by name. "You are in the great English Egress; the waystation to the afterworld; the access portal to Arcadia. These fine fellow spirits you see about you are readying themselves to pass on, to leave the mortal plane and find their place beyond." Newton then threw his arms up in the air as an expression of the grandeur of the surroundings.

"Are they all going to heaven?" asked William, looking up at the many different directional signs.

"For all intents, yes, my dear boy, but being a large egress, we accommodate all beliefs here; after all, we have to keep everyone's spirits up!" Newton chuckled at his own pun and continued. "People of good nature and true hearts all end up together, William, but we like to give them the comfort of leaving here with what they have known best." Newton paused for a moment to ponder what he had just said and then continued with another thought. "Of course, there are those here who have chosen to stay on this plane of existence and also those who could never go on. They may never reach heaven, William, but they find solace in their afterlives here."

"Why would someone stay out of heaven?" asked Thomas,

knowing that he was again violating Newton's restrictions on the number of questions allowed but being too curious not to ask.

Newton paused and looked at Thomas as if he wished to answer. But, frustratingly for the boy, without a word and in a flash, the ghost was off the pew on which he had perched and was heading further into the abbey. As he strode away, he called back to the boys, "Oh, you just wait. You just wait. They won't believe you are here. I have some very special spirits for you to meet. You really must follow. If you don't, I will use some force to move your mass. Ha!" Newton burst out laughing. "Get it? The first law of motion? Hawking cannot lay claim to that one either!" he added as an apparent indignant afterthought. Still, Newton seemed pleased with himself as he chuckled at his own joke and shook his head in delight. He had been waiting for years to use that on a mortal.

The ghost now flew quickly, through the sanctuary walls and in and out of view. The boys ran after him and past a variety of other ethereal walkways and storefronts, all of which up until just a few minutes ago had seemed so strange but now appeared to them as just a part of the abbey. The fleeting spirit stopped just as quickly as he had started out and stood in front of a series of marble markers. He took a deep breath and grinned with a mixed sense of peace and nervous excitement. The moment he had waited for was finally here. Actually, "It is the moment we have all waited for," Newton thought to himself and beamed.

CHAPTER 3 | A Gathering of Spirits

"BOYS," NEWTON DECLARED, "We have arrived!" William and Thomas jogged up just in time to hear his announcement. They bent over to begin to catch their breath. The ghost looked behind, nodded, and seemed unfazed by the plight of the boys. Turning back to the stone, he mustered up his firmest voice, stomped his boots, and dramatically intoned, "Arise, spirits!" He kicked the marble burial display to his right.

Almost immediately, a haphazard-looking gentleman in a tussled suit ascended through the stone. His tired eyes weren't the only thing that made it apparent he had been sound asleep. His hair was shaggy on top and curled in a million directions, mirroring the unruly goatee that appeared glued to his chin. "Good heavens, Newton! Is that you making all that infernal noise? And such theatrics. 'Arise, Spirits?' A simple good morning might do!"

"Hello, Charles. Sorry for the drama, but I thought it appropriate to impress our guests." Newton nodded to the boys behind him who were staring at the newly joined ghost. It was Charles Dickens who stood trying to dust off his garment and successfully removing what appeared to be spirit lint. Stopping at what Newton had said, the English writer looked up. "Guests? What guests? Newton, my good man. It is just us two!"

Newton, in a voice lower than normal, whispered, "It's the

boys." He motioned with his finger, pointing over his shoulder and simultaneously tilting his head several times to divert Dickens' attention to the mortal boys at his back. William and Thomas both did deep, elaborate bows, reminiscent of the one they had seen Newton perform.

"The boys!" exclaimed Dickens, looking around and through Newton's ghostly form. "They know we are here?" Dickens hurriedly tussled his hair and attempted to smooth it into place. His hands pulled at his overgrown and disheveled goatee in an effort to shape himself into a presentable display.

"Good day, Mister Dickens," said William.

"Newton, are they...?" the mathematician broke into Dickens' question.

"Charles, I think they might be," he replied.

"Huzzah! What in all heavens are you waiting for? Gather the others!" Dickens roared. Readdressing William and Thomas, he quieted and matter-of-factly stated, "Lads, come here. We'll need to talk." Dickens raised his arms to gather William and Thomas, and the boys took the gesture as an effort to get them to follow. The three headed back out into the abbey and away from the renowned mathematician.

Newton ignored Dickens, and he focused instead on rousing the spirit resting under a nearby altar. "Hawking, get up. Rise and shine," he announced with his usual degree of grandeur. The room stayed silent. Newton had little patience for noncompliance. He began stomping his feet and clapping his hands to make a maximum amount of noise.

Dust flew as a lithe ghostly frame slowly rose from the floor. As a mortal, he was clearly lanky and thin. His spirit mirrored the frail figure he was in life, as his horned rim glasses sat slightly crooked on his narrow face. His smile took up the width of his jaw and his lips sat in a natural pout. It took him nearly a full minute to stand upright, and he lightly alternated between tapping his feet and testing his legs' ability to bear weight.

"Newton," Stephan Hawking queried, "What are you doing? I must say, sometimes your behaviors simply don't add up!" The famous physicist laughed aloud while Newton pulled a handkerchief from his sleeve to flag in frustration at the ghost he just woke. Hawking looked away from his nemesis and stared at his hands. First at the back and then he carefully examined his palms as he wriggled his fingers. With sheer joy and awe, he began to squat in place, alternating his legs for lunges and reaching from the floor to the sky to stretch his body.

"Seriously, Stephen? Every time? Do you have to do this every time? You can walk again. Get over yourself," snapped Newton.

"Calm down, Isaac. Isn't it your own philosophy that a body at rest, stays at rest? Thus, my body in motion, will stay in motion," asserted Hawking.

"As does your mouth!" spouted Newton.

"Life would be tragic if it weren't so funny," said Hawking, not seeming to care about Isaac's frustration. He continued his various exercises to warm up for whatever event had caused Newton to wake him from his peaceful slumber. As his leg kicked to the side, his worn dress shoe accidentally tapped a fellow spirit who had just wandered up to the little gathering.

"To be or not to be? That is the question," announced the devilishly handsome gentleman, slightly floating into the air. He said the line deliciously, as only a master in the theater arts could. His dark hair was perfectly styled, and his thin, well-groomed mustache turned downward as he frowned. He stood silently for a moment, trying to think of what to say next. He huffed and loudly boomed "Lines?" as he threw his hands into the air for dramatic effect and laughed out loud.

"Gads, Olivier!" exclaimed Hawking. "Can you never write your own dialog?"

Sir Laurence Olivier looked down at the floor. "Life...is a tale told by an idiot, full of sound and fury, signifying nothing."

Clearly angered by Olivier's apparent inability to use anything but lines from his plays for conversation, William Shakespeare walked into the room scowling at the actor. His long hair, beard, and mustache compensated for the deep receding hairline that left the top of his head nearly bare. A sharp flat collar sat at the shoulders of his tight, intricate coat that covered the top of his tights. "Fie! Learneth thy lines, Olivier. Wilt I at each moment remind thee? To be, or not to be, that is the question: Whether 'tis nobler in the mind to suffer, the slings and arrows of outrageous fortune, or to take arms against a sea of troubles and by opposing end them: to die, to sleep no more."

"Listen here, Will." Olivier abbreviated the playwright's name in a clear effort to annoy. "Maybe if you wrote—nonetheless spoke—in the Queen's English, I could remember your words with more clarity. But I agree, clearly, we shall sleep no more. Loosen your collar, and you might not feel as grumpy," Sir Laurence responded.

"Would thou be clean enough to spit upon sir! Mine own name is William, not Will. Make me not to ask thee again," Shakespeare carefully warned. "And for thy record, why would I speak in the Queen's English when I have an entire manner of speech named after me? 'Tis my deepest conviction to honor my own earthly accomplishments by adhering to my own style even after death. Olivier, thee always were and continue to be so dramatic and difficult."

A spirit woman approached them both. She looked about for a moment and then sat carefully folded into a chair, repositioning her bonnet to cover the hair that was carefully tucked inside. Her long, flowing blue linen dress draped down to the floor. She yawned and politely stated, "My idea of pleasurable acquaintance is the company of clever, well-informed people who have a great deal of conversation. That is what I call good company."

"Well, sorry to disappoint, Jane," chuckled Olivier.

The woman scoffed and rolled her eyes in a playful manner. Jane Austen looked back at Laurence and shrugged, "There is no sense or sensibility." They both chuckled, and Olivier winked suggestively. Austen would have blushed had ghosts possessed that ability. She pulled at the strings of her bonnet as her eyes locked with the actor's before quickly looking away.

"Nonsense," said the voice of Charles Darwin, who had also come up from the marble. He gently dusted off his black bowler cap and placed it atop his head. His full grey beard hugged his face and would surely make any man jealous, except of course Santa Claus, who was the only other figure around the abbey who so routinely sported such a perfectly grown set of whiskers. "We may not be good company as we awaken, but as I have learned, we can all evolve and adapt into the creatures that we were meant to be!" The famed naturalist winked at the beautiful author. "Jane, I believe you have found yourself amidst a fine collection of gentlemen. It may just take us a little time to find our bearings."

A soldier emerged from another tomb situated in the room. He was wearing a British Army uniform from World War I, complete with a light brown wool jacket, matching pants, dark brown leather boots, and a khaki rucksack. A rifle lay slung across his back. The soldier was still wearing his dark green metal Brodie helmet. He shouted "Attention!" and stood in perfect form. "Forward march," he commanded as he hoisted his weapon over his other shoulder and marched in a regimented military cadence. "Fall in, comrades," he demanded to the other ghosts as they watched him pass by.

Instead of following orders, the ghosts all paused and in unison, playfully asked, "Who is that?" The soldier paused, did an about-face, and grinned. The soldier and all of the ghosts simply shrugged their shoulders. He then retreated back to a spot near his tomb and stood at attention in front of the plaque that read "Unknown Soldier."

"Fig Newton, sir?" the soldier asked Newton. "I found them in my sack, and I assume they are your favorite." The soldier rummaged through his canvas bag and held the cake-like cookie out for his fellow spirit to try, a half-smile quivering on his face.

Sir Newton was never sure what to make of that assumption nor the joke he had heard so many times before but, in any event, he had far more important plans than eating a cookie treat disguised as fruit. He looked at the group of spirits that had formed around him. Ignoring the solider and addressing the rest, he proclaimed in what he hoped was an austere and authoritative voice, "I've summoned you all together for the most miraculous event. Living boys approached me in the sanctuary. They could see and hear me, even after I tried to trick them and boggle their mortal minds. They've asked me for help, but in that asking, I think they have revealed themselves as what they are."

"They are precious mortal boys," Jane Austen said sweetly as she gathered her skirt in her hand and proceeded to fix her hair. "Let us all remember our manners and their young age while we talk to the dears."

"Where are they?" asked Darwin flatly. The sternness of his voice suggested he wanted to test the idea of survival of the fittest.

"With Dickens," answered Sir Isaac.

With that answer, Jane began walking out into the abbey and the other spirits funneled in behind her. She was far more convincing in directing than the Unknown Soldier, who had fallen to the end of the line and followed the other ghosts in a disciplined march. The gathered group of spirits strode out of Westminster's Poets' Corner and into the abbey's sanctuary to meet their young visitors.

Standing with Dickens, William and Thomas saw them well before they arrived. "Look," said Thomas, nudging William. Heading their way was Sir Isaac Newton's familiar face, escorting a beautiful woman.

William leaned over to Thomas and quietly asked, "What have we gotten ourselves into?"

Thomas responded with conviction, "I have no idea, but whatever it is, we are in too deep to back out now. We made a promise."

"Hello, my sweet boys. What are the names of the precious mortals we are so honored to meet?" asked Austen in a soft, calming voice. She bent forward towards the boys to be closer to William's height.

"I am Thomas Darlington, and this is William, my little brother," noted Thomas. He was comforted by Jane's gentle voice and sweet demeanor and for the first time felt at ease.

"Well met, Thomas and William. I am Jane Austen, an English novelist. I would like to introduce to you the ghosts of the abbey. Gentlemen," she motioned with her hand for the ghosts behind her to move forward and introduce themselves.

The Unknown Soldier stepped forward and saluted the boys in a rigid, formal manner. He nodded to acknowledge them and stepped back into the loosely formed circle of ghosts.

"Who is that?" asked William. The ghosts chuckled reflexively.

"We like to give him a hard time, because the poor chap's name died with him in battle," said Darwin, explaining the shared levity. "The blokes at the Department of Defense buried him here to honor all of the unidentified dead from the war. They named him just 'The Unknown Solider.' Since we all exist as family now, that title seems too much a formality. We just call him 'Unk,'" continued the naturalist.

"Unk?" asked Thomas.

"You mean he doesn't even know who he was?" William added.

"He does not remember," Darwin quickly replied while nodding. "Unfortunately, if one is buried in a consecrated grave without a name, the person's identity is stripped from the remaining spirit. The revenant will still have some knowledge of who they were and what they did, but they can't quite fully place themselves into their mortal life. For him, we shortened the name on the plaque to sound more like everyone's favorite uncle—'Unc'—and 'Unk' respectfully became our friend's moniker."

Thomas glanced at William as both were entertained by sentiment. They together looked respectfully to the solider, who acknowledged his acceptance of their greeting.

Breaking into the moment, Hawking placed his hands on his hips, stood tall, and announced, "Hello. I am Stephen Hawking. You should know me for developing the theory of... well, everything, if you want to be thorough. Unlike some other simple people here, I am a complicated man, proudly serving as a cosmologist, theoretical physicist, author, researcher, and mathematician when I was a mere mortal."

"Simple? Mere mortals? You always have been a condescending pleasure, Stephen, so quick to list your accomplishments in the presence of others. Not to distract from my friend, but William and Thomas, I am Laurence Olivier, breathtaking actor of the stage and screen." He threw his arms out as if he was making his grand entrance stage left. "I am pleased to meet you. Pardon Stephen's self-inflated ego. He is easily intimidated around handsome, socially charming men like the three of us." Olivier winked at the boys, while dramatically motioning that he was referring to them. William and Thomas stood a little taller. They felt empowered by the actor's compliment and smiled a bit at the irony of the introduction.

"Olivier did fail to mention his success come'th with the assistance of mine own written word. I am William Shakespeare, English playwright, poet, and actor. While I may not hath Olivier's striking features, that gent forgot to mention I am regarded as the single greatest writer in the English language and touted as the world's greatest thespian."

Shakespeare took a graceful bow.

"Let me formally introduce myself. Good evening, gents. I'm Charles Darwin," the next ghost said matter-of-factly with a mild growl. "Now that the theatrics are over, let's focus on the issues at hand. We have been told you need our help, and we certainly have some questions of you. But let's deal with one issue at a time. How can we be of service?" The boys were overwhelmed by the impressive group of ghosts. They were well aware that they stood amongst giants, but when Darwin stepped forward, they felt like they had truly met a celebrity. They had learned much of his life in their classes. In fact, he was still quite a controversial scientist within the church boarding school, but the brothers were fascinated by the idea of evolution. They had often sought out his work and frequented used bookstores in London to read about his ideas.

As Darwin yielded the group's focus to the mortals, Thomas took the lead. He looked to Dickens, who motioned an affirmation that the boy should start at the tale's beginning even though it had been shared with the author already. The older Darlington cleared his voice. "We were at the Tower of London today, and we saw ghosts. I mean, we can see ghosts, obviously, but it had been many years since we had last seen one."

William interrupted in excitement, "And we didn't just see one, we saw many! We especially talked to two young princes. We didn't get to speak to them for very long, but they said they had been trapped in the tower for hundreds of years, and they were not alone. Evil spirits have been terrorizing the tower and all of the good ghosts within. They said there was a darkness residing there and it was growing more and more violent, and more and more evil. They were scared and begged us to help them."

"Slow down. Did you say 'princes?' Terrorized spirits? Evil darkness?" questioned Olivier. He averted his eyes. "The dread. The fear. The horror!" The actor was whispering now, and his words were born of concern and not theatrics.

"They were scared," said William timidly. "I could see it in their faces. I was scared too."

"We wanted to help but we had no real idea what they are talking about..." Thomas responded, but was cut short.

"It was the best of times, it was the worst of times," mused Dickens under his breath while looking to each of his fellow ghosts. "We all knew that The Bloody Tower had fallen into evil. Our friends Thomas and William confirm it. Come, lads, sit." The author motioned the boys to an abbey bench. "Let me catch you up on a bit of history. Then you can more fully add your tale to what we already know. Everyone, make yourselves comfortable. This could take a while." The gathering settled in seeming agreement that the whole account needed to be told.

Darwin remained standing in mild protest. "Hurry, Dickens. We have opportunity with these two and from what we have already heard, time is not on our side." As Dickens took a deep breath, Thomas could feel a deep sense of pain coming from the author.

CHAPTER 4 | A History Lesson

EVEN DICKENS, EVER the storyteller, struggled with where to start in the tangled and long history that led to the current state of affairs. It was a tale all the ghosts felt William and Thomas needed to know, and Charles wanted to be clear in his account. The author stood carefully, sorting through the immense amount of information in his head to establish the most logical and cohesive explanation. The boys sat in the pew eagerly awaiting, as most of the ghosts settled in beside them. Stephen Hawking, however, continued to be enamored with the ability to move his limbs and struggled to sit still. The Unknown Soldier stood at attention nearby, fulfilling his most comfortable role as guard and protector of the group. Newton collapsed into a seat next to the brothers, breathing through what appeared to be a scented handkerchief, while Darwin was perched on the back of the bench maintaining a sense of stern authority. Jane Austen settled gracefully near him with her legs crossed at the ankles and her hands resting gently in her lap. Olivier paced about muttering to himself, seemingly practicing lines, while Shakespeare, also standing, looked on the gathered group with a rather bemused detachment.

"Let me start by saying we've suspected for quite some time that evil not only lurks in the tower but for centuries has continued to infiltrate human society from that fortress, causing much mortal devastation. That, however," said

ASHLEY WELLMAN & PATRICK KINKADE

Dickens, now pacing, "was not always the case. The tower was not built as a source of evil, and, in fact, neither was the abbey constructed to be what it is: a waystation for righteous spirits. The nature of these places simply acts as part of the natural order of things and existed long before either the castle or this church was built. As far as we can tell, from the very beginning, portals to the afterworld graced both this hallowed ground and the soil under the tower as well. Each has always been a one-way passage where spirits, either good or evil, can find their way to their next condition of being. Reapers go to collect the revenants of evil to bring them to the portal of the tower and cast them into Acheron where they would stay, only rarely finding their way back to the mortal realm. Guides, on the other hand, would bring the spirits of the good here and then on to their place in Arcadia, a reward for the sanctity of their mortal lives. Like the evil spirits I mentioned, the good, too, would only occasionally return."

"Are you talking about heaven and hell?" Thomas asked suddenly. At the same time, William, ever the good schoolchild, also raised his hand for an opportunity to ask his own question.

"It is as you suggest, young Thomas," answered Dickens patiently. "But the afterworld is so much more than that simple dichotomy. It is rather a place of all heavens and all hells as each person in every culture defines them. It is eternity: well met for the good and a horror for the bad. The afterworld is beyond space and time but tied to the mortal and ethereal worlds through spiritual passages, or portals as we call them. Understand, the abbey we are in and the tower you visited hold but two. We know of four other locations where they exist, each having separate access to Acheron and Arcadia."

"Umm, yes, child?" Dickens kindly addressed the young boy who was now waving his hand excitedly, still wanting to ask his question.

"What are reapers and guides?" asked William. Thomas nodded his curiosity, too.

Dickens noted the sensibility of the inquiry. "They have taken many forms even in the small amount of time for which we here can account. Reapers and guides may be best described as escorts. They live as the portals seem to exist, through natural law, and work toward moving the dead along to the afterworld. Their role is to help keep the balance of good and evil in place here on earth."

"But what are they? Can we see them?" asked William again.

"The ravens and the martlets, boys!" continued the writer. "Surely you have seen. Look!" pointed Dickens. "Even now!" As he gestured up, a bird flew by. It was one of the abbey's martlets that the boys had come to know since their arrival. Thomas and William also instantly remembered their experience with the ravens at the tower. "When a mortal dies, the birds collect the spirit and deliver it to the appropriate portal. As I told you, these passages exist around the world. For spirits here in Europa, the ravens reap souls to the tower and the martlets guide them to the abbey. In the Middle East, the Far East and the New World, ghosts there are led to other passages as is their destiny. Unlike these distant lands and circumstance, however, we have a dilemma. The reapers here cannot take souls except to their natural egress, and the portal at the tower is lost to them. The ravens, sadly, cannot fulfill their purpose as escorts. Even more, they have begun to dwindle."

"Simply say it, man!" Darwin abruptly interrupted as if frustrated with Dickens and his account of things.

"It is said that when the ravens leave the tower, England will fall," piped in Newton, interrupting as well.

"And, so it is," continued Dickens, forcing his way back in to control of the conversation. "Without the ravens, evil here in Europa will not leave this world, and, worse, for centuries at the fortress, it has not been able. The ravens are leaving, and the tower portal is locked. These truths, my boys, are dire in consequence. We at the abbey fear time for humanity is running out as the tide of darkness rises with no outlet to let it drain away."

Thomas and William looked around while the entire group of ghosts went silent. Even Hawking stopped moving, and Darwin held his eyes on Dickens, who was nodding his head. "Before you get to the tower portal being locked, you need to tell them about the keepers, Charles," Darwin said to Dickens with decidedly more patience.

Dickens paused for another beat and then, in apparent agreement, complied with the request. "The tower and the abbey share a similar history. Both were mortal strongholds, built by those who tended the portals. As long as these passages have existed, so were there keepers to tend them. Men and women of consecrated blood gathered in these places of transition to help the reapers and guides in their task. Eventually, structures like the tower and the abbey were built to give shelter and place to these consecrated wards. Still understand, the buildings are simple creations of man; the portals, however, appear eternal."

"Then it happened," murmured Olivier, who had stopped his own pacing and was fully focused on the story.

Dickens continued. "Millenniums ago, evil was unleashed from its cage in Acheron. The Caesars of Rome, in their mad quest for world domination, not only set out to conquer the earth but, at the same time, they also wished to tame all the heavens above. While Roman armies marched and their fleets set sail to capture new lands, Roman holy men, magicians, and alchemists sought to challenge the afterworld and assert mortal dominion over the ethereal and eternal planes. It was a mighty affront in effort and method and the ungodly forces unleashed were devastating." Dickens stopped to shake his head as if in thought. "But it all proved too much for mortal man to control. The usurpers damaged England's portal to Acheron, thus allowing the demons and evil within to pour out. It was the beginning of the Dark Ages and a time of great conflict."

"Demons!" exclaimed both boys at once. As if a world of ghosts weren't enough, the idea of demons truly frightened them.

"Oh yes, William...Thomas. Vampires, werewolves, and goblins as well," chimed in Newton without thinking. Then, looking at the boys and the distress on their faces, he added, "Buck up, now. Be good lads. Be British!"

"Shush, Isaac," said Jane, "Let Charles tell the story gently, lest we chase these young darlings away with a fright!"

The boys glanced at each other and then back to Dickens, who appeared suddenly tired and sad. "I am sorry to tell such a tale," he said, looking back and forth between Thomas and William. "It holds no pleasure nor humor, but the rest I fear must be said." Without waiting and staring not at the boys but into the distance, Dickens picked up where he let off. "Through what is known and from what we can surmise, it was then, at the beginning of our Dark Ages, that the consecrated bloodlines of the tower and abbey became more than keepers. They transformed into warriors and picked up sword and shield against the abominations that Rome's arrogance had released. While others still held fast the afterworld portals, those who were able also ventured out to war. Indeed, the keepers worked to cleanse the earth of the evil unleashed and protect its natural balance with the good that existed. Still, at the tower, the ravens brought black souls to the portal. Those few keepers who remained helped to contain the foul spirits, forcing them back through the opening to Acheron. But, with every slip of their control, evil would re-enter the world, ready to bring with it pain, horror, and chaos."

"Can you tell us more about these keepers?" asked William, not even waiting to raise his hand.

Dickens glanced at the boy, nodded, and continued. "In the beginning, they were simply referred to as 'The Blessed.' As they found each other, banded together, and their numbers grew, the commoners they served gave these congregates various other names. We here in England would eventually call them the 'Knights Templar.' Other lands and cultures gave them different monikers as their people perceived them. In the Middle East, they were known as the 'Guild of Assassins' and in the Far East, my friend Marco Polo tells us they were called 'Shaolin.'"

At the mention of the explorer's name, Thomas interrupted Dickens with an incredulous exclamation. "You know Marco Polo?!!"

Dickens mused to the boy. "Young man, you are talking to a room full of ghosts in an abbey that has become their home and that serves as a waystation to the afterworld. Does it really surprise you that I might know another spirit of such distinction?"

Thomas looked at the famous faces of Darwin, Newton, Austen, Shakespeare, Olivier, and Hawking, and then back to Dickens. "Ummmm, I guess not," stated the mortal while looking at the Unknown Soldier with some sense of embarrassment. The military man smiled back, offering some small comfort.

"Then I will continue," grinned the ghost. "Our Knights Templar, and other such groups in various lands, warred against the expanding darkness. For the unknowing, their time spent and force exerted was misperceived as conflicts between mortal men and clashes of earthly cultures. Sadly, I honestly can say 'I wish that it had been!'" Dickens again shook his head slowly. "Alas, it wasn't that simple. The Crusades embarked upon and the battles waged were between man and demonkind. Peoples and lands that were commonly seen as enemies banded together as allies in the greater good and against the unfettered evil. Tragically, history has forgotten this account, or, perhaps more accurately, those who wrote it never fully knew."

"Charles, you want to speed this story up a few centuries? If these boys don't fall asleep as you drone on, I will," snarled Darwin, glancing over at William and Thomas. The two youngsters shrugged their shoulders. They were now both fascinated with the story—but, it was true, they were also getting tired, and dinner was approaching, thought Thomas.

Dickens glared for a moment at Darwin and then reconciled himself to the accuracy of the observation. He seemed to change his direction of thought and started anew. "While the fighting raged, the Templars worked to repair the devastation that the Caesars had caused to the tower portal. Sadly, the first efforts to fix the damaged entryway only slowed the release of the evil coming back into the world and the problems casting it into Acheron got worse. Eventually, more evil was escaping the afterworld than was placed there. The demons and their like were winning."

"So, the Crusades actually started because evil was returning from the afterworld, and the Knights Templar were trying to stop it?" asked William. He had always been a history buff, and this account of those wars was far more intriguing than anything he had ever learned in any class.

"Exactly!" Dickens exclaimed excitedly. "Further, the darkness in the world began to overshadow the good. Evil was not leaving while good continued to move on into eternity. Those were bleak times..." Dickens trailed off. The writer became silent in a most ominous way. The gravity of what he had just said seemed to take him deep into his own thoughts.

"Isaac, perhaps tell the boys about 'The Binding,'" said Austen in a much more nurturing and thoughtful manner. She seemed to understand where Dickens had gone and wished him to come back of his own accord.

"As you desire, my lady," said Newton, gracefully nodding his head out of respect to Jane before giving Dickens a concerned look. "It was during the ninth and final Crusade, a defining moment for the Templars. The Knights recognized their numbers were dwindling and that their war against demonkind was growing. It left them at a precarious crossroads. Knowing the portal was beyond repair to its normal functioning, the leaders of the order called for all Templars to leave their posts and join the ongoing military effort. We assume the same happened in other places with other groups of The Blessed. It was an attempt by mortals to end the demon threat in one deciding battle. The knights also knew the potential was that once they left their posts, they may never return. Thus, they needed to ensure they halted the flow of evil back for the afterworld. To do so, they built 'The Binding,' a magical barrier placed around the tower and the passage to Acheron. This, however, was a risky decision, for the magic they harnessed was the same as that the Roman emperors had used to blow open the portal in the first place. Yet, somehow, the spells used to create The Binding worked in the Templars' favor. The hole left by the Romans' folly closed." Newton stopped his story to let the boys consider.

"Continue, Isaac," said Darwin. "Leave nothing out."

Looking first at the biologist and then at the boys, the mathematician continued. "The Binding was made from enchantments we no longer know and through a process that we do not fully understand. Mortals could pass through this restraint freely and without notice, but ghosts and those from the afterworld could not. So, the Templars also built a gate in the barrier. They created it to allow evil to be pushed through The Binding to Acheron. But, with few left to turn to, the Knights handed the gate's key over to royalty as they and others like them left for battle. The tower's key was almost certainly given to King Edward IV with the intention that a Knight Templar retrieve it and begin again their work of casting evil out of this world once the crusade ended and victory against darkness on the mortal plane was secured."

Newton sighed and stopped. He looked around at the ghostly gathering slightly lost and trying to determine where the story should go from here.

The Unknown Solider stepped forward and stood at ease. Sir Isaac and the other ghosts accepted his willingness as he picked up the tale's telling. "Things in the Crusades did not go as planned. The Templars fought heroically, as did their allies in The Guild, though it came at a high cost. Entire villages were destroyed, complete armies fell, and the earth was scorched. Nonetheless, in that utter loss, the demons were wiped from the world. It is also sadly true that no Templars returned. The consecrated blood that flowed through the veins of some mortals and had made them 'The Blessed' and Templar seemed to be eradicated. Since the day the Knights fell, the abbey's portal, the one that allows the good to freely flow out of this world, has remained active. Spirits like us and the good men of faith that attend to the mortal realm manage it. Evil spirits destined for the tower's portal, however, have faced quite a different fate. They are locked out of their afterworld or left waiting in the fortress waystation, generally bound in isolation from mortal man except for those who would visit their tower haunt or who are found roaming the world still at large."

"So, we are safe from them?" asked Thomas hopefully.

Newton looked at the young boy. "It is not so simple, lad. While what has been recounted is true, just as good does, evil is still coming into the world as it always has and always will."

"Evil is coming into the world?" asked William with a bit of nervousness in his voice.

"Through birth and the general way of things," answered Darwin. "Evil is born into existence, and then, in some mortals, it evolves."

"Without a way for evil to leave here, the balance between it and good in the mortal and ethereal worlds will eventually shatter. When the Knights Templar created The Binding to keep Acheron's darkness trapped, they did not anticipate they would be locking corruption into the world and out of hell as well. Thus, evil remains in the world with us." Newton had again joined the conversation

"And it's only getting worse," noted Austen, with a sense of worry and dread. "In my time here in the abbey, I've watched the evil grow. It has stolen so much good from all of us."

"She's right," the Unknown Solider stated flatly. "We've seen more war, famine, disease, and violence in the mortal plane than ever before. So many tragedies and so many good souls flooding the abbey as they transition into Arcadia. Evil, however, can no longer leave and the balance is lost. I fear darkness will soon overwhelm everything and everyone who is left, mortal and ethereal alike." All who were gathered glanced over to Unk. Having seen war before, he truly understood the magnitude of the situation brewing.

Hawking froze in a lunge, stretched his arms overhead, and slowly leaned to the right before concluding, "Since the beginning of time, darkness and light have co-existed. Yet the light that stood against the darkness is beginning to fade."

"Enough," said Darwin kindly, noticing the tears beginning to well in William's eyes. He raised his hand as if motioning to stop a car. "The point, I see, has been well taken."

The urgency of the situation was clear to the boys. So much so, Thomas was confident he knew the answer to his question before it even left his lips. "So, if the darkness had its way, would it take control of Arcadia, too?"

"If it did, we would never get to see our mom and dad. I would never see my parents again," William whispered. The ghosts looked on in silence. Each debated how to respond without furthering the horrific reality their young audience was just now beginning to face.

"So, what are we going to do to stop it?" Thomas replied with confidence. Despite his own fears, he purposefully tried to show a courageous front for his little brother.

"Well, boys," said Newton, looking at Hawking as if he were trying to steal an equation, "This is where you come in. No mortal has been able to effectively see or hear ghosts for hundreds of years. We here and many others have chosen not to cross over to our eternities until we know that the Templar key is in safekeeping and that the balance between good and evil can be restored. We were convinced that none of the Knight's bloodlines existed anymore, but the fact that you can see us may prove us wrong. Further, your account of meeting two young princes in the Tower of London and what you know of their plight inside is something we need to hear."

"We didn't learn much," Thomas began as if cued by Sir Isaac. "The princes we met described a terrible evil that seems to be consuming the tower, but you already knew that."

"Tell them about the key," William remarked.

"Well, we also don't know much about that," Thomas shrugged to his brother. "And, in truth, it seemed that the princes didn't either."

"But the key they were looking for...could it be the same one the Templars created to lock The Binding?" William interjected. "It has to be pretty powerful because they said they weren't the only ones looking for it. The evil ghosts they talked about being trapped in the tower were hunting for it, too."

The gathered spirits looked at each other and immediately began talking between themselves.

"This confirms what we suspected," said Darwin, turning from the collection of conversations that had erupted. "The key was lost when King Edward passed and has clearly not been found or, at least, has not been used, as The Binding stays in place and what is within remains beyond us. William, you are right. The key does hold great power. In fact, it might hold the very fates of both the mortal and ethereal worlds in its use."

"Knowing evil ghosts are present in the tower only makes the situation even more dire. Those vile spirits are assuredly still searching for the key. With its control, they could open the gate and unleash Acheron," offered a re-engaged Dickens.

"Do the ghosts in the tower know where the key is? Or can we retrieve it and bring it out of that fortress and through The Binding?" asked Austen.

"That needs to be determined," stated Darwin, "and assuredly it also suggests our next step."

"Indeed, it implies a simple formula for success!" said Newton, smirking a bit at Hawking and anticipating Darwin. "You boys have to return to the tower. We need more information. I believe the young princes there may hold the precise insight required to rid the world of its growing madness. We might be able to restore the natural balance."

"But I still don't understand The Binding very well," said a hesitant William.

"Neither do we, at least not fully," added Darwin. "As ghosts of science, we've been struggling to understand what the barrier between the mortal world and the afterworld even is. It does not fit into our areas of study nor our scientific expectations. We have, however, found a few who understand magic quite well. I think you two will be of particular interest to them and they to you. If you will indulge our little group a bit longer, come with us and learn more." Darwin stood and began walking away from the gathering.

"Don't forget! No shortcuts! The boys can't go through walls, so we will have to take the long way down," Austen called out to remind the group. Her gentle ways made up for the gruff and serious tone of the Darwin. William found her particularly warm.

As the group of spirits walked through the pews, William and Thomas attempted to follow. They all made their way down the abbey's long hall near the earthly chapel and past several more ethereal businesses. They eventually paused just outside an obscure door in the church's physical structure. Somehow, in all the time the boys had been at school here, they had never noticed the entrance that seemed to almost fade into the stone wall.

"Go on. Open it," suggested Darwin. "It is far easier for you mortal boys to move physical objects than for a ghost, I fear. We try to conserve our ethereal energy and that door is a heavy burden."

Thomas had noticed that ghosts, by their nature, seem to pass through things, though they also seemed quite capable of moving physical objects. Heeding Darwin, William opened the door, which revealed a staircase that began to wind steeply with its very first step. So steep in fact, the sunlight through the door faded just a few feet inside. The boys' eyes had to adjust to the darkness to find their footing. They were the last two to enter after the parade of ghosts that had already begun to make their way down into the gloom. Once all were in, and as if on cue, the door slammed shut by itself behind them. Magic was apparently a private affair.

CHAPTER 5 | Making Magic

THE MADNESS SWIRLED around the room as the wizard hovered over a long wooden table. The chamber was a mixture of magic and chaos, complete with candelabras, potion bottles, spell books, jars of unidentifiable contents, and animal skeletons positioned for inspiration and as macabre décor. Dust and cobwebs clung to bookcases that served as a backdrop to the magician's workstation. A boiling liquid popped from a cauldron in the corner as if it were a hot pot of angry mud. An incense burner smelling of burned patchouli and cloves gave off a thin stream of smoke as it worked to cover the pungent smell of old books and the aging contents that filled the shelves lining the walls.

Sparkles of bright crackling light and streams of color circled around the wizard. His face was slightly covered by the oversized conical hat that sat crooked atop his head. Despite much of his face being obstructed, it was easy to see the wisdom and passion he exuded through his kind eyes. The current chaos seemed to deepen the wrinkles and furrowed lines that defined his features as he clearly pondered what was happening before him. The cap on his head matched his oversized dark blue velvet robe that gathered on the floor at his feet. His long white beard was full and disheveled as it stretched from his chin down to his belt. Oddly, a small bird sat perched in its fullness.

The wizard was circling a large table in the center of the

room. Despite the other clutter on its surface, a bright blue dome glowed with a neon hue and was immediately apparent at the center of the worktop. As if being cast from a projector, the flickering blue light was functioning as a cover to what appeared to be a three-dimensional translucent replica of the Tower of London. It looked almost like a dollhouse under a glass cover. At first glance, the cupola seemed robust and solid, but upon closer inspection, that impression faded. Sparks of electric shock jumped from its surface and black patches opened and disappeared, dimming the brightness of the blue light as they did so. Something was definitely wrong or at least not working as it should.

"You've come at a bad time!" screamed the wizard. "I've officially lost my ability to connect with The Binding. It's breaking down, and my usual remedies are failing me miserably! I've tried dragon's tongue, hair of a newt, belly of a snake, hummingbird feathers, lips of a duck, and leopard spots. Of course, today is the day I'm out of unicorn tears. How does this happen?" The wizard wiped sweat from his brow before placing his hands to his mouth in disbelief. "I need a phoenix feather!" he suddenly proclaimed as if expecting someone to bring it to him.

"Boys, meet Merlin," Darwin said, looking toward the frantic figure in front of the gathering. "He's our resident magician tasked with maintaining the integrity of The Binding until we can find a way to control it. We all hope he can discover the spell that will allow us to open that blasted barrier and close it again safely. Its secrets have alluded we men of science for centuries. We have found ourselves better equipped to manage the spirits crossing into Arcadia, while Merlin monitors and works to repair the barrier to Acheron. What you see on the table over the model of the tower is the state of the restraint the Templars left so long ago. We have tried many other wizards over the years, but only Merlin here seems to have any facility at all with the magic of the knights."

"Though there was one young lad who seemed promising," Newton chimed in. "I can't seem to remember his name...a schoolboy apparently, with a nasty scar above his glasses and a fervor for magic that wouldn't quit. Harvey Putter or Henry Tubber, maybe? He continually asked to see Dusseldorf. Why he wanted to visit that infernal German town is beyond me!"

"Nevertheless," continued Darwin, forcibly taking the stage back from Sir Isaac, "Merlin came at a time of great need, and he has been a fixture in the abbey for many years."

William looked at Thomas and furrowed his brow in disbelief. Thomas, equally confused, blurted out, "Wait! Merlin isn't real. How can he be a ghost?"

"I'm not? I feel real." Merlin began patting his own body as if to check for a substantive validation of his reality. "In fact, this current situation is having me feel like a 'real' failure, but real nonetheless," Merlin rattled on in response. His breath grew short, and he began panting rapidly. He sounded as if at any second, he would succumb to tears. "Maybe I'm not real. Could that be why my magic is no longer working? Am I a fraud? Egad...I'm a fraud. I'm a pitiful fraud."

Merlin's growing anxiety became even more apparent through his frantic movement. While waving his hands, the sleeve of his robe had caught the top of a glass beaker, causing it to topple over and extinguishing the candle closest to the glowing blue hemisphere. The dome's appearance seemed to grow brighter with the loss of the candle's light and further highlighted the cracks that were beginning to grow across its curved plane.

The gathered ghosts' expressions mirrored the boys. They were confused, but not because they questioned Merlin's presence. Instead, they were uneasy that his usual ability to quickly solve any problem with his wand, a potion, or a spell appeared to be on the fritz. The brothers, on the other hand, looked as if they had seen a ghost...if seeing a ghost hadn't become a normal occurrence for them both.

Shaking off his own concerns about the abbey's resident magician, Darwin again addressed the boys. He had forgotten that Thomas and William had just become acquainted with the ethereal world and that some more explanation would be required about the nature of things. "I can sense your confusion, lads. The wizard got you stumped?" The scientist nodded to Merlin. "Let me try and explain," Darwin paused. "Our friend here is real, but not in the sense you are thinking. Unlike us, he is not a revenant of his mortal self. Rather, he is purely a creature of the ether."

"'Apparitions,' we call them!" Newton said, pushing himself into the conversation.

"Apparition?" echoed Merlin in a more composed manner. "Indeed, I may be that, but I am also every bit the ghost you are. You know we of the 'Affirmation for Apparitions Movement' prefer to be called 'Mortally Challenged Spirits.' We are not merely apparitions!"

"My dear fellow," followed Newton, "a fine wizard you have proven to be and a distinguished apparition you are, but a ghost you most assuredly are not."

"I'll have you know..." Darwin cut Merlin off mid-sentence with a wave of his hand and another short growl, leaving it fully to Newton to guess what Merlin might have wanted him to know. "Gentlemen, let us discuss our politics later. We have far more pressing issues to deal with here."

Thomas and William looked at all three of the specters standing in front of them, and they all looked back.

"Charles dear, please continue about our mortally challenged friends for the boys. No more blustering. These fine young gentlemen have enough to think about." Jane's soothing voice calmed the group and returned the focus to Darwin. He grabbed his lapels as if to straighten his jacket and then continued his explanation.

"For Merlin, or any appari...mortally challenged being to

exist"—Darwin quickly corrected himself while Merlin raised an eyebrow—"it takes a deep interest or love from mortals. Boys, it is often said, one should never underestimate the power of the human mind or heart, and truer words were never spoken. Together, the energies of those wonderful biologies are capable of miraculous things. Merlin and those like him are drawn from the ether. The mortal heart and mind energize that process. You see ether in our world all around you, in the abbey, and, indeed, you would now notice it on the streets of London were you to look. It is the very substance of this reality. Lads, the structures we ghosts visit or the things we use are all ethereal. They are not of the mortal world, but they are real nonetheless, and we who stay on this plane of existence can use ether to create them as mortals might use brick or iron. But we cannot do what mortals do, even though they don't know they are doing it. We cannot create ethereals. The physically bound can give life to characters they love and believe in, while ghosts cannot. It is not known how many of the mortally challenged there are, but they are many. Some characters are good like our fine magician here and some are evil, but all are born of human interest and concern. As such, they have the characteristics, talents, and personalities a mortal might expect. And, when summoned by human hearts, the mortally challenged make their own decisions, choosing for themselves where they might go, who they might communicate with, and what actions they will take. On their own accord, many have become friends and allies in mortal causes and some others have worked in ways that are more sinister. Still, more simply remain aloof and seem beyond caring for anything but their own miraculous existence."

"Like that Mad Hatter chap," offered Newton. "Quite the eccentric."

Darwin paused, "Good or evil, these beings are created only out of mortal imagination and sensibilities. But they are nonetheless real, and what they do has real consequences here in the ethereal world and for those still living on the mortal plane." The scientist concluded his statement sternly.

"Why don't they leave like the ghosts?" asked Thomas. "Don't they want to go to heaven, too?"

"Alas boys, we cannot." It was Merlin talking. "We are tied to mortals and their curiosities. To leave the ethereal world, we believe, would stop our existence. Indeed, a few have even tried and have simply disappeared."

"Disappeared?" asked Thomas. "What happens to them if they disappear?"

"In the same way very few mortals truly know what happens to them at their own demise, we do not know what happens to those who disappear. Perhaps they go on to another plane of existence or perhaps they simply cease to be, returning to the void or into the unattached ether."

"So, the mortally challenged like you," said William, mindful of Merlin's feelings, "can die?"

"In a manner of speaking, boys, yes." Merlin's voice had grown low and somber.

"All ghosts can," said Darwin, picking up on William's question. "If we stay on this plane and don't pass on to Arcadia, we are vulnerable to attack from evil or from misguided good. Our existence here can end by a severe corporeal attack as with an ethereal blade. Even with the danger, however, some would choose to stay. The group of spirits you see before you along with our other allies stay only to try to end the threat posed by the tower. Others stay to wait for family still mortal to transition so that they might all pass on to Arcadia together and yet others stay by simple choice. When one dies, you see, our spirits come back in the form of our best, most successful selves. For many, that is a state to be enjoyed and so they stay. However, for others, even if they returned at their best, they just have unfinished business. Thus, they may use extended time in the terminal or the mortal world beyond to rebuild or create a life they wanted while alive, seek a new or lost love, or pursue knowledge they never acquired. But, whatever the reason, all who remain do so at their own peril. We are able to witness the world around us on both a mortal and metaphysical plane, but by existing in the spiritual world, ghosts and the 'mortally challenged' are governed by the rules of the ethereal afterlife."

"What rules?" asked Thomas.

"Well, there aren't many. The afterworld is rather simple. It is entirely comprised of ether and ether is both substance and energy. Every being and every item is composed of it, and every move made by anything uses ether to make it. Ghosts and apparitions can move about and transport physical objects, but it consumes our ethereal energy. So, just like a mortal might, we recharge with food—though ours is ethereal in nature—and rest to regenerate. But lose too much energy and our souls will dissipate, no longer existing on this plane and unable to cross over to the next."

The boys grew quiet and reserved as they pondered this morbid detail.

"Don't look discouraged. As long as we are careful, it is rather easy to balance the energy we consume and exert," Darwin assured. "Just as your stomachs call out for dinner, we all know when to eat and sleep!"

William looked relieved. "How do you buy things?"

"It's simple. Ethereal earnings. As we gather a surplus of ether, we can convert it into cosmic coins. These coins can be used to purchase food and goods or to trade and negotiate with other ghosts for services," Darwin explained.

"Can you be hurt? What happens then?" Thomas asked with some hesitation from fear of offending.

"Why...yes, we can, and it works as it would for you. We take time to heal, seek out a doctor, and utilize what medicines there are to restore the ether inside of us until we are full." The naturalist paused. "Really, the only injuries that we fear are catastrophic in nature, but it is rare to face such a threat."

"I saw a store sign in the abbey," said William, thinking aloud. "It claimed that the advertised establishment carried the finest of all ghost blades."

"Hm, yes." It was Merlin speaking again, "Indeed. 'Happy Hunting Ground.' They make a fine weapon that can be used for a host of purposes. Their designs are made from the ether too, and when created, they are carefully tailored with energy extracted from its future owner. These swords hold great power, for just as a mortal sword will draw blood, an ethereal blade will consume the ether of whatever it slices. 'Happy Hunting Ground' is quite reputable, but for a truly magnificent blade, you need a master at the ethereal forge."

"Like who?" chimed the boys together. A chuckle spread softly through the crowd of gathered ghosts.

"Why, me!" exclaimed the old wizard. "I am the man who smithed Excalibur. The greatest sword in history."

"Excalibur wasn't real!" said Thomas.

"Details!" exclaimed Merlin, pointing his finger to the ceiling. "But those surely are!" He directed that same finger toward what appeared to be two swords hung on the wall. Both were beautifully crafted with carved scabbards and ornate hilts.

"I can make a sword for any occasion!" Merlin stopped in his thoughts and again, with a sudden start, began pacing feverishly about the room. He attempted to wield his magic by slinging his arms and a wizard's wand towards the blue dome. "I am not sure if that other skill will matter if I can't save The Binding. After it crumbles, so will we all." The old wizard lashed out with his hand and red bolts flew from his palm into the model of the tower. "Nothing is working. Why?!" he screamed worriedly, thrusting his hands in frustration up into the air.

In that instant, a large, soap-like bubble appeared, shining with iridescent shifting colors. As the sphere floated into the room, it grew larger upon approach. When it popped, a stunning woman in a floor-length pink ball gown, complete with gloves, and a wand gracefully stepped forward. Her crown stood nearly a foot high and sat atop her billowing red hair. The gentle nature of her smile and the softness of her face only matched Jane's in the warmth it created in the otherwise cold basement lair.

"Merlin, my dear. There's no need to worry. After all, I am here," she said playfully as she stepped from behind Merlin, clasped his hand, and kissed him on the cheek. The old sorcerer's face began to blush, and his beard curled ever so slightly while the bird living there began to coo.

"You can't be serious. Glinda the Good Witch?" questioned Thomas with a mixture of incredulity and bewilderment. "I feel like I'm losing my mind."

"Nonsense. No one here is crazy. Unless you equate being ancient with being crazy." Glinda shot Merlin an affectionate look and then glanced at the boys as if telling them Merlin's age might make him slightly mad. "Merlin, is this what you needed?" continued the enchantress from Oz. She handed Merlin a feather the likes of which the boys had never seen. "Freshly plucked!"

Merlin gently took the plume from Glinda's hands. It appeared to the boys as if it were glowing in all colors, yet not in any color they had ever seen before. "Yes," said the wizard in clear satisfaction. "How do you always know?" he whispered.

"My sweet enchanter," she laughed, "I am magic! And if you keep using me to secure your success, I might just need to take charge! You know, many scarecrows, lions, tin woodsmen, and a land full of munchkins already consider me the greatest sorcerous of all the cardinal directions." Her eyes truly twinkled in the glee at such a statement. "But, for now, I am willing to simply assist."

"Munchkins indeed!" roared Merlin. The magician quickly disregarded her banter, took the feather to task, and stuck it in the top of his hat. "Back away," he commanded with a voice that seemed amplified and filled with authority. All the ghosts stepped back, some even ducking behind the table and chairs. Jane gathered the boys to the stairwell and stood in front of them as if she could shield them from what was about to happen, and even Glinda floated back a few feet in anticipation. The sorcerer, meanwhile, began to pinwheel his arms and speak in odd incantations. Thomas and William stood transfixed, looking through Jane with wide-eyed amazement. Neither could hear nor understand what Merlin was saying until the very end when he boomed, "Bibbidi-Bobbidi-Boo!" and threw out his arms. A bolt of energy shot down from the ceiling of the abbey and hit the feather on top the wizard's hat as lightning would hit a metal rod. A moment later, that same energy, amplified, shot out of both of Merlin's hands and into the model of the tower that sat on the table. It glowed with the discharge and seemed to drink the energy, as one dying of thirst would swallow fresh water. The light in the room went suddenly dark and then flashed back on again. Merlin stood gazing at the model of the tower glowing gold. He, on the other hand, had smoke coming from his clothing that was covered in soot as if he had been working in a coal mine. "Well," he stated in a matter-of-fact manner, "that seemed to do the trick." As he spoke, smoke came from his mouth and nose before he fell straight back onto the floor below.

✦ ✦ ✦

"And from where do you precious munchkins hail?" Glinda asked, looking at the two boys. She had Merlin's head on her lap and was fanning him. The wizard seemed fully recovered but remained still as he was clearly enjoying the witch's attention.

"We aren't munchkins—or witches, if that was the next

question. Although, I was always a fan of The Lollipop Guild," said Thomas as he grimaced. William simply rolled his eyes.

"My silly, sweet child, there are no male witches, so I had already ruled that out. And considering you two are taller than most of the munchkins I've dealt with in the past, I'll accept that you are just two adorable mortal boys." William and Thomas both nodded their agreement with Glinda and their shoulders relaxed a bit for the recognition.

"But, now that we've established that, a more important question exists." Glinda's gentle eyes were focused solely on the boys. "What urgency do you bring which demands Merlin's attention?"

"We think we might be able to help with The Binding," piped in William, who seemed comforted by Glinda's presence. "On our field trip to the Tower of London, we met two ghost princes. They seemed to be about our age but said they had been trapped for hundreds of years unable to escape the evil that is growing stronger there." The brothers then recounted what they knew from their time spent in the castle.

Glinda and Merlin were clearly interested. "Well, that is quite a story indeed and the young ghosts you met would certainly be able to impart new knowledge on our dilemma."

Darwin moved forward as Glinda and Merlin finished their questions. He looked at Dickens, who met his gaze for a moment and slowly nodded as if in unspoken agreement. He then averted his eyes as the scientist spoke. "My boys, I am afraid I must ask you a service. You must again seek out the princes and bring back more of their story so we might better determine our course of action and how to get the key they speak of." All of the ghosts gathered looked to each other and then to the boys. "In fact," continued Darwin, "you may be able to bring them back to the abbey. For hundreds of years, we haven't met a single mortal who has been able to see or hear us. If we had, we would have simply explained the problem and asked them to invite us in. The ghosts in the tower likely would have done the same if they could be seen and might have convinced a vessel with a mortal body that any ghost can cross The Binding," the naturalist stated flatly.

"I don't understand," said William.

"Invite the two princes in and let them possess you, and I believe you can bring them out of The Binding and to the abbey," Dickens clarified. "It is simple, really. Invite a ghost in and they may occupy your body simultaneously with your own spirit. Do these lads you met seem trustworthy?"

"Yes," said Thomas, though the look on William's face seemed less sure.

"Should we allow this?" said Jane.

"Boys," said Darwin, "if these two ghosts are willing, and if you believe them to be good souls, there is no danger. Simply invite them into your mind and heart and you should be able to bring them to us across The Binding. They can leave your bodies here as easily as they entered there. But take heed, the choice to leave your bodies will be the spirits'. They could choose to stay or have to be forced out, though an exorcism is quite a messy affair." The naturalist looked at each of the boys as if to gage their courage. "In any event, we need more information before we reveal ourselves to any of those in the tower. It would be best for us to meet here. Will you contact the princes? Can you do this?"

"We will try, Mister Darwin, though we might need some time to get free from the school to do so." It was Thomas stepping back up to the lead. William shook his head as his older brother once again committed them to something of which he was rather unsure.

"We all understand," Darwin said, looking to the ghosts to get their affirmation. "Good. It is settled." He nodded to each of those present but the concern in his eyes made it clear he thought haste was needed.

"Then, follow the cobblestone road," Glinda said, interrupting the moment and motioning her wand toward the stairs of Merlin's lab.

"Should they take their little dog, too?" cackled Merlin as he jumped up and waved his hand into the air. He proceeded to create a scruffy dog in front of him with a seemingly simple spell. Toto appeared and instantly tinkled on the floor. "No!" shouted Merlin as he fell to the floor to wipe up the mess. He looked up at Glinda. "Too much?"

"A tad, my dear. I think the dog is an unnecessary burden for the boys," responded Glinda, softly discouraging Merlin's enthusiastic ideas and eccentric humor.

"As you wish." Merlin scooped up the dog and spun in a circle, and by the time he had made a complete turn the dog had vanished, just as quickly as it had appeared.

Glinda cleared her throat in a delicate fashion and proceeded to repeat her instructions. "Return to the tower. Don't stop for strangers along the way. Follow the cobblestone path."

"I guess we're off to see the princes." William began to laugh but stopped as he felt the glares of the ghosts and apparitions staring down at him.

"Well stated, my boy," said Olivier with a theatrical intonation.

William furrowed his brow and recognized what he had just said. He stood up a bit straighter and shifted his face to a more serious expression. "We will do just that. The moment we get a chance, we will return to the tower and learn what we can."

CHAPTER 6 | Rules are Rules

IN LONDON, BOARDING schools are as common as the red phone booths that once peppered the city's brick-lined streets. The Westminster Abbey Choir School is, in many ways, a carbon copy of most of these preparatory academies, rich in legacy, history, and prestige. Its campus is located within the historic grounds of Westminster Abbey itself, allowing the boys, ages eight to thirteen, to live, study, and play within the cathedral's holy walls. However, one of the more distinctive aspects of this particular institute is that it is the last remaining choir school in the United Kingdom. That is not surprising when one considers the often less-than-ideal pairing of prepubescent boys and song. However, to hear Thomas and William Darlington sing was different. They both had voices that were strong and pure, despite being of different octaves.

For the boys, music had always been a rich part of their childhood. Memories of singing and dancing alongside their mother as their father played the piano filled their minds and hearts. It was in these moments that the boys missed them the most, if they allowed themselves to think of the loss of their parents at all. When their voices cooperated and didn't crack due to rapid changes taking place in their bodies, the brothers' vocals served as perfect complements. Amongst the elite group of thirty students chosen to serve in the Boys' Choir, William had been selected as a soprano with soft, high-pitched vocals. Thomas, on the other hand, had a lower range, providing a rich sound that with training and age would likely develop him as a baritone singer.

Choir practice was held in a large, bleak room that had elevated platforms layered to provide a stadium-like effect. They were angled in a semi-circle shape to allow all students to see the choir director's instruction. Tall ceilings gave way to better acoustics, and a piano sat in the middle of the room for accompaniment. During practice, the carefully selected students would arrive in their school uniform. For more than six centuries, the choir had participated in daily choral services at the abbey. This required the boys to slip into long white robes finished with a rich red band that brushed against their polished school shoes and a burgundy stole that draped around their necks. Red folders held their sheet music and provided a stark contrast to the black and white marble floor as they performed.

Having already finished their concert for the day, William and Thomas hung their robes carefully in the vestibule and watched as their classmates began the walk back to the dormitory. The other boys gathered their things before heading to "quiet time" back in their rooms. This period was set aside to allow all the resident choirboys to work on unfinished projects and to review coursework. Thomas and William, however, also assumed this was the most likely time that they could leave the school undetected. It had been a day since they had left the company of the ghosts of the abbey and both were anxious to set about their agreed-upon business. William, in fact, had already crafted a story. To anyone who asked, they would simply say they stayed after practice in the choir room to work on their choral arrangements.

As their classmates faded down the hallway, William and Thomas turned the other direction, opened the ornate wooden doors that led into the courtyard, and proceeded towards one of the main gates of the old church. They walked through the opening in the abbey fencing with confidence, driven by a deep desire to find the nearest bus to take them to the tower so they could reconnect with the two ghostly princes they had met. But just as they turned the corner and lost sight of Westminster, William let out a high-pitched scream. "Ouch!" Thomas glanced over to see that Mr. Hammond, the boys' math teacher, had a tight hold of William's ear.

"Fancy seeing you boys out and about on this fine afternoon. If I recall correctly, it is quiet time, and you seem far from your dormitory or from any endeavor worthy of gentlemen," Mr. Hammond scolded. He reached his hand out to grab ahold of Thomas as well, but the boy dodged his grip. "Thomas Darlington, you walk yourself directly back through those gates immediately," directed Mr. Hammond, pointing with one hand while continuing to hold William's ear with the other. The young captive was hunched over and squinting in pain. "I believe you both now have a date with Headmaster Rattlebag. He will be excited to hear why his pupils believed they could break the rules and leave campus without permission."

Mr. Hammond walked the boys back into the school, carefully trailing behind them with his quiet judgment pushing them on. The boys could feel the teacher's pleasure as he anticipated the headmaster's reaction. The three entered the administrative wing of the building. William felt his knees go weak, and Thomas' stomach turned slightly in discomfort. Mr. Hammond walked to the door of the abbey's main office and gave it three sharp raps.

"Come!" called an agitated voice from the other side of the door.

Mr. Hammond disappeared into the private office for what seemed like an eternity. As he emerged, he shook the headmaster's hand and then shot the boys a menacing grin, proud that he had been the one to catch them off school grounds.

Headmaster Rattlebag pulled the boys into his office with a stern glance. The room was drab and cold, just as the boys perceived the man who occupied it. His large, heavy wooden desk sat perfectly positioned at the back of the narrow room in front of an expansive bookcase that stretched from floor to ceiling. The formal nature of the office almost created a feeling that they were sitting down for an admittance interview at Oxford University rather than being chastised for an infraction at the abbey's small boarding school.

"Let me start by saying I am incredibly disappointed in both of you boys," Headmaster Rattlebag noted. It was the standard message all adults must say when they begin their 'you're in trouble' speech. The boys felt the exact reaction the stinging sentence was designed to have. Their stomachs sank, tears filled William's eyes as he hated to disappoint, and Thomas shifted awkwardly in his seat as he loathed confrontation and events that seemed to be a waste of time.

"This school has rules," Rattlebag continued. "We are attempting to raise gentlemen. Do you understand the sacrifices and expectations that surround your education? The utter disgrace and disrespect that you show by knowingly violating rules we have designed to keep you safe and enhance your education appalls me. Were your parents alive, I know they would feel the same. I'm tempted to call the priest at the orphanage who recommended your admittance. Father Holyfield, I believe..." As the headmaster spoke, he looked about his desk as if in search of a telephone number. William was now in pure panic mode, and Thomas was quickly following suit. They both felt it was crucial for the old administrator to know the important reason for their failed truancy attempt.

Thomas jumped from his seat. "Headmaster Rattlebag, please don't call Father Holyfield. We can explain." As the words came out of his mouth, Thomas recognized they were just as cliché as the headmaster's harsh speech about disappointment, but still, they could not be truer. In an emotional blurting of facts, Thomas attempted to make their case. "On the field trip to The Tower of London, we met two ghost princes who need us to return. They are trapped in the tower, and the world's very existence relies on us helping find the key to The Binding, the protection that exists between worlds. Spirits have been searching for it for hundreds of years." William hung his head against his chest, recognizing how crazy his brother's words sounded. From the look on the headmaster's face, he was in complete agreement with William's own assessment of Thomas' tale.

The headmaster waved off any more of the story. "Your imagination has always been one for the books, Thomas Darlington, but I will not have you filling even your own head with this utter poppycock. Even more so, the way in which you so easily spun this fiction and used it to excuse yourself from the reality that you broke the school rules is unsettling. How do you respond to that?" Rattlebag's voice boomed the last statement in a manner that surprised the two boys. His age had made him seem feeble at times, but now he filled the room with his authority. The boys glanced at each other with little more than a look to express that they both knew that they were likely facing major punishment and a call home to the orphanage. They both hung their heads in remorse.

After a minute and in unplanned unison, Thomas and William lifted their eyes with shame and dismay. As they steadied themselves to embrace the headmaster's wrath, William Shakespeare's ghost floated softly down to stand behind the office desk. He situated himself against the left shoulder of Rattlebag.

"Mine boys, 'tis time to calleth in some help! Thy acting is in need of much work, but I believeth I can assist, for all the world is a stage and no one knows that better than the Bard of Avon." The ghost, seemingly pleased with his own entrance, took a deep bow and with a quick flourish popped up to address the boys. "I will direct thee as if you were on thy own stage. Repeat after me..." Shakespeare began to direct William and Thomas as his hands gestured a new approach to the headmaster and a grand dramatic entrance for the two. The boys weren't sure if Shakespeare's expectations were going to be a relief to their situation or if they might add to their punishment. In fact, they had only understood half of the words that the ghost had just said, but they were out of options. Shakespeare proceeded to look to Thomas for the recitation, "Master, thee must believeth me. We art not falsing nor telling an odious dammed lie! To thine own self thou must be true, and it must follow, as night the day, thou canst not be false to any man."

Thomas shifted in his seat and sat forward as he carefully tried to repeat the words. "Thee musted believeth me-eth. We art not falsifying-eth to thee-eth." With that, Shakespeare and the headmaster simultaneously, and as if in tandem, shook their heads. Shakespeare added an eye roll to indicate his disappointment in the boy's inability to mirror his direction, while Headmaster Rattlebag's eyes partially closed. His nose and lips curled to paint confusion across his face.

William and Thomas both readied themselves to simply throw their fate to the mercy of the court, but before they could, yet another player entered the stage. At that very moment, Laurence Olivier emerged from the back wall and assumed a position behind Rattlebag's right shoulder, leaning up against him in a proud and confident pose. "My fine bard, you in no way can be the one to provide these boys with advice to help them out of this situation. Your pretentious language is nearly as off-putting as your questionable style in clothing!"

"And I suppose that thee bethink thou hast the solution, thee washed-up celebrity," Shakespeare shot back with a sidewise angry glance. "Tis in their best interest to tell the truth. Remember, truth is truth to the end of reckoning!"

"My dear, Will," Olivier let each word drip from his mouth

like honey. "This isn't one of your elaborate scripts. Only on stage would someone believe that the boys see and hear ghosts, are on an adventure to help two dead princes, and are the only ones summoned for this extraordinary mission. There is no option but to fib. With a little sparkle of my magical showmanship"—Olivier proceeded to provide an overly dramatic bow midsentence—"there is no way we don't convince this stiff man that the boys are innocent."

"Falsing is an unbecoming and distasteful art, but I fear thee art correct," Shakespeare conceded after a moment of thought. "I believe we should hast the boys state that they art nearly halfway to death. As men only live to be'est thirty years of age, so peradventure these lads wast sneaking out to find their wives and to secure their careers."

The boys again couldn't understand much of Shakespeare's discourse, but they were confident he had said they wouldn't live past 30 years old and so they should tell the headmaster they were sneaking out to marry immediately and start careers. Confusion and fear spread across their faces. The abrupt change in their demeanor caused Rattlebag to shift in his seat.

"Gads, Will, you miserable soul. Men only died young in your day because life was so mundane. In my time, men wore brilliant suits, smoked cigars, enjoyed fine spirits, bathed with beauties at pool parties, and packed their days with adventure. Perhaps the boys should say they were sneaking out to find the perfect glass of scotch to pair with a lovely cigar."

William chuckled and Thomas leaned his elbow on the arm of his chair, resting his face on his palm. "Seriously?" the older boy said as he rolled his eyes and shook his head. He and William would be in even bigger trouble if they used Olivier's defense.

"Pardon me, son?" Headmaster Rattlebag scolded. "How dare you speak to me like that? Not only am I more 'serious' than you can imagine, but my frustration with you both is escalating even as we speak."

Shakespeare and Olivier both began to become more animated behind the desk, shaking their heads and waving hands as if to signal for the boys to quickly apologize and divert the situation. The boys were stupefied watching the two ghosts almost dancing in hysterics. William and Thomas looked from left to right and from right to left, back and forth, as if observing a competitive ping-pong match. The headmaster began to mirror their pivoting heads. "Whatever are you two doing?" bellowed Rattlebag.

Shakespeare gasped, "Oh, for the love of all things holy. Apologize, lads! Sayeth this: Oh, greatest apologies thou gallant tiger-booted wafer-cake." It was Thomas who spouted out that last bit to Rattlebag at Shakespeare's request. The room went silent, and the ghosts stopped moving.

Olivier seemed to place his hands on his temples in sheer panic "Dear God...Wafer-cake? Boys! I fear we are sunk." And, with one last considered suggestion, Olivier shouted, "Save yourselves, lads! Run!"

"Enough! Silence." Headmaster Rattlebag was glaring at Thomas and William. "I am finished with this conversation. The reality is, you broke the rules and there are consequences for doing so. You both will be required to assist the kitchen staff for the next two weeks, collecting and cleaning dinner dishes of your peers. Additionally, you must write a letter detailing your transgressions, the importance of following our rules, and describe your commitment to the legacy of our school. Depending on your behavior over this two-week punishment period, I will decide whether Father Holyfield should be privy to your poor behavior."

Hearing this, the boys relaxed and succumbed to the idea that while it was a failed rescue effort by all involved, they at least were going to get out of this fiasco still enrolled at the school. Simply put, the quicker they could acknowledge their failed escape and receive their punishment, the quicker they could begin to plan their next trip to see the princes. "Yes, sir. We are sorry." Thomas and William slowly stood up, bowed to the headmaster, and carefully moved towards the door.

Olivier and Shakespeare, however, were far less accepting of the afternoon's ghastly and disappointing performance. Shakespeare clenched his fists before brushing the peplum of his shirt to try and release his tension. Olivier threw his hands up in the air and then shook them like tambourines before he positioned them on the corner of the headmaster's desk. Olivier stared at Shakespeare, fixating on him with a look of disdain. The bard caught his eyes and shifted his body to glare back at the actor.

"I blame a terrible script," Olivier scoffed as he tossed one hand into the air and then carefully laid the back of it across his forehead in disgust while he placed the other hand firmly on his hip.

"I censure an overly dramatic actor and poor delivery. Mine script wast flawless," Shakespeare sharply responded, crossing his arms delicately across his chest and raising his nose into the air. "I'd beat thee, but I wish not to infect my hands," muttered the playwright to the actor.

"Your wit's as thick as a Tewkesbury mustard," countered the thespian to the bard.

The boys paused at the door, looking over their shoulders to hear the ghosts' parting shots. William made eye contact with the headmaster, who still looked rather bothered by the meeting and the comment on his shoes.

"'Tiger-booted' indeed," huffed the headmaster, looking down at his footwear.

Thomas put his hand against William's shoulder and shoved him fully through the door. They had to be cleverer then they had considered. And it would take even more careful planning to get back to the tower given the additional supervision and suspicion that would now be upon them. But their father had always said, Thomas thought, "When there is a *Will*, there is a way." Of course, Father didn't know Shakespeare, Thomas chuckled to himself as he and his brother both hurried back to the dorm.

CHAPTER 7 | Free Day with the Princes

"FREE SATURDAYS" NEARLY mirrored the same excitement as Christmas day for the boys of the Westminster Abbey Choir School. Due to their rarity, all of the students would extensively plan what their next adventures let loose in London would include. Over the last several days, the debate of where to go had become resolved. William and Thomas' friends had decided on visiting Madame Tussauds famous wax museum to take a peek at their favorite pop culture characters and historical figures. William and Thomas secretly knew that many of the ghosts of these famous individuals made in wax were waiting for them to retrieve information from the tower and return it to the abbey. The boys stressed about the important mission they would attempt that day while their classmates seemed most worried about whether they would be able to capture the perfect "selfie" with notable celebrities. The brothers planned to sneak away from their assigned group of boys in the crowds of the museum and make their way quickly to the tower. After the fiasco with Headmaster Rattlebag, they had told Darwin and Dickens of their plan to get their approval. Both had agreed it seemed the most prudent course of action.

Dickens, Darwin, Hawking, and Shakespeare sat propped

up on one of the perfectly made dorm beds, hoping to help send the Darlingtons off to their task. While the ghosts waited on Thomas and William, they also began to listen for their names to be mentioned by the other boys heading to Tussauds. "Gads...I don't understand it. Surely, we are popular amongst visitors in the museum. Who wouldn't want their picture taken alongside the world's greatest scientist?" asked Newton while vainly waiting for his name to be said. "And who is this Beyoncé character? Everyone keeps mentioning him!"

"He is a she," whispered Thomas to the ghost, "and she is quite lovely and sings beautifully. But, you are very interesting too." He added the compliment as an afterthought in an attempt to please the mathematician.

"My God, man! The lads hath mentioned already that Einstein fellow on whom Hawking keeps ruminating. These boys seem to think him of grand scientific importance so, indeed, you, Newton, may be second most interesting at best," mocked Shakespeare. He had learned who Einstein was years ago from the "World History Since Your Death" class he had taken from an ethereal historian.

"Surely you aren't serious? Einstein? He's a pedestrian mind who had a significant stroke of luck...relatively speaking," Hawking laughed to himself and to the confusion of the others. Looking around at the gathered ghosts for acknowledgment and finding none, he shrugged. "Besides, as I've said before, it is never smart to boast about your IQ, and that is all he did! I must say, I am utterly surprised that my own brilliant figure is not at the forefront of these young scholars' minds and interests." He lowered his knee, placed his left foot onto the floor, and raised the right knee to his chest while maintaining his look of disbelief.

"Receiveth not thy panties in a bunch," warned Shakespeare to Newton. "By the time those gents finish examining mine own statue, so prominently displayed for its artistry, p'rhaps they shall accidentally walketh past your statue on the way to the loo." The writer was teasing, yet Sir Isaac found little humor in his delivery.

"How clever. By now, perhaps, the curators have evaluated your life's work and they've moved your statue into the loo where it belongs," responded Darwin with a growing look of disdain for the conversation of the entire group. Shakespeare waved off the insult as if to suggest it was meaningless but broke into a half-smile at the retort while doing so.

"Touché!" exclaimed Hawking, "Well played, sir." He stopped exercising for a moment to bow to Darwin and to acknowledge his wit. The hiatus from exercise, however, was short-lived as he almost as quickly started doing toe-touches in sets of twenty.

While the ghosts fussed and bantered, the boys buttoned their uniform jackets and eagerly exited the room at the precise moment the clock hit nine. Their free time had begun, and they had few constraints on the fun they could have as long as they were back to the abbey in time for supper. All of the classmates made their way into the courtyard and out of the gates of the choir school to the corner bus stop. The museum was waiting, and as their ride arrived, the boys flooded on, carefully navigating around the few already seated passengers. The brothers slid onto a bench at the rear of the double-decker, with William crammed against the window so Thomas could entertain and converse with their classmates. The younger boy stared through the glass and tried to imagine what the city looked like before all of the added commercialization and modernization. "When the two princes were playing near the tower, what was their view?" he wondered. Then he turned to his brother and said, "If we are going to find the princes, we will need as much time as possible."

"Which one do you want to see first? Prince Harry, Duke of Sussex, or Prince William, Duke of Cambridge? I heard that the William one is ugly and looks awful. Oh, wait! That was about you! I am sure the royal William looks far less hideous than you do," laughed Nigel as he overheard William's comment about "finding the princes" and leaned over the seat in front of the boys. Nigel was a fidgety redhead who was stretched thin like a string bean. He liked to pick at William, who was often his competition in the classroom. William disregarded his comments and reminded himself that Nigel was a spoiled child who likely hadn't been taught any social cues, thus making his opinion hold very little weight. Will turned his head to sit quietly.

"Stand up for yourself, boy!" William heard Newton's voice at almost the same time he saw his head pop through the ceiling of the bus.

"What are you doing here?" William exclaimed to the ghost. He immediately shrank into himself while the surrounding schoolboys looked at him quizzically.

"I'm riding a bus to the wax museum," answered Nigel, shaking his head and answering what he assumed was a question directed toward him. "You've gone daft!" he added to the amusement of the other boys.

"Quiet, lad." Dickens' head had dropped though the ceiling at this point and addressed William and the situation. "Remember, they can't see us."

"Nor me!" said Hawking's head, suddenly appearing next to Dickens.

"What is this? Much ado about nothing?" quipped Shakespeare, his head pushing out from behind Hawking.

"I hope they have Banshee Brandy at the museum. I could use a drink, and I know there is a poltergeist pub there." Olivier sounded as though he could really use the libation as his head appeared beside Shakespeare's and the actor began looking about. "Wonderful party..." he quipped.

"Are you all here?" William blurted the query out to the ghosts again before he thought through how such a question might appear to the bus full of mortal boys.

"Just the same as when we started!" responded Nigel's voice and then he addressed the bus as a whole. "I am telling you, he is not right in the head." At which point, Newton reached down from above and flicked Nigel in the ear. The obnoxious schoolboy jumped, as if he had been shocked, and slapped his own head.

"Who's the loon now!" laughed Thomas, pointing to Nigel as the other boys joined in the humor.

"Miserable child," stated Newton.

"I guess we are all here." It was Darwin talking as he and Jane emerged in full form from the floor. "We all decided to come to see the museum. It's been quite a while since we have been on an outing. Discussion over whose statue would be placed where and who would be viewed most acutely seemed to consume us all. The vanity of the dead knows no bounds, young William." Darwin shook his head while Jane looked on, smiling sweetly.

"My dear friends, while we are all here in good humor, we are also a distraction to the boys. We have tasked them with a mission of grave importance and here we are diverting them from their cause." Jane's voice quieted the rabble of other ghosts. "Let us retire back up to the roof of this fine motor-stage and leave Thomas and William to their business."

With only a bit of grumbling, the gathered group of ghosts receded out and up to the roof of the bus where they had apparently been riding. Jane was the last to leave. "Thomas and William, do be careful. It worries me that two so young are left with such a large responsibility. Do what you can, and hurry back to the abbey. Please take no chances. We shall be waiting." With her last word of advice, she too disappeared up onto the roof.

The boys around William and Thomas continued their conversation, discussing who in the royal family their favorite was and whether or not they should pay the extra money to have the "Tea with the Queen" photo made at the museum. Within minutes, the large green dome of Madame Tussauds rose against the sky as the gathered group of riders turned onto Marylebone Road. The driver stopped the bus, and as it barely pulled to the curb, the stream of perfectly dressed students pushed their way out onto the sidewalk. A red carpet rolled out of the building as if the arriving guests were celebrities in their own right. Some of the boys pretended like they were famous, asking classmates to take their picture as they posed in a stance to show off their swagger, while others headed straight to the ticket window to purchase entry. Thomas held William at the end of the line. As the last boy disappeared through the doors to find the wax casts of favorite royals and famous celebrities, William and Thomas abruptly changed direction and began their walk to the tower.

"Farewell! Farewell! Parting is such sweet sorrow." Shakespeare was waving as Thomas turned back to see who had called out.

"Come on, Will," Olivier clapped the bard on his shoulder. "Let's go find that brandy. I'll buy."

✦ ✦ ✦

As the boys arrived at the gates of the tower, William gulped. He remembered how the hairs had stood up on the back of his neck the last time they exited the old fortress. The haunting sounds, the pleas from the ghosts, and the whistle. Oh, the whistle. Both boys had found it intoxicating. Today they had to stand in line for tickets and watched as the many tourists gathered in groups to have their chance to visit the historic landmark. "If these people knew of the ethereal world and demonic presence inside the tower walls, would they continue in? Ghostly adventures are more fun," Thomas thought, "when reading about them from the safety of your own bed under the covers at night." After the gate attendant passed the boys their tickets, they rushed into the tower and headed straight for the anteroom to the gallery of the crown jewels.

Before walking through the last doorway to the where they had met the two young princes, Thomas and William glanced around to see if other patrons were heading in with them. They had noticed several ghosts standing about on their walk there, but the ethereals had not seemed to notice, probably only thinking them typical tourists. It was the best reaction the boys could hope for. The last thing they needed was onlookers: living or dead. Thomas strode into their destination first and wasted no time. It was momentarily empty and seemed to have a haze lingering in the air. He immediately began summoning the princes. "We've come back as we promised. Are you here?" When no immediate answer came, he again asked the question. Silence was the only reply. Thomas glanced over at William as a group of visitors moved through the room looking to gawk at more jewels. They did not linger, and Thomas called out to the princes for a third time, much louder than before.

A chill came into the room along with the silhouettes of familiar faces. As they emerged, the transparent outlines formed into more strongly defined figures. The two princes had been waiting and were eager to reunite with the boys. They seemed almost gleeful as they approached the mortals. "I think this may be the first time in hundreds of years that there is hope in the castle. Our fellow spirits have not stopped talking about you both, doubting you would come back, but desperately anticipating the day you did. We are so thankful you have returned," Edward beamed.

"Darlingtons always honor their word," Thomas said with attempted authority. "And we have important news! When we returned to the abbey, our ability to see ghosts and spirits expanded immensely," he continued. "We started seeing them everywhere. It's like we've been introduced to an entirely new world. We had no idea how active or complex the spirit life was at our school or around London."

"And there is a group of ghosts in Westminster Abbey who have been dying to meet you. No pun intended," teased William.

"They are very worried about what has happened at the tower. Many important people have remained in the abbey to help everyone here, to open the fortress and restore the natural balance. And they now also wish to protect us all from this evil you have described. They feel there must be a reckoning with the darkness, whatever it may be. Sir Isaac Newton, Charles Darwin, Charles Dickens, Stephen Hawking, and Jane Austen to name just a few!" Thomas professed the names of the ghosts he and William had met in a manner to impress but saw only confusion on the princes' faces.

"Sadly, Thomas, we do not know of these ghosts," remarked Edward. "Nonetheless, if they can see you, then they could help us, too."

"Before we met you, the spirits here were helpless. We have all been trapped within the walls of the tower since the death of our father." Rake's reiteration of this core fact gave both Darlingtons a sense of the young ghost's desperation.

Edward picked up the conversation. "You see, before our father died, the Knights Templar managed the gate that keeps evil here."

"The ghosts we met in the abbey called it 'The Binding,' and they told us of the Templars," offered Thomas.

"Did they? That is a good name for it," answered Rake.

"It is also good you know that history, for it tells you of the importance of the key," added Edward. He continued, "The Templars left and then our uncle turned on our family. He killed our father and then us out of greed. As we said, our father tried to tell us about a key that would protect the tower, but he died before we could understand what the key was and where it was hidden. So, we've been looking for it ever since."

"Wait! Your uncle killed you and your dad?" asked

Thomas, who was intrigued, startled, and simultaneously saddened by this information. He attempted to put his hand on Edward's shoulder in consolation, but it passed through the spirit. William had gone silent in concern.

"He did," affirmed Edward. "He thought if he killed us, he would become king. With the crown, he believed he would also be given the key. Once he killed our father, he killed the one person who knew where and what the key was. Our uncle wasn't himself anymore, and we watched as he became consumed with greed, jealousy, and rage. When he died, we first saw the demon that possessed him."

"And," whispered Rake as if it could hear him, "it stayed behind in the tower."

"Demon?!" said William and Thomas together. A new and terrible sense of dread began filling them. The ghosts back at their school knew nothing of this.

"Yes," said Rake, picking up where his brother had left off. "It had possessed our uncle, and, unlike us, it can cross The Binding. We believe he came through the walls of Acheron to enter the tower, and we've watched him step through The Binding to move beyond its gate. He uses mortal vessels seduced into carrying his black spirit. Once outside, he transforms himself into a man. He also sometimes walks the tower with the visitors, calling himself 'Jack,' manipulating and convincing people to do whatever he wants. Here in the tower, he also sometimes takes the form of a dark, evil presence with glowing eyes, tentacles, and hoofed feet. His consuming rage torments all of us inside as he has been on the quest to find the key, too."

"We saw The Binding back at the abbey. It's cracking. The ghosts there fear that evil is gaining more power here and that this cage will fail. Is that because of the demon?" asked William.

"I think that the good in the tower has grown weary and is becoming resigned to the fact that the demon is far stronger than we are. The hope that we will find the key has almost disappeared. I do not know the answer to your question William, but I know the demon is darker and more powerful than the rest of the evil here combined..." Edward's voice trailed off. "Do you really think the ghosts in the abbey could help us?" he eventually asked.

William was sure of it. "I don't see why not. I actually think you might be able to help each other," he said. "But they need to hear this story themselves. They are some of history's greatest minds, and I am sure they will have plenty of questions and insight."

"I am not sure how this works, but the ghosts in the abbey sent us to bring you back to them," offered Thomas.

"I can't believe this is finally happening," said Rake. "All you have to do is invite us in, and then we can travel with you back to the abbey." Both Princes seemed excited at what they had just heard.

"That's what they told us. Just 'invite you in,'" shuttered William. He was always anxious about the unknown and added "So you understand what must be done?"

"We do," said Edward and Rake in unison.

"Well, what are you waiting for? Come in. We've got places to go and people, or at least ghosts, to see," exclaimed Thomas. He had been wanting to use that line. It reminded him of his father, who always used cliché sayings but somehow sounded profound and in control when doing so.

The ghost princes nodded and walked to stand in front of the schoolboys, nearly touching them nose to nose. Rake stood before William as Edward was before Thomas. Together they took one final step to enter the bodies of the boys. As they did, Thomas and William felt a powerful thrill flooding them from head to toe. It was a paralyzing feeling that froze them in their stance before fading into a burst of energy. Their limbs began to shake involuntarily in an effort to spread the current that was pulsating through their veins.

"This is so incredibly awesome!" shouted Thomas, who felt an almost uncontrolled strength and power race through him.

"It is a divine feeling, indeed," remarked Edward, taking control.

The spirits were gone from the room, and yet, were still there. William and Thomas were closed off from control and reality in their own bodies, only experiencing it as the ghosts allowed.

The princes stood looking at each other from within their vessel possessions. "Are we really free from the tower now?" asked Rake.

"I believe we are," answered his older brother. "William? Thomas? Are you ready to go to the abbey?" At once, Thomas felt himself back in control of his body. He knew that Edward was still there and could even talk with him inside his thoughts, but the prince had receded. Edward was a stowaway in his body.

"Yeah, we better get going to the abbey. Our time is limited," said Thomas.

Inside Thomas' thoughts, Edward suggested, "The demon makes his rounds at sunset to ensure that none of the good tower ghosts are on the hunt for the key. We have no option but to be securely back in this location by then or be found missing."

"I get it. Back before sunset," said Thomas aloud as if answering Edward, "and it's pizza night at school. We have to be back by dinnertime, or I will be depressed that I missed my favorite greasy goodness! Also, William will panic because he hates to be in trouble," teased Thomas.

"Whatever. Someone has to follow the rules," said William. "Come on, let's get you guys back to the abbey."

In William's mind, Rake laughed, "We're leaving!"

The two boys with their "live-in" guests walked down the corridor, out to the tower gates, and onto the cobblestone streets. Through their hosts, it was the first time in centuries the princes had felt the bright, limitless sunlight and smelled the crisp fresh London air outside of the tower. They were filled with new hope.

"What is pizza?" Edward popped the question into Thomas' head.

Thomas nearly began to drool thinking of his favorite food. "If I can, I will show you before we go back into the tower. You think Arcadia is heaven? You have no idea."

CHAPTER 8 | The Princes at the Abbey

AS WILLIAM, THOMAS, and their two spectral guests approached the abbey, they could sense something unusual was happening. Small groups of students were gathered outside the church's doors talking energetically or simply standing and staring as if in some mild form of shock. The urgency the mortal boys felt from Edward and Rake precluded them from stopping to find out the scuttlebutt; however, they couldn't help but hear some of the comments of concern as they passed through the gatherings.

"They bloody-well came to life," said Nigel, William's nemesis, who was standing in the courtyard in front of the main abbey doors. "I saw it with my own eyes. Hawking got up from his chair and attacked Einstein." William and Thomas looked at each other in surprise at the thought.

Going into the abbey, they heard another. "It was all just robotics," declared Burt, an older boy with carefully styled brown hair, known for his sensibility and leadership. His large, athletic frame was enough to command respect, but Burt was better known for his cool head and his ability to help in nearly any situation. He had his circle of friends closer to the side entrance traditionally used by those working in Westminster and wishing to avoid the queue of tourists. "The museum is just trying to boost attendance."

William and Thomas looked dubiously at that group and moved on.

Further on in the vestibule, they passed the largest collection of choirboys yet, one that surrounded James, a natural storyteller and recognized class comedian. His curly black hair fell onto his forehead, and his belt barely buckled around his waist. His antics, hand motions, and vocal inflections added to the excitement of his account. "So...Einstein is tackled by Hawking who is then tackled by Newton. And, when Beyoncé arrived and started trying to pull them all up and off each other, she finally managed to disarm them. Not that they had weapons, mind you. She literally pulled off their blooming arms! She looked a bit taken back dealing with that brainy brawl."

While the crowd seemed pleased with James' account, William could only look at Thomas and mutter, "It had to be them." They pressed on into the abbey.

The boys heard their new ghostly friends before they actually saw them. Newton and Hawking were bickering in the corner of the sanctuary. The afternoon had clearly turned into a nightmare at Madame Tussauds, and the spirits seemed to be trying to cast blame on each other for the events as they occurred. While the free day had been an incredible experience for the schoolboys, for the group of ethereals, it had turned into an utter fiasco with tricks, torment, and destruction all brought about because of the ghosts themselves.

"Olivier! Get over here immediately," shouted Newton with great command and newfound authority. He made eye contact with the actor and fixed his look upon him with frustration as Olivier made his way to the agitated mathematician.

"I had a feeling you wouldn't just let it go, could you, Newt?" replied Olivier as he strolled up to the conversation. "We all know I had no intentions of causing trouble today. I simply had one too many cocktails at the spirits bar and thought I could put on a show for our little troupe and the gathered schoolboys. They all claimed that they don't believe in ghosts, so I wanted to show them that we are both real and present. I thought the idea of a partial possession was inspired. Why, I have friends who live at Tussauds and I felt the sting of the insult for them. I simply wanted to put the boys all to the test." The actor took a swallow from the glass that Thomas and William had just noticed he was holding. Clearly, the actor had not fully quenched his thirst at the museum.

"A show? What you did was humiliating," piped in Hawking. "You were a prime example of why we don't leave the abbey much. A partial possession of an object is not a trifling ability. Who knows what kind of ideas you put into the heads of dark spirits? Without your theatrics, we would have attracted very little, if any, attention. You never seem to be able to control yourself. If any of our evil ethereal brethren find inspiration in the mess you created, we could have an entire army of department store mannequins marching on parliament by tomorrow! Not to mention what might come out of the museum's chamber of wax horrors!!"

"Is that really what it is about, Stephen?" asked Olivier in a condescending manner. "I have a feeling you and Newton are just mad that I took it upon myself to engage in friendly banter as Albert Einstein. My good man, you two seem so intimidated by him. I thought it might be a lark to let you two finally face your fears and give you a jab or two. You both certainly jabbed back. All in good fun, boys!"

"You bounder! It has nothing to do with insecurity, for, indeed, I have none!" responded Newton, who then motioned to Hawking. "My colleague and I were enjoying the sensation of being back into our own bodies and you ruined it. I am sorry you aren't famous enough to have your own wax statue, but by walking around in Einstein and taunting us, you made an absolute spectacle of things. Good heavens, sir! Poor Hawking may never be the same. His museum figure was broken."

"Now, I can't take all the credit for that, Steve," said Olivier, looking at Hawking.

"You broke my glasses, you goon, and the fall took a large sliver out of my nose. Now my figure will be housed in some dark hole waiting to be repaired." Hawking shook his head in disappointment and for the moment he stood still, clearly feeling quite defeated.

"They may just trash you all together, Hawking, as you surely were not amongst the most popular attractions," Olivier continued. "And it was not I who so abruptly removed your arms. That Beyoncé creature was an absolute reaper."

"Less that and more a naturalist," came Darwin's voice from behind the proceedings. "And let us hope I have the chance to ask the poor lady's forgiveness for absconding with her likeness to try and stop the fray."

"Charles!" exclaimed Olivier, "So good to see that you are back to yourself. Curious... why ever did you select her to join the fun?"

"She was just there, Laurence. Nothing to make of it," said Darwin, glaring at the actor.

"I have had it, Olivier, you D-list celebrity," barked Hawking, wanting the group focused solely on his perceived injuries. With that proclamation, he made use of the nimble nature of his spirit form and charged at Olivier, knocking the actor's ghostly frame to the floor. The thespian howled in amusement as the thin spirit of Hawking tried with all his might to hold him down.

Just as the mathematician was losing his grip, Darwin shouted out, "Enough, you fools! Can't you see our young friends have returned? Get up and act like the gentlemen you are supposed to be. I will not have these lads seeing you in this distasteful manner." The naturalist was looking directly at William and Thomas. The boys, for their part, were standing quietly behind the gathering, listening to the argument. At this point, they did not even bother trying to hide their smiles.

Dickens was silently sitting on an ethereal bench, wearing a top hat and smoking a pipe. He held a quill pen and tapped it against a notepad. He had purposefully removed himself from the argument at bay and shot the boys a look of relief as they came into view.

Thomas and William stepped forward towards the tussling ghosts, who were now making their way to their feet. Hawking shifted his glasses, and Olivier fixed his hair.

"My boys! You are back. Are the princes with you?" Newton inquired with his usual flamboyance of tone while trying to pretend that nothing unusual was happening. The mortal boys both nodded their affirmation to the inquiry and stopped in their tracks.

Thomas and William stood still as the now familiar electric current pulsed through their bodies. A cool sensation had embraced the boys from the moment the princes had entered them as hosts. As the princes slowly emerged from their borrowed flesh and bone frames, William and Thom felt a calming heat return to their bodies. Standing beside the two mortal boys were similar-sized ethereals. Their outline was radiant, glowing fiercely. The hue of their ghostly shapes appeared as a reflection of the intensity and urgency of purpose they carried within them.

At first, the gathered ghosts and the ethereal princes simply stared at each other in amazement. And then, in unison, the abbey ghosts bowed to the princes. "Your Royal Highnesses, it is an honor to stand in your company," stated Newton, rising up from his signature obeisance. "We thought it might be you two from the descriptions given by young William and Thomas, but we could not be sure. So much of what is happening and has happened is lost to us behind the veil of The Binding. Prince Edward and Prince Richard, is it not?" The two young ghosts both nodded to the mathematician in their most regal manner and released him from the courtesies with a gesture of their hands.

"You can call me Rake," said the younger of the two ghosts.

"Rake it is then," said Newton, smiling as he continued.

"My friends, if you would like, please come with me. We here are eager to know what is happening in the tower," the affable ghost remarked. "I thought you might also be curious about the abbey. Let us walk and talk for a few minutes, and I will show you about." He then turned to the other spirits, "Shall you gather the rest of our little cadre while I take the princes strolling? We could meet you shortly."

"Good God, Newton!" roared Darwin. His voice made all those gathered freeze in the moment. "You are actually making sense!"

Newton waved at Darwin in a dismissive fashion. "I assure you, sir, my sensibilities are now, and always have been, as highly calibrated as the striking of the great bell of the tower clock!"

"Sir," piped up Thomas without much thought, "The tower clock isn't working!"

"Details!" retorted the mathematician, quickly raising his finger into a now-familiar point straight up.

"Get about your business, Newton, before I retract my earlier observation," rejoined Darwin. "We here shall convene the others."

As Newton and the ghost princes wandered out into the abbey, the mortal boys and the remaining spirits set about to round up those who were missing. "Let us not forget Merlin and Glinda in this!" said Darwin to Olivier, who had an unfamiliar look of seriousness on his face.

"The details from the princes might help them deduce why The Binding is failing." A tinge of desperation had crept into Darwin's voice that Olivier well understood. If the two magically- disposed apparitions could not soon find a long-term solution to the gaps that were appearing in the ethereal barrier, there would be no stopping the pending catastrophe. Olivier assumed it was his directive to go find the witch and magician. He walked out of the sanctuary and down the hall to the passageway that led to the basement.

Hawking had taken it upon himself to look for Shakespeare and Unk. Earlier, they had both noted their desire to visit Ghostly Grinds, the ethereal coffee shop. Shakespeare had been exhausted by the incident at Madame Tussauds, and while Olivier preferred a "spirit" in moments like this, the Bard preferred a double-spirit espresso to reset his senses. Beyond the coffee, however, the writer had grown close to the Unknown Soldier. Both enjoyed discussing history, and, when feeling generous, Shakespeare would even read some of his own poetry to the military man. Unk would drink tea, sometimes enjoy a short cigar, and close his eyes as he listened to Shakespeare's words. In rare circumstances, Shakespeare would work on new material, asking the soldier for feedback. On occasion, he took some of the military man's suggestions to heart, but more importantly to the writer, something about sharing his work made Shakespeare feel alive again. Hawking proceeded to the café to see if the two ghosts were there.

"William and Thomas, I recently saw Jane in Poets' Corner. Why not see if she is still enjoying that visit?" Darwin continued. Just as the others had left to find their assigned ghosts, the brothers set out to look for her. The hunt, however, did not take long. They quickly found Jane where Darwin had felt she might be, standing gracefully by her remembrance in the abbey. A look of melancholy left her face as she saw the boys.

"William and Thomas. Oh, my heart. You are back," she said as her mouth curled into a delighted grin. It was clear their safe return had brought her much happiness. The change in expression, however, had not been lost to William. Something was bothering the gentle spirit.

"Miss Jane," the young boy asked shyly, "Are you sad? We didn't mean to disturb you."

Jane's smile widened at the question, and her eyes pooled in potential tears. "No, dear William, you did not disturb," the ghost sweetly replied. "I just sometimes miss Hampshire and my friends at Winchester Cathedral. When I came here to move on, I had no idea I would be staying so long. Sometimes one just misses home, do they not? Though"—Jane paused to consider her thought—"it is so nice to be remembered here. People have been so kind. There was such a lovely sermon given that day. How I wish you had seen it." The boys knew of the ceremony to place Austen's commemorative stone in the abbey and could only surmise she had the privilege of seeing the dedication.

Both brothers were now smiling at the kind soul before them. It was Thomas who broke the moment. "Miss Jane. The princes have come here with us and Mister Darwin asked us to find you. I think he wants everyone to hear their story firsthand."

Jane nodded with understanding. "Come, boys. The time for my reverie has passed. Let us continue to the gathering and hear all that is known. Will you lead me? I am feeling rather tired." Holding both hands out as if she wanted each of the boys to take one, Jane started walking forward. Thomas instinctively reached for the ghost's extended hand and was surprised to find that he could take it gently in his. William, looking at his brother, followed suit. He walked to the other side of Jane, reached out his hand, and held onto hers.

"Sir Isaac took the princes to acquaint them with the abbey. Mister Hawking went to fetch Merlin and Glinda, Mister Olivier set off to find Mister Shakespeare and Mister Unk, and Mister Dickens and Mister Darwin are waiting in the sanctuary for all of us to return," informed Thomas. He wanted to refocus Jane's attention. Seeing her homesick had made his heart heavy.

"I can't wait for you to meet the princes," added William with an optimistic, eager tone in his voice. "They are so brave and smart. They might have the exact information Merlin needs to help with The Binding."

"Good, my darlings," whispered Jane as Thomas guided their walk. "Let us not keep them waiting."

CHAPTER 9 | Meetings and Discoveries

IT HAD BEEN nearly an hour before the mortal boys returned to the sanctuary with Jane in tow and they were enthusiastic to rejoin the princes. As they approached, they could see that their two young ghostly friends looked refreshed but miserably full.

Edward, who was holding his stomach that was about to burst, exclaimed, "You were right about the pizza, Thomas!" Barely able to stand upright, the young ghost waddled over to a bench and plopped himself down with a mild thud.

"Gads, Newton! What did you do to those poor boys?" questioned an approaching Darwin.

Newton looked a bit flustered and guilt was painted on his face. He attempted to explain. "It has been centuries since they last enjoyed a proper meal, so I took them to Phantasmal Foods. Can you believe there wasn't even a wait? There is always a line out the door, but not today." Newton looked up in hopes of finding a group of impressed peers, but when the other ghosts looked back with blank stares, he began to ramble. "They both requested pizza, but I made sure to also present them with a diversified collection of other abbey classics. We shared the Banshee Bacon Macaroni and Cheese, split the Bogey Burger, and finished it all off with a Church Chocolate Sundae, complete with a warm brownie."

Darwin shook his head in disgust. "For creatures who have ostensibly died, that galley of ghostly gastronomists has moved gluttony to new heights," he muttered. "Why, that eatery is becoming positively American. Keep a diet like that up, and the princes won't be able to fit inside Thomas and William for their return trip." Both the princes sucked in their stomachs and tried to hide their swollen bellies.

Thomas and William decided to break the tension by introducing Edward and Rake to Jane and by taking a moment for they themselves to acknowledge the ghosts newly gathered.

"Enough with the niceties and formalities, my dear gathered ghosts." It was Dickens serving as the group's moderator. "Please let us attend the issues at hand, lest we run out of time. It is not long before we have to send these boys away back behind The Binding." Then addressing the princes specifically, he added, "Please lads, tell us what has been happening in the tower these many years."

The princes started at the very beginning, describing their once joyful relationship with their uncle, their father's reign, his death, and the many bizarre and dark events that had happened since. Rake and Edward took their time to include as many details as possible, as they weren't sure when they'd have another chance to recruit the ghosts for help. Yet, both princes wondered if they could find the right words to accurately describe the horror they experienced and the evil they witnessed so many centuries ago. They told what they knew about the demon who called himself Jack.

✦ ✦ ✦

(Year 1483 – Depths of Acheron)

The souls who reside in Acheron add the most piercing sound to its wicked din. The shrill pleas of those abandoned here freeze the heart. Ghosts that never stop burning. Never stop begging. Never stop crying out and never rest. Their screams are not human anymore but are torn from the eternal spirit; a manifest cry to the universe for their release back to the mortal world. Yet, this blood-curdling noise will never cease. Acheron is a forever destination, where all within are constantly being consumed by fire. It is eternally apart from the ethereal and mortal worlds that are beyond its bounds and different from Arcadia in the Afterword where the righteous find their eternal peace. The sounds here are of those being tortured for their sins in life, and they echo in this hell of their own making.

While the symphony of the damned continues to score the gut-wrenching reality of their own existence, one creature seems unphased in this mournful gloom. In fact, for this fell spirit who walks the pit, the sounds, smells, and visions of Acheron seem to delight as he strengthens with the sense of agony that surrounds him. Suffering feeds him as he licks his lips for the meal of emotion he has eaten and for the feast of despair he will continue to consume. The demon, a lord of Acheron, is a menacing, formidable figure, looming larger than any human could. To the mortal eye, his physique would be an abomination; a patchwork of features that might only be drawn from a nightmare. His chest resembles that of a chiseled man, muscled and thick, but his scaled skin appears reptilian. Tentacles that protrude from his back drape against his frame idly, save as he uses them as appendages in concert with his more human-like arms. Adorned with only a breechcloth to preserve some perverse sense of modesty, his overtly strong legs are capped with hooved feet that tap against the rock and the occasional skull of some unnamed, unrecognized creature. The result of his gait is an almost rhythmic cadence. His thick arms give way to sinister hands with elongated fingers and claw-like nails that could easily summon death. His neck fades into a face dark as night. His red eyes are but small slits of light in the darkness, but they glow with such intensity that they appear as bright as the flames that crash against his shadow. Two twisted ram-like horns take the place of hair, their calcification mimicking the rock formations that line the path he walks through in the underworld.

Although the tortured souls of this netherworld would never be allowed to crawl to the wall that separates Acheron from the mortal and ethereal worlds beyond, the demon spent untold centuries there walking and searching. He had come to know something was amiss in the other worlds; that something had changed on those planes of existence. The rate of evil souls that streamed into Acheron from the ethereal plane had slowed as if a spigot had been tightened and even more, the magical binding that had stood against Acheron's evil denizens returning to the mortal world felt different, weakened somehow. The black spirit agonized over this change as if it were his own personal torment. It had been hundreds of years since the worlds of mortal man and the ether had felt so accessible. He had roamed those worlds before and wished to be back to again spread pain and destruction.

He stopped and placed his gnarled hand on the wall. He had been captive in this realm for far too long, subjected to the rule of Lucifer. "What a waste of potential. Lucifer has the ability to destroy all good and even more, all things that live beyond The Binding in the mortal world, if he only got himself free. Why does he hesitate to try? Why would he keep his power confined inside of hell?" The demon relished in the idea of his own escape. "If The Binding gave way and a hole was opened, I could again leave Acheron and become lord of all of those beyond it." The demon's brow furled as he continued to reflect. "All the heavens and earth would then open unto me and, even more delightfully, I could bring others here to share in my delicious visions there. Together we might even assail the gates of Arcadia." The demon paused his walk as if to slow his thinking and lessen the emotion of anticipation. He, a lord of Acheron, would become a king outside in the ethereal plane and of the mortal world. And, his kingdom would be of his own design, serving to torture all those he ruled. The demon unfurled what passed as a smile. "The devil," he thought, "be damned. I will rule as dark lord."

So, the demon continued walking the wall, dragging his hand along the layered stratum of rock that gave boundary to Acheron and marked the edge of The Binding. Sparks flew as his nails dug into the stone and left five long tracks behind. The passage of time could be seen in this well-walked path, for the scars left there suggested age akin to rings on a tree. Eons had passed since he began. The demon clacked his hooves along the rock as he wandered on. Tap, tap, tap, tap. Often as he walked, he whistled a curious tune. He knew that it was an odd habit, and contradictory to his malicious nature, but it was something he learned before he was trapped behind The Binding and while he still had access to the other worlds.

On the earthly plane, the beast had prided himself on possessing mankind. As much as the demon could understand emotion, the sound of the whistling had long given him pleasure. It had been jaunty when it came from the men he embodied, but from the demon, the sound was now like the wind blowing through the confines of a broken mausoleum or perhaps the beckoning call of a reaper. It was dark and no longer of the world of men. It soothed, hypnotized, seduced, and enveloped the mind of the listener but eventually would lead its audience to their death.

The demon continued to enjoy his walk. He began to alternate between dragging his entire palm against the wall and using a single cracked nail to pull its way along the rock. It was then that it happened. The demon halted abruptly. He was certain he had felt something. The wall gave way ever so slightly. His tapping hooves stopped, and the whistle died on his lips. He lowered into a crouch, with his tentacles billowing and his red eyes lowering in the darkness. The wall's rock looked solid. The demon pressed it again. His hand slightly sank into the stone. He pulled back, surprised, and then a malicious grin slid across his jagged yellow teeth. This time, with force, he pressed on the rock until his oversized fingers disappeared into the wall. The demon shuddered in excitement, his horns vacillating from side to side. A piercing yell erupted from within his throat as he pulled his hand back from what he had discovered. For centuries, he had looked without avail. But he had finally found it, a hole in The Binding, a portal to the world beyond. He sank his back against the wall, and his crooked mouth formed into another hideous smile. He held it for only a moment and then slowly closed his eyes, leaning his head back. He felt The Binding snap ever so slightly, and he started to whistle again. But this time he did so with a new purpose.

CHAPTER 10 | An Evil Invitation

(Year 1483 – Tower of London)

LORD RICHARD AWOKE in his elaborate gold four-poster bed with worrisome thoughts plaguing his mind. For months, he had stewed on the fact that the boys he had once rough-housed and who relied on him to inspire roaring laughter were next in line for the throne. "How," he wondered, "has my fate been so misguided?" All the years he had supported and helped run the kingdom now left him at risk of bowing down to a child, as his nephew Edward would reign as the king should Richard's own brother pass. Richard himself would only be allowed to serve as a royal consult to the new king. He grimaced. Even the coupling of the words "Edward" and "king" made his skin crawl. "Why should I have to work so hard, fulfill the basic duties of the high ruler, and not reap the benefits?" he griped to himself as he considered the kingdom and its future. He envisioned the military strength that he could rally, the empires he could create with the kingdoms he would conquer, and how, unlike his brother, he could expand his homeland far beyond its current boundaries to what had been lost in the great wars. The territory and wealth could assuredly be recaptured, and he would even resurrect the Templars and the security they brought to the realm. It could all be again under him. Resentment had slowly taken the place of the love Richard once had for his two nephews, and he had a distaste for his plight. He knew he had to end it.

Though Lord Richard did not know it at the time, that "end" he sought started on one of his private walks. As would-be king, he used these rambles around the tower to steer his considerations and think to himself about what he should do in relation to the succession of the king. Thinking was all he did in the beginning. But as his anger grew, his methods of reflection transformed. Private thoughts became low-toned mutterings and eventually, those had evolved into audible, manic conversations with himself. He had been able to justify this behavior as normal, as anyone in his circumstance would do. He trusted no one with his thoughts, and indeed, he doubted anyone could understand him even if he did. So, he kept his own company and enjoyed his personal discourse, filling the castle's empty halls with his ideas, schemes, and dreams. It was after months of that private torment that he first heard it...a whistle. He thought the sound was just a figment of his own imagination. It was slow and seductive, begging him to respond, and, at first, he didn't. "Who would do such a thing? Call out to what must certainly be a trick of echoes?" he thought. But the whistle continued, and he began trying to trace it to its source. "I am mad," he had feared each time he heard it, "or soon will be if this siren song does not stop." It did not stop. In fact, the whistle grew louder and clearer each time he heard it. Just a few days prior, he would have sworn he had heard a voice along with it, whispering his name, calling to him for release.

Richard swung his legs over the side of his elevated bed and slid from the silk sheets onto the chilled cobblestone floor before finding his slippers to warm his feet. He started a fire in the hearth and watched as the flames danced like fiery guests in a demonic ballroom. It was hypnotic and only with great effort was he able to avert his gaze.

Richard was turning from the mantle when it happened.

The whistling began filtering through the flames he had just ignited and brought to life. It was the same sound that had been luring him for months, but this morning it was the strongest and most distinct it had ever been. It filled the air around him and seemed to burrow deep into his mind. Lord Richard cocked his head as he continued to watch the flames swirl with heat. The whistle mimicked the sound of wind rushing across the chimney that allowed the smoke to billow from his room. As he listened, the whistle turned into a melody, changing from the sharp, distinct sound to a more pronounced musical presence. "Is someone in my room? Perhaps a guard whistling in the halls?" he thought to himself. It seemed far too early for that kind of activity, but Lord Richard shuffled to his chamber door and opened it, ready to demand silence from the offender. The hall was empty and dark. No guards. Confused, he closed the heavy wooden entry and latched the iron lock.

"Richard? Come here." A low deep voice rattled from the corner of his room. The whistling had stopped.

"Who's there?" the lord called out in a voice a pitch higher than his normal range. Richard moved away and nervously reached for the door he had just closed.

"Come here, Richard. I want to help you," the voice proclaimed a tad louder than its previous summon.

"By royal order, I demand that you show yourself and identify who you are," commanded Richard. His words sounded hollow and of no consequence.

"Calm yourself, Richard. I am here to help you gain what is rightfully yours. You are wise, my Lord. You are strong. You deserve to be king." Richard walked towards the voice, so melodic and tempered. "That's right, Richard. Come closer to me. I have listened to you these past months, heard your thoughts of your nephews, your brother, and the throne. I know your desires, Richard, and I believe in you."

"You do?" Richard's voice sounded childlike in its plea.

"Yes, Richard, and I want great things for you," the voice assured.

Richard found himself pressed against the wall bordering his fireplace. His ear rested on the stone, intrigued by the voice coming from within. "Richard, your brother doesn't have the courage to guide this realm. His ways will surely destroy it if he is allowed to continue on his current path. And, your nephew? A child? How can a child possibly lead a kingdom?" the voice slyly inquired.

Lord Richard could not comprehend how this was happening, but his head was slowly nodding. "Who knew so much about what he had only acknowledged to himself?" he thought about what the voice had said. Perhaps his thoughts were not a fiction at all. He had just heard confirmation that his brother and his nephews were not fit to run this kingdom. "Who are you?" the royal questioned again.

The voice was clear and crisp as it said, "I am your only friend, Richard, and I have heard your thoughts. Consider me your royal advisor. My Lord, you can be king. You should be king. The throne belongs to you. All you must do is invite me in. Let me show you how to declare this kingdom in your name and to take what is rightfully yours. Will you let me in?"

Lord Richard's heart began to swell with greed. The voice articulated his exact beliefs. He needed to be king. If the kingdom's health and viability relied on a strong leader, was it not his responsibility to protect the crown?

"Richard, invite me in. You deserve to be king, and I will make it so. Invite me in. Let me help you," the voiced seduced and cajoled. This next request became a little more forceful than the last. "LET ME IN," it rang.

"Make me king! Come to me," exclaimed Richard, with bold confidence mixed with sheer delight.

As his lips finished the request and pressed together, a loud straining groan filled the room. It was as if metal was being stretched and tested to the point of its snap. A rugged boot followed by haggard pants and a black trench coat emerged from the stone. A striking figure popped his head from the rock and then stepped through, shaking off the dust that came from the broken mortar. Standing before Richard was a strikingly handsome man. His face was angled with sharp edges, well defined by a carefully crafted beard and handlebar mustache that ever so slightly curled at the tips. The collar of his trench coat was popped straight up to frame his face. His hair was somehow perfectly combed to one side, as it swooped across his forehead and grazed the side of his right eye. It all gave him a look of cunning and maybe even malice. "Good, Richard," the figure stated as an owner might praise a dog. The man standing before Richard let out a soft whistle. "You inviting me here was the last bit of pull I needed."

Richard stood quietly, his eyes flicking about the man. He was reconsidering what he had just done and with whom he had done it.

"Richard?" the stranger questioned, "My good fellow, why are you staring? We have things to do and preparations to make. You want to be king, don't you?"

"Well...certainly," Richard stammered as he tried to regain his composure. "But I don't see how..."

The man in front of him raised his hand as if to signal silence, and Richard's voice went mute. Richard looked perplexed. He was uncertain if he had acted out of courtesy or if he had chosen to act at all. "I suppose we might start with introductions," the visitor suggested as Richard stood silent. "I am"—the man's voice trailed off as he seemed to consider—"Jackin or Jack. Yes, that's it. I have been named that and you may use it for now. You can call me Jack."

Richard nodded an acknowledgment; again, not completely sure if he was acting for himself or being made to do a bidding.

"And," Jack continued, "I want to thank you. I am only here because you invited me in. It is not generally necessary you know, but with that infernal barrier...!" The newly arrived man trailed off and began to study Lord Richard carefully.

Richard looked at Jack blankly. He did have some memory of that request but was uncertain how long ago it had been since he had asked or even what time of day it was right now.

"We"—Jack approached Richard and slid his arm around his shoulder—"are going to do great things, yes?" Richard again nodded. "Good, Richard," Jack again spoke to the lord as one might assure a pet. "I have questions you will answer." This was less request and more statement of fact. "The damnable Templars—where are they in this 'place'?" Jack asked, looking around the room and in some contempt of his surroundings. "And how many are there?"

"There are none..." Richard's voice trailed off to a somnambulant slur.

"None?" Jack did not or could not hide his surprise.

"They left for the war and none returned," Richard assured.

Jack's eyes glowed suddenly red with what appeared to be excitement and anticipation. "And they left your brother, the king, here, in this place, without any guard?" Jack stroked his beard and chortled. He paced around Richard and again looked him over. "It all makes sense," he hissed, any vestige of seduction falling from his voice. "So simple."

Lord Richard began to tremble. Jack looked at the mortal in front of him as if he were seeing him for the first time. "Richard," he smiled and calmed, "we are going to kill your brother."

The words hung in the air around the lord. He, himself, had said the same on many occasions before, but hearing them from another voice stung him. He could feel panic inside. He suddenly wished to be far away.

"So, my dear, dear Richard, it is again time for you to invite me in."

"But you are already here," Richard whimpered.

"So I am," Jack feigned surprise, "Yet still, you will invite me in." He purred in the royal's ear. "Say it, Richard. Say it."

"Come in," Richard's head dropped dejectedly as the words passed his lips.

At once, the handsome figure of Jack erupted into a black mass, tentacles protruding from the darkness and seemingly searching for Richard. The clever human facade that had served to hold the demon in had completely vanished. It had transformed into its true self, a vision of hell as had never before been seen in the tower. With supernatural speed, what had been Jack had disappeared entirely and turned into a cloud of evil that rushed into the terrified Lord Richard. The creature's tentacles pried open Richard's mouth, and the dark mass dove deep into his body and heart. The lord's figure crumbled and went limp. His potbelly frame contorted, and his skin thickened as it turned a shade of ash. His teeth gnashed with anger. The demon from Acheron had discovered a hole in The Binding, and it had found a mortal foolish enough to allow him both into the world and into his soul. At that moment, Lord Richard's mind snapped.

The demon shivered as he held out his new arms and surveyed his newly occupied mortal body up and down. "My dear Richard," he spoke aloud to himself, "well done! Though you might have taken better care of yourself!" With this last muse, he patted his stomach.

It took a moment, but the creature inside Richard's comfortably rotund body shrugged his vanity away as he crossed to the room's only cabinet to find clothes. Dressed and satisfied, he released the chamber's iron lock, opened the heavy wooden door, and began a nonchalant walk down the hallway.

"To kill the king," the demon thought to himself, "I must be subtle. It would do no good to raise alarms and lose poor Richard's body to the executioner's blade until I am done with it." The demon laughed to himself, "Poison will work." His 'brother' would die slowly. As the creature turned a corner, the fates were with him and he fortunately found just who he needed. A young scullery maid was walking directly toward him. Her eyes were averted from the lord as was her practice but, today, keeping her gaze down felt even more a need.

"My lady," the demon summoned the girl with his tender voice.

"Yes, my Lord?" she inquired. The maid saw only Richard before her but knew him to be different somehow.

"Would you escort me to the kitchen?" he asked as he held out his hand. The maid curtsied and then with some effort took her lord's hand in her own.

As they walked, the demon made light conversation. Once they reached the kitchen, however, he instinctually thought to kill his guide to appease his appetites but, instead, let the thought and her hand go. "So kind of you, my dear," said her royal companion. The young woman smiled and hurried away, disquieted by the contact but uncertain why.

The demon ignored all of the other tower staff he saw in the large culinary workspace that stood before him. He knew just what he sought, hemlock. The leaves and the roots of the poisonous plant were left around castle kitchens to tempt and kill vermin. Its well-stocked availability would grant him ample opportunity to serve it in the king's food. It was perfect, and it would only take a mere moment to add to any dish the kitchen staff prepared. Slowly, the poison would consume the monarch of the tower and his vessel's brother, and no one would suspect the murder.

And so it went, day after day, Lord Richard returned to the kitchen, and with each passing day, the king grew sicker. Edward was dying; the demon made sure of it. And, he knew, as the king passed from this mortal earth, so would he leave behind what the demon wanted most, knowledge of The Binding and the entrance to the worlds beyond. "If the Templars had abandoned their posts," the demon had reasoned, "they must have left information about that cursed cage with the king and tower ward. The Binding is surely known to Edward and the power to open it must be here with him. Edward will not let that die as he does. He will secure that information with this body, his presumed trusted counselor. I will very soon be able to unleash all evil back into the world." The demon smiled a grin of self-satisfaction.

Time passed as he mused and grew confident of his plan. On one of his trips to the kitchen, he leered as he spied the same maid who had first guided him about the castle. "My dear," he called to her. "Would you mind walking with me to my room? I seem to be a bit faint." His work was nearly done, and he felt no reason to deny his appetites any longer. The demon began to whistle softly as he and the girl neared his chamber. It would be the last time the maid was seen within the castle.

CHAPTER 11 | The Princes in the Tower

(Year 1483 – Tower of London)

THE DARK CLOUDS hung low against the consuming ivy that clung tightly to the cobblestone walls of the Tower of London as if in an eerie foreshadowing of the days to come. All corners of the castle were filled with this gloom; it seemed to the fortress' inhabitants that the sunlight had not touched the tower in months. Once a bright, lively home full of joyful bustle, laughter, and song, the castle had of late been filled with chilling rumors and secreted conversation. Edward and Richard, two of the youngest in the castle, were most keen to the transformation. Something was amiss in the tower; something foul had taken hold.

Born Edward V and Richard of Shrewsbury, the brothers were the sons of King Edward IV of England and Queen Elizabeth Woodville. Thus, as young princes, the boys found their daily lives to be dictated by those lessons that in time would train them to sit on the throne. Still, in the monotony of daily duties and teachings, they found rare moments to be children—playing pranks on the staff, riding horses, and cahooting with their favorite uncle, Lord Protector Richard, Duke of Gloucester. He was, after all, the man after whom young Richard, known as "Rake," had been named.

Edward was 12 and the next in line to the throne in the

event of his father's death. He resembled a porcelain statue of a Greek god, even as a young boy. His sharp jawline framed his childlike features and thick flowing blonde hair cascaded down his broad shoulders. As years went by, he was morphing into a young man who embodied the commanding frame of a king. The strength and charm he carried served him well as he positioned himself in royal company.

Rake was younger, and although only nine years of age, was cleverer and far more cunning than was his older brother. His physical presence, however, paled in comparison to the strapping build of Edward. Rake was gentler and more thoughtful both in demeanor and the relationships he cultivated. His round face and strawberry blonde hair, which was often tussled and out of place, engrained a sense of innocence and vulnerability and left the young prince often underestimated by those who didn't know him. These initial impressions, however, self-corrected with the discovery of his brilliance and the power his intellect harnessed. While he would not attempt physically to command a room, he was perceptive and aware of his positioning within most any situation. He was the perfect complement to his brother, who had always served as his protector.

It was Rake that first pointed out the change to his older brother. The king, their father, had always been a robust, bulky man who looked as if he could carry the weight of the world with ease. He ruled with a stern presence. The boys knew his love for them but also recognized that the responsibilities of the king's position would always take priority, removing him from their day-to-day lives. And Edward and Rake in turn loved their father. It was the reason they were both so concerned about the changes they were seeing. Their father now resembled a shell of who he once was, and over the past few months, his health and presence had progressively declined with rapid weight loss, crippling frailty, and fierce bouts of confusion. In the night, the boys would often hear his screams of horrible agony or an incorrigible, incoherent rant. This was especially true when their Uncle Richard spent time with him. What had once been a relationship firmly based on brotherly affection between the king and his counsel now seemed to be one stationed in the dynamic between the tormented and his torturer. It frightened the boys.

"No!" the king would scream over and over again, "You'll not have it!" Such pronouncements would often be followed with accusations of evil being done and the names of corrupt and ungodly sounding places and things.

Beyond their father's decline, their Uncle Richard, once a stark contrast to the king and whose company was a welcome treat for the two young princes, had also changed. In recent weeks, the boys had witnessed a strange metamorphosis that seemed to elude others in the castle.

It was subtle at first, small changes that perhaps only the boys would recognize in their uncle's behavior. He stopped having time for them and instead more often wandered alone about the castle. Then, he suddenly became curious about the tower's scheduling, security, and safe keeps as if he had not lived in the castle's confines for years and did not already know the answers to his questions. And, of course, there was the whistling.

"Perhaps it's the case that he is just happy," Edward hopefully suggested to his younger brother, while knowing it in his heart to not be true.

Rake shook his head. "There is something amiss there, Edward." The last few days in particular had confirmed that suspicion. The changes in behavior were rapidly becoming matched by a marked physical transformation. Their uncle, Lord Richard, was short in stature and clearly had not missed many meals, yet had always carried himself in a lighthearted manner. His jovial presence outshone his lack of comeliness, though he was not considered handsome. But that once convivial demeanor was now lost, and his physical frame had become gnarled. He no longer stood upright as his spine bent him forward. His skin had tallowed and the twinkle in his eye had been replaced with reflections of loss and anger. The man the boys saw before them no longer resembled their beloved uncle.

It was winter now, and Edward and Rake spent long hours huddled around their fireplace. They talked, played, or simply watched the golden, shimmering flames crackle over the logs. They laughed as bursts of tree pitch shot into the air before its ash blew out as smoke through the chimney. The fire had become a calming presence from the seemly frantic confusion that stirred around their father's bedroom. Quiet whispers of his inevitable death lingered in the damp, cold hallways while dark and sinister cackles poured out from under their uncle's chambers onto the hard, stone floor like a malicious vapor. The boys found themselves questioning what would become of the throne if tragedy did indeed strike. Edward, while mature for his age, was overwhelmed with the idea that his father's health was all that stood between him and the responsibility to run an entire kingdom.

It was on one such day when the intense concerns of their conversation were suddenly shattered by their father's voice, once again screaming in pain while pleading for the young princes to hurry to his room. Leaving their safe solitude and thoughts behind, the boys ran down the hall between their private quarters and their father's. In both of their minds, a knowing fear emerged. Something was about to change. They paused in their tracks as they approached the room, sensing that their lives and childhoods as they knew them were ending. In that moment they heard someone approaching. From deep within the dark and rushing through the hallway's flickering candlelight, a dark figure passed them with a force that nearly knocked them down to the floor and stole the flames from the candles of nearby sconces. The rest of the journey to their father's chamber would now be much darker and felt even more ominous. Edward and Rake slowed their pace to navigate the dim.

The door was open when they arrived at the king's chamber entrance, and their father's eyes set upon to their presence immediately. He was lying on an elaborate bed that seemed to engulf the entirety of his frail body. With great effort, the unnaturally old monarch weakly raised his hand to motion for the boys to come closer. Edward gently pushed Rake through the entry, sensing his brother's reluctance to be near his father. The boys knelt on an ivory bench that was perfectly positioned at the foot of the bed. Edward reached out and touched his father's cover. "Come closer," the lord said, his voice weak and dry. Rake sat frozen on the bench. Edward crawled over the intricate bed's railing and eased himself close to his father's face. As he looked at the man before him, the king was unrecognizable. His sunken cheeks seemed to collapse against his skull and many of his teeth were missing, leaving his mouth a painful cavern. Edward felt pained at the state of his father's cracked lips and reached across the king's body to a vial on his nightstand. It was filled with bergamot oil, and Edward carefully dressed his patient's skin with it. As his fingers left his father's mouth, he could barely make out the words that followed. "The keys are the king's to command. Pass them." The king's eyes glowed with urgency as he whispered the words. He grabbed Edwards' arm with surprising strength.

Edward glanced at Rake, who quickly climbed onto the bed and hovered over his father as his brother did. "Tell us again, papa," Rake said.

"Protect the key. It is more powerful than the throne. Do not be fooled by my brother. They are the king's to command. Pass them." With these last words and a death rattle that stole what was left of his mortality, King Edward IV left this world.

At the moment of the royal's passing, the tower shook. It

felt as though a large door had been slammed shut and the entire structure groaned under the weight of its closure. Within the king's chamber, the boys, stunned and grief-stricken, held to each other for comfort as they cried for the loss of their father. It was then that the dark figure that had nearly knocked the princes down in the hallway stepped out from the shadows. Removing the large wool cloak that adorned his dark mass, the boys were startled as they recognized the figure's eyes and crooked shape as their uncle's.

"ENOUGH!" Lord Richard exclaimed with a deep, seething boom. He rushed towards the bed and the room was instantly filled with utter darkness. The last that either Edward or Rake remembered from that moment was the feel of their uncle's hands around their throats and the suffering while they both gasped for air.

✦ ✦ ✦

The two boys awoke on the cold, dirt-covered floor of the castle's dungeon. Rake regained consciousness first, with a ringing in his ears so intense that he could barely open his eyes. He felt his way through the dusty room and found Edward passed out with drying blood matting his blonde hair. The young prince shook him, and Edward rolled over groggy and disoriented. "What happened?" he asked.

"Uncle Richard," Rake muttered. "I think he may have killed father." Edward didn't want to worry his little brother, but he knew that if his uncle had, in fact, killed the king, he did it for one reason and one reason alone. He wanted the throne. Edward also knew that such a succession was currently impossible, as he and Rake were the true heirs to their father's lost reign. They both in turn would inherit the throne before their uncle, the king's brother.

Edward's mused concerns ended abruptly as both boys

heard a noise approaching their current cell. The oversized metal keys of the yeoman guards clanked as they were carried down the dungeon's echoing hallway. Their rattle was only silenced as a key was placed in the door to their room and its heavy lock was opened.

"Good afternoon, my dears. How are you feeling?" Uncle Richard ogled in a way that suggested far more menace than concern.

Edward grabbed Rake, pulled him into the corner of the cell furthest from the door, and stood in front of him. "What have you done to our father?" Edward demanded an answer in his attempt at a kingly voice.

As Lord Richard entered the room, there was no trace left of the man who had loved and cared for the two princes. Instead, his eyes had an evil red glow, his skin had turned from ashy to grey, and he could barely stand upright. He inched his way towards the boys, getting so close to their bodies that his foul, musky breath warmed their faces. "I killed him," he answered in a manner devoid of emotion, "and have since locked his soul away in a place beyond your concern. He is of no more help to you or anyone."

The princes were confused. "Locked his soul away?' asked Rake, looking back and forth between his brother and the thing that had been his uncle. Edward stood stone-faced, unsure what to say while the dark creature slid his lips over teeth that had seemed to grow in the moment, creating a most ghastly smile.

"Uncle Richard, please," Rake cried. "Take the throne. It is yours. We can run away. You will never hear from us again."

The lord cocked his head to the side and sneered. "You think I want the throne? You naïve little brat. The throne is the least of what I seek. It is the world I desire, and it is the key I want now. I would destroy this castle stone by stone and salt the earth beneath it to find the key. I would let all of England burn to have it. I will have the key and you pitiful things will help me get it."

"The key?" Edward wondered to himself. "Was this the same key that their father had warned them about as he lay dying in his bed?"

The glow of Uncle Richard's eyes intensified, and his lips slid back over his face, opening a gaping hole. A black cloud shot from his throat, rushing towards the boys as it divided into four large ribbons wrapping themselves around their necks like venomous snakes. They were lifted from the floor and up to the ceiling before being slammed back into the cold dirt. The boys kicked and struggled to break the bond of the beast consuming them, but their efforts got weaker and their struggle softer as the demon tightened its grip. Within seconds, the princes' bodies went limp, their eyes closed, and the blood within them began to cool. The demon retracted back into Uncle Richard's throat, his mouth returned to its normal size, and his demonic growl exclaimed, "Time to get up, my dears." Lord Richard looked at the lifeless bodies at his feet. "GET UP!" he commanded.

"Edward?" It was Rake's voice that broke the silence. "Edward, what is happening?"

Edward bolted up and sat looking about. His brother was lying next to him as if asleep, but yet, he also seemed to be sitting upright and glancing about. In fact, after a moment, the prince came to realize that he, himself, seemed to share the same position as his brother and he must look the same to him.

"What are we?" Rake was now standing looking through his own hand that he held in front of his face and what appeared to be himself still lying on the chamber floor.

"What you are is 'mine,' young prince. Bound to this place and me forever if we cannot find the key. But we will find it. Together." Lord Richard's voice paused in consideration. "Let us start with what your father said at his end." He hissed the words this time and made no attempt to hide his malice.

The two boys stared at each other as ravens dove past their cell's lone window to the outside. The birds were welcoming the two new ghosts to the tower. Their low croaking sounds alternated with high-pitched shrills as the beat of their wings filled the air. Edward and Rake shuddered as their gaze shifted back towards their uncle.

"Edward!" The tone of Rake's voice was now nearly hysterical. Their uncle's body fell to the floor and now, standing before them was an imposing, yet dapper, male figure.

The stranger simpered slyly. "Please, call me 'Jack.'"

CHAPTER 12 | The Beginnings of a Plan

"SO, JACK, OR whatever name you call the beast, hasn't rested since," Edward concluded.

The ghosts were just as appalled as the mortal boys to learn that the king and the princes had been killed by Lord Richard. After hearing the princes' account, a deeper, different level of horror surrounded the details of the demon. The threat of this evil lording over the old castle felt paralyzing.

"So, this demon," inquired Dickens. "Is he alone or has he summoned more of his kind to help him in his quest for the key?"

"We have not seen any other demons," noted Edward, "but he does not act alone. He has enlisted the evil ghosts that reside in the tower to help him in his search. Most of these villainous creatures come from a time when the tower was a prison. Evil mortals were held there and died, turning to dark spirits that didn't want to leave this world. They have roamed the tower ever since. There are also those damned spirits who were made to travel to the tower by reapers but who were left trapped unwilling to cross over. The demon screams at night, making threats that he will build a hell here in the mortal world with the key. He is right to say so. The tower is a bloody hell!"

"Master Edward, language please!" It was Jane who

pointed out the prince's salty turn of phrase.

Edward blushed as much as a ghost can, and, despite his royal status, lowered his gaze and apologized, "Sorry, mum." He stood for a moment, as tears began welling in his eyes.

"Quite all right, my young prince," Jane assured. "I know this has been hard on you." Then, in an act of quiet kindness, she hugged the young spirit to herself tightly. Edward at first stiffened and then hugged her back while sobbing heartily.

"We've spent much of our time trying to avoid the demon and often too scared to hunt for the key. He has killed others who stood in his way or who have challenged his power." Rake picked up the tale, glancing at his brother with mild concern. "Many of the spirits who have helped and protected us have fallen to him. The living have fallen to him as well. He kills the unsuspecting for seemingly nothing but his pleasure. At other times, he consumes the living as a black cloud that has glowing red eyes, snake-like arms, and a tooth-filled mouth that stretches, allowing him to swallow his prey. In yet other moments, he embodies the vessel he is using after seducing them into possession," continued Rake.

"Once inside the possessed vessel, he can leave the tower, walking freely through The Binding," Edward added. He had composed himself but still stood next to Jane, drawing strength from her presence.

The ghosts of the abbey stood quietly, unsure of what to do with the newly discovered and fully disheartening information.

Dickens spoke first. He cleared his throat and gently stated, "This is worse than what we had imagined. We have been able to manage The Binding and its faltering lines thus far with our good friends Merlin and Glinda. We knew if it failed entirely, catastrophe would certainly follow. Still, we managed." The writer motioned to the two magical apparitions who nodded their attention. "But this demon is beyond what we can control in our current circumstance. If that vile thing were to find the key, hope, I fear, would be entirely lost. It holds the power to protecting this world and the worlds beyond it from the terror currently plaguing the tower. We must uncover where this key is for the safety of all existence," Dickens surmised for the group.

"It's harder than that," piped in Edward. "We don't know what the key is. Our father told us that it held a power greater than the throne, but he died before he could tell us what and where it was. I don't even know what exactly we would be looking for. Regardless, we have still searched when we can and have found nothing. We have taken it as our task for centuries."

"We felt the situation was hopeless until we met Thomas and William. They felt you kind people might help us find what was lost, or perhaps you can help with Jack. We don't have the strength to rid the tower of the demon and dispel the evil under its sway," Rake said quietly.

"I fear I do not feel comfortable sending any of these poor boys into that tower alone. We should attend them and travel to that horrid place to deal with this demon ourselves," offered Austen, overwhelmed with worry and looking toward William, Thomas, Edward, and Rake.

"It would have to be at night," stated Darwin. "We don't want the type of commotion we had at the museum in public view again, and the boys will be questioned if they are acting suspiciously during the day."

"How are we supposed to get into the tower at night?" asked Thomas.

"Never mind that. How are we supposed to get out of here at night? The headmaster and dorm parents will never let us out," William noted what he perceived to be an even greater obstacle.

"Why, my silly boy!" Newton exclaimed, "You have some of the cleverest minds in the history of the world before you. Escaping the abbey is an easy task for such formidable minds as ours!"

"Perhaps we borrow wax dummies!" offered Olivier with just a hint of amusement in his voice. "Nonetheless, I agree with Isaac. We can get the mortal boys out of the abbey, but through the gates of the tower after visiting hours? That is another question entirely. Unlike us, the boys cannot move through walls."

"And let us not forget The Binding. While the boys may walk through it, we would be trapped outside, unable to help them once they are in." From the look on Newton's face, he was stumped. At that and after a moment, everyone began talking at once and it did not take long for the combined tone of the gathering to give one a sense of desperation.

Stepping forward, and ignoring the growing concerns of others, it was Shakespeare who took the stage, confident they could come up with a solution. "We shall findeth a way, rest assur'd mine own cater-cousins. We might not but simply put our minds togeth'r and develop a plan."

As the bard attempted to regather the group's hope and refocus the conversation, the two ghost boys huddled together in a whisper. It took a few minutes before Edward turned back to address the gathering. He cleared his throat shyly to gain everyone's attention. "There is an old beefeater who might know how to help us. He is a mortal man who works at the tower to guard the gates. We've only had a few opportunities to interact with him, but when we do, he can sense us. He has called out to us many times, and I can tell he wants to help. He is a believer in ghosts, so he might be easily convinced to render aid. Trust me, if anyone knows a secret way into the tower, it would be him. What if William and Thomas went to him and asked for help?" suggested Rake.

"Do you have his name, lads?" Dickens asked with some small hope gleaming in his eyes. "With it, we might be able to find his lodging and pay him a visit. Mortals have this marvelous invention called a 'telephone book.' It lets you look up anyone's address by simply knowing the alphabet!" The author had true excitement in his voice with the observation and the chance to use a telephone directory.

"Mister Dickens," suggested William, "I'll just look him up on my laptop."

"Nonsense! Why would his address be in your lap?" Dickens looked bewildered but pressed on. He turned to address the princes. "Your highnesses, what is the name of said beefeater?"

"Basil Flounderbee," answered Rake.

"I shall find the book and will return with knowledge of our Mister Flounderbee's whereabouts!" Dickens announced proudly as he turned and began to stride off.

"Mister Dickens!" It was William again, who was now sitting on a bench and putting down the just opened backpack he routinely carried. "Mister Flounderbee lives at 438 Kingsrow Court, and his home is in between the abbey and the tower."

Dickens stopped in his tracks, looking at William dumbfounded. Shifting his stare to Hawking, the scientist halted his perpetual movement only to raise one eyebrow in amusement. "He did have it in his lap," pondered the author.

Darwin's head was spinning with thoughts. "I am leery to trust another mortal with these young lads or even the information we now have about The Binding, but I fear we may have no other choice."

"How well can you take orders, boys?" The whole group turned in confusion as the Unknown Soldier had stepped forward and bellowed out the question.

"Pretty well, I think," replied William, slightly intimidated by the stern presence of the soldier.

"Good. Fall in line. You will march to the tower, return the princes, and then find your way back to the abbey. While you are on your mission, we will be here strategizing your next steps," Unk instructed.

Thomas looked at William and nodded.

"But why must they go back?" asked Olivier of the young ghosts. "Surely, they are better here with us."

"Laurence," said Darwin, "If they do not return, we will have given some warning to the demon. This is the first time in centuries we have had a single bit of information that may allow us to protect England."

"God save the Queen!" bellowed the Unknown Soldier.

Darwin looked up a bit surprised, shook his head, and then continued, "If the boys are missing, the demon will sense something is awry. We must not raise suspicion as we seek a solution to this dilemma. Our young noblemen surely understand the need."

Darwin looked at the princes while they resolutely nodded.

"We have to get back by dark. The demon will be patrolling, and we don't want to be caught out when he does," offered Rake.

"Agreed, and we also must be sure that our friends William and Thomas are back for pizza tonight. With what I learned at Phantasmal Foods, it is not a meal you'd voluntarily miss," said Edward with a grin on his face, hoping to mask his personal dread.

"Spoken like a future king," gushed Newton.

The gathered ghosts each embraced the young princes in turn and offered last-minute words of advice. Jane Austen held tightly to them, reluctant to let them go. She kissed the top of their heads before hurrying them back to Thom and William.

"Come in, Edward," Thomas said with newfound confidence. No encouragement was needed, as Edward quickly took his place inside him.

William stepped forward to stand near Rake. "Your turn. Come in." The ghost took a large step towards William and disappeared into his body.

"By God, I have it!" shouted Dickens as Thomas and Edward turned to go. "The boys...The Binding...they can be our shuttle service!" As the author went on to explain, true hope was born again in the voices of those gathered.

The sun was beginning to set. Without waiting a moment longer, the boys began their journey back towards the tower. They knew they had to move quickly. The demon would be preparing for his walk around the castle that he used to keep the spirits there in line with his strict demands. The path to return to the tower included a bus ride, which thankfully was uneventful. The boys pulled on the rope to signal their intent to get off to the driver. The bus stopped at the corner of the public square that sat just in front of the gates to the tower. As it was nearing dinnertime, the square was packed with people buzzing through the shops and entering the restaurants that opened onto its walkways.

The boys were on a mission. They pushed through the crowds and dodged around people leisurely strolling the square. A sense of urgency was growing as the sky darkened, and their pace quickened. Nearly running through the gates of the tower, the mortal brothers flashed their tickets from their visit earlier in the day to the guard on duty. Just inside, a rush of energy left them, and the two ghost princes exited their bodies. Thomas and William had crossed The Binding and successfully returned their passengers as promised.

"Thank you, both. Waste no time in returning to the abbey. We are counting on you to come back with the others." Edward's voice was calm, somehow comforted by the idea that help would soon be on its way. The two young ghosts turned and walked into their prison home.

Just as quickly as they had entered the gates, Thomas and William left. Knowing that the ghosts back at the abbey had been strategizing their next moves had them eager to return. However, it was the thought of pizza that had them in a hurry.

CHAPTER 13 | An Elaborate Breakout

NEWTON AND HAWKING came to gather William and Thomas early. The ghosts were excited to share their plans with the boys and the rest of the small spectral conspiracy who were already graciously waiting to hear their ideas. The thought of the beefeater being able to provide insight about a secret or at least an unobvious entry into the tower had kept the two mathematicians up and talking all night. The scientists had huddled together to develop the perfect plan, so they claimed, to get the boys out of the abbey and to the home of the beefeater.

It was barely five in the morning when a thud startled Thomas. As he opened his eyes, Hawking was sitting on the end of his bed. "Good morning, chap! It's a beautiful day to plot an escape," exclaimed the gangly ghost. The mathematician's energy was too much for Thomas at such an early hour. He had barely had a chance to orient himself, and Hawking was acting as if he had already consumed two massive cups of espresso from Ghostly Grinds Coffee Shop.

Newton nudged William, who was sleeping nearby. "Up and at 'em, lad. We have the most marvelous idea. Get your britches on, grab a pen and paper, and meet us in the abbey." William was far more enthusiastic to hear the spirits' ideas than his brother was. He sprang from his bed and began getting dressed. Thomas remained lying down, watching with eyes half-closed and an unwillingness to get out from beneath his warm blankets.

"Come on, Thom! Get up," begged William. This was a routine all too common. William was always the one to hurry. It was in his nature to be obedient, inquisitive, and punctual.

Thom, on the other hand, was never in much of a hurry. Few things could rouse him to rush outside of dinner. However, William's excitement and drive to hear the ghosts pulled him from bed this morning. "No need to upset my brother," Thomas thought. And to be quite honest, he too was intrigued by what the ghosts had planned.

When all was done and the two boys headed out of their dormitory, William looked ready to take on the day, with his shirt perfectly tucked into his pressed trousers. Thomas, on the other hand, had barely taken time to fix his hair and looked disheveled and groggy.

The two mortal boys were clearly the last to arrive at the place where they had left the ethereals the night before. All the ghosts were already gathered. As Thomas and William nodded their hellos to the others, Newton addressed them all. "Dear friends, we have been at it all night." Darwin and Dickens both nodded their approval at the effort, while the rest of those present simply waited for the description of the plan to begin. "Boys, did you bring your writing instrument?" asked Sir Isaac as he got set to continue his oratory.

"Yes, sir," noted William as he held a pen and paper up for the ghost to see. He was pleased to show that he could be counted on to get things done. Hawking nodded.

"Excellent," said Newton, "Then let us begin. First, I need you boys to make a list of all the materials that we will need to execute our plan. Please take note. We must acquire: a standard wooden ruler, a perfectly inflated basketball, a metered scale, a calm feline." William had been scribbling down the items but paused at the mention of a cat. He shot Thomas a look of concern as animals were rare in the abbey, but Thomas shook his head to encourage his brother to pay

GHOSTS OF THE ABBEY

attention. Sir Isaac continued, undeterred by the boys' interaction, "A hanging basket, a set of dry matches, an operating Bunsen burner, and one golf club, preferably a nine-iron. Additionally, you will need several strong cords, four metal pulleys, wiring, and string."

Newton and Hawking looked first at the mortal boys and then to the other gathered ghosts with eager faces. They were clearly proud of the work that had been done over the course of the night, and the excitement they had sharing their idea with the others was palpable in their discussion. Thomas, on the other hand, looked perplexed and was decidedly confused by the list of items. Most would be readily available around the abbey, but he wasn't fully sure why or how the things asked for would be useful to help get himself and his brother out of the old church at night and undetected.

"So, what are we supposed to do after we find these things?" asked Thomas.

"Yes, Newton, what are they supposed to do after they find these things?" asked Darwin sternly. Thomas looked at the ghost, who was clearly losing patience with what he was hearing. He also noticed that Dickens was now simply standing behind the naturalist holding his face in his hands while shaking his head.

"Patience, Thomas Darlington. We have carefully designed blueprints for the mechanism that will allow you two to exit the abbey later tonight," noted Hawking. "I am really quite excited to see it work. I haven't had this much fun since I came up with the theory of everything!"

"Nor I since I postulated the nature of gravity! This is just so exciting! The math of it all. I feel alive! Every equation sorted out in relation to each associated motion, weight, force, and friction," Newton added giddily. He gathered a large translucent cylinder leaning against an ethereal bench and centered himself in the middle of the group. He proudly stood in front of his entire audience, mortal and otherwise, and shook a rolled-up ghost-like paper from the container where it had been secreted. Grabbing the document as it slid out of the tube, he held it forward with delight on his face. "William and Thomas, behold! I am proud to unveil 'Newton's Knocker.'" He grabbed the corner edges of the paper and slung out the ethereal roll, revealing a massive plan that took up nearly six feet on the abbey floor. The ghostly ink glowed as it depicted an elaborate, scientific contraption, complete with instructions, dimensions, and tracks of motion. The sheet clearly contained enough calculation to fill an engineering student's notebook.

"Actually, we are calling it 'Hawking's Hammer!'" added Hawking, taking the floor from Newton.

"Knocker!" exclaimed Newton.

"Hammer!" said Hawking.

"What in the world?" asked William, perplexed by the intricacy of the plans. Darwin had by this point joined Dickens with visible worry, now bringing his hands to his own mouth and slowly shaking his head as Dickens did, in confusion.

"Phenomenal, isn't it? Please, try to follow along. If you boys can construct and execute this marvelous machine, you will be walking down the streets of London and into the beefeater's house this very evening." Newton looked pleased with the idea. "Hawking, please come take the boys through the plan for my knocker!" Newton stepped back, apparently wanting to spend time preening and posturing in what he clearly viewed as a moment of ascendant victory. Thomas and William noted from the stares of the other ghosts present and the schematics lying on the abbey floor that the vote of confidence in the presented machine was going to result in well less than unanimous count.

Hawking sprung from the bench where he had been seated. "Of course. I'd be honored to show these fine lads how the machine will operate." He pulled an ethereal pointer from somewhere up his sleeve and held it into the air. "First, for this plan to work and our machine to open your way out of the abbey, we must remove all known obstacles. This being so, we encourage you to find a sleeping aid to place in the headmaster's tea. He always brews an Earl Grey at approximately four o'clock, so slip the powder into his drink, and he will sleep through your escape."

Thomas was unsettled by this idea. "Sleeping aids?" he thought. Where were they supposed to find these, and, even more difficult, how would they get them into the headmaster's drink? He ignored his own hesitation about drugging adults and waited anxiously to hear exactly what else the plans being put forth required.

"As you can see, this blueprint reveals a fantastic model that once assembled will be your key to escaping. To start, you will be required to remove the glass cover from the wall clock in your dorm, at which point you will affix the wooden ruler to the minute hand of said timepiece. At exactly 8:31 p.m., the ruler will hit the basketball placed on the shelf below the clock. Note the basketball must be fully inflated with air to allow for maximum effectiveness. We have a helium model as well," said Hawking as an apparent aside to the gathered group of ghosts who were by this point all standing aghast at the description.

"We decided against that inert noble gas because we didn't want to complicate things," added Newton as an affirmation.

Speaking over Newton, Hawking again started instructing. "The basketball will be rolled from the shelf onto the metric beam balance scale that is carefully situated below it. The scale must be placed exactly six inches to the right of the shelf's edge. Atop the right side of the scale, you will place the patient, relaxed feline. This will leave the left side of the scale empty and elevated. At the moment the basketball drops from the shelf, it will fall upon the scale, decompressing the left side and rocketing the cat into the air."

"The cat will essentially be catapulted," Newton added,

laughing at the idea of the flying feline. The boys' faces grew with confusion while the general assembly of ghosts brewed with bewilderment. Newton seemed pleased with himself and Hawking continued.

"As cats always do, our feline accomplice will land gracefully on its feet in a basket that you have suspended from the ceiling with a pulley. Its weight will allow the wickerwork to drop with the force needed to pull a match with such precise energy that it will strike on the ignition strip adhered to the side of the box, causing a flame to rise. The fire from the match will light a Bunsen burner that has been left on..."

In a panicked voice, William interrupted Newton and questioned, "Leave it on?" In his mind, all he could envision was the abbey exploding into flames.

Newton, ignoring his concern, continued. "As I was saying, you will place the Bunsen burner below a taut rope tied securely to one of the coat hooks on the wall. This line will be tied with equal tightness to the golf club hanging nearly perpendicular to the floor and two feet from the window. Within seconds of the Bunsen burner being engaged, its blue flame will scorch through the coarse rope, releasing the golf club. The rigid, heavy iron will strike the window, shattering its double-paned glass, thus creating an opening through which you boys will carefully crawl. You will then shimmy down the fire escape and begin your pursuit of the beefeater." The spirits surrounding Newton and Hawking were either whispering back and forth between themselves or had joined Dickens and Darwin with perplexed looks on their faces.

"We must also establish a way in which your classmates can be incapacitated to eliminate the chance that they will foil your escape," interjected Olivier dryly. "Perhaps Shakespeare could do a reading for them, which would surely have them sleeping in no time."

"Start'eth not, Olivier. The present-day is not about thee," Shakespeare responded.

"Agreed. Perhaps we should have Merlin create a concoction that will place the boys in a slumber," noted Newton.

"Drug them!" concurred Hawking, with a certain amount of mischief in his voice.

"This all sounds so illegal," cried William, who felt great distress when thinking about dosing the headmaster, potentially blowing up the church, and, at the very least, poisoning his classmates with gas from the burner.

"Details!" retorted Newton with his finger pointing to the ceiling.

Thomas blurted out, "This really all seems far too complex. Why don't we simply wait for our classmates to fall asleep, distract the headmaster, open the window, and walk down the fire escape?"

"Well, there you have it, and I have asserted it before! Children these days are always seeking the easy way out." Newton was clearly upset that he may not be able to launch a cat and disappointed that the boys had not celebrated the complex and surely effective plan he and Hawking had labored over. "Have it your way. If your simple chicanery doesn't work, just remember that we told you so." With that, he huffed and sat with Hawking, who had also taken a seat and was clearly amused at Newton's upset.

"The Newton Knocker was a bit overengineered," jabbed Hawking.

"Given a name like the Hawking Hammer, it was flawed at conception," frowned Newton.

"Don't mind them," Austen comforted the boys. "These geniuses have never had minds for simplicity, and, while they were only trying to help, a lack of complexity more often leads to the greatest result." Jane was now looking at the two mathematicians. "Sometimes I think they forget that."

"Indeed," said Darwin, echoing Jane's observation.

"Clearly," said Dickens.

"Hear, hear," said Shakespeare.

"Cocktails?" asked Olivier.

While it took a degree of discussion and some consolation toward Newton, the gathering did eventually settle on a plan that seemed to satisfy the needs of the day with the least amount of risk. Clear on their instructions, the boys decided to head back toward their dorm, excited to get started but nervous that they would be caught. Olivier had offered to create a distraction to draw the headmaster away and Unk agreed to assist him. Darwin seemed very relieved that the military man would accompany the actor, apparently fearing another theatrical debacle like the one they all had experienced at the wax museum. As the boys proceeded back to the dorms, the last words they heard were from Newton asking again about using the cat. What sounded almost as a growl from Darwin seemed to put an end to his request.

While the other residents were awake and milling about in their schools housing, William and Thomas began making small adjustments to allow for their escape. William made their beds, while Thomas slowly slid a desk closer to the window. He then placed a chair to the left of it, which would allow them to quietly step onto the work surface, placing them at the perfect height to raise the window. Thomas checked the dormer to make sure he could open it easily and without much noise.

"What ya doing, Thom?" Nigel was standing behind him, running a comb through his red hair. Thomas' shoulders dropped. Of all the people who might inquire about his actions, Nigel was the one who in most circumstances would serve to be the most annoying.

"Nothing important, Nigel," said Thomas. "But you are just the person I wanted to see."

"I am?" asked Nigel, surprised at what appeared to be a sudden change of heart in the older Darlington brother.

Despite their history of conflict, Thomas thought Nigel had

the potential to be an asset to him and his brother. He also believed the truth about Nigel was exactly what their mother had told them about tattletales: They are just jealous of being left out and clearly want to feel somehow included. So, here was a chance to win Nigel over. By giving him a role, the traditional pest would feel important and a part of Thomas and William's plan. Against his normal tattletale nature, Nigel would hopefully feel sneaky and excited to help. "Besides," Thomas mused to himself, "you should always keep your friends close, and your enemies closer."

"Come over here. No one else can hear us. I have a story I want to tell you and need your help to make it all turn out for the good," lured Thomas. Intrigued, Nigel followed. As the two made their way into a quiet corner of the dorm, Thomas whispered, "Do you believe in ghosts?"

"Naw," said Nigel, "You have to be daff to believe in them. Nothin' but ole tales and tourist foolery to me." As Nigel said it, William walked up with Newton, who immediately took the opportunity to flick Nigel in the ear.

"Old tale, indeed," said Newton.

"Ouch!" yelled the boy. "Who keeps doing that?" Nigel's head was looking from side to side while the other boys in the dorm turned to look at him.

"That was a friend of ours, Nigel," said Thomas. "He wants to show you he is real so that you will believe in him."

"He does? Believe in what, exactly?" Nigel inquired fearfully.

"In ghosts, Nigel," William tried to say it in a comforting tone and then proceeded to introduce Nigel to Sir Isaac Newton. Noting a slight hesitation in accepting his existence as fact, Newton promptly tugged at a tuft of the boy's red hair to remind him of his presence. Nigel's eyes went wide; he was quickly coming around to a new reality accepting of ghosts and remarkably was transforming from adversary to ally.

"Okay! Okay, I believe. I believe you! Now leave my

bloomin' ears, hair, and head alone, Mister Newton!" Nigel had taken several minutes to accept the fact that he was in the presence of Sir Isaac Newton, but when the flicks to the ear evolved into full-fledged swats at the side of the head, he gave in to the assertion. Newton gave him one more whap for the last comment.

"He likes to be called 'Sir,'" said Thomas.

"Sir, then," huffed Nigel, rubbing the side of his face.

Though boys living in the dorm still wondered why Nigel kept screaming in pain while holding his ear, they all had, nonetheless, wandered off to the common areas to watch television or play games. The Darlingtons and their newfound accomplice, then, were left to their own for a private conversation, with Newton overlooking the dialog.

"What we need is really quite simple, Nigel," said William. "Tonight, after first rounds are made, we will be leaving on an errand of utmost importance to Sir Isaac and the rest of the abbey ghosts." William saw no reason to give a full explanation to Nigel. "All we need you to do is to watch our door. If the dormitory monitors go by, that is fine. They never enter and won't notice anything is amiss, but you have to keep the other boys away. We shouldn't be long, so there shouldn't be a problem, but, if there is, you can handle it, right?"

Nigel nodded, and Thomas added, "Sir Isaac has offered to stay with you to help." The ghost was really staying to watch Nigel, but William, thinking politically, left that fact out of his request.

"Nothing to worry about. I've got your backs, friends," said Nigel with a proud grin. William and Thomas looked at each other. With the redhead on their side, the brothers were ready to find the beefeater. They knew he'd be vital in their fight against the demon.

CHAPTER 14 | An Evening of Unfortunate Events

OLIVIER AND THE Unknown Solider found little comfort in Nigel keeping watch at the dormitory while William and Thomas were away. Still, noting that Newton would be supervising the young sentinel, the two ghosts set about to plan their promised distraction. The goal of the operation was clear enough: actively prevent the house parents and the headmaster from coming by Thomas and William's room. The Unknown Solider proposed that they keep their plans to themselves as to alert the ghostly troops would only cause concern and unneeded suggestion. They both knew to rely on the strength of the other.

Olivier recognized that the soldier's strategic nature would serve them well in finding and capturing the needed abbey audience. "If he could do that," the actor thought to himself, "I can handle the rest." The old army shade, on the other hand, understood that he had elected perhaps the riskiest partner in the abbey to help execute this 'mission.' "The actor at times is impulsive and self-indulgent, which could lead to problems in a controlled operation," considered the solider. But Unk was willing to assume those high stakes. He also noted that Olivier had one of the most creative and clever minds he had ever encountered. The solider also understood that the theatrical strengths of Olivier would create a large enough spectacle to buy the boys all the time they needed to get back. Indeed, the actor could be good in a pinch.

The military ghost was ready. He stood in a powerful stance, his legs spread, his hands folded behind his back and his chest and chin pointed out. In a commanding voice, he addressed the thespian. "Listen, Olivier. You must be disciplined in your approach tonight. We have already raised eyebrows outside of the abbey while at the museum. The boys are counting on us to help aid in their planned escape. We can contribute directly to their success, but we also could cause them to fail. We have to be controlled in our approach. Do you copy me, private?"

"Sir, yes sir!" said Olivier, with a less than proper salute of his hand. "But can I be a lieutenant, at least?" implored the actor and then continued, "I have a perfectly delicious idea, my strapping companion. We are going to give the most spectacular performance."

"I am not sure we need spectacular, Olivier," warned the soldier. "Distracting is quite enough."

"On the contrary, chap. Spectacular is exactly what we need," Olivier said the line with gusto and with it, seemingly from nowhere, he shook what looked to be two large, printed drapes out into the air, watching them fall open onto the floor. He produced a pair of shiny scissors in his hand and quickly went to work cutting the material. First one circle, and then another. He repeated the process with a second sheet. "As unfortunate as it is to cover our handsome faces," noted Olivier with disappointment, "we are going to embrace the human fascination with ghosts. This fine cloth is a Templar tapestry. I found it rummaging through the abbey. Appears the Templar touch allows us to wear them without much loss of ether, and I must say, I'm quite fond of the way the colors complement my skin tone." He tossed one of the bolts of dog cloth up into the air and slid underneath it. He carefully positioned the two awkwardly placed and haphazardly cut holes over his eyes. He stood before the soldier looking like a young child ready to set off for an evening of trick or treating. The tapestry draped over the spirit had created a classic ghost costume. "What are you waiting for?" he asked the soldier, as he tossed him his sheet.

The Unknown Soldier held the cut tapestry in his hand, looking at Olivier and then down to the cloth several times. The intricacy of the woven pattern was now destroyed by Olivier's handy work, but the damage had already been done so the soldier dismissed any concern of the tapestry's value. "I can't believe I am doing this," remarked the disciplined man. Still, at this point, he was committed to working with Olivier, so he removed his helmet and carefully slipped the sheet over his head.

"Perfect!" exclaimed Olivier. "You practically could pass for that Peanut fellow... 'Charlie Brown.'" The actor's attempt to rile the solider had good effect.

"Just say one more thing, Olivier, and see what happens. Just one more thing." With that, the Unk turned and stomped out into the abbey. He clearly thought corralling school monitors and security would require some noise. "Laurence," he called over his shoulder, "Follow the nut."

"I always have," Olivier answered.

The thespian and the soldier walked to an area far from Nigel and Newton but still on the security routes of the church's staffing. They waited patiently. As the dormitory monitor, Mr. Harold Wiggins, rounded the corner, Olivier and Unk stepped into the middle of the hallway wearing their 'ghost' costumes. Mr. Wiggins was a pleasant man, who stood barely five feet tall and had a waist nearly as round as he was high. His walk mirrored more of a shuffle and his evening rounds were most likely the sole form of exercise he experienced each day. He had a receding hairline and his dated glasses sat towards the end of his ever-widening nose.

The dim lights lining the hallway and his poor eyesight made it difficult for Mr. Wiggins to make out the two figures in the hall. As his eyes adjusted, the illusion of two floating spirits began to take shape. While he failed to recognize that the tapestries were truly hovering off the ground, he quickly turned on his flashlight and showed it towards Olivier and the solider. In an effort to identify which boys might be playing a prank on him, Mr. Wiggins shined a beam directly towards the eye holes of the sheets and was perplexed when the light revealed an empty dome.

"Alright, boys, enough. Take off the blankets. You know you can't be out of your rooms at night," Mr. Wiggins noted, raising the pitch of his voice on the last word. The ghosts, however, just simply stood and stared.

Frustrated, Mr. Wiggins stepped forward. "Boys! Enough! Back to the dorm or the headmaster will be hearing of this."

Now having the monitor's attention, the two spirits began walking backward. At first, their steps were long and slow, and then they began to quicken the pace, creating distance between themselves and Mr. Wiggins. Olivier let out a long and soulful moan. Whether the mortal heard the sound was not as important to the ghost as the feeling it provided him. Laurence loved method acting.

"I know you are not disobeying my orders," the monitor hollered after them. He began to shuffle faster, nearly breaking into a jog. Almost instantly, he was out of breath. He slowed and placed his hands against his knees to still his panting. He looked up just in time to see the two figures disappear as they turned to go down the main hallway.

Laughing, The Unknown Solider glanced at Olivier and said, "That wasn't even fair. The poor man needs some military physical training. He nearly collapsed at the simple idea of chasing after us. His effort to actually do so was almost painful to watch."

Olivier let out a loud, joyful chuckle. "So perfect," he exclaimed as he spun across the floor, enjoying the sheet as it dramatically flared around him with each twirl.

Another bright light stopped the actor from his short-lived celebration.

"Brace yourself, Olivier. This one will not be nearly as easy as the last. Headmaster Rattlebag is a relentless oppositional force."

"Rattlebag?!" shouted the actor. "Oh, this will be grand."

"Freeze, boys," ordered the headmaster. He stood with his flashlight out in an aggressive stance. It was as if he was a police officer who had just pulled his gun on a criminal, and he was shining his light directly into Olivier's eyes.

Olivier was stunned and blinded. He stepped backward, caught his shoe on the edge of the tapestry, and struggled to find his footing. He teetered trying to regain his stability and as he stumbled forward, the sheet caught a candleholder mounted to the wall, tipping it forward. Flames jumped from the candle onto the cloth, and Olivier found himself rapidly consumed by fire. Taking the moment as an opportunity to be truly spectacular, the actor began to spin like a fire wheel set off to celebrate the New Year as he suddenly began to sing show tunes.

"Blimey!" Rattlebag went into crisis mode, running towards the fire extinguisher hanging on a nearby wall. He was praying he would know how to use it. This was the first time in his tenure he would be battling fire as opposed to the usual schoolboy messes. He grabbed the nozzle and aimed it towards Olivier.

The Unknown Solider flung his sheet off his body, dropping it to the floor. He charged towards Olivier. The actor was fully flailing now, trying to get the tapestry off of his frame, and, as he did, he was met with two forces. The soldier knocked him to the ground as a blast from the fire extinguisher sprayed in his face. The white foam instantly put out the flames, but had also completely exposed the two ghosts. Most dramatically, the haze and residue of the spray fully illuminated the features of Olivier. As the headmaster looked at the figures before him, he could see the full detail of a strangely familiar translucent human face. Olivier made direct eye contact with Rattlebag and both mortal man and ghost froze. The soldier stood back and looked on in horror. Running out of options, Olivier rose and took a menacing stance, reaching out as if to embrace an unlucky victim before screaming, "BOO!"

Headmaster Rattlebag dropped his flashlight and ran from the foyer, heading straight towards his quarters. Mister Wiggins and the two other abbey monitors who had been drawn to the scene on hearing the commotion also followed suit. One of the monitors momentarily halted his hasty exit just long enough to kick the cloth that had been so animated moments before. It did not move save for the force of the mortal's effort. Nonetheless, even that motion seemed to further unsettle its viewer. A burst of panicked speed sent the man fully past his running workmates and out of the building.

Too frightened to turn around until he reached his room, Rattlebag flung open his door, locked it tightly behind him, and hurried to his bed. He pulled his sheets all the way up to his neck and lay there silently with his eyes wide open. "It was a dream. Or a nightmare. It had to be. Ghosts aren't real. I did not see a ghost. I am going to close my eyes, and when I wake up, this will all have been a bad dream." The headmaster continued to chant various versions of this mantra until he drifted to sleep.

"Well, that seemed to work despite the disastrous delivery," Unk was musing to Olivier as the pair walked back toward Newton and Nigel.

"Disaster!" scuffed the actor. "My good sir, it was a perfectly executed plan, though I may have been a bit pitchy in my opening to 'Oklahoma!'"

"You were in good voice, Olivier," chuckled Unk, "Though I would have preferred something from, 'South Pacific.'"

"Noted for next time," the actor yielded to the request.

It appeared that both soldier and thespian were correct in their general assessments of success as they met no abbey staff on their walk back to the boys' room. When there, Olivier told their story to Newton and then retired to clean himself off. For his part, the mathematician laughed heartily at Olivier's account but seemed to genuinely lament not being present to see the fireworks himself. The Unknown Soldier, however, stood stiffly at attention and watched out the window. He would remain at this post for hours, waiting for William and Thomas to return.

✦ ✦ ✦

Inside the tower, the Ravenmaster was finishing feeding time for his avian charges and was about to retire his post. As he placed the final bird into its cage, the beefeater glanced down at his hand. Drops of bright red blood sat atop his pale skin. They must have fallen from the birds' mouths as they enjoyed a meal of gore-soaked biscuits. A twisted sneer began to sprout upon his face. With his crooked teeth exposed as his lips parted, he lifted his hand to his mouth, and he proceeded to lick the life fluid from his skin. He had been bitten by a vampire and so needed the fresh blood of the living to survive but sometime the "juice" of the dead had to suffice. He now wished only to turn completely into a night-lord with another bite. "My master has promised he would make me so," he thought to himself.

His head tilted back slowly, and his eyes closed as he relished the iron flavor. The very taste of blood sent a surge of energy through his body. After a moment, he raised his head up and opened his eyes. His body ached as if it was suffering from withdrawals. While the small amount of ichor would not be enough to sustain him, for now, the Ravenmaster had regained energy and a feeling of warmth had returned to his blackened soul. He might be able to feed his physical hunger with some insects or perhaps one of the mice that still inhabited the tower lawns.

On most nights, the old guard left the tower to return to his home in the country. Tonight, however, he needed to deliver an important message. He entered the stone castle and descended into a dark passageway. He paused his stroll ever so often, listening before continuing on his path. During one of his rests, he heard it. The whistle. The Ravenmaster quickly rushed towards the sound. He loved its seduction.

In the flicker of candlelight, red eyes shown from the darkness.

"I am here, my lord," announced the Ravenmaster, as he knelt to the ground with his head hung in a sign of obedience. A hoof emerged from the shadows before horns pierced through the darkness, bringing the demon's full body into view.

"My sweet pet, what causes you to disturb my peace tonight?" said the demon with a liquid, snakelike hiss to his deep voice. A single black tentacle slithered out of the darkness to wrap itself around the minion. It stroked him slightly while the demon waited for a reply.

"My lord, I have sensed a new threat in the tower," replied the Ravenmaster.

"Go on," the demon said, using the tentacle to lift the mortal into a standing position.

The yeoman looked forward, avoiding direct eye contact with the demon as he delivered the news. "There is a beefeater that stands guard just outside the Crown Jewel Room. Over the course of many months, I have heard him rambling. At first, I suspected he was filling the time in his lonely position, but I began to listen to his rants. This one is sensitive to the spirit world. He knows ghosts exist, and from his conversations, it seems as if he can feel the agony and fear the weaker spirits carry with them."

"Has he made contact?" The demon inquired, with growing anger in his tone.

"I can't be sure. I do not think so from his blather. He does seem to long for the spirits to show themselves to him. He shares his own openness to the spiritual realm and begs them to trust him. However, I cannot be sure if he has been successful in his attempts." The tentacle uncoiled itself from around the Ravenmaster, and, again, as a servant to his master, he fell supine to the ground.

The demon gnashed his teeth, seethed in anger, and beat his tentacles against the ground before he calmed himself and snarled, "I suppose I need to pay this sensitive a visit then, don't I? Do you know where he lives?"

"Yes, my lord. I have found him for you," the Ravenmaster affirmed.

The demon hissed and again a tentacle reached out to stroke the Ravenmaster. "You will need to take me out tonight. Will you let me in?"

"Yes, my lord. Please, my lord," cried the servant in ecstasy.

"Good, my pet." A small snap could be heard as the demon talked and a rat's body was dropped before the Ravenmaster.

"Dinner before we go?" the creature asked.

CHAPTER 15 | Finding the Beefeater

DETAILS NEVER ESCAPED William Darlington. As the princes described the beefeater and the valuable information he may be able to provide at the gathering of ghosts, William had been meticulously taking notes on directions from the internet in hopes of finding the castle guard's home. It was exciting to think about meeting another human who had at least sensed the princes' presence. William was amazed that the beefeater would talk so frequently with the spirits in the off chance they were real. Indeed, in these musings, he had even expressed a hope that the ghosts of the tower may sense him in return and might one day reveal themselves. The boys could not wait to meet the guard. They wished to tell him he had been right about the spirit world in the old fortress and to find out if he could help in their cause.

From the map they had seen on their computer, the two boys knew that they would need to pass Big Ben, cross the River Thames, and make their way towards Archbishop's Park. From that point on, there were many quiet avenues and public walking paths that would allow them to get to the beefeater's house safely. Big Ben was situated just by the abbey, so that part was easy. The Thames divided the city, so to get to the park, they made their way to the pedestrian walking path that lined Westminster Bridge. The abbey and "Ben" served as a backdrop to the stunning architecture of the crossing. The water below, particularly at night, created a peaceful scene, while the lights of the nearby buildings danced off the ripples in the waves. The boys continued towards Archbishop's Park. This public park was legendary. It was a beautifully maintained green staple in the city, providing playgrounds, sports fields, and spaces to escape urban life. It was usually buzzing with people, but tonight it was quiet. The boys took a shortcut through one of the soccer fields and noticed a woman walking her dog while talking on her cell phone. William held out the map he had drawn. The beefeater lived just three blocks from the park near the train tracks, but this was foreign territory for the boys. William directed Thomas to follow him. At each intersection, he carefully studied his map and contemplated each turn before committing to a direction.

"One more left, and we should be there," William noted. As they turned onto the block, the brothers could see their destination. It was a modest flat built from light brown bricks. The front door was framed in white and consumed the slight width of the home. As narrow as the structure was, it spanned three floors and had windows wrapping around the second and third level. A red door popped against the dull-colored bricks, and a low wall held a small gate that granted entrance to the property.

Out of nowhere, a man entered the glow of the streetlight that stood just down from the house and a couple blocks ahead. William hid behind Thomas, who slowly backed towards the bushes lining the walkway. The figure continued their way. His unique dress caught Thomas by surprise. He had a long, structured jacket, popped at the collar. From underneath, slim black pants tucked into heavy boots that were pounding against the pavement. All his clothes seemed somehow mottled with darker hues of black than the night surrounding him, and they glistened as though wet if such a thing were possible. Beyond his dress, his face was striking. It was chiseled, and his jawline was razor-sharp. His eyes peeked out from behind perfectly swept and styled hair, and his mustache added a sharp complement to his features.

William could not see the details of the man, but as the sound of the boots grew louder, another haunting sound filled the air. Both boys froze as the man let out an ominous whistle. It almost did not sound human. Each note would cause one to shutter, capable of sending chills down the spine of anyone within earshot. To watch the man stroll, you could tell it was soothing, peaceful, and rewarding to him. He walked with a confidence that made you want to know him, but at the same time, his boastful stride carried with it a sense of threat. As the figure veered off down a side street, he stopped and turned to look in the direction of where the boys now hid. Thomas and William sank deeper into the bushes. The man seemed to scan the surrounding area and then started his walk again. His whistle disappeared into the darkness.

"Did you hear it? Did you feel it?" William asked his older brother. "The whistle was the same as I heard in the tower the day we met the princes."

"I know, Will," said Thomas, shivering from the encounter and then regrouping a bit before he continued. "Come on, let's get to the house before anything else happens or before that thing comes back." William looked at his brother with a startle. He had not even pretended and chose not to use the word "man."

As they approached the address, William repeated the street number, "1497."

"This is it," pointed Thomas.

They both entered through the waist-high gate that separated the sidewalk from the home's small lawn. As they walked the final distance to the front door, the boys found that it was ajar, exposing them to the first few feet of the home's entryway. It was dark and eerily quiet inside the house. Two lanterns that welcomed guests to the home flickered, and the dancing of the flames reflected through the window onto the wooden floor. Despite the glow, the boys could not make out anything much beyond where they stood.

"Hello?" called Thomas in a shaking voice. He took a deep breath and called again. "Hello? Sir? Is anyone home?"

William could sense something was off. "Maybe we should go. If he isn't here, I don't want to be caught inside his house. We can come back. Come on, Thom. We shouldn't be here. It's a waste of our time."

"Calm down. It isn't a waste. He could be inside, and if he isn't, maybe we can find something that could help the princes." Thomas didn't wait for William to protest. Instead, he pushed the front door open, allowing himself to walk in. He felt near the doorframe for a light switch. As he flipped it on, a yellow brightness filled the room, temporarily providing relief and a sense of familiar comfort for the boys. Right off the main entrance was the kitchen, which was stark white and minimal, with tiny pops of red appliances giving the room a sense of personality. Everything was in its place, which didn't come as a surprise. Given the nature of his royal position, the Darlingtons expected the beefeater's home to be tidy. Even more, it had a homey feel, despite the crisp, clean display. Pictures of relatives and postcards hung on his fridge. At the far corner, the wall gave way to a darkened hallway. Thomas walked through the kitchen to explore it. William followed close behind.

As the hall opened into a small room, William and Thomas both fumbled to find another light switch. William was the first to feel it at hand. As he flipped it on, both boys surveyed their surroundings and William screamed in horror. He dropped his head, could barely catch his breath, and covered his eyes calling for his brother. "THOM! Get me out of here. Please. Get me out." Thomas was usually the one to remedy any difficult situation, but he stood paralyzed as his eyes caught the image William was begging to escape.

The beefeater, or what was left of him, lay across a chair at the dining room table. His legs were positioned as if he had just taken a seat but had yet to swing his feet under the table. His torso was twisted to the side and hanging from the base of the chair, causing his back to be arched and his head to be elevated slightly above the ground. His rib cage was fully exposed, as his torso looked as though it was slashed from his belt to his neck. The bones were almost glowing white against the reddish, purple blood that lined the cavern of his chest. It appeared they had almost been stripped of the meat and muscles that would have surrounded them. The stomach was empty, as the contents sat in a thick pool of blood that was forming around the table like an area rug. His head hung at an inhuman angle, falling away from a perfect incision that nearly severed his neck completely. The man's eyes had been removed with aggression, no longer filling the empty holes that sat in his skull. His mouth was raw and dripping blood, with teeth sprinkled throughout the viscous mess on the floor.

Both boys were frozen in horror. They had never witnessed real violence before, much less the atrocity that sat before them. The smell was overwhelmingly pungent. The image was one that could not adequately be captured in a horror film. And the silence. The complete and utter silence of it all added to the terror before them. They were transfixed, petrified, and unable to move. Thomas' mouth hung open and his eyes could barely blink. William looked up, only to pierce the silence with another round of screams and a fit of tears.

For Thomas, it was not until he could hear the sirens in the far-off distance that his trance broke. It sounded like a fleet of emergency vehicles that were growing closer. His fear shifted. They couldn't be here in this place when the police arrived. It would be too suspicious, and the consequences would be too high. He grabbed William by the wrist and physically pulled him towards the front door. "William, come on! Move!" he demanded.

The younger boy was so scared that the color had drained from his face. He simply locked eyes with Thomas, and without saying a word was begging for his brother's help. It took all of Thomas' strength to guide him from the house. As they stepped outside, red and blue lights were flashing through the tree line. The brothers stumbled beyond the gate and made their way down the sidewalk to the end of the next block before Thomas allowed William to sit.

"I can't breathe. Thom. I can't breathe. Help me. Please." William's body was shaking, and tears continued to fall from his eyes. He was in shock and clearly having a panic attack.

Thomas felt helpless. "It's okay, William. It's okay." He tried to regulate his own breathing and fear to calm his brother. "Breathe with me." Thomas' father had taught them both this trick. He kneeled next to William, dipping down to make eye contact with him. Grabbing his brother's hands, Thomas took deep, purposeful breaths, and William began to follow. In time, his body relaxed, and he was able to slow his gasping to a normal rhythm of inhale.

Tires from the police cars, fire trucks, and ambulances screeched to a halt in front of the beefeater's house. The sounds and the rush of people triggered both boys to move and get further away from the scene.

"What are we going to do? I don't know what to do," said William, barely speaking above a whisper and almost talking to himself.

"I am not sure, but I know we have to get back to the abbey," whispered Thomas.

William grabbed at the back of Thomas' shirt. "Thom, we have to tell someone what we saw. We have to tell them what happened."

Thomas pivoted with almost a sense of anger. "No, we don't, and we won't. Do you understand that, William? No one can know what we saw. No one will believe that we just stumbled across a murder. It won't be just the headmaster punishing us for being out. The police will be the ones to come and get us if we don't keep this secret. Got it?" The volume of his voice had nearly grown to a holler.

William crumbled. Thomas had not meant to be so hard on him. "I'm sorry. I'm sorry, William. I didn't mean to yell at you. I'm going to get us back to the abbey. When we get there, we will go straight to see the ghosts. I think you should be with Jane, while I talk to the rest of the group. Okay?" William looked down at his feet. "Okay, William?"

"Okay. Let's just go. I don't want to be out here anymore," William said with meek obedience.

Thomas put his arm around his brother, and they set off to find the safety of the school and the familiarity of their newfound friends. They would know how to calm the boys, how to fix the situation, and what to do next. At least, that is what Thomas continued to tell himself as the sounds of the emergency vehicles dulled in the distance.

✦ ✦ ✦

Detective Mulroney shook her head as Sergeant Grant looked straight ahead into the crime scene with steely blue eyes. The detective had shown the sergeant her badge. It was inscribed with a gold 221-B. Sargent Grant had glanced at it and nodded, "Baker Street Department, huh? I thought your team would be here," he stated flatly.

The detective looked back at the crime scene and then down to scribble more notes. "Bloody hell! I had hoped it wouldn't happen again in my life, but I somehow knew it would," said the detective.

"Every few years, for the last century and a half," murmured Grant.

"And who knows how long before that," posited Mulroney. "The Ripper is back."

"God help us all," Grant whispered under his breath. It was as if the sergeant had released a genuine prayer to help with the evil before them.

CHAPTER 16 | Unusual Help

THOMAS PULLED AT the heavy side door to the abbey. He had given up the caution of sneaking back into the dorm though the window and hoped that the entrance used for deliveries would allow him and his brother an ease of access. He was not disappointed. The door was both open and presently unwatched. He did not question his good fortune. In his mind, he was trying to put together the best way to explain to the spirits what they had just witnessed. Beyond the trauma, he was disappointed that he and William could not come bounding in with details of how they would all gain entry into the tower. He had none of the important information the beefeater would have surely shared with them. William was still in shock and was slowly following his brother into the great hall in an almost trancelike state.

"My poor darlings. Come here, my angels." Upon seeing them, Jane Austen immediately went to embrace the boys, seeming to forget that her spiritual arms could not physically hold them close to her chest or as dearly as she would wish. She stepped back and placed her hands to her mouth as if nearly unable to speak. "My heart aches that you precious boys witnessed such tragedy and horror. We will get through this. I am here and we are all going to help you."

William began to cry again. "Miss Jane, I was so scared. I can't get the torture of his body and the blood out of my head." He sat down on a bench sobbing while Jane gracefully joined him to offer whispers of comfort.

Thomas, on the other hand, was confused. "How did Jane

know? Was it a spiritual ability?" he wondered. Regardless, she was providing the comfort William so desperately needed. Leaving his brother's side, the older boy wasted no time and began searching for the other ghosts. In many ways, he thought their wisdom and assurance would be as healing for him as Jane's soft-spoken assurances was a consolation for his brother. He was quickly approaching panic mode as he struggled to find them.

Laughter caught Thomas' ear. It seemed so out of place given all he had been through, but still, he was drawn to the sound. He was sure he could make out Darwin's rumble in the general guffaw and certainly, he heard Newton's high-pitched chortle. It was all coming from inside the confessional booth that offered the "Highway to Heaven." It was where he and William had first met Sir Isaac.

Thomas approached the wooden box at the side of the abbey with some trepidation. As he opened the door and attempted to enter, he saw the spirits piled on top of each other almost like prankish teenagers crammed into a photo booth. The moment they saw the young mortal, the group billowed out to meet him. Thomas would have turned to address the gathered spirits that had convened behind him, but he stood transfixed at what he saw beyond what had been the jumble of ghosts laughing in the confessional. Peering into the booth, he saw a landscape that only gave way to a light on the far, far horizon. Tall flowers of every color filled fields in a perspective that stretched well beyond Thomas' imagination. The pallet of floral hues was broken only by a roadway leading to the light and a station of sorts where ghosts were apparently waiting to catch a ride into the distance. Antique cars drove along the road, jauntily coming from someplace before the abbey and Thomas' vantage point. It was a beautiful and happy scene.

Thomas felt a slight pressure on his shoulder, much like the experience he had while holding Jane's hand the day that the two princes had paid a visit. He looked back and found that Dickens had come to stand next to him and was resting his hand on his shoulder. "Lovely, isn't it, child?" asked the kindly author. "Someday, we all wish to take that drive to its end."

"But not today," interjected Darwin softly. "Thomas, you made it back, my good lad. We were so very worried about your whereabouts and are so very sorry for your experience. Trust me. It's all going to be fine. No need to worry or be downhearted," encouraged the naturalist. "We would have come to you, but our friends the martlets were watching. They said you would be here before we could find you on the streets. So, we waited. Poor Jane nearly had to be restrained to stop her from rushing out to find you and William." The ghost so often gruff in demeanor smiled warmly at the boy.

Thomas could contain himself no longer and turned to face the ghosts. It had become clear to him that they all knew what he and William had found at the beefeater's house and yet, they did not seem concerned with the loss or its implications. "What is happening? 'Don't worry? It will be ok?' The beefeater is dead. Not just dead, he was murdered. It was so horrible, Mister Darwin. How are you so calm? The poor man died, and beyond that, we have lost our only chance to be secreted into the tower," Thomas stated in a frustrated tone.

"Nonsense," muttered an unfamiliar voice.

Thomas began looking around the group, searching for the person who was challenging him. "How could you know? You were not even there. It was ghastly." Thomas cried out so loud that several ghosts walking to the confessional station turned their heads to shush him.

"Young Thomas, is it?" said the stranger. "I must beg to differ in your assertion, but I certainly understand your upset. I was there, my young friend." The recently slain beefeater stepped out from behind Hawking and Olivier. "I may not have my physical body to prove it, but that demon couldn't take my mind or spirit. The martlets brought me here as soon as I left my body, such a thrilling experience with the birds. They are absolutely delightful creatures. Most importantly, my dear boy, I can still help you. I think I know a way to get you in the tower. As for all else, I have no family to speak of, and it has been my life's desire to connect with the spiritual world. While I would have preferred a less extreme measure, I've arrived." There was a hint of joy in the old guard's voice.

"But you..." Thomas stood in awe.

"I know, son. I was murdered. Trust me, it is not something I will soon forget, and I would take great pleasure in ending that thing that killed me," he responded.

"But you were all laughing. I heard you," Thomas said in a pleading tone and trying to find some reconciliation in all that had happened.

The beefeater comforted, "I was just telling the lads that I didn't like my flat anyway, and that in my human form, this uniform was quite restrictive. Now it seems I've lost weight: a two-hundred-and-twenty-pound body, to be exact. Just as I was when I first joined the tower company," he said with a wink. Thomas could tell the ghost was trying to make him smile to relieve the fear in his heart.

"Isn't life magnificent?" Olivier said with a grand theatrical flourish. "Meet Carl Langinberry. He has been here the last two hours telling us about his life, his run-in with the demon, and the layout of the tower. I must say, I cannot tell which tale is more exciting. He's quite the fellow and tells quite a story." Olivier nodded at the beefeater.

Hawking had just stretched his legs, pulling each to his chest, and appeared to be making himself ready to run a race. As he dropped his right ankle from his hand and began to again work on his left, the physicist chimed in, "Gathered ghosts, I believe what we have said is enough of an introduction for now. Carl, why not tell the boys about the demon."

"Gently," admonished Jane as she approached the group

with William in tow. She saw no reason to relive the gory details.

Carl shuddered before regaining his composure to speak. "During my time at the tower, I could feel what you all refer to as the ethereal world. I sensed this plane of existence. I knew I was never alone at my post and I felt both positive and negative energies around me. There was always something, but most often it was a mild in impact. From time to time, I could also sense a dark force within the walls. It was different, more powerful, consuming, and malevolent than what was typical to my experience. I came face to face with that darkness tonight."

The beefeater continued, "Shortly after arriving home, I heard a knock at the door. A fine-looking fellow stood on my stoop, introducing himself as 'Jack.' He stated he was with a historical society and wanted to know if I would consent to a short interview about my job at the tower. He told me Henry Wigworth, a fellow beefeater, had recommended me to him. He was articulate and sharply dressed, so I had no initial concern about inviting him in for tea and conversation. Besides, I have known Henry at the tower for decades now and I am always willing to back up another guardsman. In all, I was intrigued, so opened my door to him fully. As I went to pull up a seat to join him at my table, his frame shifted, and my world was ripped apart. 'Jack's' eyes became a bright red, as tentacles rose from his back and they reached forward to trap me and draw me into the transforming abomination my visitor was becoming. It is one of the last things I remember in the flesh. Moments later, I was watching from above what could only be described as a demon disemboweling my body. I think the teeth and eyes he pulled were to be more of a statement to those who might find me or maybe just a personal pleasure because the big job had long been done." He rolled his eyes and made a cynical laugh as if unimpressed by the demon's work. "I think the evil beast wanted my soul."

"Kind sir, please," protested Jane, "Remember the children!" Jane looked at the boys, fearing their upset.

"Aye, gentle lady," replied the beefeater contritely.

"We can only assume he somehow found out our plan to talk with Carl here. How he might have done so, we can only hope to ascertain. In any event, he beat the boys to the house and left his body for them or maybe just anyone to find." It was Dickens who was pointing out a reality that was clearly causing confusion and concern among the ghosts.

"Mister Dickens," said William meekly. "We saw him. We saw the demon. He passed a little distance in front of us on the street as we made our way to your house." William was now looking shyly at the beefeater.

"Did you hear his whistle?" whispered Thomas, who was now looking directly at Carl.

The beefeater seemed overwhelmed. The beast had whistled throughout the entire ordeal of his murder, serenading himself as he worked. "Yes, I did. If I close my eyes, I can still hear that sound. I fear I always may."

Thomas was still trying to process all of this. "Why did he spare us? Why didn't the demon kill us too?"

"We can only speculate. Fate and the darkness likely have saved the day. It simply may not have seen you," remarked Darwin.

"Or you may not be perceived as a threat," guessed Dickens.

"Or he has a bigger purpose for keeping you alive," suggested Newton.

"But what we do know is that the demon has unwittingly given us an opportunity beyond hope and expectation." It was again Darwin speaking.

"Aye, contrary to his goal of silencing me, the demon simply altered my existence. Now I've been pulled towards the abbey." The beefeater took a moment to look around at the magnitude of the place. "It may have taken my body, but the demon won't stop me from sharing what I know. I will tell you how to enter the tower secretly and as you wish."

"A man after my own heart. You truly understand survival of the fittest, my friend. We have adapted." Darwin placed his arm around Carl and exuded great pride as he said, "A mere modification in the plan will not deter our quest. In fact, having you with us will actually enhance our efforts."

Thomas looked at William at the mention of a plan. Neither boy had heard much, if any, thought of what may be done to help the princes beyond finding a way for the ghosts to get into the tower. What the clutch of conspiratorial spirits would do about finding the key or dealing with a demon once they gained access to the old fortress had been lost to the boys in the general discussion. Clearly the ghostly group had been working on all the issues at hand. Even William shook off some of his emotional trauma and showed a real interest in the discussion to come.

Darwin started. "For the first order of business, we will be sending Unk and Olivier to St George's Chapel at Windsor Castle. Together, they will retrieve the skull of King Edward the IV."

"With Merlin's magic and that royal remnant, we are hopeful we will be able to resurrect the king's spirit. Then we will simply ask him where he has hidden the key. What he would apparently not give the demon, he might be able to give to us. Simple and straightforward may be the best way to achieve our end," noted Dickens as he looked to Merlin for approval. The wizard gave a slight bow to acknowledge his responsibility.

Darwin then continued. "The rest of us will be heading to the tower to seek our own clues on the key's whereabouts. This is where Carl's knowledge becomes indispensable. Go on, chap. Tell them your idea," encouraged the naturalist to the group's newest accomplice.

Carl asked the spirits to gather around, and he pulled an

ethereal map from his coat. Somehow, it was in pristine condition despite the fact that the tight fit of the guard's jacket would have crushed a mortal document. As he unfolded the reference, his face revealed a familiarity with it. It was a map of London, showing Westminster Abbey on the far left and the tower on the far right.

Seeing the map, William and Thomas looked a bit confused about how the beefeater came about such a prop. "He picked it up at the Seven to Heaven convenience store," informed Olivier, sensing their confusion and offering explanation. Both the boys nodded their understanding, silently amazed at the wonder of the ethereal world.

"We must be smart about where and when we enter the tower, lads. Luckily, for us all, I am privy to the tunnel system that spans underneath the fortress and extends to the edge of the city. It, at one time, was used to move prisoners quietly out of the tower and was left intact in modern times to allow for secreted acts of policing. There are few access areas to it from the outside the wall, but once underground, you will have many points of entry to emerge within the tower." The beefeater scratched his head, contemplating where the boys would have the easiest way in. He knew the shuttling of the spirits would take some time but did not want the mortals to be exposed for a moment more than necessary. "There it is," he finally pointed. The entire group clustered to see where the efforts to rid the world of the demon's threat would begin to fully unfold.

CHAPTER 17 | The Secret Tunnel

THE RED PHONE booths of London had served for years as a practical convenience, doors opening and closing to those who needed to make calls while they were out and away from home. Now that practically everybody carried a cell phone, they act most frequently as a tourist attraction. The beefeater knew, however, that beyond photo opportunities, there was another very significant role the booths served for both queen and country. While the public was unaware of their dual purpose, he knew that a few select booths worked as entry points to the tunnel system. They were the latest in a long line of facades used by the English government to protect the knowledge of the tunnels' existence. The booths had not been used in decades for this purpose, but the one closest to the abbey would be the ideal egress to send the boys into the tower.

The booth of interest was located at Parliament Square, Westminster. It was perfect. The boys could easily access it and quickly take cover underground. From there, they could move with the spirits to the tower and shuttle them beyond The Binding.

Carl pointed to a spot on the left side of the map, slightly above the abbey. "Here. This is where you will enter the tunnel system, the Royal Labyrinth we guards call it. On the square, you will find two red phone booths. The first is down the block from here on this corner and is nothing special. It has too much traffic to be used as an entrance. However, a block away from it on this side street, Horse Guard Road, a second booth sits against the corner of the old Cabinet War Rooms, just out of view of the main square. When you arrive at that spot, search for a section of bricks that are slightly out of place and embossed with a royal seal. That is how you will know you are at the correct box."

William was taking notes as the beefeater provided directions.

"Once at the booth, step inside and close the door. Be sure no one is watching, as you can't afford to have anyone follow or alert the tower. Once fully inside, pick up the phone and dial 13975 to form a star on the keypad. The floor will loosen, and you will be able to slide the heavy bottom towards the building and away from the street. Get quickly down onto the revealed ladder beneath and close the entryway immediately. We don't want any of the mortal guardsmen to come snooping around to see what opened the booth." The beefeater ended his account.

At this point, Dickens, looking directly at the young boys, took over the substance of the conversation. "I want to make sure you two understand what is needed once we are in the tunnels. The Binding is intact and will not allow us entrance beyond the perimeter of the tower. In order for us to cross over, you will have to escort us two at a time by inviting us in. It is not a small thing to ask, boys, and we all know this. Just a single possession requires great energy and sacrifice, but you will be tasked with many and in rapid succession on this trip. If you are hesitant, we fully understand, but I fear there may be no other way to accomplish our end."

"We understand, Mister Dickens, and we know the importance of the responsibility. We can do this," answered Thomas.

"Now that we have agreed where you will enter the tunnels, let me show you the rest," commented the beefeater.

He then lifted and flipped the ethereal map he had been using as if he was turning the page of a book. The back of his chart was covered in a large depiction of the tower.

"At first glance, the fortress layout resembles a pentagon," thought Thomas, referring back to his geometry class. The choirboy leaned forward to carefully study the schematic in full detail. The tower seemed a simple design. The building was surrounded by a moat and high walls to protect its grounds and treasured contents. However, upon closer inspection, many intricate subsections became apparent in the larger structure, each providing an entry point and built-in modes of protection. "It would, in fact, be quite easy to get lost there," Thomas surmised and stepped back.

"I believe it is wisest to have you emerge via the passageway at Brass Mount Battery, here," the beefeater instructed as he pointed to the top right corner of the map. "The tunnel will guide you nearly three miles from the phone booth to the tower. It will take you under Little Tower Hill and deliver you below the moat to the walls of the battery. When you get to this point, you will see a winding iron staircase that will guide you up to a heavy grate in the tower floor. We ghosts can float through it, but unfortunately you boys cannot. It will take both of you to lift the grate, but once you do, you will be able to climb out into the keep. It is a quiet part of the tower, with very little supervision needed as its contents have long been removed. You should be safe there."

"That is perfect," noted Newton. "We will travel with you as a troop through the tunnels. Once we are at The Binding, we meet our biggest hurdle. We will enter your bodies two by two to step through the barrier. Once we are inside, you can drop us, step back through, and retrieve other pairs. If we work as a team, this phase of the plan should not take long."

The conversation continued for an hour, but, even with the new knowledge shared and the emergent plan, Newton and the other ghosts knew it was much too soon to head to the tower. After witnessing the beefeater's dead body displayed in such a hideous way, the boys needed time to heal. Over the next few evenings, William in particular continued to have an intense reaction to the experience, with stomach pains and trouble sleeping. Jane made it her routine to take a place at the side of his bed to comfort him. More so, this also allowed her an opportunity to check on Thomas. His stoic demeanor worried her. She knew he had bottled his emotions away to be strong for his brother but also recognized that simply ignoring their reality would not serve the young boy. While she kept watch over the both the Darlingtons, the rest of the group strategized, identifying the risks associated with entrance to the tower, ways to protect the boys from what waited inside for them, and what was at stake if they failed to aid the princes. It was clear the demon would waste no time in attacking the ethereal group once he discovered their presence. The ghost planned for that reality, and then, they too waited as they gathered their courage. They knew what lay ahead and were rightly afraid.

✦ ✦ ✦

To help with the tower search, Darwin planned ahead. In the afterlife, one of the first spirits he connected with was a longtime fascination and professional inspiration, Leonardo Da Vinci. While most of the world had been fascinated by Da Vinci's art, Darwin intimately knew of his inventive nature and was incredibly impressed with the host of creations Da Vinci had designed. From air and watercraft to weaponry and architectural engineering, the Italian Renaissance man had developed and sketched visionary ideas that wouldn't be completely realized until hundreds of years after his death. Once he became part of the ethereal world, Darwin was convinced that many modern developments were, in fact, the result of Da Vinci's spiritual guidance of several mortal creators. The naturalist, however, was most fascinated with the inventor's study of nature and the biology of the animal kingdom, especially, his work on birds. The avian world become important to Darwin's own work and created in him a mild affinity for Da Vinci. "Birds of a feather flock together," Darwin often thought and would rumble a laugh. Eventually, he contacted the inventor to learn of him and his work since his death. Despite the obstacle of Da Vinci residing in Amboise, France, in the Chapel of Saint-Hubert, ethereal technology and communications had allowed the two to talk, and across many conversations they became close friends.

"Meeting Leo was one of the true joys of my death!" Darwin always claimed to those close to him.

Once the plan of the tower search had been set in motion, Darwin had reached out to Da Vinci to request he send him a special tool to aid in the hunt. Once it arrived, Darwin recruited Newton to go with him to retrieve a package from the 'DeadEX Shipping Depot' in the abbey's ethereal terminal. The artist had not failed him.

The ghost behind the counter disappeared into the back storage room, quickly reappearing with a package, and Darwin carefully examined the box. The label was written in calligraphy and addressed to a Mr. C. Darwin from Da Vinci's personal assistant, M. Lisa. He nodded in approval, signed the pick-up receipt, and turned to leave the shop.

"Aren't you going to open it?" asked Newton as he skipped to keep up with Darwin.

"Of course," Darwin said, continuing to walk. He was clearly set on getting to some specific destination to do it, so Newton remained quiet and followed closely behind.

As they arrived at Poets' Corner, Darwin carefully looked about the area for prying ears and eyes. After confirming he and Newton were alone, he wasted no time. The naturalist ripped off the tape and dug into the box as the mathematician looked on in anticipation. Darwin pulled out a black ether bag from the shipping container and quickly worked to untie the tedious knots holding the sack closed. Once he unraveled the lacing, Darwin reached in and brought out two odd gadgets. "Well done, friend!" he called to an unhearing Da Vinci as he held out the mechanisms for Newton to see.

"Without further ado, may I present Da Vinci's original and innovative 'X-Ray Specs'?" Smiling with pride and anticipation, the evolutionist placed the pairs of oversized goggles on a nearby stone ledge. The so-called 'specs' looked more like steampunk-inspired oversized scuba masks than traditional eyewear.

"I never learned to swim," noted Newton, "so if you plan to explore under the water in the tower moat, you are going to have to find a new partner to search with."

Darwin shook his head. "Not swimming, Newton. But these scientific marvels are sure to make a splash during the search," Darwin stated matter-of-factly but clearly, making a rare attempt at humor. "These are vital tools to advance our cause."

Grabbing up one set of the ethereal eyewear, the scientist pulled them onto his head and adjusted the black-leather strap that bound them. The goggles magnified the features of their wearer to ridiculous proportions. Darwin's eyes resembled the massive, protruding optics of a tarsier. As he turned around to hand Isaac his pair, Newton laughed at the sight. Still, the mathematician's reaction paled in comparison to Darwin's as he looked at Newton.

"Good God, sir!" roared the biologist. "Have you no shame?!"

Newton, feeling that someone had walked up behind him without his notice, immediately spun and turned his back on his colleague.

Again, Darwin roared, "An even less attractive side! Newton, you bounder! Put back on your clothes!"

Newton reached back and put both hands on the seat of

his pants as if to assure himself he hadn't forgotten to buckle his trousers and then turned again to face his companion.

"Ugh, enough," stated Darwin. "Please, let me see no more of your natural state."

"I assure you, sir, it is your own imagination that serves you these images. I am quite dressed, and you would only gasp in awe if I were not!" Newton's inflection of voice signified his indignation at Darwin's apparent affront of sensibilities.

Grabbing up his own goggles and snapping them in place, Newton followed Darwin's lead and screamed. "Bloody hell, Charles! It is you who seems to have become free-floating in the buff." Newton placed both hands on his hips and surveyed the biologist. "I think that your friend Da Vinci may have succeeded all too well in allowing us to see through things. Perhaps one of these tiny side knobs might adjust the view." Newton reached up and began turning a small control marked 'In/Out.' "Simply amazing," Sir Isaac muttered. "Charles, my dear friend, I had no idea you had suffered a broken rib in the past. As a child, perhaps?"

"Why yes, I did," replied a much-calmed Darwin, who himself was now playing with the controls found on his own goggles. "But how did you know?"

"Your skeleton. I am looking directly at it," responded Newton, with his eyes appearing as if they were about to break through the lenses.

This time it was Darwin's turn to pat himself in disbelief. "I didn't even know I still had a skeleton to look at," Charles posited. As he continued to play with the capabilities of his mask, he, like Newton, became entranced with all they could see. "These will serve perfectly in our efforts to see inside the walls of the tower. Nothing shall remain hidden from us for long!"

Newton nodded and noted fondly, "Charles, you really must introduce me to Leo when you have the chance."

"Happily, Isaac. However, for now we should return to the

others." The ghosts placed the goggles back in their original sack and set back towards the abbey's chapel. Soon, Darwin realized, the ghosts would be starting the hunt for the key. He hoped they would be ready. Dead or not, spirits could be killed again, and the demon would surely test that fact were it given the opportunity.

CHAPTER 18 | Back and Forth

THE DORMITORY WAS silent, except for the sounds of soft snoring and gentle breathing from the sleeping choirboys. The sun was barely rising over the Thames River, and warm light was beginning to shine through the window at the far end of the room. Shadows played off the floor and flickered over the beds.

William awoke with peace in his soul. As he opened his eyes, Jane was seated in her usual spot at the foot of his bed with her soft gown and her legs hanging over the side. Her hands were folded in her lap, and her gaze was fixed on William. She had found comfort in this place, feeling as if she had gained new purpose caring for the young boy. For nights, William had woken up in screaming fits, covered in sweat, and shaking with fear. The boys in his dorm were quite concerned but believed Thomas when he told them that William sometimes went through these phases because of the death of their parents. Moreover, had it not been for Jane, William may not have been able to close his eyes again in those moments without the scenes of the beefeater's body consuming his thoughts. Now, however, as he focused his look on Jane, she could tell his eyes had returned to their innocent default. Fear had faded, and the trauma had processed to a more manageable state.

"Good morning, my sweet William," she softly stated.

"Good morning, Miss Jane. I think I'm ready to return to

the tower," William whispered.

Jane was cautious, and inquired, "Are you sure, my precious boy? I want to be confident your heart and mind are ready."

"I'm sure. If you want, you can tell the other the ghosts, and I'll tell Thomas we can leave tonight." He looked at the gentle spirit with hope of approval.

Jane smiled graciously and arose from the bed to go and share the news. She turned back and made eye contact with William. He nodded his head, providing her additional reassurance that it was time to make the announcement. With one more glance at her young charge, Jane left the room.

William rolled out of his bed. Thomas slept above him, so he climbed up the ladder and grabbed his brother's foot, shaking it for him to wake up. A rough, grizzly groan came from underneath the sheets.

"Go away. It's not even daylight yet," Thomas barked.

William rolled his eyes. Why did his brother have to be such a grump? He shook Thomas' foot again.

"Thom, get up," instructed William. "Tonight's the night."

Thomas sat straight up in the bed, throwing the sheet off his body. "Are you serious?"

"Naw, I'm joking," said William in a dull, sarcastic voice. "Yes, I'm serious. I asked Miss Jane to tell the others. I think we need to leave tonight to get them into the tower."

Thomas thought for a minute, rubbed the sleep from his eyes, and nodded his agreement. Leaving would not be easy, though. It would require a large amount of assistance to be out for another night without raising eyebrows. The older boy had made the decision to ask even more of his classmates for help. "I'm going to wake some of the others. We can't do this on our own."

"You trust them? You don't think they will rat us out? The last thing we need is for them to tell on us," William reminded Thomas. The young boy felt desperately obligated to help the abbey ghosts and the princes. If he and his brother blew this, William knew there were huge consequences—and not simply to themselves.

Thomas was putting on his clothes to get ready for the day. As he tucked his shirt into his pants, he paused, looked at William, and said, "You know we don't have another choice. I'm going to wake up a couple of guys." With that, Thomas quietly gathered Nigel, James, and Burt, and despite their complaints about being awakened, led them, along with William, to the bathroom. They were far enough away from the dorm beds to talk privately and the boys could close the dormitory doors so that they wouldn't wake the others.

While Nigel had been a potential threat to expose the recent events concerning the tower, he now was one of the brothers' biggest supporters and a clear ally. Not only had he accepted the reality of the ghosts, but he was already implicated in the previous night's subversive activity. He now had a stake in the success of what he called 'The Cause.' More so, being a part of Thomas and William's adventure gave Nigel a sense of being needed and accepted. His adopted façade of being a bully and tattletale was simply to disguise feeling out of place and it fully fell away. Now, he was a part of something bigger, and it had softened his attitude with his peers.

Thomas quietly surveyed the other two boys. James rarely took anything seriously, but he also had the ability to be quite clever and charming. He had been in trouble more times than the brothers could count. "If anyone knows how to talk his way out of a difficult situation," thought Thomas, "it is James."

Burt would be able to supervise Nigel, the rule follower, and James, the class clown. It was difficult to get a rise out of him because he always focused on the mechanics of a situation. If he could fix a problem, it was nothing to cause worry. He would simply do so. If he could not control an outcome, then again, why worry? Thomas assumed Burt would be the one he would most rely on to aid in their cover and keep a cool head should difficulties emerge.

The group had stumbled into the bathroom wearing their pajamas, barely able to adjust their eyes to the light. They took a seat on the shower benches, and Thomas stood before them, ready to share his big idea. "Ok, guys. Here is the deal. Tonight, William and I are going to leave school. We have a very important task to complete, and we need your help." Thomas went on to explain the existence of the ghosts in the abbey and their need to get inside the Tower of London. Nigel interjected and told of meeting Sir Isaac Newton. He went so far as to flick his own ear as a demonstration of his experience, as if to provide needed proof. At the story's end, both Burt and James sat completely quiet, looking back and forth between William, Thomas, and Nigel.

Burt spoke first. "You all sound like loons, but for some reason, I believe every word. Maybe I'm a bit of a loon myself," he joked.

"This is magnificent!" piped in James. "Ghosts or not, I am all for helping in this plan. 'Her Majesty's Secret Service' I shall call it! This is going to be fun. I'm going to be 007. Bond, James Bond," he announced while doing his best Bond pose. James looked around to his co-conspirators for approval but only got annoyed looks. "Tough crowd," he shrugged.

"Nigel, you were an awesome lookout last time we left you in charge of security. Think you could keep watch again?" asked Thomas, trying to move on.

"Absolutely!" affirmed Nigel. He stood up straighter with a proud look on his face. He felt important because unlike the other boys, this would be his second time to aid William and Thomas.

"Great. Thank goodness," said the older Darlington to his former nemesis. William looked at his brother, impressed by his ability to manage their classmates. Thomas had roped in the biggest risk to their plan as an ally not once, but twice, so any doubts William held about the night fully slipped away.

ASHLEY WELLMAN & PATRICK KINKADE

His brother knew what he was doing, and Thomas continued his instructions with equal assuredness in relation to the other boys. "Burt and James. We need you to develop a way to have it look like we are in our beds when the house parents make their rounds."

"YESSSSSS! I've always wanted to do this. I saw it in a movie once," blurted out James, almost giggling with excitement. "We can take all of our weekend sacks, stuff them with shower towels, and use them for your legs and torso. I can grab two volleyballs from the gym to use for your heads. With blankets over the top of our 'straw men,' nobody will be the wiser about you two being off and about!"

Burt nodded, noting that James, typically a prankster, was actually onto something. "What if we tied fishing line to the bags to move them ever so slightly if someone came to check the beds? My phone would allow us to record you snoring, Thom! We could play it for effect during the monitor's rounds."

Thom looked bewildered and asked, "Wait, I snore?"

"Yes!" exclaimed the whole group in unison.

"Well, I had no idea," said Thomas, breaking a half smile. "But, since I clearly saw logs when I sleep, that sounds like an awesome idea. To recap: Nigel, you'll keep watch, waiting for the house parents to make their rounds. When you see them coming towards the dormitory, it will be up to you to signal the others. Burt, if any of the other guys wake up tonight, you'll need to throw your weight around and convince them that nothing is happening. James, we will need you to be the one to intercept any adult who might look too closely at the situation. You are the world's best at spinning a convincing story. William and I have a lot to do before tonight, but we are trusting that you guys will have our backs. Can we count on you?"

"Of course, you can," said Nigel. "You picked the best group of friends to help." The word "friends" took William by surprise, but he turned to Nigel and shook his hand.

"Thank you...truly" said William with a sincerity that hardened the resolve of all those enlisted.

With that, Thomas and William left others in the conspiratorial group behind. The three classmates were huddled together strategizing, talking about the items they would need, and how they would avoid arousing the other boys' suspicions later that night.

✦ ✦ ✦

Back in the abbey, the ghosts had planned the needed tasks for the evening. They identified the groupings that would see those jobs done once they all made it through The Binding. Recognizing nightfall allowed for less chance of detection, Olivier and The Unknown Solider had also packed themselves up and set off on their 'SpiritCycles' on their assigned task, to retrieve King Edward's skull from Windsor Castle. This traditional mode of ghostly transportation had first appeared in the mid-1800s with the introduction of penny-farthing high wheel bikes but the bikes had developed with their physical counterparts to their current sleek state. The ride Unk and Olivier planned would take mortals nearly two and a half hours to complete, but with the aerodynamics of their ethereal bikes and their own weightlessness, it would take the ghosts less than half of that time to make the trip from Westminster to Windsor.

Olivier, happy to be with his friend, the warrior, and heading away from the church, was absolutely chipper about taking the ride. "What a delightful night to be out and about and away from the gloom of towers and abbeys," said the thespian to his often dower companion. With a ring of the bell on the bike's handlebar and a donning of a roguishly styled hat, Sir Laurence headed off into the city.

Unk stood and looked after his chosen accomplice. A small

grin broke the usual somber look on his face. "He's right. It is a nice night," he chuckled to himself. Throwing his leg over the SpiritCycle from habit, as it would have passed right through the bike had the ghost moved the limb accordingly, the soldier focused his will on staying seated. He pedaled away from Westminster, and, for reasons unclear to even himself, he also rang the bike's bell. "Actually, it is a beautiful night," he thought, reconsidering his initial assessment. He smiled fully this time and headed after Olivier. For the first time in decades, he started to hum then fully sing his favorite tune. Folks who were out walking and quiet in their own thoughts that evening swore they heard the Rolling Stones' "Sympathy for the Devil" rushing by in the wind. "I always liked Mick's work when I heard the mortals play it," thought the old solider.

✦ ✦ ✦

The abbey carillon erupted in a glorious, gothic ring as the hands on the clock turned to 10 p.m. Within minutes, Thomas and William, dressed in dark street clothes, trotted into the vestibule and met the spirits. Thomas had a look of sheer excitement on his face. William was slightly anxious but, nonetheless, eager to begin the trip.

Despite his desire to come along and even with the loss of the help he might have provided, Darwin had declared the beefeater, the abbey's newest conspirator, unable to travel. Given the recent nature of his demise and his unfamiliarity with his spiritual body, the scientist decided it would be best for Carl to stay, relax, and decompress after his horrific death. He had suggested that the tower guard explore the abbey, check out a few shops, or maybe pursue a meeting with a spiritual counselor at one of the existing clinics. "Getting used to your own afterlife can be almost as traumatic as what put you there," observed the naturalist, and Carl, despite his immediate protest, knew Darwin was right. He was not quite feeling himself, whatever exactly that "self" currently was, and so yielded to the naturalist's suggestion.

The remaining ethereals had gathered. After the boys made their way to them, the group as a whole set off, following the directions the beefeater dictated. William was familiar with the landmarks, so he guided the effort to find the red telephone booth. Given that the ghosts had not been out in the city much and were not intimately familiar with any new additions since their deaths, they allowed the boy to lead. The decision was sound as they arrived at the square where the abbey and Big Ben were perfectly lined up for a postcard photograph and where the beefeater had directed them to go. Thomas stood still while William wandered down a couple of side streets searching for the exact red box.

"There!" Will called and pointed down a small lane. Within a second of identifying the booth slightly tucked out of view, Dickens took charge of the group and led them over to what he presumed would be an egress to the tower. The beefeater had instructed them to enter the corner numbers on the phone pad in a clockwise fashion before hitting the middle key. 1-3-9-7-5. It was Thomas who carried out the sequence. Instantly, an unlatching sound came from the base of the booth, and as directed, the young boy leaned forward and pushed the floor towards the adjacent building. Sure enough, underneath was a deep, dark hole with a metal ladder descending underground. The boys, one after the other, climbed down into the dim while their ghost companions floated beside them. Once they were all inside, Thomas pushed the cover to the opening shut. It closed with a click, making Thomas a bit nervous because he was not sure how to reopen the door as an exit. Shrugging off his doubt, however, Thomas whispered "Details" to himself, and as a mimic of Sir Isaac, he pointed his finger straight up into the air. He laughed under his breath as he climbed down to join the others.

Allowing their eyes to adjust to the low lighting provided by Merlin's staff and the two flashlights they carried, William and Thomas looked around their present confines. The tunnel to which the phone booth led was dark, damp, and cold, smelling of the moss that clung to its walls. It had archways that shaped the various twists and turns of the tunnels the troop could take from this particular entry point into the tower. Luckily, the beefeater had carefully dictated, and William had perfectly transcribed, which arches to pass through and how to identify their next direction to reach their prescribed destination. Rats scurried past the boys' feet, and echoes filled the air. Still, despite the frightening backdrop, the map William had created left little question about how to proceed. All remained quietly waiting as the tunnels seemed to demand it.

It was Darwin who broke the hushed silence, muttering, "Now for it." He strode forward into the gloom. The others slowly followed. As they grew closer to their ultimate destination, the collection of spirits could feel a powerful sensation slowing their progress. It was as if they were walking through deeper and deeper mud. The boys could sense something too, an electric feeling pulsing from their heads down to their toes. It was much like what they first felt in the tower when they met the princes, but it was being doled out in a more controlled manner. Like a subtle tickle, the sensation resided on the border between pleasure and pain.

"That is The Binding," announced Thomas, familiar with the feeling from carrying the princes through it twice.

Dickens approached William. "I think it is time, young sir." William nodded understanding of the comment and immediately he invited the author 'in.' With a flash, Dickens disappeared and William shuddered. The possession had worked.

Darwin was next. He stood before Thomas and made ready to enter his host and cross The Binding alongside

Dickens. "Come in, Mister Darwin," welcomed Thomas and then, it was done. Darwin and Dickens, inside their young vessels, turned toward the other ghosts.

"Wait here," said Darwin in the voice of Thomas. "The boys will be back for you." Leaving the others behind, the vessels and their two passengers moved forward.

The tunnel dipped lower, creating a steep path. "This must be the moat," noted Dickens through William. A few more steps forward beyond the depression and suddenly, the force disappeared like someone had turned off a light switch. The boys could feel it and so could the ghosts inside them. Hesitating and to be sure they had cleared the barrier, the two moved further down the corridor. Then, as quickly as they had entered, Darwin and Dickens exited the boys.

"My dear, lads. You did it. I can't believe it. We are through that confounding barrier!" Dickens was smiling and slapped Darwin on his back, who himself was offering a Cheshire grin. "Quickly retrieve the next couple."

Two by two, the other ghosts crossed through the barrier to join Darwin and Dickens. First, Jane and Hawking, and then Newton and Shakespeare. The princes waited patiently and then took their familiar place inside the boys to pass through. This left Glinda and Merlin as the last to break through the magical wall.

Once the entire group had entered inside the Binding's perimeter, Darwin wasted no time taking the lead and giving directives. "Now, the stairs. Where are the stairs?" he questioned.

Dickens cleared his throat to gather Darwin's attention. As all eyes were fixated on him, Dickens pointed towards a small tunnel to the right of the main corridor. Sure enough, through the blackness of the underground maze, cast iron stairs wrapped towards the roof of the tunnel. Directly above was Brass Mount Battery, surmised the crowd. The beefeater said it would be so, and he had yet to be in error. William and

Thomas knew all that stood between them and the horror inside the tower was the iron grate at the top of the stairs. But it was also all that stood between them and the hoped-for completion of their night's objective.

Carl had warned the boys that the grate was far too heavy for just one lad to open. William and Thom both walked up the stairs, prepared to use their strength to pry open the access point. Yet, as they reached for the grate, Newton called them back down.

"Change of plans, boys," he said in a stern voice. "You two are staying here in the tunnels."

"No. We can't. We are the only way you all can come back," argued Thomas.

"Stop!" interrupted Hawking. "This is not up for discussion. We may be ghosts, but we are still adults, and you are children. We decided at the abbey that it was far too much of a risk to allow you back inside the tower. We cannot afford for anything to happen to you. Heaven forbid we lost you two boys," he paused in horror at the simple idea and choked back the sad upset of the thought before regaining control and dispassionately continuing. "We would be trapped here forever." His attempted pretense did not fool any of those gathered.

"Do you two understand? It is critical that you stay at the base of the stairs so that when our search is over, we will be able to find you and shuttle home." Dickens was also speaking as if the ghosts were concerned about their own safety when it was clear that their only desire was to protect the boys. He put his hand on Hawking's shoulder to give comfort to the physicist, who was wiping an eye in a furtive manner. "As for our princes, we need you two to escort us into the tower as we begin the hunt. Then, you shall return to watch over, no, entertain our boys." No words were needed. The princes acknowledged their role with a simple nod of their heads.

Thomas and William were frustrated but understood why

the ghosts wanted them to stay. They watched as their friends ascended into the tower ready to hunt for the key. As the last of the spirits left, the boys sat side-by-side on the bottom step of the staircase. They wondered how long they would be sitting in the cold, damp, and dirty tunnel waiting for the "adults" to return. However long, the boys feared, they would simply be waiting and worrying until they were reunited.

✦ ✦ ✦

It may have been an hour or possibly more, but William was sure he heard it. It was a shuffling sound that was coming from behind them. "Do you think it's Mister Darwin and the others?" asked Thomas.

William shook his head. "It's coming from the wrong direction, and ghosts don't shuffle." That much he knew for sure.

Through the darkness, Thomas could see a shifting figure. As he squinted to try to make out who or what it was, he whispered to William, "Can you see that?" William could. He instinctively leaned into the wall, hoping to hide from the thing that was approaching. Thomas did the same.

Whatever was coming stopped and bent quickly as if to pick something up. It seemed to freeze for a moment and then looked up into the ceiling. "I feel you," whispered a voice oddly familiar. The figure began to turn slowly. "I smell you." Whoever it was said the words as a child playing a game and wishing to scare. Then, with another step toward them, it spat, "I see you."

William shrank further behind his brother. Not knowing what else to do, Thomas turned his flashlight on and pointed it at the now rapidly approaching figure. He recognized the Ravenmaster immediately, though his face seemed more gnarled and grimmer than remembered. In the beam thrown, the tower guard seemed to be covered in a brown syrup that dripped from his chin. It was then the young boy screamed.

When the man, now turned creature, raised his hands to cover his face from the light, he dropped the body of the rat he had been eating.

"My master will be so pleased," the old tower guard exclaimed with glee. Much like what the princes had experienced with the demon so many centuries before, it was the last thing either boy would remember before everything went black.

CHAPTER 19 | The King's Tomb

FOR THE UNKNOWN Soldier, the thought of an undercover mission made him feel alive. Darwin and Merlin had approached him with an idea days earlier, asking that he plan and execute a trip to Windsor Palace, where he would be tasked with retrieving the skull of King Edward IV. This was right in his wheelhouse, and he knew exactly who to recruit to aid in the recovery. Olivier, who had become his partner in crime, was the obvious choice. The soldier chuckled as he made a mental note to keep the poor bloke away from fire. As he pedaled onward, the immense presence of Buckingham Palace was coming into view. Upon approach, he could see the bright colors of flowers from the Memorial Gardens even in the growing gloom of the late afternoon sky. They painted a beautiful landscape that popped against the red brick streets, golden iron gates, and the stately face of the palace. Unk was mesmerized. It was the look of the soldiers who protected the palace, on the other hand, that fascinated Olivier. As the ghosts rode by the stately landmark, the thespian called out to the Unknown Soldier, "I'd make a fabulous addition to The Queen's Guard. The fit of that coat, those impeccable trousers, and the avant-garde hat make one sharp vision."

The solider scoffed at the idea. "You know they pee in those trousers, right? Plus, you can't move or talk. You would be helpless and also the first on your shift to faint at attention and without any theatrics. I think you were perfectly suited for many roles, Olivier, but Queen's Guard is not one of them," remarked Unk with brutal honesty.

Olivier paused the conversation for a moment. To get one last look at his fancy, the actor slowed his circling legs as he and his riding companion passed between the palace and the Queen Victoria Memorial. The intricate figures of the statue seemed to welcome visitors, with the golden angel on top appearing as a protector and guide to those who stood in her presence. "Preposterous!" called back Olivier after apparently reaching a conclusion about his military potentials. "I can hold it longer than most, and, if not, I have a boot flask I could use. It's a trick I learned from the boys in the Rat Pack."

"What do rodents have to do with the Queen's guard? Bugger me blind!" retorted the military man as he quickened his pedaling pace.

Proceeding through a roundabout, the two continued on their route past Kensington Palace. Unk studied the brilliant gates of the homestead and its statue of William III. The cast likeness looked regal, yet inviting, perfectly positioned to welcome guests onto the property. The royal residence was also breathtaking. A tour group of the living stood in front of the monument with a guide talking of the haunts that graced the estate. Olivier fought an urge to stop and introduce the palace guide to a real ghost, but Unk forbade it. "We are carrying explosives," noted the old soldier. "Probably a bad idea to stay and create a ruckus." However, he did look back with a small amount of mischief in his voice. "Of course, we could plan a special trip," he called to his partner.

The pair passed the National Archives, smiling at the swans floating in the reflecting pool. The delicate smell of honeysuckle and lavender offered a calming scent as they rode alongside the Royal Botanical Garden before passing the expansive footprint of Heathrow Airport. For others, this ride might have seemed daunting, but for Olivier and the Unknown Soldier, it was refreshing to have the chance to see the cityscape and to feel the wind rush through their faces. The sound of jets taking off and the bright pops of the planes' navigation lights pierced the quiet darkness of the evening. As the two ghosts rode, they passed an advertisement for one of the ethereal airlines that used Heathrow as a hub. "Fly Banshee Air," the sign read, "And leave the screaming to us!" Soon they found themselves crossing over the Thames River, and, within minutes, they were pulling up to Windsor Palace.

This royal edifice was massive, but the ghosts knew exactly where they needed to go. St. George's Chapel was located in the Lower Ward, so they rode their bikes through the King Henry VIII Gate and propped them up against the stonewall of the chapel itself. The irony of their directed foray was that almost their entire plan could be completed with ease and without drawing any attention to themselves. Unlike the tasks of the other ghosts, few threats existed for the two until they had the king's skull in hand. For now, they could easily walk straight through the shut and locked doors to the great hall at the front of the chapel. Moreover, should they find the need to pass through walls, ceilings, or floors, that could be accommodated as well. They were ghosts, after all.

Entering the ceremonial sanctum, both spirits were impressed with the opulence of the architecture. Heavy wooden pews sat stationed on the black and white diamond pattern of the marble floor. Colorful garter banners of knights, both living and dead, hung high above, drawing one's eyes to the labyrinthine vaulted roof. A vibrant altar sat against elaborate tapestries, carvings, and metalwork, serving as a foundation for the picturesque stained-glass window that spanned to the top of the high ceiling. Olivier and Unk now floated down to the northeast corner of the chapel where they knew the Monument of King Edward the IV to be. A carefully carved partition sat between two delicate columns with matching engraved woodwork marking the final resting place of the royal. The two spirits looked at each other and simultaneously descended into the catacomb below.

Completing the quick sink through the floor, Unk and Olivier found themselves standing in a dark, cold, and dusty tomb before the remains of his majesty. It was humbling to recall the moment they themselves had left their mortal bodies. A skeleton was all that remained of Edward. It was hard to disturb this hallowed resting place for the king's body. Yet, the spirits believed Merlin when the wizard suggested he could conjure the sovereign's spirit if he had the monarch's skull to work with. "I did it with Arthur," the apparition had claimed. While there was some concern about how the old magician procured the skull of a fictional character, no one pressed the issue too far. "Desperate times allow for desperate measures" was the consensus among the ghosts and so the plan hatched. Surely, the king's spirit would be able to guide them to the key. If the magician could summon him, many of their troubles would soon be solved. Merlin's instructions had been simple and specific: bring back Edward IV's skull intact, and he could set his summoning spell into motion.

Unk and Olivier only hesitated for a moment. It was time to begin the more difficult part of their trip. While getting in was easy, getting out with a physical object of the mortal world would be more problematic. They would be unable to pass through walls, floors, or doors holding the skull. To add to the complications, while both ghosts could easily manipulate physical objects, to do so for long periods of time was draining to their ethereal energies. They would have to move quickly once their plan was set into motion.

"So, this is it?" asked Olivier. There was a decided twinkle in his eye.

"It's showtime, mate," remarked Unk.

As the Unknown Soldier gave his approval, Olivier reached over to the burial bed, carefully removed the skull, and held it in his hands. He turned the skull towards him with his arm outstretched, as if making eye contact with a dear friend. In his bold and artistic Shakespearean accent, he exclaimed, "Alas, poor Yorick! I knew him, Horatio, a fellow of infinite jest, of most excellent fancy."

"Cut!" interrupted the soldier. "Olivier, do not call me Horatio—or Yorick, for that matter. While I do not know my name, I should hope it is not one of those abhorred monikers. If I were to select my own, it would be far grander. Something like Beardsley, Cromwell, Zebedee, or Bertie." He froze for a moment in thought, proud of the names he envisioned for himself. The moment, however, passed quickly. Recognizing he had been distracted, a serious scowl passed the military man's face as he refocused on the current affair. "A name for me is neither here nor there. We won't be solving that mystery today. Let's do this, Laurence. We have to be back to the abbey with our trove."

The tomb was solid stone, thus posing the first issue for the spirits. Merlin and the Unknown Soldier had anticipated this dilemma, and thus, the soldier was ready. He rummaged through his ghostly rucksack and pulled out a fiery, glowing orb. A grin and a devious look spread across his face. "Time to blow this gaff to smithereens," he chuckled. The orb spun an inch above his hand before he extended his fingers and held the energy like a baseball. A flash of nostalgia ran through the old soldier's head as he thought back to his days on Brighton Beach. As a young lad, he and his friends would buy fireworks to blow up sandcastles by the ocean. "A slightly bigger knock," he said to himself, "but, the same idea." He stood amazed that Merlin was able to create an ethereal explosive that while spiritual in nature packed so much power in the mortal realm.

The Unknown Solider took a deep breath and turned towards his friend. In a more somber mood, he gave final direction to initiate their plan. "Now listen, Olivier. If you follow my lead, we have little risk of being caught. With this bomb, we should be able to create a hole in the floor of the chapel. It was hard to calibrate the explosive strength exactly not knowing the thickness of the stone, but the wizard made this little beauty to minimize the damage to the palace. God save the queen!" Unk blurted while simultaneously patting the explosive with real affection. "I am confident the chapel-keeps will be able to patch the damage we cause. The hole left should only take a few pieces of marble to patch." While the anticipated detonation would result in a controlled and insulated blast, the soldier's ethereal form was literally glowing with excitement. It had been far too long since he had been able to play with weaponry. "This opening will allow us to escape the tomb with the skull. Once we are clear of the crypt, we need to rise directly to the height of the ceiling. The explosion should cause enough commotion to rouse the guards, who will open the doors to the chapel. With their entrance, we should be allowed to float inconspicuously outside and to retrieve our bikes without problem. Are you ready, private?" The Unknown Soldier was standing at attention as if he were waiting for he, himself, to answer in subordination to his own question.

"Ready, willing, and able, my friend. Bombs away!" boasted Olivier with a twist of his moustache and in resignation to his ascribed rank.

"Keep your head on a swivel," shouted the soldier. "Fire in the hole!" Unk spun his hands around the glowing orb to heighten its energy before smashing it into the ceiling where it stuck. Both ghosts covered their ears and crouched instinctively as if they feared for their own safety. A moment passed that seemed to drag forever and then the ceiling above them shattered with a boom. Concrete and marble came crashing down onto the floor of the tomb. As Unk and Olivier looked up through the dust and smoke, they both sighed with a sense of relief and satisfaction. A jagged hole opened in the chapel floor. Unk went straight up to survey the room for structural damage and to get a notion of the current location of the guards who were assuredly coming. As the echoes of the blast settled, Olivier dusted off the skull and ascended to stand beside the Unknown Soldier.

As carrying the skull was already draining significant energy from the thespian, Olivier almost immediately decided to pause and rest after he approached the altar where Unk had stationed himself. Clumsy with the mortal mass, Olivier fumbled the one task he had and dropped the skull on the black and white marble tiles. The soldier watched in horror as the king's head bounced down the stairs from his perch and into the main aisle of the chapel. "Damn it all," cursed the actor, "Shakespeare was right. I need to get into shape!" His head was nodding up and down as his gaze followed the bouncing skull.

Sounds of pounding feet and heavy doors being slung open echoed through the historic church, coming from the opposite direction of the skull's roll. Unk jetted to the royal head that had come to rest at the foot of the first pew. "To the top, Olivier," he screamed as he scrambled to grab the stolen skeletal remains. Following his own orders, he shot to the ceiling of the chapel just as the massive entry doors were thrown open, and a dozen officers flooded into the church. If they had come just moments earlier, the guards would have seen a floating skull rising through the air, but instead, they were fixated on the settling disturbance towards the far corner of the room.

There was a sounded relief as the guards evaluated the damage to the flooring. Given the magnitude of the explosion they heard, they had feared the damage would be immense, but from the look of the hole, it could be easily patched, and Windsor would survive. As the officers lowered themselves into the tomb, however, a new hysteria arose. It only took a moment before they recognized the king's resting place had been disturbed.

"The grave has been robbed!" yelled up one of the guards. "Tell the captain. He might want to get the folks at Baker

ASHLEY WELLMAN & PATRICK KINKADE

Street in on this immediately." Hearing the words "Baker Street," another one of the entering guards who was waiting up top ran from the chapel. The message was urgent and needed a speedy delivery.

Wasting no time themselves, the two ghosts carefully passed through the intricate decorative work on the ceiling of the chapel and quickly slipped through the doors that had been propped open by the guards. As they exited the church, they picked up their phantom bikes and sped through the gates that were slowly closing behind the metropolitan police just arriving on the scene.

Once outside and down the street, the ghosts took a moment to compose themselves. Glancing at each other, they erupted in nervous laughter. "We did it! By God, we did it," exclaimed Olivier.

With a chuckle, Unk said, "We did do it." He placed his hand on Olivier's shoulder and gave him a look of satisfaction. "Now, lieutenant, just a quick ride back. No time to waste getting this precious possession to the abbey."

With that, Olivier beamed with pride as he asked Unk, "I got promoted?"

"Indeed, sir," Unk replied.

"What an honor. I was sure I had lost that opportunity when I dropped the king's head." Olivier paused for a moment to relish his new title. With that, they both took a moment to ring their bells before they began pedaling.

On the way to Windsor, the two ghosts had basked in the scenery and the joyfulness of their ride. On the return trip, they had no time to enjoy the sights and surroundings. They slipped back into the abbey and used their last bit of strength to open the door to Merlin's lair. They rested the skull on his table and settled in as they waited for the others to return from the tower. It surprised them that they had made the trip safely back with a physical skull and without detection. Unk laid his rucksack on the floor and used it as a pillow as he proceeded to take a nap. Olivier sat in Merlin's chair and propped his feet up on the table, watching the flickering blue hue of his model of The Binding through the darkness. The actor relished how suave and elusive he and the solider had been. Their colleagues would be suitably impressed, and queen and country were none the worse for the escapade.

"Indeed," thought Olivier while his feet remained propped up and resting after the long ride back. "We pulled it off without a single hitch. It is as though we never left the abbey!" His pride remained as he fell into an easy slumber.

✦ ✦ ✦

Outside the calm of the abbey, the city was in a panic. Phones were ringing off the hook with calls coming into emergency services and the media. Cars, trucks, and buses were littered across London streets with their flashers piercing the night, waiting for towing crews to respond to countless accidents. Planes were grounded as passengers sat flabbergasted on the runway. Heathrow had shut down. A floating skull had been seen throughout the city. It moved with speed, but social media was lit up with photos of it darting around corners and passing by heavily touristed monuments and landmarks. It took just a few hours for some to claim that the flying bone was a sign for an impending apocalypse. Others suggested it was a hoax carried out by bored hackers. In either case, the consequences of 'The Event,' as it became known, were entirely real.

For the first time in years, London printing presses were stopped at night and a new front page was prepared to sell a host of British newspapers for the following morning. As stacks of tabloids were distributed around the city, everyone woke to the shocking headline: "Planes grounded, flights canceled as flying skull hits Heathrow Airport. Metropolitan

Police Service remains on high alert." Before the slumbering ghosts woke from their fitful nap, the story had spread worldwide.

CHAPTER 20 | The Hunt for the Key

FROM THE MOMENT they fully entered the tower, the ghosts broke off into three predetermined groups. At the abbey, the spirits identified specific areas that the individual parties would search, each in their own way and each with a given task to accomplish. Beyond the search, all were keenly aware that they needed to avoid detection. Being found out by the ghosts of the tower or the demon himself would only lead to disaster. Indeed, they all recognized the risk and made themselves ready for unforeseen and unwanted encounters. In truth, however, stealth would be their best ally and greatest advantage in their quest for the key.

Hawking agreed to hunt alongside Glinda and Merlin in the Crown Jewel Room. Should they run into a situation where spiritual ability was needed, and the magic of apparitions simply could not substitute, his ghostly strengths might be necessary. Glinda had been the one to plan their strategy of discovery once they reached their selected destination. They were going to construct a divining rod to help locate the keys. Hawking, as a man of science, was skeptical of the utility of the effort and knew little about its operation. Yet, he was still willing to try the stick. He also recognized with a smile that Glinda could manage Merlin. The old wizard was a gentle soul but could be cantankerous if made to feel that he was not in charge.

The first goal upon entering the Crown Jewel Room was

to retrieve a particular royal item: The Coronation Spoon. As the sole royal treasure from the time of King Edward the IV, Glinda and Merlin thought it may hold a spiritual resonance from the time of his reign and thereby be of use in finding likewise temporally bound items. Glinda, passing as a ghost would, swung her dress through the security door that protected the jewels and walked directly towards the case that held the spoon. Although she typically defaulted to Merlin and the strength of his magic, a 'divining rod' is also called a 'witching stick.' Being a witch, albeit a beautiful, good witch, its construction was a bit more of her forte. Merlin, for his part, yielded to Glinda's expertise in its manufacture. Truthfully, Merlin seemed otherwise distracted, examining several royal swords that also remained part of the tower's crown jewel collection.

For centuries, many names have been given to this divining practice, but the technique remains the same. A witching stick is a forked twig that guides its user to lost or yet unfound things and ultimately their heart's desire. Although there are those who believe that the devil guides the rod, Glinda knew better than anyone that this magic was often simply misunderstood. Good energy was as likely to guide the stick to its directed goal as bad—as devils might do, so might angels. She believed with the help of The Coronation Spoon, they may be able to harness enough spiritual and magical connection to have the witching stick literally guide them directly to the key.

Hawking stepped toward Glinda and pulled a perfectly sanded ethereal dowel from his sleeve. Merlin looked up from the sword he was examining and glanced at his colleague inquisitively.

"What?" Hawking asked defensively. "We are making a witching stick. It seems necessary to have a stick, so I went shopping at Heavenly Hardware and got us the closest thing I could find."

"It's utterly perfect, my dear," said Glinda as she took the dowel from Hawking's hand and turned to pass it to the conjurer. "Merlin, can you please split this into a wooden wishbone?"

The wizard took the piece of ethereal wood from the witch and held it out in his left hand. He pulled his right hand up to his shoulder, aimed it at the stick, closed his eyes and, after a moment of concentration, shot a bolt of lightning from his fingertips. Startled, Hawking ducked to the ground. As he uncovered his eyes and slowly rose back to a standing position, the mathematician could see that Merlin had perfectly split the wooden rod into the shape of the letter "Y." Merlin winked at Glinda before holding the stick out for her to use.

"Don't be silly, Merlin. Your wisdom and experience give you significant power. I think you should lead the search," she encouraged while waving off the stick being handed to her. She moved beside Merlin as he was left holding the rod's two split ends in his hands. "Now, all we need is the spoon. When I lift it, an alarm will sound and alert the guards, so we must act fast." She carefully took The Coronation Spoon from its case, and as she had expected, a loud siren seemed to fill the tower around them.

Glinda at first held the absconded utensil and then slipped it into the wizard's right hand. She wrapped his fingers around both the spoon and one of the twig's two ending points, which composed the head of the Y. She could sense the wizard's hesitation and nerves. "Concentrate, Merlin. We have time. All you have to do is focus on the key, and if your mind is in tune with your desire, you should feel the pull of the stick guiding you." Merlin's body relaxed, and Glinda was confident he was ready. She whispered a few incantations over the rod to fully activate it and turned to begin her own visual exploration of the room, wondering if the key might be there. Hawking had done the same, intrigued by the historical items around them, but keenly aware that he was not to be distracted from the hunt for the item they so desperately needed.

Merlin stood peacefully still, intently watching the witching stick before him. It began to slowly bounce. He felt an overwhelming sense of excitement. "What if an apparition was the one to find the key?" Merlin mused. It would be such a proud moment and a way to vindicate their standing within the ethereal world. Even more than that, the protection of the physical world would also be at least partially credited to their kind, and more mortals loving apparitions would only be better for that ethereal population. Most of all, Glinda would be impressed. Her approval was deeply important to Merlin though he did not fully understand why. His mind now had truly started to drift, but the rise and fall of the stick quickened into a quiver and then it pulled at the wizard, directing him to his heart's desire.

Glinda and Hawking turned to watch where the witching stick was guiding its magical handler. Merlin nearly tripped on his robe as he followed the energy directly towards Glinda. The witching stick pulled up towards her chin before resting on her chest, directly over her heart.

"I was thinking of the key. I promise I was," Merlin whispered somewhat sheepishly, looking back and forth between his two comrades.

"Merlin! Good fellow! Give me that infernal thing. You are quite distracted," Hawking pleaded, taking the stick and spoon from his hands. He in fact was somewhat offended that Glinda and Merlin had assumed their magical powers were somehow superior to his spiritual nature for witching.

Glinda recognized the blow to Merlin's ego and contemplated comforting him but feared it might embarrass him all the more. She instead proceeded towards Hawking to consult the apparent former "unbeliever" on the use of the rod he now was holding. She was only interrupted as the stick physically pulled the physicist towards the door.

"Good God!" yelled Hawking. "This bloody thing actually works!" At the same time, the pounding of boots neared the door. The three conspirators rose to the top of the room, and as the door opened and guards rushed in, Hawking called to the others, "Here we go! Follow me!" With that, the physicist was dragged out the door by the stick, which was now behaving like a bloodhound hot on a scent.

After several quick turns, long hallways, and a rapid descent down a small flight of stairs, the three spirits were standing in the middle of the tower's kitchen. The stick was moving so forcibly that they all became overwhelmed with hope that the key was near. Like a strong magnet, the spoon and tip of the twig pulled Hawking to a drawer built directly into the wall of the fortress. There, its bouncing movement turned into a banging as the stick hit the handles and face of the cupboard over and over.

"Open it!" Merlin's voice thundered. "Open it!"

Hawking placed the stick and the spoon on the countertop and pulled open the tray from the wall. A large serving fork, butcher knife, and a few other random kitchen utensils lay within its confine. The spoon levitated on the counter before quickly diving into the opened drawer, which slammed shut on its own. As if it was taking a cue from the spoon, the witching stick flew up into the air and burst into flames, apparently concluding that its work had been done. The three ethereal beings looked at each other in complete disappointment.

Glinda spoke first. "I am so sorry, my dears. It seems as if we are at a loss here. We can only hope the others are faring better in their search."

Merlin then cleared his throat and teased, "Gads, it certainly found its heart's desire. Do you think the other utensils like to *spoon*? It seems as if it was a *whisk* that blasted dip was willing to take." Hawking turned around, groaned, and began the walk back to the tunnel. Glinda smiled at the old wizard's jest, and they both hurried to catch up to the unamused physicist.

✦ ✦ ✦

Dickens, Austen, and Shakespeare had requested to work together given the nature of their search. They were going to the King's Library and Royal Archives to do their part in the ghostly group's overall efforts to find the key. They would be looking for Edward the IV's personal writings that were stored within the preserved stacks of Kings' Diaries. There was no doubt the role of the ruler was isolating. Many times, the pages of their personal diaries were the only outlet to express concern or ponder ideas for members of the royal family. These journals held key information about the royals' most intimate thoughts, struggles, successes, secrets, and predictions. To protect royal privacy and history, only select passages of these volumes had ever been released to society at large. While it was true that historians and researchers of all intent had explored the contents of these books for centuries, they had not known about the key and so would not have found nor publicized any germane findings in relation to it. Looking for information about the key specifically, they believed, would make a major difference in this particular search.

Further, for the first time in several hundred years, there was some access to firsthand knowledge of the king and his intimate thoughts. As literary agents with an educated eye for metaphor and allusion and the firsthand information gained from the two princes, the group of spiritual authors hoped to have a more sophisticated perspective than others who had thought to examine the diaries before them. Even the demon, had it thought to look, seemed to have left the diaries with no new knowledge of the key. But the beast did not have their acumen and the princes were not as forthcoming in their knowledge of the key to Jack as they were to the abbey's illustrious authors. In any event, their plan was to gather copies of Edward's writings and take them from the tower to the abbey. There, the journal entries might be read and discussed fully with each other and the young ghostly princes in hopes the passages could lead the group to the key they so desperately sought.

Much like with the other search parties, there would be very little difficulty in gaining access to the books. The ghosts passed through mortal security screens undetected. Moreover, and fortunately for this particular group, it was determined that there was no real advantage in trying to bring the physical books back. Reproductions would do and with a short visit to the 'Phantasmal Photo Shop,' three ethereal picture boxes were procured. Not quite a camera in a mortal sense of the word, a picture box could gather free-floating ether to capture impressions of what was seen through its lenses. So, as a purely spectral process, the ghost authors could, in effect, take pictures of the pages needed and simply carry those copies back to the abbey for study.

Entering the library, the three spirits immediately set about their business. The required texts were located, and the copy work started with but a single interruption. A huff of dismay came from Dickens, and it nearly filled the room. "Blast it!" he proclaimed. "I knew I should not have let Olivier test my picture box. He has filled it with captures of him and Newton preening at the lens."

Stopping his work, the Bard of Avon looked at the source of Dicken's complaint. "They puckerth their lips like ducks," he observed, looking at the image that was captured. Turning back to the pages he was working to copy, he added, "I beliveth young mortals call them 'selfies.'"

"Call them what you might, Master Shakespeare, I will call both these perpetrators 'ugsome marplots!'" said Dickens with some satisfaction in his voice. Austen and the bard both looked at each other following Dickins' proclamation. Even among other brilliant authors, the writer of *Oliver Twist* could turn a phrase.

An hour passed, and the three authors turned photographers were finishing their raid on the archive when Dickens again turned to address his colleagues. This time, however, he simply asked for their patience. "There is another volume I think we might collect here. It may provide us much-needed guidance. Can you give me a moment?"

Jane nodded her agreement, but added, "Charles, please let us hurry though. I am concerned about the boys." With a wave of a reassuring hand from Shakespeare giving his acquiescence, Dickens set back out into the archive.

Sitting quietly, Jane and Shakespeare could hear Dickens as he moved about the shelves muttering to himself. After several minutes, they heard a loud bang that sounded like an entire bookcase had toppled to the floor. From around the corner came the disheveled author.

"I have found it," Dickens chimed. "Success is ours!" He held out a sleeve of what appeared to be handwritten vellum sheets. The title page read in French, *Les Propheties par Michel de Nostradamus.*

"The writings of a seer?" questioned Shakespeare, looking at what Dickens held.

"Indeed, my good sir. Nostradamus is a seer who has predicted catastrophes to befall this fragile human world on many occasions. It occurs to me we may be pushing up on Armageddon should the demon break free. These are his original verses that few have seen. My hope is that reading directly from his pen will shed light in our darkest hours." Wasting no time, Dickens placed the prophet's writings on their worktable, untied the sleeve, and all three ghosts began to quickly copy its contents. Before the trio headed back to the tunnel, they had finished the entire volume.

✦ ✦ ✦

Darwin and Newton had agreed that the best use of their time would be a thorough exploration of the king's death room. They both reasoned that King Edward would not ever want to be too far from the key left to him by the Templars. That being true, the room where he was convalescing would seem a likely place to hide it. The two ghostly scientists agreed they would not simply explore the room, however. Over the centuries, assuredly the key would have been found by mortal concerns or by the demon's own searching were it only casually hidden. Rather, they planned a meticulous and extreme hunt. They knew the walls throughout the tower were incredibly dense, often concealing hidden compartments and small obscured rooms of which only a few knew if not privy to the secreted floorplans of the tower.

"Could the king have hidden the key within the stone walls surrounding his deathbed? Perhaps once he had begun to fall ill, he somehow placed it within the rock," Darwin had proposed. Now in the room, he slipped his X-ray specs over his eyes.

Newton, for his part, had agreed. He removed his goggles from a satchel that hung across his chest. As he tightened the strap to secure the specs to his head, he jumped and immediately turned around so that his back faced Darwin. "Darwin, forgive me. Seems these blasted specs are on the wrong setting again." He nervously fumbled with the contraption.

"Set the distance knob to four feet, and let us start," Darwin instructed, brushing off the exposure.

Newton and Darwin knew exactly what to do. They were to follow a plan drawn by the mathematician that would provide the most comprehensive scan of the environment. He had carefully mapped directional patterns that would allow the pair to walk side by side to search the conceptualized grid, first horizontally crossing through the room, and then shifting their directionality to scan again in a vertical nature. As ghosts, they could cross through solid objects, but now they would have a full view of any matter within the structure of the walls and potentially inside any hidden compartments. The spirits began the search, slowly and carefully making the zig-zag journey from one side of the room to the other, through the walls and then back out into the room before the next linear search path was started. An hour passed, and the ghosts had not found a thing of interest. Floating up, both spirits put their feet on the wall and began walking it like a floor to scan the remainder of the room. Again, they found nothing except numerous piles of rodent droppings and a mischief of rats that had gathered. The vermin, it seemed, were almost aware of the ghosts and making sense of their observations.

When they were done, Darwin sat on a chair in the corner of the room with his goggles off, slowly rubbing his head. He had resigned himself to failure when Newton walked over to stand beside him. "It was worth the try, dear friend." He consoled Darwin as he, himself, took off his specs.

"Aye, Isaac, it was. I just wish we had turned something up. Time, I fear, is beginning to work against us in this matter," replied Darwin in a frustrated tone.

"Perhaps the others had better luck in their approaches." Newton's voice had the sound of someone trying to be encouraging while battling his own feelings of defeat. The two sat quietly for a moment when the mood was rightly broken by a slight noise. There was a scurrying sound running down inside the wall. Both companions looked to where the din was originating, and a rat appeared inside a flooring vent.

Darwin and Newton looked at it as the rat's beady eyes peered back at them through the grate in the wall.

"Cheeky little beast," commented Newton. However, before he even finished his thought another appeared. "What's that? You brought a friend?" he continued. And again, as soon as that thought was stated, more rats appeared, truly beginning to multiply. One after another, their chittering squeaks began to fill the air.

Darwin shook his head dumbstruck and slowly put back on his goggles. Looking through the wall, his already pale continence went another shade white. "My Lord, Newton! There must be thousands of them."

Newton slipped his eyewear back on as well. Seeing what Darwin saw, he gasped. The wall venting was full of rodents and those in front were chewing at the vent grate to break through. "Charles, can they see us? Is that even possible? I fear this is not of the natural order. There is something sinister brewing here in those little beasts. Let us depart before they fully arrive."

"I could not agree more, dear fellow," said the biologist.

With a sudden snap, and as if to punctuate Darwin's thought, one side of the wall grate broke free. A rat, its mouth bloodied from its driven effort to chew itself out, stuck its head through the created opening. The squealing sound it made was not of this world.

The ghosts rushed from the room. "Let's find the others. I think we have officially overstayed our welcome." Darwin's voice was grim. Both fled from the room in the direction of the tunnel grate and their exit across The Binding. The tower was awakening.

CHAPTER 21 | The Dungeon

AS GLINDA, MERLIN, and Hawking floated down into the tunnel where they entered the tower, they were met with silence and utter darkness. "Where are the boys?" they all asked in almost perfect unison to the stillness into which they descended. Merlin lit a small glowing orb in his hands and set it floating to the tunnel's ceiling. As the gloom receded, William and Thomas were nowhere to be seen. The boys had been given explicit instructions to remain here, where the spirits had left them. They had either ignored the instructions on their own or something else had happened and the plan had gone terribly wrong. Moments later, Darwin and Newton joined the already gathered group. Before they had the chance to inquire about the boys' whereabouts, Austen, Shakespeare, and Dickens flew into the tunnel holding the captured images they had taken on their visit to the library.

Almost immediately, Austen asked, "Where are the boys? Please tell me, where are our boys?" As she echoed the earlier arrivals, the concern in her voice was obvious and her desire for their safety made clear in the tense tone of each word spoken.

Instantly and almost as if in response to Jane's plea, the two princes emerged from the tunnel wall. Edward stepped forward and with a heaviness in his voice said, "We tried to find you. The Ravenmaster has them. He hit them both on the head and carried them up the stairs right after you left."

"If I had to guess, he took them to the dungeon as a gift for the demon," added Rake. "He has used that area to hold mortals before."

"Then you will take us there," instructed Darwin. Edward nodded to the naturalist and without another word, the princes turned and led the entire troupe of spirits back deeper into the tunnels. Merlin kept his light aloft and in front of the hurried group while Glinda lit another. Darwin drew an ethereal blade from a scabbard hidden within his coat. His grim look and purposeful demeanor reflected on the faces and pace of the line of spirts who followed.

✦ ✦ ✦

The dirt-covered stone floor was like ice. The darkness that consumed the space was broken by only a small sliver of candlelight being cast through the barred window at the top of the door. A damp, stale musk filled the room.

As Thomas regained consciousness, he could barely think due to the pain in his head. He lay silently still, trying to assess his surroundings before his fear that William may be hurt took over. Groaning, he tried to push his body to a sitting position. "What just happened?" he thought to himself. He could not remember seeing or hearing anything. Rubbing his head, the blackness in the room lightened as his eyes adjusted. His mind was spinning, and a dull pulsing throb came from behind his left ear. His heart began to race, and his breath grew short. Thomas knew he and William were in danger. His hands began to shake, and he felt lightheaded. This was no time to panic. The older boy squeezed his eyes closed and began to count to slow his breath. He knew that if he could not calm his nerves, he would not be able to find William or a way out of his current circumstance. As he again opened his eyes, he began scanning the room for William. Against the door, he could see the outline of a small heap crumpled on the floor. Crawling on his hands and knees, he felt his way along as he moved towards the pile. He could now see his brother's face with some clarity. He scooted close to William's body and pulled him into his arms.

"William?" he whispered softly. Whatever had happened left Thomas terrified of who or what could be listening. "William?" he repeated. Anxiety rushed over the boy as he pulled his brother's head into his lap and began to rock back and forth. "Please wake up, Will. Please, wake up. I need you," he pleaded.

William moaned in agony as he came to and tried to regain his bearings. His body ached from head to toe. He could hear his brother's voice and found comfort resting in his arms. He was fearful of what he would see when he opened his eyes, but after hearing the worry in Thomas' voice, he forced the view. He at first could see nothing but the dark but then caught glimpse of how stark their confines were. "This is not a cell," the young boy thought. "We have been thrown into a dungeon." Making eye contact with Thomas, they sat silently for a moment, each trying to organize their own thoughts. Quietly, William asked Thomas, "What happened? My head is killing me."

"Mine is too. Someone or something must have hit us, but I don't remember a thing," replied Thomas.

"We have to get out of here. Where are Mister Darwin and the others?" William inquired with urgency. Looking at his brother, Thomas just shook his head. He would have offered some form of speculation as hope but for the smell that assaulted his nose. "What is that?" he said as he sniffed.

In the instant that followed, smoke began to creep inside the room. From underneath the door, the boys could now see tendrils of grey vapor quickly beginning to fill the dungeon. The burning smell was sweet and pungent, but it made it hard to breathe. Beginning to cough, William panicked. "Is there a fire?"

"The fumes are coming from somewhere," stuttered Thomas between coughs in his own battle to catch his breath.

William ran to the back of the room and dropped to the floor. "This can't be happening. We are being smoked out. This will suffocate us. Thom! I didn't want to die like this." Thomas thought quickly and took off his shirt to stuff it under the door. He hoped to slow the gathering cloud in their room, but, ultimately, he retreated to the far corner of the small space to be with William. He too, sank to the ground, pulled his knees into his chest, and began to pray. There was little more to be done.

Though time was passing slowly, it did not take long. As the boys looked on and through the shroud of smoke, a large figure emerged and approached the cowering brothers.

"Thomas!" cried William again, "It's the demon!"

"What's this, lads? Demon? No, not quite that bad though the ladies have called me a handsome devil before," came a booming voice. A kind face pushed through the tendrils of smoke to gaze directly at the boys. "Why, you two look as if you had seen a ghost!" The figure roared with laughter at the thought and his apparent jest. Pausing, the translucent man struck a match and deeply inhaled several puffs through a pipe he held before exhaling another extremely large cloud of smoke. From the glow provided by the burn, in what appeared to be a meerschaum pipe, the ghost could be more clearly seen. He was a jaunty-looking gentleman. His thin face had a perfectly groomed, short beard that came to a point at his chin, and a well-styled moustache that was wound tight at the ends. A black hat with a pearl band and black feather sat atop his head. The white beads on his hat matched the earrings that hung from his lobes. He wore a decorative white shirt that had puffy sleeves, a whimsical design sewn into the fabric, and overstated buttons. His black and white cape was lined with fur, which slid beneath his linen cartwheel neck ruffle. The voluminous nature of the man's clothing made his upper half look disproportionate as the shirt's peplum gave way to a thin, tight pair of pants and pointed shoes.

"Care for a smoke, gents?" the figure offered congenially as he extended his pipe and again bent forward to greet William and Thomas.

"No, sir. We don't smoke," said Thomas, suddenly feeling safe and at ease with the grandiose character that stood before them. He could now smell hints of vanilla and cherry within the clouds of vapor and recognized there was little threat of actual fire.

"That's a shame, as I built my fortune around men who adored tobacco. I call it my 'brown gold,'" the spirit noted.

"That stuff will kill you," said William in a judgmental tone to the figure. Thomas looked down in a mild shame as he had been reconsidering the man's offer for a puff.

The ghost chuckled, "Too late for that."

"There are worse fates," said a female voice that instilled such a surety in Thomas that he knew he was safe. As the boys turned, another spirit appeared through the door of their cell. She used a fan made of peacock feathers to whiff the smoke and clear the air around her face. The woman was strikingly beautiful. A black velvet headdress adorned with a border of gold covered her head. Her dark hair was pulled taut and tucked carefully under the hat. In addition to a thick choker piece that was marked with a finely embroidered letter B embellishment, several strands of silver and delicate jeweled chains hung from her neck. Her fashion accents complemented the decorative square neckline of her billowing gown. "I must say, the physical world was quite the challenge for me," the ghost noted, rubbing her throat with gentle strokes. "I have found my greatest joy being my complete self in the spiritual world."

"Who are you?" asked William in a clearly vexed voice while looking back and forth between the two ethereal visitors.

"Oh my. How rude I've become. I thought you had recognized us. I am Anne Boleyn, one of Henry VIII's many wives—though our marriage didn't stop him from ordering me to be killed when he grew tired of me. As it turns out, I lost my head over Henry as I fell in love with him, then I lost it again as he fell out of it with me. I like to think I was simply too strong a force for him to reckon with. The story, I am afraid, is long and sordid and of no consequence now. Perhaps later, if you are interested, I can tell you more of my thousand-day reign," she said this all with a kind smile and firm delivery. "But really, my sweet boys, that is enough about me. You are the points of our concern! I always longed for a son, so just having you two young fellows here warms my heart. On top of that, the very thought I might leave this ghastly place with you gives me chills of delight. We have heard rumors of your earlier visit and are very gratified to see that many appear to be true."

"And sir, you are?" politely questioned Thomas, looking away from Anne and at the man who continued to smoke his pipe in a regal fashion.

The spirit coughed as he acknowledged the boy was now speaking to him, smoke blowing from his mouth, nose, and, oddly, both ears. Clearing his throat, he tilted the brim of his hat and responded, "Sir Walter Raleigh at your service. I was once a great explorer, quite the romantic with royal women, and the reason tobacco became such a popular commodity here in England. A wonderful product, my leaf, though my understanding is once you start with it, you have a hard time giving it up," said the ghost as he packed another bowl. "It took me a while to discern how to make the glorious plant ethereally, but really, I had nothing but time to do it and now nothing but time to smoke it. Oh! For the record, please do not believe the gossip you hear about me in relation to treason and conspiracy. I am one of the most loyal comrades you can have." He again offered a smoke to Thomas, who looked at William, shrugged, and this time took a pull from the pipe. "That's a good lad," said Raleigh. "It will strengthen your constitution and make you a man even as a ghost!" And, so saying, Raleigh again put the tip of the meerschaum to his mouth and inhaled. Thomas, meanwhile, was trying to hold his cough to the point his eyes had reddened. William, looking at his brother, shook his head in a most 'I told you so' manner.

As this happened, a third figure entered the room. She gently placed her hand on Raleigh's arm, forcing him to lower the pipe from his face. "Perhaps the smoking could cease with the boys here," she stated with a stern look. "Apologies for Walter. He tends to forget his audience," she winked at William and Thomas. "I wouldn't want to miss out on meeting mortal visitors and I know the value of a proper introduction. I am Lady Arbella Stuart."

"'The White Woman,'" Thomas gasped, remembering the ghost stories he had read about the tower before their very first visit with the choir.

The name seemed fitting. Unlike Anne, who had very tightly kept hair, this ghost's red locks were thick, curly, and somewhat untamed, highlighting her pale face and falling nearly to her waist. Yet, her red hair was the sole note of pigment in her ethereal presence. The rest of her was solid white. The top of her hair was pulled back ever so slightly to allow for the placement of an ivory jewel at the crown of her head. A series of precious stone necklaces hung at varying levels against her chest. She wore a synched white dress that nearly matched her fair skin tone. The corset was so visibly tight that William and Thomas shifted uncomfortably thinking of how painful it would be to wear a garment like that.

Noticing their concern and quick looks toward her waist, Lady Arbella continued, "I was starved to death here in the tower, so this actually fits quite comfortably now." She pointed at the constricting garment. "But imagine the agony of trying to tie myself into this torturous device after an afternoon of tea and crumpets," she stated with a hollow laugh, purposefully trying to break the tension.

"They do say beauty is pain," noted William. He was not quite sure why he was offering fashion advice to the woman. Still, he felt inclined to say something to distract himself from the fact that all of the three ghosts before him had each died a tragic death in the tower.

"Do they?" the White Woman was considering Thomas' observation. "I will say, men's clothing is far more comfortable than women's, but the one time I tried to disguise myself as a chap, it got me killed. I have since embraced the idea that I fancy dresses far more than a pair of trousers. After all, starving to death was far more painful than this dreaded corset. I will stick with beauty and try to avoid the pain!" The White Woman blushed a bit at the self-recognition. "But that is neither here nor there," she said without further batting an eye.

William shot Thomas a look of discomfort and regret for opening his mouth. Arbella, however, did not seem fazed. She continued, "Since my passing, I've been one of the more rebellious ghosts in the tower, constantly challenging mortals to accept their ability to sense spirits. A few visitors have caught glimpses of me, but I've never been able to fully connect to ask for help. Then, I heard the news. Two young schoolboys had come to pay the tower a visit and met with our precious princes. The excitement has yet to cease, as we knew you two could be key to our release. There was claim that you had Templar blood and could see us. Now, I know what was said to be true. With your help, we will flee the tower. There may even be chance to put to rights what we lost so long ago with the poisoning of King Edward."

A rush of cold air filled the room as the entire band of abbey ghosts forcefully, and without much grace, flew into the chamber. "You won't be fleeing with these boys! Hands off! We come armed and ready!" exclaimed Merlin, holding his wand out like a swordsman's blade.

The three ghosts from the tower looked completely

unimpressed. They stood composed and undaunted by the aggressive arrival of the pack of spirits before them. "Back away from the children," growled Darwin in a voice so low and feral that all in the room drew a shallow breath in response. He moved past Merlin with his sword drawn, lowered, and almost dragging. The menace of the posture was palpable.

"Calm yourselves. The boys are perfectly fine. Why not ask the princes of our intent? They will tell you there is nothing worth losing your head over happening here," the White Woman suggested while raising her hands as a gesture of placation.

"Trust me, she's right. Losing your head is not something you wish to do," stated Boleyn. She again placed her hands around her neck and checked the security of her choker.

Sir Walter Raleigh nodded in agreement before concurring with Anne by adding, "'Tis best we all keep our wits and our heads intact. I can tell you it was quite an unpleasant experience to lose mine, and I wish not to repeat that horror."

"Back away from the children," Darwin said again, adding the word "now" after a moment. Even though ethereal, the veins on his hand were showing the tightness of the grip he had on the blade.

Edward stepped forward and tried to reassure Darwin. "We know these ghosts."

Darwin quickly barked back, "But we do not!"

The look of the biologist's posture was not lost to Raleigh. He returned Darwin's gaze for a beat and then, breaking the tension, he replied, "Of course we will, good fellow." He puffed his pipe as he examined the ghostly intruders. "Blimey!" he exclaimed, nearly choking. "William Shakespeare. My, my, my. I can't even escape you in death. Have you lingered behind in the spiritual world to insure no one discovered you had other scribes write most of your famous works, myself included? I'm still chaffed you never gave proper credit to those who aided your success." Shakespeare looked around at the rest of the group and shook his head in confusion, pretending not to know what the ghost was talking about.

"Raleigh, I believe we have more important things to worry about," Anne added abruptly to redirect the group's attention. Shakespeare looked relieved by her interjection.

"So, we do." Raleigh acknowledged, shaking off any disdain for his old friend. "Ladies, let us all relax a bit and stand here against the wall. We have little time before discovery, but let us take the moment we have for introductions. So important in these dark days."

With that, each of the tower ghosts moved back to the wall furthest from the boys and reiterated their identities. Each also offered assurance of their own concern about the demon and the malfunction of The Binding. They further recognized the threat to the world should all of Acheron be released into the reality of mortal men. William, Thomas, and the young princes also all voiced their support for the intentions and characters of the newly met spirits.

The abbey ghosts, at first suspicious, were all nodding their heads in approval by the end of the conversation. It was Darwin who stepped forward first and offered his hand to Sir Walter. "Dark days, indeed," he stated flatly.

Newton followed suit by bowing and kissing the hands of the two ladies standing in wait. "So nice to have more refinement in our little band," complimented the mathematician. "Without our dear Jane and Glinda, I fear, we would soon degenerate into a troop of baboons." The two spirit women smiled their acceptance of the intended compliment and nodded their acknowledgement of the three new members of their party.

Dickens then brushed aside both Newton and Darwin. He proceeded to give a quick introductory account of all the abbey ghosts and their search for the key. The tower spirits returned the nods of approval they had been given earlier to display their pledge of solidarity.

Hawking, clearly showing a desire to move from the tower and get back to the abbey, started a mild routine of exercise. "Well met, all," he chided. "Now that we are on the same page, lest we forget, we have to make our way back to the abbey for any of this to matter. Perhaps most pressing, we have a demon currently stalking this fortress and looking to return us all to the ether for good."

Anne stepped in front of the group of ghosts and commanded, "For anyone who would like to meddle for my cause, let's figure out how to get us all out of here in one piece."

"Spoken like a true queen," offered Shakespeare. With that admiration, the entire group left the room with vigor, leaving the boys standing in the sudden quiet.

Thomas and William, alone in the cell, looked at each other. "I hope they remember we can't walk through walls," said William with a shrug of mild concern.

"Silly boys." It was Jane's head that popped back through the door to the cell. "Sir Walter knew where the dungeon key was and went to fetch it. He will be back presently," she said before her head disappeared.

It took a moment, and smoke again began to fill the room. There was a solid sounding "clank" and the door swung open. Raleigh stood outside with his pipe in hand. As the boys walked past, he held it out to Thomas. "Quick puff?" he asked as the dungeon door slowly closed. As his brother was already walking well to the front of the group, Thomas took the pipe and drew. "Good lad," Sir Walter chuckled.

CHAPTER 22 | Crossing Tower Green

THE ENTIRE GROUP of ghosts had agreed the tunnel was no longer an option to exit the tower. The Ravenmaster was clearly roaming the area and had discovered the boys at the base of the stairs. Given that egress was found out, the risk that the yeoman—or even worse, the demon—could be waiting in the darkness was too high. It was Sir Walter Raleigh who convinced the gathering that departing through the front gates of the tower would be their best chance of quick escape. He had pinpointed where their exposure would be minimal and their journey to The Binding would be the shortest. They would exit the Bloody Tower, cross Tower Green, and head for the touristed exit.

Anne Boleyn recoiled at the thought of crossing the green. While historically other prisoners of the fortress were hung beyond its walls at Tower Hill for spectators to see, royals and others of particular status were spared the ridicule and humiliation of public execution and instead were killed inside the gates. Anne had been one of the ones who walked to the scaffold at Tower Green, meeting her final moments as a mortal there in some privacy. Where she once hung, there was now a monument giving notice of the morbid use of that land. A small, paved plot of granite marked the execution location, while a plaque described the horrific sentences that were carried out on that soil. Anne, again, shuddered while starting the walk on which the group set out.

As to the ghost's current concern, the plan was relatively simple. William and Thomas would reinitiate the shuttling process, starting with the two princes. Even before leaving the security of the tower walls, the princes would assume their now familiar position within the boys' bodies to be the first beyond The Binding. William and Thomas would then return through the enchantment to bring the rest, two by two until all were out. Once delivering the entire group safely through the magic of the barrier, they all could return to the abbey together by whatever means possible.

As Sir Walter Raleigh and the boys stepped into the open air of the green, all present, both mortal and ethereal, felt an immediate sense of dread. The night was complete, and a thunderhead of clouds was beginning to form overhead. An unkindness of ravens was circling above, exalting in a sinister song of darkness. The boys ducked in fear. The chattering and squawking birds terrified them. The spirits, however, felt an even more profound sense of ill-ease. These blackbirds' caws were a siren's song to the evil dead. The ravens, themselves, were the reapers who brought souls here to the doors of hell before they were locked away inside Acheron forever. No ghost ever wanted to be visited by such a being.

Looking up and listening to the avian cacophony, those fleeing were distracted from another more immediate threat forming on the grass across from them. From deep within the ground, and through the walls of surrounding buildings, came a host of souls marred with scars and rope burns around their necks. "Charles," whispered Raleigh, looking down from the birds to what was blocking their escape. Darwin followed Sir Walter's gaze to a rapidly growing gathering of ghosts. "We have been discovered. We are in it now, I fear." The tower spirit finished his thought while furiously puffing his pipe.

As the whole group watched, a singular ghost stepped forward to take control. "Anyone recognize the one in front?" asked Dickens to all listening.

"Guy Fawkes," answered The White Woman, "a terrorist and scoundrel if there ever was one. He is of the demon."

Fawkes glared ahead at those before him. A smirk slowly curled up from his thin translucent lips. His neck was cocked to the side, still in the same position from when it had broken as he hung in this very place a century earlier. His dark, ominous eyes and thick, furrowed brows peeked out from beneath the rim of his oversized hat, creating a sense of fear and anxiety in those who saw him. He proudly drew an ethereal sword from his waistband and pointed it to the ground. Seemingly in jest, he leaned on it as one infirmed would a cane. "I think that we have some birds that want to flee that nest," he glowered.

"Let us pass, foul ghost," said Dickens. "We are not unprepared."

"My good fellow, I would be more than pleased to do just that!" the criminal responded. "My master, however, might take exception to that decision."

"He is stalling, Dickens," whispered Darwin. "He is waiting for something." Then, looking at the mortal boys, the scientist murmured, "Now is your time to run. Take the princes all the way out and wait for us. Stay as hidden as you can from other mortals at The Binding. We need you in position to help us get out." Without a moment of hesitation, the boys, with the two princes inside, ran faster than they had ever moved before.

"You will not escape the devil's army. You are ours." Fawkes intoned the threat almost to himself. In unison, and as if by some agreed-upon signal, the entire company of gathered dark soldiers unsheathed their ethereal swords.

Recognizing the inevitable clash in the scene that was unfolding before them, the host of abbey spirits and their newfound allies began to draw their own weaponry. They were prepared to fight. Almost knocking Sir Walter Raleigh to the side, Anne Boleyn masterfully swung out a double-headed battle-ax with ease. The aristocratic Virginian paused with some wonder as to where the ax had come from as he pulled his own rapier from his side. Shakespeare pulled thin stiletto daggers from the cuffs of his sleeves. Jane suddenly had a knife that she held tightly against her right hip. Newton reached over his shoulder, retrieving the parts of a knight's pike. He tightly screwed the two pieces together and lowered the end to the ground, steadying himself before he had to put the weapon to use. The remaining spirits pulled their own swords and weapons of choice. Glinda's and Merlin's wands both started glowing with power. The music of the blades leaving their sheaths was sharp and crisp against the still of the night. The boys watched from the far side of the green as their ethereal friends had formed a solid line of defense between themselves and their spectral antagonists. The ghosts all knew that if they were to survive this moment, they would have to fight a retreating action together and towards the exit.

Slowly, screams erupted from both sides as Fawkes and his company ran forward. When the shrillness of the warrior cries quieted and the combatants ran out of breath, the troops collided. Individual battles ensued. Newton ducked down as a demonic shade ran towards him. As the dark soul came close to his body, Newton impaled him with the pike, nearly raising him from the ground before the spirit slid down the pole. Within seconds, the evil spirit crackled into bright, brilliant particles that gently fell to the ground. The entire spirit had dissolved, and as the final bits of him faded into the air, nothing remained. Death and dying had come to those already dead. No one really knew what happened to a ghost who left the ethereal world through dissolution, but the fear of it was as real as a mortal's trepidation about passing from his or her own plane of existence to what might lay beyond.

As Jane watched the encounter, she knew the importance of getting the photo boxes to the boys. Should the spirits all fade at this moment, she wanted the king's journal and Nostradamus' writings to be securely out of the tower. She could see the two mortal boys and the princes now beyond the glowing blue force of The Binding that served as a backdrop to the violence unfolding. The princes were as safe as could be given the circumstance. Sheathing her knife, Jane lifted the three boxes to her chest. She looked across the green in fear, acknowledging to herself that unarmed, her chances of making it to the boys would be low. Seeing Jane's distress, Lady Arbella raced towards her. Sword drawn, The White Woman offered some protection as Jane ran closely behind her hugging her precious cargo. Nearly at the wall, one of the dark soldiers dove at Jane, grabbing her dress. As he pulled his hand back to plunge his weapon into the author's side, Lady Arbella swiftly wielded her sword. In a single chop, she sliced his arm off at the shoulder and in an upward thrust planted her sword in his head. Before the attacking ghost's severed appendage could settle on the ground, the spirit as a whole evaporated. The two mortal boys ran into The Binding and out the other side to gather Jane and Arbella. Immediately allowing the two women to take possession, William and Thomas dove back through the barrier. Jane was still clinging to the photo boxes as the boys released the women alongside the two princes. Thomas and William then returned to the edge of The Binding to watch for the next spirits needing to cross.

The battle on the green had become pitched, but, from the Darlingtons' perspective, their side seemed to have gained the upper hand. Shakespeare and Dickens ran beside each other, and in tandem swung their weapons in a forceful arc. Like a scythe cutting through wheat, the legs of three of the demon's army were cut out from under their bodies. The howls of pain and rage dissipated only as the three evil spirits eventually dissolved back into the ether. The move formed a glowing streak that followed behind the two authors before fading into nothingness. As Dickens and Shakespeare neared The Binding, the boys once again stepped through. They retrieved the exhausted souls of the writers before retreating back through the protective force.

Merlin and Glinda fought together, their magic wands shooting fireballs and punching holes in the ethereal bodies of the gathered soldiers comprising the army of evil. Over and over small bands of the vile spirits attacked the two magicians, only to be repelled with blinding flashes of light that lit up the dark and revealed the carnage left from the attempt. But magic like physical strength dwindles if it is overused, and both of the apparitions were beginning to fade in their abilities. Dickens saw the change and called to his enchanted friends from the far side of the barrier. "Flee, fools!" he shouted.

"Boys! Catch them!" the author further implored, now looking to Thomas and William.

Merlin saw his chance as William ran forward. "Get through, my dear!" he implored. And with that, the old sorcerer lit a wall of fire between himself and Glinda and the wave of rapidly approaching foes. In that moment, the witch found herself able to get inside the young boy and was rapidly heading back out towards the barrier. Merlin fell to his knees in exhaustion. He knew the cost of his last act but had accepted his fate. He had allowed Glinda to escape but his fire had gone out. As the evil approached, his head slumped forward. The last the wizard heard was "Gotcha, Mister Merlin" before he passed out, utterly exhausted.

Sir Walter Raleigh, Anne Boleyn, and Charles Darwin had formed a circle, turning their backs to each other, thus eliminating the risk that a member of the demon's hoard could attack them from behind. Nearly shoulder to shoulder, the men swung their blades and Anne slashed with her ax. It was becoming clear that these three had every intent to be the last through The Binding should they make it that far.

Guy Fawkes stared down Newton and Hawking, who were fighting off combatants as they retreated towards the exit. Instead of running towards them, he walked slowly and confidently with his sword held at his side. As he approached,

Hawking swung his rapier mightily in an attempt to end the terrorist in one fell swing. Fawkes watched and anticipated the move, knowing it would turn the mathematician's back ever so slightly to him, leaving Hawking exposed. When it happened, Fawkes raised his sword and plunged it forcefully through his opponent. Hawking gasped, looked down, and dropped his own weapon. Putting both of his hands on the blade of the sword that had impaled him, he fell to his knees. Fawkes let loose the weapon's hilt. Leaving the blade inside Hawking, and adding a decided vileness to the act, the ghost smiled. Fawkes turned and simply walked away, heading back to his allies in the fray.

"Hawking, no! God, no!" Newton screamed and dove to catch his friend as he nearly collapsed forward against the grass. Newton broke his fall, pulled the sword from his back, and knelt to the ground. He helped his wounded colleague into a sitting position, holding Hawking's head against his chest to stabilize his breath.

Seeing what had happened, Anne, Walter, and Charles ran towards their fallen friend. The trio stood between Hawking and Newton, now forming a straight line and holding their enemies away from the two mathematicians. "Don't look back," instructed Raleigh. "We fight for him." Anne twirled her ax above her head with both hands, before dropping it solidly against the neck of blackness. Through the crackle of the spirit's evaporation, her blade continued to claim the heads of those before her. Darwin and Raleigh both fought with a renewed ferocity, slashing and stabbing those who ran against them. In the moment, they all almost believed they alone could clear the tower of evil as the popping lights of the spirits' souls filled the air.

It was Darwin who first recognized the folly of the thought. Even though many of their enemies had fallen, Fawkes seemed to be mustering an even larger group to rush those still within the border of The Binding. Darwin stepped in front of Anne. "Go to the exit, your highness," he spoke with urgency. "We can't hold them." Anne lowered her ax, noting the futility of their circumstance and the finality of what had just occurred behind her. She retreated towards Newton. He sat with Hawking, who was crumpled on the ground almost within reach of The Binding.

Rocking back and forth, Newton tried to remain calm.

"Isaac, we must go," the young queen whispered, as she stood over the two scientists.

"Anne is right," coughed Hawking "I am on a different path now."

Newton continued to gently whisper to Hawking, "Shhh, Shhhh, Shhhh, my dear friend. I am here." Looking down at Hawking, Newton could tell his colleague did not have long. Hawking's body had gone limp, and his strength depleted as a slow ooze of light ran from the hole in his torso.

Struggling to keep his eyes open, Hawking gazed up at Newton and said, "Since I was a boy, you always were my inspiration for greatness."

A tear fell from Newton's cheek. "And ever since we met, you have been mine," he confessed to his friend with his own voice cracking.

"Go," Hawking gravely whispered, finding it difficult to breathe. "You must go before they take you, too." Hawking took one more deep breath and exhaled, "I'll be alright. The grand design awaits. I hope I'm allowed my calisthenics at my next stop, wherever that may be." With that, he closed his eyes. The fight within him was finished.

"Goodbye, Stephen," said Newton through gritted teeth. His heartbreak was turning to rage.

With tears in her eyes, Anne reached down again for her grieving ally. "Come, Isaac. He is at peace now. We must leave this cursed place."

Grabbing one last moment, Newton whispered into Hawking's ear, "I will always remember you, and I will honor your name. Find peace, my dear friend." Newton lowered Hawking's body to the ground, and before he could rise, Hawking was consumed with a bright light that broke into a flurry of fiery particles. A breeze blew and within an instant, he was gone.

Anne grabbed Newton's arm, helped him to his feet, and rushed him to the exit. The mortal boys had tears streaming down their faces as they emerged from The Binding. Grief consumed their young hearts, but, nonetheless, they stood firmly awaiting the spirits. Before they were met, the anger that filled Newton's body also captured his mind. Shrugging off Anne's kindness, he turned back to where Darwin and Raleigh still fought. Fawkes was there and had reengaged. As Newton moved to go back, Anne forcefully placed her hand against his chest. "Enough!" she cried, as she shoved him against Thomas. They both pressed back through The Binding. She, herself, quickly stepped inside William. All were on the outside looking back in at the tower. She left her vessel as Newton left his, and the boys jumped back through the barrier to catch their last passengers.

Raleigh and Darwin had made their way to the edge of the force as well. The demon's army had regathered under Fawkes and was working to cut them off. "Run!" cried Darwin. Simultaneously, he and Sir Walter both turned their backs on their foes to sprint to the boys. The two ghosts slammed into the mortal bodies as William and Thom both offered the needed welcome to the possession. The four tumbled through the magic of the barrier and wound up on the other side in a tangle.

It was done. As Darwin and Raleigh stepped out of William and Thomas, the boys broke into tears. Jane ran to their sides, hugging both as hard as she could, expending all of her ethereal energies to provide a physical sense to her embrace. The boys sobbed in her arms. As the other ghosts gathered themselves and took consolation in each other, Newton simply stood and stared out to the green.

The tower's ghosts had been depleted, but the remaining ethereal soldiers slowly gathered in front of The Binding staring out to those beyond. Other than the shushing consolation of Jane and the staggered breath of the calming boys, complete silence fell over the tower as the two opposing forces stood just feet away from each other as if awaiting the start of a second battle.

The eerie quiet was broken suddenly and thoroughly. An unnerving whistle filled the tower. It appeared to come from everywhere but started dimly, sounding like the remembrance of a forgotten dream. Still, it was growing. It took only a minute, but, for the abbey ghosts, it felt an eternity. The volume of the melody had met a crescendo. At that peak, a well-dressed, perfectly groomed man in a trench coat appeared from nowhere and stepped alongside Guy Fawkes. "Well done," he praised, slowly applauding as he made his way to the front of the tower army.

The mortal boys immediately recognized the man and his whistle. He had killed the beefeater. The princes and the tower ghosts also shuddered. The entire collective knew the demon was standing before them. "Welcome, friends!' he announced with his arms wide open. "I am Jack, Lord of the Tower and the host of our little party." To taunt them, Jack walked along the force of The Binding, slowly dragging an ethereal dagger against it to create the shrill sound of nails on a chalkboard. He smirked with an evil grin as he accompanied the sound with his whistle before stopping in front of Newton. He cocked his head back and forth as he looked at the ghost.

Leaving his head tilted to one side, he tapped the dagger against The Binding. "Your friend was just the beginning. I revel in your loss, Newton, and I tasted your friend's fear as he dissolved into the nothing. He was just the first; I will be taking others. But you always remember your first," the demon provoked. "Your little friend was a welcomed sacrifice, even if only an appetizer."

Newton couldn't control his rage. A feral cry escaped his body as he threw himself at The Binding. He tried to dive through its energy, but it threw him back, burning his body to punish him for the attempt. He fell to the floor, holding his face and arm in agony.

Jack looked down through the magical barrier, addressing Newton. "Calm yourself, you scorched stump. Save your energy, for we will be coming for you soon. It's a pity my mortal help is not near, for I could come and play now." With that, he turned his back to The Binding. As if rehearsed, the remaining soldiers parted to create a clear pathway, and Jack began the walk towards The Bloody Tower. The ghosts and the boys watched as he and the whistle faded within its walls.

Newton screamed. His heart was breaking, and the rest of the group began to grieve as the adrenaline of the fight faded from their body. "It is done," said Darwin as he placed his hand on Newton's arm. "We will grieve at the abbey. We still risk the boys being seen or heard by mortal guards, and I fear we may have created a stir. I will distract the beefeaters as you all leave the gates. I will not have us lose anyone else."

CHAPTER 23 | The Conjuring of a King

UNK COULD HEAR their echoing voices and footsteps long before they reached the abbey. This was it. The group from the tower was returning. He quickly left his vantage point outside the church and rounded up the beefeater and Olivier to herd them into Merlin's laboratory. They were all eager to hear what the others had learned about the key or maybe even if it had been found. Regardless, if the key remained lost, they had their own news to share and a real opportunity for its discovery. Each took a seat and waited. The three sat only briefly before the others appeared at the top of the stairs. As they all rose from their chairs to cheerfully meet the returning spirits, their hopes of solution were dimmed by the somber, downtrodden group that entered.

The two mortal boys entered first and were barely able to place one step in front of the other. They were exhausted from moving the spirits back and forth across The Binding and emotionally spent from the outcome of the night. Glinda was gently whispering to them, as she paused to wipe William's cheek. Tears had exposed streams of clean skin against the dirt that covered his face. Thomas appeared to be listening to the witch, but the trauma experienced was evident in the deadpan of his eyes.

Behind them, Newton appeared despondent and injured,

an emptied wreck from the ghost he typically was. Merlin was nearly supporting the mathematician's entire body weight. As the pair got closer to those waiting, they could see that Sir Isaac was burned on the left side of his face and body.

"What happened?" thought the Unknown Soldier, his own mind racing with anger, frustration, and remorse.

The rest of the group was not much better off. Cloth wraps were tied around Anne's hands that were marred with blisters from her ax. A makeshift sling was supporting Dickens' shoulder that had dislocated during the fight. Shakespeare applied pressure to his leg as he limped to the closest seat. Sir Walter was smoking his pipe in an anxious fashion as he tried to appear strong. The White Lady was on his arm, clearly shaken, smudged, and grey from the fray. Jane was carrying three photo boxes in her hands, while the two princes walked alongside her, holding on to her skirt that had been ripped and covered in soot and dirt. From the read of her face, her heart was heavier than a library full of books. The grim procession ended as Darwin pulled the door shut behind him and walked down the stairs. While he did, all eyes were on him, and he took the moment to look at each of his friends. The fight they had experienced had been devastating, but the causalities they could realize in the future would only get worse, he feared.

"Where is Stephen?" asked Olivier.

"He is lost to us," answered Darwin blankly. It took a moment, but after introductions were made all around, the biologist recounted the tale of the day for all involved. The failure of the witching stick and the room search drew murmurs from the group while the capture of the king's diary drew a modicum of praise. Finally, Darwin's account of the battle covered the gathering in a shroud of silence. The quiet in the room was profound and palpable.

The Unknown Soldier, clearly despondent, was the first to speak. He was pacing back and forth across the abbey floor before he stopped and finally addressed the group. "I have failed in my calling. How could I see you head into such dangerous territory without being there myself to fight? My God, to think Hawking might still be here if I had been there to help. I swear it shall not happen again. My deepest apologies." Wiping his eyes, the ghostly solider turned from the group to gather himself.

"I was his friend, and I couldn't save him," Newton muttered. "This was beyond you, Unk. If any failed Stephan, it was me—or maybe, us all." The once lively, energetic spirit had become overwhelmed with guilt and could hardly bear the reality that Hawking had literally vanished beside him. The fact that his friend's soul was lost forever rocked him at his core.

Dickens, looking down, asked no one in particular, "Who were we to think that we would have the ability to find the key? Is it just arrogance that keeps us so inclined? Are we so special? The plan was flawed from the beginning. We were found lacking and were always doomed to fail. Maybe it is just time for us to go." The last statement hung in the air over all those gathered.

Darwin stood up in frustration. "Hold there a second, Charles. We did not fail. We tried something heroic. It didn't go according to plan, but dammit, we tried. That is a hell of a lot more than most other souls have done. Our friend knew what he was risking. He knew what he might be sacrificing. But he went anyway. You want to know why? He knew the evil that we met on the green. He knew that if it gets out, the world as we know it will end. He has family and friends still living and, like us all, more descendants to come. So, do you want to know what I think? I think we get ourselves together and regroup. If you want to honor Hawking, we need to finish this. I am not done. We are not done. Not by a long shot." The ghost's voice rose in anger.

The Unknown Soldier turned back to the gathering, thought for a moment, unwrapped the king's skull, and laid it in front of Merlin. "Here then, let us start with this. You said you could conjure Edward, and there is still hope we can find the key's whereabouts from this bone. Well, here it is. Do it!" He paused for a moment to calm the agitation in his voice, and after he apparently contemplated his request, suddenly exclaimed, "God save the queen!"

Merlin looked at the soldier and shook off his own somber state of mind. Unk was clearly not ready to retreat either. The wizard took heart in that recognition and Darwin's adamancy. If the old military man and the naturalist were not ready to give up, then how could he, Merlin the Great Wizard, embrace defeat? He had, in fact, promised the group that he would attempt to connect magically with the king and, "In the name of Arthur," the old conjurer thought, "I will do it!" He gathered himself, took a deep breath, and picked up the skull. "For Stephen," he stated flatly as he handled the dead king's head and inspected it fully. He carefully studied the intricate suture markings that ran zigzag across the bone, hoping they would tell him a story. Finally, he bowed his head, only to suddenly look back up to address the gathered spirits.

"I will do it now." Energies began cracking around the magician. The ghostly group and the two mortal boys gathered in a semicircle around Merlin to watch his conjuring. There was no longer any desire to leave or stop in those gathered. Death had come to their family and a new resolve had galvanized them all.

"Everyone, move back! These energies are unfamiliar. Harnessing them may create a certain danger. All powers, light and dark, are needed to call King Edward back to this plane of existence." The wizard seemed to be reminding himself of what he was undertaking. Glinda approached Merlin and placed her hand on his shoulder, falling into a deep concentration. It appeared to the others she was adding her magic and substance to the effort being displayed. The two ghost princes looked at each other in frightened anticipation but also moved forward toward the sorcerer in hopes that they might see their father. Merlin placed the skull on a small table that stood at knee height beside him. The positioning allowed him to stand directly over the greyed cranium. The sleeves of his heavy, blue velvet robe exposed his strong hands, which were perfectly cupped and hovering just inches above the royal's head. So situated, Merlin began to rock back and forth as he let out a slow, low chant, starting softly and then growing in volume.

Spirits beyond I hail to thee.
Hear my summons and heed my call.
Break the veil, I set you free.
Gather here to please us all.
Let us speak of that unknown.
Let us do what must be done.
Release thy will from flesh and bone.
To me appear, no longer gone.

After several rounds of his verse, Merlin's hands separated and began to swirl around the skull in opposing directions, creating the force of a tornado above it. "King Edward the IV of England, from the deepest depths of my soul, with all the power of the earth and the magic of the heavens, I call on the afterworld to bring you forth to us. Come to us, Edward. Come to us!"

His movements did not slow in the circular vortex he was creating, and he once again began to chant. The time was short before a deep green projection began to flicker and swirl within his hands. As he continued to rock his body and louden his recited verse, the projection grew high into the air. It crackled and sparked with a now brilliant glow as swirling mists of ether began to gather. Small bolts of lightning discharged across the face of the growing funnel. Papers started to fly about Merlin's laboratory as the wizard continued his spell. The other ghosts and apparitions stepped even further back from the magical tempest. The mortal boys, at Darwin's firm direction, ducked behind a couch. As the tornado grew, a light from within it began to reveal the broken outline of a male figure. His arms were outstretched, and the image appeared welcoming and peaceful. As the soft form began to gain definition, the princes could make out their father's face. He looked like the robust ruler who they lovingly remembered before his health had so rapidly declined. It jolted their young hearts to see him and to feel a connection with him after so long.

"Papa!" screamed Rake, putting his arms out towards the projection and clearly hoping to embrace his father in their spiritual forms. But, as the ghost prince reached out for his father, burning red and orange sparks ripped through the summoned presence and scorching heat suddenly radiated from the still churning maelstrom. All of the onlooking spirits were nearly knocked to the floor. Instinctively, Merlin stepped back from the vision he had created, allowing it to wane slowly. Glinda held fast her position, but her eyes darted up to the wizard and then to the conjured king. The group of ghosts also refocused their eyes upon the image, but it was changing. King Edward had wilted from the strong, strapping, peaceful man first presented into a sickly, tormented, and anguished shell, bound with shackles on his wrists and ankles. The serenity of his face had dissipated entirely. He now screamed in torment, begging for release and pleading for final death. His eyes seemed to fixate on the group who was watching him. "Mercy!" he beseeched. "Mercy! I can stand no more!" His look was wild in the wanting for the horror to stop. Behind his image, glowing red eyes showed against a black rock background. Three-headed dogs barked, and slithering snakes wrapped their way up and down the king's body. Flames then engulfed his frame.

"Rake!" the image cried with seemingly singular recognition. "My son...save me." The cry in his voice and the tears in his eyes gave all the spirits pause as the image reached toward his youngest heir. "I can take no more. Find me! Release me! The pain!"

The princes screamed in a terror that nearly matched the sound of the tortured soul of King Edward. Rake rushed towards the image, excreting a wail that sounded inhuman. In an effort to reach his father, he tripped over a stool, knocking all contents off the table. Jane hurried over, lifting Rake from the floor into her arms. "Let me go," he screamed, kicking to free himself from her embrace. "Let me go! My father needs me."

Merlin stepped forward again, standing in between Rake and the image of the king. The young ghost continued to wail and beg for the torture of his father to stop. Merlin attempted to take command of the circumstance that was beginning to feel beyond all control. Firmly regaining his position above the skull, the wizard's hair blew back from his face as he confronted the now gale-forced wind. Pointing his wand into the heart of the conflagrating image, Merlin exalted, "Release him. I, Merlinus Caledonensis Ambrosius, command that the lasting bonds of the damned that bind you in Acheron be broken. I command that your spirit be freed. Shackles break. Spirit soar. I conjure thee to me." The screams of King Edward grew as competing forces were ripping his body in half. As the group watched silently, the image began to shake. Then, like a film strip struggling to play, the figure bounced and broke before them. The red glow faded. Just as quickly as it had appeared, the vortex, the image, and all its intensity were instantly consumed back through the eye sockets of the skull, nearly knocking it off the table. Before Merlin could touch it, the blackened and scarred head bone of King Edward the IV shattered and turned to dust. The wizard seemed to age a lifetime at that moment. He clutched the table and dropped his head. The magnitude of his failure washed over him fully.

"Oh my God. No! Father, come back," hollered Edward,

who had tried to grab the image before it had fully retreated into the skull. "What have you done?" he screamed as he turned in anger, staring down Merlin.

Rake broke away from Jane and collapsed against the floor. "Why didn't you let me go to him? How dare you. My father is trapped. I needed to save him, and you stopped me. You all were supposed to help. Now look what you have done," he screamed, addressing the entire group of spirits. Completely exhausted, he crumpled to the floor in utter devastation. Edward crouched down and tightly held his brother in an effort to calm his hysteria. "He needed me to help him," Rake whispered in his brother's ear.

"I'm so sorry. I'm so sorry." Merlin's voice trembled in shock as he locked eyes with the two princes. "I thought I...I thought I could..." Merlin walked backward and fell onto a nearby stool, disappointed and embarrassed he had been unable to fulfill the confident promise he had made to the group. Mostly, however, he was horrified at what had happened, at what he had just put the princes through. Rake stood absolutely still and rigid. Jane hugged him, but the wizard could see something had snapped inside the boy. Merlin did not know what to say. Glinda approached him with concern in her eyes. She hugged the old magician to her and stood quietly while he wept.

Anne cleared her throat and adjusted her collar. She could feel many of the spirits were losing any shred of hope they had once held. The thought of what might happen if they gave up scared her. She looked at the boys, mortal and ghost, as well, and saw the strain on their faces. It was clear significant damage had been done to the strength of their young resolve. "Jane, my dear," she said kindly, addressing the author. "Might you take the boys back to the abbey? I think the adults should talk. It is nearly daylight, and the mortals, as I understand things, should be back to their beds. Perhaps our young princes could be accommodated somewhere close by. I vow to keep you well informed." She smiled, speaking lightly in an attempt to give some assurance to all of the children. Jane understood Anne's intent completely and gathered Thomas, William, Edward, and Rake back up the stairs. The remaining group of ghosts heard the door latch behind them as the boys left.

With the children gone, Anne looked to what remained of the group. They were battered, burned, and quiet, all lost in their own thoughts. She, however, was still a Queen of England and these were forever her subjects. Every bit the royal she was, Anne commanded their attention. They may be tired and hurt, but she believed they still were willing to fight. She stood before them all and picked up where she had left off. "While the spectacle we saw is troubling, no doubt, it is not surprising that the king is trapped. Inside the tower, we have watched as spirits of the damned and souls of the faithful have both been stolen and used by the demon. Those who refuse him are bound in the horrors of their own personal hell in the tower, or possibly even pushed through to Acheron, which is what I believe we just witnessed with King Edward. Perhaps the fortunate few are the ones he kills completely. I cannot say," she stated, shaking her head. "But what I can say," the queen continued, "is that the man you saw tonight during the battle, Jack as he called himself, is a type of evil that this world cannot bear to face, even if fully united. We have only seen a small fraction of the carnage and disasters he can so easily unleash. He is seeking the key to free the souls of the damned by opening the gates of Acheron. The army we saw tonight was nothing in terms of the size or brutality we are sure to face if the demon has his way and releases all the evil afterworld to do his bidding. So, while Merlin's magic didn't work to our end and your other efforts proved fruitless, we still must continue to try and find the key. We must do everything we can. If we are not successful, it could be the end of all things."

As Anne sat down, the other ghosts slowly began to talk in small groups, making suggestions to each other and discussing possibilities. Unk took Sir Isaac aside and began to minister to his needs. After doing what he could for the mathematician, the solider then went ghost to ghost completing a triage of injuries before heading to the apothecary to retrieve medicines, ointments, and other needed medical supplies. "Strategies can wait," he thought while leaving, "I must attend to the wounded dead."

✦ ✦ ✦

Hours had passed. And, while Unk doctored as he could, Dickens had been sitting off to side of Merlin's lab by himself quietly examining Nostradamus' writings that he had worked to retrieve from the library. He had been a student of mystics during his mortal life, and since his death had taken time to talk to any passing spirits that shared his fascination with prophecy. Of all the prophets, oracles, and seers he knew or knew of, none compared to Nostradamus. After hearing Anne's fears, Dickens looked up several passages he had remembered from the text as he read it in the past. It was becoming clear in his mind.

"Her majesty is right, and our long-held worst fears may soon be realized," he stated firmly to the group as he stood up. "I know that many of you disbelieve or at least doubt the mystics, but Nostradamus was unchallenged in his capacity to 'see' and had long ago predicted a brutal war. From his writings, it seems a battle of an epic magnitude is inevitable."

"I need no mystic to know that, Charles," Darwin agreed in frustration.

"But there is more, my friend," Dickins continued ignoring the tone of the scientist's voice and paused for effect. "I am also fearful that a misstep in our efforts may cause the predicted upheaval. Perhaps it is a blessing that this key is unobtainable to us. While in the hands of the demon, it could unleash hell. However, what if our discovery of the key allowed for that devastation? What if our actions allowed the demon his prize?"

"What in the world are you talking about, Dickens?" said Darwin. "Elaborate your concern. How would our control of the gate allow for such calamity? The gate needs to be used. We all agree to that! This plane must be able to rid itself of the dark."

"This is true, but that certainty does not suggest we here should have it or even find it to give to someone else. The responsibility of the key could belong to others." The author paused to let the notion of their possible mistake sink in. "There are several verses and writings of Nostradamus that I can recall and which have long troubled me. Only now, they seem far more relevant and ominous than I had ever imagined." He flipped through the pages. "Here, for example..." Dickens pointed to a passage as he read it aloud. *"So come, my son, strive to understand what I have found out through my calculations which accord with revealed inspiration, because now the sword of death approaches us, with pestilence and war more horrible than there has ever been—because of three men's work."*

The group sat bewildered, looking at Dickens. "Don't you get it?" the author said excitedly. "We've been so focused on the demon. What if we have been naïve to the fact that we all hold a significant role in this whole event, too? Reading this now, I worry the three men may be our very own King Edward, Prince Edward, and Prince Rake. Perhaps Nostradamus was predicting the hiding and retrieval of the key there."

"Dickens, even if I were to believe in prophecy and to agree with what you take from this particular writing, we could just have the princes end their involvement at any time," scoffed Darwin. "It would seem to solve the problem."

Dickens shook his head and continued. "Let me read another one... *'The great Royal one of gold, augmented by brass, the agreement broken, war opened by a young man: People afflicted because of a lamented grief, The land will be covered with barbarian blood.'*"

"Care to giveth us your interpretation of this verse too, Dickens?" Shakespeare inquired.

"Of course. It is hard and obviously open to interpretation, but I've spent a great deal of time contemplating its meaning so as to explain myself to you all. To me, this passage is about our dear Thomas or William. The princes are gold, but have they been augmented by the common or 'brass' as it is alluded to? The royals have used the commoners, William and Thomas, as vessels. You see, should we find the key, it will be one of our mortal boys who will be doing much of that work. We have a king who was betrayed by his brother who broke a bloodline promise of protection and servitude by his own hand. Recognize the nature of the grief and tie it to the mortal boys' delivery of the key, and this augury may tell us that we are putting the world at great risk."

Unk stepped in and interjected with disagreement. "That seems nonsensical, Dickens. You really believe that those two young lads are going to unleash a bloody war? I think not."

"Think what you might, but a war is coming, and Nostradamus knew that Satan and evil would be major players in the game. Here. Right here," Dicken pointed as he glanced again at the copied pages of the book. A shadow of fear and dread fell upon his face.

"*Wars and battles will be more grievous and towns, cities, castles and all other edifices will be burned, desolated and destroyed, with great effusion of vestal blood. By means of Satan, Prince Infernal, so many evils will be committed that nearly all the world will find itself undone and desolated. Before these events, some rare birds will cry in the air, 'Today, today!' and sometime later will vanish. Satan will remain bound for hundreds of years and then unbound."*

This last passage needed no further comment. It was all too clear. The group sat quietly as they processed the predictions.

Lady Arbella quietly whispered, "We've all heard the birds and the cry of those reapers as ravens. The seer is right about one thing. The flock grows thin."

"I wish Nostradamus was here to explain what he saw in his visions," noted Olivier. "The old boy could make things a bit easier!"

"He would be of no further help to us," noted Dickens. "I met him once before he crossed over to his afterlife. Several of us spirits intercepted him to tell him of our cause, fears, and specific efforts. While he honored the noble nature of our endeavor, he believed he had written and exposed all that he could. On the day he left the terminal to move on, he was confident his work here was done."

Newton was tired of the banter and had run out of tolerance for the entire effort. "The only thing I am confident about is that the hunt for the key is pointless. Our labor has been without result, and, even worse, it seems to have expedited the demon's plans. You just heard it for yourselves. Rapture and devastation at the hands of the demon are inevitable. Nostradamus said it loud and clear. If we are to believe him, then we are doomed."

✦ ✦ ✦

When the boys reached the dorm, their waiting comrades looked at them with some fear and sense of wonder. It had become so late; the three enlisted conspirators were considering options on how to cover for the Darlingtons should they not return for the day soon to break. In looking at the two as they returned, Nigel, Burt, and James saw immediately there was no energy for discussion nor time left to have it. Burt clapped Thomas on the back and simply assured, "All is well here, so there is no need to talk. Let's off to bed now. We can talk later."

Thomas offered his thanks and pushed William off towards his bed.

As the Darlingtons left, James turned to the other two boys. "I am glad we helped, but I fear we are in it now!"

✦ ✦ ✦

Satisfied with what she heard from the gathered mortals and needing to help the princes find rest, Jane walked the two young ghosts away from the dorm. They could sleep fitfully at the small inn her friend Conrad Hilton had built at the other end of the abbey.

CHAPTER 24 | Merlin's Plan

"WELL, THAT SETTLES it," Merlin said as he stepped to the center of the group. He had calmed himself and shaken off the disappointment and trauma of the failed conjuring and was now determined to guide the spirits towards a new solution. "If we can't find the key—or maybe, as Charles suggests, 'shouldn't find it'—and the demon's war is inevitable, we are left with only one option. To tamper with fate, we must kill that abomination."

Merlin's suggestion had rattled Newton, who was still visibility grieving and processing the loss of Hawking. "Merlin, my good man! We just kill him, you say? We have neither the skill nor the weaponry. That foul creature is not a ghost, and our ethereal blades will be as nothing to him," scowled Newton. He made no attempt to hide the tone of anger and disbelief in his voice.

Looking steadfastly at Sir Isaac and recognizing his pain, Merlin replied calmly, "We will kill him the same way he would kill us: with a sword. But we will use one of the physical world."

"A mortal sword will not kill him either, even if one of us had the capacity and skill to wield it. In his natural form, the demon is a horrific, terrifying beast," broke in Lady Arbella, who then added, "There are none here to do this deed."

Raleigh stepped forward to confirm what had been said. "He won't fight us as Jack. He will fight as a monster. We in the tower know that form all too well. Imagine a living nightmare, a thing with tentacles that protrude from his back and dance across his shoulders and can be used as extra arms. His ram horns and his hooved feet add to his height. His red eyes shine with power and when he drags his long fingernails across stone, he leaves an evil mark. So strong and sharp are those daggers." Raleigh took another long drag from his pipe. Shaking his head, he continued, "No, Merlin. Unfortunately, we cannot kill the demon with a blade. If I thought we could, we spirits at the tower would have tried to do so a long time ago."

Merlin let the idea settle. He paused for a moment as if to consider his own thoughts. So much had happened and so much had been lost. He wanted to be sure of his words before he spoke them. Looking at the tension in the faces of his friends, the mage continued carefully, "Dear spirits, in what I want to suggest, we will not be killing the demon ourselves nor will just any blade be used."

Glinda quickly approached Merlin, "What are you doing?" the witch asked plaintively. She clearly felt he was going to again suggest they count on his magic to answer the dilemma. Just as apparent was her worry that he was not consulting with her prior to offering his suggestion to the group.

"I am trying to save us here, London, and perhaps the world. That's what I am doing," he said, smiling with an apparently undiminished confidence.

"And how do you propose we kill him?" asked Dickens, drawing the conversation back to the entire group. "From what we just heard and what we all survived, this is no small task, even for a wizard and a witch!"

"Please," implored Merlin, "I know it is hard to have any hope or faith. Yet, that is exactly what we need to hold onto in our hearts and minds. We must trust the strength we have and in the forces we can muster. We are not as alone in our concerns as it may seem, and there are others who might be willing to help. We need only ask." Merlin was nearly pleading with the group to rally around his charge. "Perhaps if we have had any fault at all in this endeavor thus far, it has been in the arrogance of thinking we needed no one else. I, for one, will not make that mistake again. There are several mortally challenged beings who I count as dear friends and who are uniquely qualified to help given the current situation. I will seek them out if we can all come to an agreement."

"Dear God, this seems more a prescription for catastrophe than a resolution to our dilemma. Add more apparitions to the mix amid utter disaster? Brilliant," Newton said in disgust. "There is little I can think of that any apparition could do to help."

Merlin bit his tongue, but the pain from Newton's words was evident in his eyes. "Sir Isaac, I am only trying to help. I am sorry you are hurting. In fact, I am sorry we all are hurting, but bickering between ourselves will do nothing towards our end. Hawking is gone. We can't bring him back, and, even more, we need to move forward. He would want that." Merlin offered more condolence in his voice for the mathematician. "For those we have lost, and those we might lose, we need to finish what we have started. I assume we all agree, at this point, that we need help." The wizard looked into the eyes of each of the gathered ghosts.

Newton knew his outburst had been misguided. He apologized to the magician and removed himself to the back of the gathering to avoid any other aggressions that his friends did not deserve. He was not himself, and he knew it. Lady Arbella followed and sat near him silently, not wanting him to be alone.

Darwin tried to redirect the conversation. "Merlin, go on. Tell us what you've envisioned." With tensions high and emotions raw, the biologist felt they needed to get back to simple logistics before another personal battle erupted and further fractured the group that for so long had survived here at the abbey.

Merlin refocused himself before again addressing the

gathering. "We have said it. Mortal swords and the ethereal blades we can comfortably carry will not be lethal to the monster who roams the tower. It is most clear then, we need a different weapon more than anything: one that can lay waste to our adversary. My plan is simply to kill Jack, and to do so I need to create demon killer swords; blades so powerfully hewn with the mystic arts that a cleaving stroke or plunge into the demon will end him and his threat forever."

The group began murmuring at Merlin's words, but Darwin again brought it back to a focus. "And what makes you so confident you can create these so-called 'demon killers?'" Charles asked.

"I created the legendary sword, Excalibur, a weapon so powerful that, even today, it could control the fate of a kingdom and the life of the person wielding it. You may think the weapon a fiction, but you would have said the same about me before I came into existence. Indeed, you would have felt magic a topic of fairy tales at a time, but here you sit before The Binding and in conversation with a conjurer and a witch. What need I say or do to convince you? I can create the blade." Merlin eyed the biologist for a reaction but got nothing more than a slight cock of the head. Raising an eyebrow, he continued, "What I cannot do is build these swords on my own. In fact, I can only start the work with the swords of a king. It is the base that will bind my other enchantments and incantations to the blade."

"Merlin, dear friend." It was Olivier talking. "That then seems a major obstacle to it all. We have no such weaponry available."

"But we do, Laurence," answered Merlin quickly and with confidence. "The swords needed are in the tower. In fact, there were three such weapons in the Crown Jewel Room. I studied them during our search for the spoon. I will simply need to retrieve them."

The Unknown Soldier stepped forward and stood at

attention in front of Merlin. "I should have been there with you on your last visit. I insist that I go retrieve the swords," he commanded. The tone in his voice made his pronouncement unlikely to be challenged.

"I have no problem with that," said Raleigh as he stepped alongside Unk, "but I'll be going with you. I know the Crown Jewel Room well and will be able to lead you to the swords. I have looked at those blades myself. Merlin, you must stay here. It is unwise to risk getting you hurt when you are so essential to our plans and future."

Darwin fell into formation as well. "I agree. Merlin and Glinda need to be protected, but I will attend also. The transport of the swords will be trying and there is no reason to carry more than one each. We should distribute the necessary energy this trip will take. So, one blade for each of us."

Merlin was about to complain about being left behind but instead nodded in approval. "Wise decision. Please be careful in your selection of the swords. It is critical they be the weapon of a king. No others will do."

"Gentlemen," said Anne, breaking into the conversation. "Might I suggest we all rest a few days before we take on this endeavor? The tower is awake, and we are all but spent. Let us heal, consider our decisions, and make plans for their execution."

"My dear Majesty," chuckled Olivier, "That is a turn of phrase I never thought to hear coming from you!" He began stroking the ascot he wore on his neck.

The gathered ghosts all looked at the queen and then back at the actor. It took a moment, but she laughed, rubbing her own neck. "You are quite right, Sir Laurence," she quipped. "I just think we each may have our own ax to grind in this endeavor, and I want them to be sharp when we swing them."

The laughter that ensued from the two swept across the group to the point that even Newton broke a smile.

As Merlin worked to elaborate his plan, all of the ghosts sat quietly, intent in their listening and relieved to have a new direction to follow. Even the rat that scurried across the floor of the old cellar stopped to take notice. There was a gravity in the air and it seemed to intensify with each word the conjurer spoke. The rodent made his way through Darwin's and Raleigh's boots, while Unk careful waited for him to draw near. As the rat stepped upon his foot, Unk expended the necessary ethereal energy to kick the creature across the floor. "Disgusting vermin," he noted.

"We will need the boys again, I am afraid," Darwin commented to the gathered group. "They should rest as much as they can, but we will leave as soon as it is practical."

"Give them some time," suggested Dickens. "We have asked much already and pushing them to go back to the tower too soon might break the poor lads. Two of us, perhaps, should go to the boys, inform them of our plan, and better assess their readiness." The author stopped and turned to the wizard. "Merlin, set the rest into motion so that we may act as soon as our young wards are able."

The nodding heads of all those there left talking assured a new direction had been found. As each ghost left Merlin's lab in their own thoughts and to their own place of rest, the rat turned back from the hole in the wall from which he had emerged and peeked its head out. With a final look at the magician, who was now lost in his own mind, the animal whipped its tail, turned once again, and ran into the darkness.

✦ ✦ ✦

Communication throughout the spiritual realm is as unique as each spirit's journey to the afterlife. Clever devices and services are available on the ethereal plane for ghosts to connect to each other across the world. Merlin preferred the most flamboyant and magical form of contact available: The

Crank Crypt Caller. Stepping past the device's formal operator and the ghostly message boys who gathered call recipients, the wizard approached the machine with excitement. At first glance, it looked to be a relatively nondescript translucent metal box. It had a mild military style to it and two tiny nubs attached: one emerging from its front panel and the other coming out the back. Beyond these, there was also a small crank adorning the left side of the box and a large-handled earphone hanging from the right. It might have even passed for a prototype of an older field radio used during the mortal's Great War. Upon closer inspection, however, one could see that such a general assumption simply did not hold up. The crank was attached to an intricate and finely engraved set of gears that served only the most obscure of purposes. It was clearly not a utilitarian army relic. Merlin tensed his shoulders, ready for the exertion, and then he began to turn the handle. By rotating the crank, he set in motion the mechanics within the box, and the device began to transform. The nub on the front started to expand and produced a flower-shaped horn that grew with each turn of the bar. The phantasmal metal-looking sheets that formed the ornate cone were soon available for full inspection and were held together with nail head embellishments that added to its already Victorian look. While the front of the box sprouted the horn, the nub on the back of the box also began to take shape. An extension of ghostly nature suddenly protruded from the flat plane of the box, and as it grew it twisted like an unkempt garden hose. At the end of the tangle, a mouthpiece appeared that took the shape and size of an old-time radio microphone. Apparitions and ghosts admired the whimsical, and so their gadgets were often as visually stunning as they were useful. Merlin was no different. The Crank Crypt Caller, when completely expanded, resembled a most chaotic-looking electric trumpet built for either a very large man or a singularly small giant. Its look made the old apparition beam in delight and admiration.

Merlin continued turning the handle, and, with each revolution, his action gained in speed. He began huffing a bit with the exertion and small beads of ghostly perspiration began to rise on his forehead. With a small "ping" that arose from the machine, the wizard stopped the turning and bent over slightly to rest his hands on his knees as a runner would after a sprint.

Shakespeare, just happening by and seeing the wizard's activity, walked up from behind, hailed Merlin, and immediately queried, "Good sir, why art thou heaving so and in such a way? You have no working lungs."

Merlin looked back at the playwright, mildly embarrassed for the discovery. "Quite so, William. I honestly just like the sensation. It makes me feel young and virile. My manhood in full bloom!" Before he could give any further elaboration, however, another ping came from the box, and the wizard turned his back to the playwright to address it. "Sorry, my dear fellow. I really must handle this call." Merlin reached for the earphone on the side of the 'caller.' Shakespeare, looking at his friend and thinking only for a moment, walked away from the scene. Once out of view he immediately leaned forward, grasped his knees, and began gasping in his un-functioning, un-needed lungs. "T'would be a pleasure to blossom again," he muttered to no one.

As Merlin picked the earphone up, a long thin tendril of ether shot down from the roof of the abbey to be captured directly into the front of the flowered horn of the machine. It seemed almost a tornadic vortex as it whipped about between the crypt caller and the ceiling. Merlin immediately began to talk. "Yes, my kind lady. I would indeed like to make a call." With each word he spoke, that word, composed of ether and neatly typed, would pour quickly out of the machine's horn, where it would be sucked up into the swirling tendril. From there, it left the abbey. In a similar fashion, each word of a response coming from the intended connection shot out of the vortex, down from the ceiling of the abbey, and into the abbey machine. The messages, coming and going, were entering the spectral slipstream, a network of ethereal tubes bringing communication to the world of ghosts.

"The Basilica of Our Lady of Guadalupe. That's correct, Mexico City. I understand it is long distance. I'll hold." Merlin gave the needed information to an opaque operator at Phantom Phones who was working to direct his call. Slowly, the magician began to sway to the elevator-like music being played while the crypt caller system attempted to make his requested connection. His robe brushed back and forth against the stone floor as his hips kept time with the beat.

"Yes!" Merlin stopped his dance abruptly. "And to whom am I speaking? Juan Pablo? It's ok. Might you find Don Diego de la Vega for me?" There was a pause in the wizard's questioning, "Five minutes? That will be fine." Again, Merlin went silent, but his sway to the music started up again. This time he added his own hum into the mix he was already hearing.

"Hola, mi amigo! Como estas?" Merlin excitedly asked as he finally heard his friend on the other end of the line. "It has been too long." The magician paused. "Glinda? She is fine... still gives me a hard time about our last Affirmations for Apparitions Meeting." He grew silent listening for a response. "I know...too much Banshee Brandy would do that to anybody. She always speaks of you fondly." Merlin held. "I will...Listen, my friend, we've run into quite bad circumstance here in London. Can you spare a moment while I catch you up on what has happened?" It took time, but Don Diego heard all that he needed.

"We need your help. In fact, the reality is that the world needs you." The urgency in Merlin's voice was real. "Gracias! Gracias, mi amigo! We will all eagerly await your arrival, and I will find the others and get them to come." Merlin slowly hung up the earpiece on the side of the box and started turning the crank again. A few minutes passed, and the Crank Crypt Caller let out another ping. "Hello? Yes! I need Notre Dame Cathedral in Paris." Merlin went about making his calls.

✦ ✦ ✦

The demon scraped his gnarled hoof across the floor as he sat patiently. He softly whistled his evil melodies and waited. His glowing red eyes were fixated on a jagged crack that had formed where the stone wall met the cold rock floor. He paused his whistle as he heard light scampering coming from within the flooring. The corners of his mouth curled while he watched a dirty, dusty rat emerge from the gap. The rat shook the rubble off his fur and cleaned himself before running towards the dark creature. Reaching his master's feet, the rat stood on his hind legs with his front claws held together as if a supplicant in prayer. It paused for just a moment and then began to release a hysterical jumble of chatter, squeaking, and hissing. The demon leaned forward and listened intently, "Really? Go on." The words slithered out of the abomination's mouth like a snake. The chatter continued until the rat's sounds had ceased and it returned to a normal crouching position on all fours.

The demon stretched his massive hands towards the rat. His long, spindly fingers ending with yellowed, serrated clawlike nails reached for its fur. Gently, he scratched the rat's back and head, before sliding his nail under the rat's chin and pushing its gaze up towards. "Wonderful work, my loyal little servant." Smiling down at it, the demon leaned forward and bit off the rat's head.

✦ ✦ ✦

Days after their escape from the tower, the spirits had once again gathered in Merlin's chamber. The troop heading to the tower had left just after the boys finished dinner, hoping to retrieve the swords in the still of the night. It was thought the raid would be quick and the ghosts going would be back before midnight and the boy's first bed-check in the dormitories. The group that stayed behind grew restless. It seemed an eternity, but it wasn't more than a few hours later that the door to the chamber swung open.

"En garde!" screamed Raleigh as he dove through the door with his sword dramatically drawn. He was gripping his pipe with his teeth that were framed with a cocky grin. The three spirits made their way into the room, and the two mortal boys followed behind.

"Believe it or not, we met no resistance. We lifted the swords in unison, and as the alarms sounded, we rose to the top of the room. When the guards opened the doors to the Crown Jewel Room, we floated out. Surprisingly easy," noted Darwin.

For his part, Unk shook his head. He muttered under his breath, "Almost too easy."

"Nevertheless, here you are, and you have the swords. Please, let us all see them," requested Merlin, as he held his arms out to instruct the men to deposit the swords on his table.

The spirits laid the blades out in an orderly fashion. Merlin again inquired about their integrity. "You are sure these are the king's swords, correct?"

"Of course. That is what we were ordered to find, and so I assure you that before us are three king's swords, as per the mission," defended Unk as he snapped a salute.

Raleigh ruffled through his pocket and dumped three plaques on the table.

"You stole those too?" exclaimed Darwin.

Raleigh lit his pipe and as he drew strong, quick puffs into his mouth, he noted, "Assumed the wizard wouldn't believe us, so I figured if we are going to be thieves, may as well be thorough ones."

Merlin found comfort having Sir Walter's evidence that the correct swords lay before him. He arranged the plaques alongside their respective blades. "Beautiful, are they not?" asked the wizard. "Before us are the three ceremonial swords of the English kings. Here lie the blades of Temporal Justice, Spiritual Justice, and Mercy." He shifted from addressing the group to examining the swords. Almost talking to himself, Merlin held the sword of Mercy up for inspection and noted, "I had forgotten that the tip of this particular blade was so dull. I'll have to make some adjustments to it later."

Raleigh set his pipe on the table and asked Merlin, "Now that you have your swords, where are these friends you were talking about?"

CHAPTER 25 | The Demon Killers

DAYS HAD PASSED, and the time had finally come to put Merlin's plan into motion. When the boys could sneak away from their classmates, the abbey ghosts asked them back to Merlin's laboratory and the entire cadre of spirits, who they now considered friends, came to meet them at the entrance.

"So, you all trust Mister Merlin's plan? You really think we can kill the demon?" William asked skeptically.

Newton placed his arm around Will's shoulder and replied, "Lad, I fear there is no other choice but to try. I'm just as concerned as you are, but at this point, we don't have another option."

"And, don't forget, the wizard has arranged help; we won't attempt to kill that abomination alone," Darwin reminded the group, as Thomas turned the handle on the heavy wooden door that would take them into the cellar laboratory. "Merlin's friends are here, and though we have not met, it is in them that my trust and our hope now lies."

"No worries, I am here!" came the voice of Olivier as he drew up to the gathered group. The actor was waving his hand from behind Shakespeare and Unk, who were standing together.

Darwin gave a hard look to the late arriving ghost but only nodded his recognition of his late appearance. With the entire conspiracy assembled and without further delay, the naturalist turned toward the entrance to the wizard's lair.

The little group pushed through the arched doorway that gave access to the stairs down to the dimly lit room. Here the spirits had grown accustomed to Merlin's efforts at magic and enchantment. As their eyes adjusted to the ambiance of the candlelight, they could all see Merlin was engaged in a conversation with three figures the assembled ghosts did not recognize, at least by sight. The boys' shoes made a pronounced tapping sound on the stone floor as they were the last to enter the room. The noise caught the gathered apparitions' attention.

With little warning, one of the figures turned abruptly. Dramatically swinging an elaborate black cape off his right arm, he revealed a sword sheath affixed to his tight cummerbund waistband. His entire outfit from head to toe was black, including his well-polished leather ankle boots and oversized silk gloves. While he came towards the ghosts, they could see that beneath his black gaucho hat, a dark domino mask partially hid his expression. If not for the smile that graced his face and the lack of concern from the remaining apparitions about his approach, the ghosts would have been worried about his intents. Instead, as the figure closed the distance between himself and the group, his look became fully light and joyful as he pulled his sword and held it directly in front of his body. He practically danced his final length to Darwin and Newton, waving his blade like a conductor's baton. "Ah-ha!" he bellowed as he swung his weapon.

The tip of his sword caught the edge of Newton's shirt and, in an instant, the Mexican Fox had used the rapier to tear a perfectly sculpted "Z" onto the white lace cloth across Newton's chest.

Sliding backward, the man continued to swing his sword in the shape of a Z and exclaimed, "Behold. I am Don Diego de la Vega, but you may call me Zorro!" He laughed and exulted muted battle sounds as he spun around the floor, blade still swinging.

Newton placed his hand through the slit in his shirt and asked with some confusion, "Zorro, do you by any chance know how to sew? Seems like, in addition to my shirt, you've left your signature on nearly every available piece of fabric in the room." The others looked around and took in the torn tapestries, tattered tablecloths, and punctured flags.

"Ah-ha!" Zorro again called out rapturously but then pointed down his sword. "Sorry, no, amigo. Don Diego only makes the holes. He does not mend them."

A second shade stood beside Merlin and chuckled at Zorro's handiwork. He seemed genuinely amused at Newton's plight and Zorro's answer to his question. "And you are?" asked Darwin as the apparition's laughter brought attention to his unknown identity. The figure was dressed in a much brighter manner than Zorro. An oversized hat adorned with a feather sat atop his head but allowed the group to see his handsome face and carefully styled facial hair. His whip-thin moustache was perfectly kept and the goatee that sat against his chin was immaculately trimmed. A billowing burgundy shirt with an accordion neck and profoundly bold, brown, thigh-high leather boots could be seen below his medallion fencing cape. One arm was covered in the cloth, while the other was free to wield the sword held at his hip. But rather than draw the weapon, he removed his hat and placed it on Merlin's table before pulling a rose from his cape.

"Perhaps the better question is, 'Who are these rapturous expressions of womanhood?'" The man looked past Darwin, not even acknowledging him as the source of the inquiry while he lightly stroked his beard and continued to flirt. He fixed his eyes upon Lady Arbella, Glinda, Jane, and Anne, seductively addressing his rebuttal question to the ladies. An electric tension immediately filled the room. Without breaking his romantic gaze, he called in a heavy Spanish accent that dripped with passion, "Hola, mis amores. You are breathtakingly beautiful. So lovely, so delicate, and so captivating. I, Don Juan, am utterly devoted to you all. Please let me only bathe in the loveliness of these flowers I see before me, for never has there been such a bouquet for a mortal man to view." He bowed down on one knee, placed the rose in his mouth, and looked up to scan the women's faces to see if he should continue his flirtatious introduction.

"You do have a way with words, kind sir, but surely you can't be devoted to all of us," said Glinda, fanning herself with her hand and looking at Merlin, who furrowed his brow.

Don Juan captured the eyes of the enchantress, "But why not? There is enough of me to go around." The swordsman twisted his moustache while considering his options.

"Really, we are not interested," said Glinda, steadying herself, her intent and resolve.

"Are you speaking for all of us when you say that, Glinda?" Lady Arbella asked somewhat sheepishly, looking for permission to pursue the romantic moment and blushing a translucent red.

Anne wasted no time exerting her confidence. "She is definitely not speaking for me. Perhaps the witch is not interested, but please go on." Her voice had slowed, and despite being a little rusty on romance, she was quite the natural. "I haven't seen a strapping man like you in centuries." Now it was she who captured the gaze of Don Juan.

"Ah-ha!" cried Zorro as he sliced another of the room's curtains. "More cloth to the attack!"

"Pardon me? Anne? I've been beside you for so long. What is wrong, my strap?" Sir Walter asked with disappointment in his voice, redirecting the conversation away from Zorro and back to the queen and her apparent suiter.

Anne brushed off her friend's inquiry. "Oh, Walter, why...nothing at all. I had no idea you wanted me to notice, but in the future, if you would like me to...who knows?"

"*Nose,* you say?!! Of course. It is the only thing that you saw when you looked at me," boomed the final guest. As he turned towards the ghosts, the group gasped, taken aback by the enormity of his beak.

"Good God!" blurted Dickens, raising the back of his hand in front of his eyes to block his view.

Sir Walter Raleigh nearly choked on the smoke from his pipe. Speaking through a coughing fit, he bellowed, "Swordsman, indeed! That protrusion is incredible!" He seemed to completely forget Don Juan and Anne.

"Is that real?" asked William.

"No way," responded Rake. "It can't be."

It was clear that all the spirits and mortals in the room would have noticed the apparition's proboscis without his own direct acknowledgment, but now that he had called attention to his nose, they found it difficult to look away. While some of those gathered could not contain their shock, others sat silently in awe. Their mouths hung open and their eyes were frozen on the man's hooter.

Time seemed to skip several beats. It became impossible for anyone to acknowledge the precision cut of the guest spirit's hair or his distinguished outfit. No one noticed his perfectly tailored black jacket that was carefully accessorized with a large white lapel neatly folded over the collar. They overlooked the man's styled broad billowing breeches, paddock boots, and the details of the cape that hung around his neck. The silence that had gathered in this last introduction was deafening, and the stares gathered at the center of his face as if his nose had its own gravitational pull.

"I am not here to be made a spectacle, Merlin. It was you who summoned me and asked for help. If I am simply an oddity to be looked at, I shall make my farewells now!"

Merlin saw the hurt in the apparition's eyes and tried to intervene. "Cyrano, these fine ghosts mean no harm nor disrespect by their actions. They are inherently uncertain about us spiritually challenged in general. It is not your nose. It's your state, dear friend, that has them so out of sorts." He looked at the spirits with such an intense glare that it began to melt their frozen gaze. Indeed, recognizing the wizard's unspoken directive, the ghosts closed their mouths and shook off the initial amazement. They turned to each other and started talking about anything but the nose of their new colleague.

"Cyrano de Bergerac? What an incredible honor," Jane said as she curtsied towards the long-nosed spirit. "You must tell me of Paris and the French countryside. I have always wanted to visit."

De Bergerac straightened his collar, gave Jane a downcast look, and huffed, "If it was such an honor, a simple curtsey and an ounce of respect would have been a much warmer welcome."

"They weren't trying to be disrespectful or discrimina- tory," chimed in Zorro, attempting to recast the reaction of the ghosts in the room. Then, directly addressing Merlin directly, he began to elaborate, "Surely he knows all of these fine ghosts by their noble purposes and good intentions!" Zorro looked at the wizard, then Cyrano, and then around the room to the other spirits for affirmation.

At the word "knows," the French swordsman again growled.

"Nose?! Now you pick up where these others left off!" Cyrano waved out his hand to indicate his disdain for the entire room. "Your crude references to my strongest feature are not unnoticed, monsieur."

"Que hombre! You are onto my scent like a bloodhound finds his quarry. What can I say!" exclaimed Zorro as he slapped Cyrano on the back and dropped his attempt at appeasement. "Stop throwing a rabieta, amigo. After all, you have reason to celebrate. You'll be able to sniff out the demon before we even see him." Zorro smiled, looked at a still unmarked tapestry, and laughed. "Dios mio!" he exclaimed, rushing toward the hanging with sword drawn.

Jane placed her hand delicately on Cyrano's forearm and

looked up slowly into his eyes. "I meant what I said. It is a true honor to meet you. For what it is worth, I think your nose is distinguished. You are incredibly handsome."

The anger in the French swordsman's eyes faded and turned ever so slightly to sadness. "Perhaps I overreact," he said mildly. Jane's calming presence and compliment seemed to quiet Cyrano, restoring his sense of pride, confidence, and humor.

Don Juan again approached Anne and tenderly slid his rose across Anne's lips, down her chin, and across her choker. He had been talking to Shakespeare across the chamber from his newly formed love interest while Cyrano had centered the attention in the room on himself. The lothario slowly whispered to the spectral queen. "Hear my soul speak, the very instant that I saw you, did my heart fly to your service." Anne accepted the overture and sighed deeply. Don Juan bowed low and kissed her hand. Shakespeare, for his part, having written the words Don Juan delivered, gave his mouthpiece a satisfied thumbs up. Sir Walter, readdressing his attention back to the budding romance that was clearly unfolding, jiggled his pipe up and down in his mouth while puffing it in such a manner that smoke bellowed out from under his shirt though his sleeves and neckline. Had he been mortal, there may have been concern about an imminent combustion.

It was Merlin who interrupted the flowering romantic landscape that was growing around the room. "Dear colleagues, please!" He raised his voice above all of the conversations of the gathering. "While this meeting was a time for introductions, I in no way intended to become a matchmaker or this to become a fraternity mixer." He used a term he had learned from the choirboys who graduated on to college.

"Pity!" offered Olivier, thinking back to his time spent as a student at St. Edward's in Oxford. "They are a jolly lot of fun!"

Ignoring the actor, the wizard continued, "Please, gentle spirits, put aside 'amour' for a time and let us focus on our shared cause. These three fine apparitions have willingly and bravely come to answer our need or, more broadly, the world's need. They are among the greatest swordsmen of all time and imagination, and some of my truest friends. I say that so you know I trust them in all things. Alone, I feel any one of them would have a real chance to topple our adversary. Together, and all at once, they are assured of victory. Our enemy will fall to their skills and my swords."

"But of course," said Don Juan, winking at Anne. "It has been too long since I held real steel in my hands. It will feel good, even though it will take from me."

"Certainly," nodded a completely calmed Cyrano while still looking at Jane, who looked fondly back at the gentle soul.

"Ah-ha!" cried out Zorro, who whipped his sword through the air and with a flick of the blade launched an ethereal flower from a vase sitting upon a nearby side table. The bud flew through the air and was caught by Lady Arbella.

"Oh my," exclaimed The White Lady.

"God help us," held Darwin as he rolled his eyes and examined the three with some trepidation.

"I still wish we had a musketeer or two," lamented Dickens.

"The trouble they were experiencing in Notre Dame forbade it," said Newton, shaking his head. "It is worrisome; our concerns are coming to the point of disaster in many places and certainly beyond what is simply happening here."

Merlin had been leafing through his spellbook and excitedly opened to the page he had marked for the group as they had formulated their plan. "Here is the rest of our answer," he chimed, holding the page out for the others to see. "With this spell, I can create demon killers."

The wizard turned to the shelves that lined the walls of his laboratory and began systematically scanning each. He shifted his glance from the page he was holding to the items on the wall and back down as he sidestepped across the various cabinets, curios, and racks. Every few moments, he would grab a bottle, canister, or jar. Eventually, he dumped an armful of items onto the table and called for the group. "The enchantment is tricky and will require much concentration." He looked at Glinda, who nodded her concern as she fully understood the complexities that were about to challenge Merlin. "Many of the ingredients needed, I have in my collection: ogre nail trimmings, dandelion dust, a vampire fang, dragon scales, and the necessary liquid emulsifier to bind the other components. However, there are several missing elements that I'm going to retrieve from the Astral Apothecary."

Dickens rose immediately and without being asked by the wizard. "What if I take the princes and our choirboys to meet Dr. List? I feel like they would benefit from a more lighthearted trip." Edward, Rake, William, and Thomas all perked up at the notion of "lighthearted" and immediately voiced their support of the idea. As Merlin handed Dickens his scribbled list of remaining ingredients, the two met eyes. "This will work, Charles," he said, almost as if he was confirming the assertion for himself.

"Sadly, my friend, Nostradamus predicted it shall not. Still, perhaps we can recast the future if we act against what the fates had planned." With that, Dickens pushed the boys up the stairs and out into the abbey.

✦ ✦ ✦

The Darlingtons and the princes could all feel the energy coming from the apothecary as they approached. Dickens had told them of the unique nature of this store. It gathered ingredients needed for magic and medicine, all having been translated from the mortal plane to the ethereal. Looking through the store's window fronting the main terminal, the old-time pharmacy stood out even from the many other curious shops to be found in the abbey. Radiant colors, bright lights, and intriguing smells poured through the massive dungeon-like doorway. Whatever item one sought to find, Astral Apothecary provided both it and an alluring experience and startling destination for the visitor. Floor to ceiling oddities, exotic ingredients, and items of arcane intent covered the wooden walls. In addition, the buyer might pick up some aspirin and vapor rub for the more mundane of needs. Bright 'Deaddison' bulbs illuminated each shelf, so the shoppers could clearly see all the offered items. Many of the liquids seemed arranged to provide a spectrum of colors from the shop's back lighting, projecting hues around the shop to the bedazzlement of the eyes of any observer. The middle of the pharmacy had boxes of dried herbs and a collection of powders that could be dispensed from a single scooping station. Another section of the store had freestanding bins and barrels of a whole array of magical paraphernalia. The final section offered standard ethereal fare, mirroring items found in mortal pharmacies. Ultimately, to anyone stumbling into the store, it looked like a mix between an eclectic candy store, a local hardware shop, and a village mercado. To a true magician, however, it was a conglomeration of wonder and endless possibilities.

Even Dickens stood transfixed on the enchanting displays of colorful liquids. Glancing around, he felt as if he was walking within a prism and looking at the rainbow of a shattered visible light beam from within it. Lost to his fascination, the author only lost his reverie when suddenly startled by a loud pop that rattled the glass on the shelves and caused the shop's brilliant bulbs to flicker. As all spirits there turned to assess the commotion, they could see the remnants of a small explosion that had occurred behind the slightly elevated pharmacy counter. A small ghost, barely able to see over the counter, stood behind it laughing. He was still holding a beaker and a test tube in his hand. Smoke was clearing around him to reveal his enormous, frizzy, and disheveled head of grey hair. It looked as though he had placed his finger in an electrical outlet and received the shock of his life. Wide-rimmed black glasses sat at the end of his nose, though at a catawampus angle with a prominent vertical crack through the left lens.

"Woooow! That was exciting," the druggist said as he peered over the ledge in front of him.

Dickens seemed entertained, jabbing, "A failed combination, Dr. List?"

"You know me better than that, Charles," Dr. List responded with a wink. "I get bored easily and sometimes I just need to mix it up a little, if you know what I mean."

His perfectly pressed white lab coat was covered with a spattering of various colors and had a stitched name tag on it that read Herbert Archibald List. "What brings you and these young lads into the apothecary today?" he questioned.

"Dr. List, is there a section of ingredients for magical sword spells?" questioned Edward while thinking of the purpose for the visit.

The pharmacist looked over his glasses at all of the boys. "Is there a section for sword spells?" He paused to think. "Lads, each and every item in this store serves a host of purposes. A spell isn't so much about specific ingredients. I need to know what your purpose is and then I can guide you in the various combinations you could mix together to meet your end. Want to break a sword? Want to render it useless? Want to make one disappear? We can do all those things in a variety of ways using a multitude of ingredients. We just need to sort it all through."

Dickens shook his head. "We are easy today, Herb." He pulled Merlin's list from his pocket. "The wizard told me what to purchase and I already saw the dragon scales as I walked in.

We are going to need some of those and then each of the following. The author read the list Merlin had provided; sheets of bark from a weeping willow tree, a vial of horse sweat, three four-leaf clovers, and a good helping of bat guano."

Rake was appalled by the final ingredient. "Bat poop?"

"Magic isn't always pretty, boys," hollered Dr. List over his shoulder, "but you have to trust the process." He had grabbed a shopping basket and several small medicine jars to begin to gather up the requested items. With a quick trip around the store, the pharmacist brought the needed ingredients to the register. As he accounted for the last of the items, he leaned over to Rake. "I had exactly three four-leaf clovers left in the shop. Those aren't always easy to find. I'd say you and your spell are going to be lucky." With a twinkle and excitement in his eyes, Dr. List called out "Happy mixing!" and watched the group push their way out of the store's door.

"Mister Dickens?" asked Edward, "Am I mistaken or is the apothecary named Herb A. List?

The author stopped in his tracks and let out a long belly laugh. "Herbalist. I never thought of it, but I guess you are right, my boy. You are absolutely right."

✦ ✦ ✦

Edward took the brown shopping bag and ran it to Merlin, who beamed at the boy as he received it. Reaching inside, Merlin took out each item purchased and carefully lined them up beside ones already pulled from his own collection. "Ah, yes! Perfect, my friends. We are nearly ready," the wizard said gravely. The ghosts, boys, and apparitions gathered around the table as the magician reached for the horse sweat and poured it into a bowl. Sprinkling in dandelion dust and dragon scales, Merlin's face began to glow. He peered down into his mortar and continued to crush the ingredients with his pestle. The work continued as Merlin combined and recombined the items he had set out for use. After an hour had passed, the mage stopped abruptly and stood back from his work. "Zorro!" he said, "Quickly man, give me what I asked you to bring to this gathering."

The apparition shrugged, a bit confused, and reached into his black drawn cloth sack, pulling out an even smaller bag. "I have only this that you requested from my abuela," he replied. The swordsman seemed a bit confused.

Merlin looked at the package, untied the sack, opened it, and nodded his approval. "I love real Spanish chorizo and you can't get it here. He took what seemed to be a bit of sausage and popped it in his mouth, rolling his eyes in pleasure. The wizard then looked back at Zorro. "Sorry if the request sounded urgent. Your grandmother is a phenomenal cook, mi amigo. Glinda, could you put this away for me?"

Glinda paused and smiled a bit at the enchanter. "My dear," she smiled, "you have legs. Go on, you can put it up yourself." Merlin looked shocked and a bit embarrassed at his unthought out presumption but took the small sack and placed it on the shelf. As he walked back towards the table, Glinda nonchalantly passed the shelf and affixed a small note to the sack that read 'Merlin's Chorizo.'

Dickens laughed to himself at enchanter's behavior while Newton asked to ignoring ears if he might try a bit of the sausage later.

Merlin hesitated and then pulled a full iron cauldron to the edge of his workstation. He intensely studied the directions written for the final spells. Glinda knew how tricky and how demanding magic could be. She softened her approach to the wizard. "You know these incantations. Trust yourself." She reached out and touched his hand to offer comfort, but he knew she was right. He knew these spells. He was a bit timid because of the failed conjuring of the king, but magic swords were his specialty. He shook off the lingering hesitation and began to pour the ingredients he had mixed so thoroughly into the pot. Putting his hands over the cauldron, Merlin began to intone:

Hilt and blade;
Of good be made.
But more is needed still.
Grant me the might
To win the fight.
And with this steel shall kill,
A royal sword
The beast be gored
Its life forever lost
A deadly brand
Is in my hand
And death shall be the cost.

A mist rose from the cauldron, spilled over its edges, and climbed onto the table. As if it were alive, it crept towards the blades Merlin had laid near, releasing electric sparks as it contacted the flat surface. As the currents connected to the tip of the swords, a blistering orange glow shot towards the hilt of each weapon. Light surged through the metal, illuminating each sword in its entirety. A wind whipped through the room. "Hold tight, everyone," screamed Merlin above the noise. The blowing gust howled in seeming anger and then the room went black and still. Light and sound had been sucked out of the chamber like air from a killing jar. The blades were left glowing with indecipherable runes etched into their surfaces. A singular engraved inscription was left on each handle and glowed well after the rest had faded; "Hoc Est Mortis" it read. The mist slowly returned to the cauldron and disappeared.

Don Juan spoke. There was a reverence to his tone. "'Hoc Est Mortis.' It is Latin. It means 'With This Comes Death.'"

"Behold the demon killers," Merlin said quietly as each of the swordsmen picked up a blade.

"It is done," marveled Cyrano as he lifted his sword and swept it horizontally to admire its grace and beauty.

"Mi amigo," said Zorro, looking at the wizard. "Now *our* work begins."

CHAPTER 26 | Extinguishing Evil

IT HAD BECOME apparent that the tower's Ravenmaster was a true creature of habit, albeit many quirky ones. For weeks now, the ghosts of the abbey had been watching him, hoping that he would serve as a vessel to bring the demon out of the tower and into the streets of London. They had learned of this practice from Queen Anne who, like some of the other ghosts trapped in the tower, had witnessed it firsthand. The swordsmen had decided their duel with the beast would be best staged away from his current confines to prevent any meddling from his allied spirits. So, they waited and watched for their opportunity. Each evening, after leaving the tower, the odd yeoman would walk away from his work whistling as if in perverse homage to his lord. He would head to his home in a meandering manner, stopping to look in select trashcans along his way. Why these particular receptacles were picked on his walk, the ghosts never surmised, but they each seemed almost territorially his.

Every night, he would also proceed down Drewbury Street, an avenue known for high-end and toney men's fashion. There, he would stop and look in the mirroring shop windows. While gazing here, he would apparently try to match his reflected face to the heads on the store mannequins on the other side of the pane. It was almost as if he were trying to see what he would look like in their clothes but, again, his followers could only speculate on what he found in that looking glass. And, finally but invariably, he would approach the doorman at the "Red Iron" club, an establishment known to be frequented by elite and secreted mortals and vampires of all classes. He would try and enter but be consistently barred. The undead doorman always turned the Ravenmaster away, hissing under his breath in a Romanian dialect about his distaste for the approach and the threat of the demon. The trailing ghosts heard this exchange with regularity. The evil in the tower was clearly known to the night lords, and so, they tolerated the Ravenmaster's taunts to avoid a confrontation with his master. The mortal would leave the doorway laughing and call back to the angered vampire that maybe he would 'drink' with him tomorrow.

Arriving home, the Ravenmaster attended to his own birds that he kept caged in the back of his house. His collection was mostly crows but also included several pigeons and even a few bats. After cleaning the cages and ensuring proper food and water, he would sit and talk to them before snapping the neck of one and locking the rest in for the evening. He would then hang his coop keys outside his back door and proceed to his kitchen for his own dinner of fresh kill. It disgusted the trail that watched the routine, but they continued to follow, hoping the demon would appear.

The tracker this night was Sir Walter Raleigh. Like the other monitors that served to watch the Ravenmaster and all those involved in the planned death of the demon, he carried a small ethereal signaling device that Glinda had devised when she lived in Oz. It used to keep her attuned to the goings-on in Munchkinland and allowed the citizens of that tiny realm to call her as needed. Leaning against the side of the building and slowly puffing his pipe, Raleigh let his thoughts wander to the witch. "Living in Oz?" he mused, "Glinda never really lived, and Oz is a place of childhood fancy, not of the mortal world. But yet she claims its reality, and who am I to doubt her. Even we ghosts can be surprised and amazed in the face of magic," he thought to himself and slowly shook his head with no attempt to mask his amusement at his own surmise.

The sun was setting on another day, and Sir Walter watched the gates for the Ravenmaster's appearance. As Big Ben chimed the turn of the eighth hour, he stepped through his usual tower exit. It was instantly clear something was amiss. Raleigh fiddled with the button on his signal but held fast, wanting to make sure he had something of importance to report. This night, the mortal vessel to the tower demon was not engaged in his usual, purposeful walk. In fact, he pivoted and turned away from his traditional routine and path.

"Something of uncertain nature is happening," Sir Walter thought to himself. "What are you about?" The ghost decided to take a closer look at the yeoman. He quickly floated up into the trees that lined the street the mortal walked on. The ghost moved from branch to branch and tree to tree as a squirrel might jump during their own kinetic activities.

Seconds after Raleigh let those thoughts pass through his mind, the Ravenmaster bent forward, reeling in pain. He let out a muffled scream of torment and collapsed to the ground. A dark smoke arose, and, from nowhere, Jack appeared, looking every bit his dapper self. He stood over his servant, glancing down at his cramping form. A deviant smirk twisted his face, like someone taking pleasure in kicking his own dog. There was no doubt what had just happened. Raleigh recognized the elusive man in the distance. Just as the ghosts had expected, the demon, in his human form "Jack," had left the tower using the Ravenmaster as his vessel. His loyal servant had again made it easy to slip through The Binding as he had whenever the demon wanted to feed or pleasure himself with human consumption. "Come now, my pet," said Jack seductively, "Do not be so pitiful. Thank me for the pain I gave you." The demon waited only a moment before he reached down and grabbed the mortal lying at his feet, lifted him as a doll, and brought his face close to his own. "What, no gratitude?" Jack asked and again waited. "You disgust me," he said, looking into his servant's eyes. "You and all your kind are as nothing. Weak, foolish, and little but cattle to be fed on." With that last statement, the demon threw the man's body against the wall of the building they had passed. "Pathetic," murmured Jack as he began to walk away.

The Ravenmaster lay whimpering, but, in a last best effort to please his lord, he gurgled, "Thank you, master," before passing completely out.

"This is it," Raleigh murmured to himself. He had seen enough. He pressed Glinda's signal and hoped that it would serve its function well. The apparitions and ghosts who meant to be part of the attack now knew that the demon was out of the tower and moving. Through the tracker, those involved could trace Sir Walter's whereabouts and find him and, by proximity, the demon. He only hoped the others would catch up to them both soon. The ghost knew he could do nothing against Jack by himself or with any weapon he now held. He also knew the group, once assembled, had to attack quickly, for if Jack got a taste of the human flesh he craved before they got to him, the dark creature would be even more powerful and difficult to kill. Moreover, from the strength shown by the demon in the manhandling of the Ravenmaster, that goal clearly was already going to be a tall order in any event. Sir Walter followed the beast at a safe distance. He did not want Jack alerted to his presence, but he was careful not to lose the creature. The demon was quick and fluid in his walk. He looked lustfully from side to side as he passed by people enjoying the beautiful London night, unaware of the evil sneaking through it. "Whatever the purpose of the demon's walk, the wander could end as quickly as it started," Sir Walter thought. The spirits in the abbey needed to act now. Raleigh was sure of it.

Darwin was the first of the ethereals to find Raleigh. "I am here, Walter," he said as he came up from behind. Raleigh had abandoned the trees since sending out the signal and simply walked after Jack as any mortal would follow another. "How goes our quarry?"

In whispered tones, Raleigh responded, "So far, he seems content to simply walk, Charles. He is looking for something, but I do not pretend to know for what. Maybe he, like us, needs a confluence of opportunity: a desirable victim, a place to feed that would be private, and the dark to full secret the act. The mortals on the street are becoming few and far between. His needs are working to our advantage as distraction, but they will also cause him to strike soon. If our apparitional friends can just arrive without creating a city-wide spectacle, like Olivier and his 'flying skull,' there may still be hope." Sir Walter continued to pace the demon moving forward without looking back over his shoulder.

"Behold! I have arrived, and so, there is hope, my friend," came the voice of Zorro. His typical exuberance quieted. His voice was low and filled with death and purpose. He joined the two ghosts carrying his wizard-forged weapon in a black sack that he moved almost magically, blending it with shadow and cover. "That is he?' the swordsman questioned, looking forward to Jack, who had become the only visible body on the street ahead. The swordsman shrugged his shoulders, "Perhaps we meet him now. I have no fear of this creature with or without the others."

Darwin put a hand on Zorro and a stop to the inclination of the Mexican weapons master. "Let us wait. We may only have a single chance for this to work. We must be prudent in our approach."

Jack continued to walk along the deadened street. The hour had grown late and shops and cafes that were once lively with customers now had emptied. Only staff remained to begin their nightly closing routines.

Several more blocks passed without a variance in direction. The demon stayed on its course. Then, it happened.

Jack turned abruptly and darted into an alleyway that stood between two old brick buildings. The swordsman and ghosts hurried forward so as not to lose the demon's route. They, however, need not have worried about losing him at all. Before the trio even turned the corner, a soft and seductive voice filled the air.

"Come out...Come out...wherever you are..." Jack implored mockingly. "I am finding it tiresome to just walk. I prefer to play." It was apparent the demon had found them.

The three spirits turned to peer down the alley where the voice wafted out, and Jack had disappeared. It was a bleak, lengthy lane, dimly lit, except for a streetlight down at the back. It looked relatively narrow, creating somewhat of a bottleneck for those going in. The alley was not ideal for a single swordsman nimble of foot relying on guile, much less three of the same, all requiring space for movement. Zorro, Cyrano, and Don Juan would have been barely able to stand side-by-side as mortals without brushing up against the bricks of the surrounding buildings. Architectural archways and clothing lines hung overhead, while several small doorways, window planters, and trash receptacles lined the way.

"Do we wait?" asked Raleigh.

"I fear we can no longer do so. We are discovered. Even more, my blade wishes to taste blood. I can feel its soul vibrating in my hand," Zorro responded to Sir Walter while unwrapping the demon-killer Merlin had given him.

Both he and Raleigh looked at Darwin, who sullenly nodded his approval. "The others will come. I am sure of it," the apparition declared with certainty. "And, if not, they will miss the fun."

Amused, Zorro unsheathed the king's sword and pulled a second ethereal blade from his sack for safe measure. The steel he carried glinted in the moonlight, and the other ghostly weapon glowed. "Yes, my darlings,'" Zorro whispered to the swords. "It is time. I will quench your thirsts. You shall both drink deeply." The swordsman, a blade in each hand, led the way down the alley. The others followed behind, quietly and carefully as they attempted to locate Jack.

The demon stepped from behind the wall where the alley widened. The light of the lamppost behind his silhouette gave him an outline of light against a darkened continence and body. Jack sinisterly acknowledged those who approached him. "I loathe spirits who can't mind their own business. You, Raleigh, should know that, above all the others in your little herd." Jack opened his arms as if he were offering to embrace them. "After all, you've seen what I do to ghosts in the tower who don't keep to themselves."

Darwin stepped out from the back of the group to stand beside Raleigh as he confidently addressed Jack. "Abomination, I am never going to keep to myself. As I both lived and died so shall I not depart this earth until you are cast back into the pit out of which you crawled."

"Bold talk," spat Jack. "I know you, Charles Darwin. You are so much better with finches and iguanas. Why bother with the likes of me? Surely I don't fit into your areas of expertise."

Zorro ran his metal blade in an arc along the wall where he stood. Sparks flew from the brick as the blade appeared to sharpen against it. "My friend, you are quite right. Charles has no expertise here. It is I who, as you say, 'came to play.'"

"Excuse me. Have we met?" asked Jack with a certain incredulity as Zorro moved slowly forward. The action clearly caught the demon off guard. "Another ghost? Who...no wait, I can feel it. You are not a ghost at all. My good fellow, you have even less reason to be here than the rest of this vanguard. My desires with the mortal kind don't concern apparitions." The demon then turned back to Raleigh and Darwin specifically. "You two, however. You'd think that when you lost so miserably at Tower Green, you'd accept the fact that your hope to control the fortress is a fool's errand. Why not pass over? Find your peace in whatever afterlife you choose. Leave this world to me," Jack stated in a most conciliatory tone as he regained his composure. He clearly did not desire a confrontation with spirits and apparitions tonight.

"I am Don Diego de la Vega, and you will know me." Zorro scowled at the perceived slight in the beast's conversation. "In fact, your last thoughts on this earth will be of me, demon," stated the swordsman as he attacked. With speed and agility that seemed beyond the possible, Zorro's blade sliced through the air, apparently intent on ending the contest with a single stroke to Jack's neck. The demon, however, was equally fast. In the moment of Zorro's assault, it produced two weapons from under its coat. As with his assailant, Jack also carried rapiers of both metal and ether. He was ready, it now seemed, to kill ghost or mortal. He parried both of Zorro's attacking blades, steel and spirit, in an impressive, defensive move. Both Darwin and Raleigh gasped, fully amazed and fascinated with the swordplay they were seeing.

Zorro and the demon disengaged and circled each other. "You might find that swords do little but to annoy me, Don Diego. In truth, though you may not know it, you have already lost. When I slice through your body, you will have no last thoughts. You will simply cease to be. Forgotten forever."

"You may find that my blades surprise you," Zorro feinted an attack to the demon's right. In a move that was nothing less than acrobatic, he managed to fully shift his momentum in midair, spin, and thrust his steel sword into the demon's left arm.

The beast let out a howling cry of pain and anger. It fell back, dislodging the swordsman's weapon still in Zorro's hand. It crouched for a moment and then circled, clearly more concentrated on his opponent than he had been before. Shaking his head, Jack hissed. "That hurt."

"Surprised?" asked Zorro, allowing himself a small bit of satisfaction while still looking as concentrated on the duel as his opponent.

This time it was the demon's turn to attack. It matched the grace of Zorro's moves with pure ferocity. Blades rang as steel clashed with steel and sparks flew from the impacts. Ethereal tendrils escaped the strikes of spirit swords as well. Between the fire, mist, and the blur of movement coming from the entangled combatants, the fight took on the look of a choreographed dance being performed during a pyrotechnic display gone horribly wrong.

Another cry of pain split the two, apparition and demon, apart from each other. This time, Zorro had sustained the wound. His arm had been gashed by Jack's ethereal sword and from the opening, his life's energy was slowly seeping. "You are done!'" Jack spat at his heavily breathing foe.

"No creature, he is not," came a voice unfamiliar to and directly behind Jack. "He is far from done, and I have yet to start." Another swordsman stepped through a door at the back of the alley.

"Don Juan, mi amigo! I am so glad you could make the party," said Zorro with true warmth in his voice. "Though, as you can see, I have the festivity well in hand!"

"Indeed, Don Diego. I only interrupt because I promised to dance with the demon. As a man of honor, I must keep my word. So sorry to be late. I came as quickly as possible. I am afraid I underestimated the time it would take to move such a divine mortal weapon."

"Apologies accepted, though I also see that there are bruises on your neck and lipstick on your cheek. Were you perhaps in a delicate moment when the signal happened?" Zorro conjectured about Don Juan. Both ignored the demon entirely.

"All my moments are delicate, my friend," nodded the Latin lover. Zorro winked his understanding.

Jack watched the two with snarled interest and disdain spread across his face. As a snake would shed his skin, Jack's physical-self ripped apart, and the demon, in its true form, stepped out of its facade. The onlooking ghosts were horrified and the two swordsmen, reattending the fray, strengthened their fixed stance.

"You look so unsettled," hissed the demon in a contemptuous tone. "Did you think I would bother to fight you as a human? I want to make sure that this is quick and effortless so that I can continue my hunt for mortal meat. Unfortunately, I have grown tired of the futility of your attack and the sound of your insipid banter."

Like an angry bull, the demon began to stomp his cracked hooves against the broken pavement. The tentacles of his back began to shake and rose like the angry tails from a bed of scorpions. His nostrils flared in rage. His eyes glowed a deep red as they slanted into an angry gaze. His mouth opened to reveal his horrific, pointed fangs, and he flicked his forked tongue about his maw with menace. He issued a ghastly, hellish howl so loud it echoed and shook the panes of windows on nearby streets.

Don Juan whipped his magic steel through the air, and, like his companion Zorro, held a second blade of ethereal make to use in defense. Zorro looked to the Spanish swordsman across the small auto turnaround, now arena, at the end of the alley. The Mexican cocked his neck to the left and then to the right, settling his gaze on the demon. As if on an unspoken cue, the two apparitions attacked simultaneously. Like the Mexican swordsman, Don Juan's speed and skill were uncanny. He, at times, seemed to appear and disappear in his personal movement. His steel sword flew so fast it could not be seen, only heard as it ripped through the night.

Four times the trio engaged, and it became clear to both Darwin and Raleigh that the apparitions were having the best of the fight. While the demon was holding its own, Don Juan had opened gashes on several of its tentacles, and Zorro, with a flurry of swordplay, had managed to carve a "Z" into the creature's chest.

"Ah-ha," he crowed with the joy of battle as he finished his lettering handiwork.

"I will autograph his other side," called Don Juan to Zorro upon seeing the triumph of his engraved moniker.

Zorro and Don Juan may have ended the battle at that moment, but disaster struck suddenly and certainly to the Spaniard. A tentacle he had severed from the demon's back had slithered its way to his feet and wrapped itself around Don Juan's legs. He had clearly not anticipated its continued animation. The swordsman's stumble was momentary, but it left him vulnerable. In that split second, another of the demon's tentacles thrust itself down through the swordsman's calf. Don Juan came back up, and, in a miraculous show of grit and determination, extracted himself from the attack. The consequence of the misfortune could not be treated in the current circumstances. Like Zorro, Don Juan's ethereal presence would slowly seep away through the wound. For the demon, time was now an ally.

"Is it bad, amigo?" asked Zorro of his comrade.

"A mere scratch," answered Don Juan, leaning against the wall while holding his swords and eyeing the demon.

The beast was not without injury. Four of the demon's tentacles had been severed, and he was bleeding a black ooze from gashes on both arms, a leg, and a now gaping "Z" wound on his chest. On his back, Don Juan had managed only to cut in a "D" on his flesh before he tripped and fell. It, like Zorro and Don Juan, seemed content to rest and eye the swordsmen as they watched him.

A sound of new steel drawn from a sheath caused the entire gathering to look away from each other and into the darkness filling the path between the two buildings. Down the alley, a figure approached Darwin and Raleigh. "Did I miss anything?" came the voice of Cyrano. The Frenchman had arrived. He walked past the two ghosts with a nod and stopped in the center of the small area where the demon and other swordsmen had contested. He looked to Zorro and Don Juan and then to the demon. "Ah," he mused after finishing the inspection. "I see that I have. Pardon. It took quite some time to find the festivities. I'll be sure to make up for the delay." He then took the apparent respite as an opportunity to kick a severed tentacle away as it slithered towards him. It landed in a trashcan beside the demon, who snorted angrily. "I do not want to make this long. Jane awaits me so that I might read her my latest verse. I shall not keep her wanting!"

"Of course," seconded Don Juan. "We must keep priorities. I, too, have a lady to attend."

"Jane and Cyrano?' asked Darwin of Raleigh. Sir Walter simply pulled out his pipe, began to puff, and shrugged.

Zorro laughed from deep within his soul. "If truth be told, I am also obligated, shall I just say, elsewhere."

Cyrano began tapping the tip of his blade on the ground. "Messieurs," said the Frenchman, "it seems then we should quickly dispatch this thing standing before us and all be gone. While I do have an appetite for swordplay, my heart yearns for the taste of my lady's lips."

"Jane's lips?" asked Darwin again of Raleigh, who remained stoically puffing and again offered only a raise of his shoulders.

Cyrano looked at the demon and arched one eyebrow nonchalantly. "I offer you a quick and painless beheading now if you will save us all the time we waste if we duel." He continued to tap his sword on the ground while awaiting an answer.

"You are offering me nothing, swordsman," the beast coldly replied.

Before the last word left the demon's mouth, Cyrano was upon him, slashing, spinning, thrusting, and turning. Zorro and Don Juan both joined the fight as they could, depleted but still skilled beyond what all other specters might be capable of doing. As had been the case with his fellow swordsmen, there was no doubt the Frenchman was winning. The demon was faltering with every new onslaught. It was clearly only a matter of time before de Bergerac would claim the day. Time, however, was rapidly become a precious commodity. It was also taking a toll on Zorro and Don Juan. Their wounds were not in and of themselves mortal. Still, the accrued effect of their injuries combined with the energy spent using mortal swords in this combat was causing a final drain of their ethereal strength.

"Cyrano," called Zorro, "I am afraid you will have to finish this dance for me." And with that, the Mexican slumped against the wall. What life he had left was slowly seeping out of him. Darwin and Raleigh immediately made their way to the fallen apparition. Darwin attempted to bind his arm to bolster Zorro's ebbing existence while Sir Walter picked up Zorro's sword and stood over them both, should the combat come close.

Cyrano looked at his fallen friend and then to Don Juan, who still engaged with what little strength he had left. He too would fall if the contest did not end quickly.

It happened suddenly. "Time's up," said Cyrano, looking into the eyes of his Spanish friend. "Tell Jane."

"Cyrano, you fool. Do not..." Don Juan's words were never completed. At that moment, the French swordsman in a single mighty swipe cut deeply into the beast's arm, nearly severing it at the elbow. The act, nonetheless, exposed the side and back of the apparition. The demon took the move as an opportunity to plunge his ethereal sword through de Bergerac. Cyrano grabbed the sword and pulled it further into himself and out of the demon's hand as he fell.

"You have failed! You maggot," exalted the demon, his massive horns rising above Cyrano's crumpled body as he kicked the Frenchman's mortal sword away from his grasping hand. The beast roared with pleasure, and its broken and shredded tentacles shook and swayed in frenzied celebration.

At the same time, the demon dropped his own metal blade from the hand attached to his ruined arm and in that moment, the beast stood defenseless and distracted with his sense of conquest. It served Cyrano's purpose.

"You are mistaken, devil, he didn't fail," said Don Juan as he plunged his king's blade into the heart of the beast. Those were the last words the demon heard on that day. It crumpled to the ground. All present went still.

The swords created by Merlin had fulfilled their purpose, and all were dripping with a black tar-like substance. Darwin broke the quiet, picking two blades up and pulling the last from the demon's body. Don Juan squatted down by Cyrano and took his hand. "Tell Jane," the Frenchman said again. "Tell her that I loved her."

"Dear friend," said the Spaniard, "she already *nose*."

"Monsieur!" warmly whispered Cyrano. "Do you mock me?"

Don Juan just winked. He carefully placed the French-man's arms across his chest, laying him to rest. He rose and stood with Zorro and the two ghosts. They all bowed their heads, each alone in their own thoughts amongst the carnage and ruin. Raleigh was holding up Zorro and the Spaniard was using his sword as a cane. The massive remains of the demon dwarfed Cyrano's body that rested just feet away from where the monster had fallen. As they all looked on, the apparition's body became more and more translucent. The slow and subtle change progressed until, with a small puff of wind, their fallen friend disappeared.

Darwin felt utter devastation that yet again, they had lost a comrade in a fight. While a success, the completed plan had ultimately come at a dreadful cost.

"Don't feel sorrow, Charles," Don Juan gently stated. "Cyrano de Bergerac died a death of valor and as a loved man."

Zorro continued, "For the first time in his life, he was complete. For a weapons master, there is no greater departure." His words brought some comfort to the ghosts, but Darwin could only think of telling Jane. Don Juan volunteered to address her, but Charles knew he had to be there, too. The loss of true love was no less heartfelt to those who may have died, and perhaps even more so to those who were never really living. With Cyrano gone, the four turned and began the walk back to Westminster Abbey. It would not be long before the demon's body was detected by mortals, and none in the group wanted anything to do with that disturbing discovery. Moreover, there was still much to talk about. The tower was now theirs for the taking.

CHAPTER 27 | Recovery and Celebration

WORD OF THE encounter between the demon and the swordsmen spread quickly. The rats that lived in the alley took the information back to the tower. The birds that had nested above the where the fray had taken place chirped their knowledge to the martlets of the abbey. The ghosts wasted no time in alerting their comrades either. Utilizing the signaling device, Darwin transmitted word to those at Westminster that both the demon and their companion, Cyrano, were dead. He also called for medical aid to be on hand when they arrived back at the abbey. The survivors were in bad shape. Raleigh had one arm each around Zorro and Don Juan as they all retraced their steps to needed help.

When they arrived, a small crowd was waiting to greet them. In addition to many of the familiar faces, a larger gathering of the concerned and curious had assembled to see the 'demon killers.' Newton was waiting for the troupe as they stumbled into the north choir aisle of the cathedral. "You did it. Men, you did it," the mathematician said in awe, looking at Darwin and Raleigh. There was a brief pause as he assessed the injuries that stood before him. "Come quickly. The doctor is waiting, and our two fellows are clearly in need."

Zorro and Don Juan, now supported by both Darwin and Raleigh, followed closely behind Newton as he made his way to a large, marble memorial. Atop the stone slab sat the effigy of a medical doctor, lounging in his academic robe. The statue was surrounded by additional carved figures, both of man and angel. Inscribed into the rock was a lengthy epitaph, but all the swordsmen cared about was whether whoever this "Doctor Hugo Chamberlen" person was, that he still remembered his profession. They both needed help quickly to continue their existence and each knew it.

"They say don't believe everything you read," announced a voice behind them. As the group turned to look at the source of the comment, the ghost who had been standing to their back, and now before them, chuckled. He nodded toward the memorial and said, "If you ask me, it's a bit much. It all seems so dramatic and terribly overblown. Not sure if I am all the things inscribed there, but I am definitely capable of patching these wounds. Sit. Let me look. Isaac, did you bring the supplies?" The doctor was relieved to see that the mathematician had done as requested. Raleigh, who was still holding Don Juan, helped to lay the swordsman on an examination table neatly tucked behind the statuary. Darwin, who had taken over the help of Zorro, allowed him to collapse on to a similar platform a few feet away from where his fellow swordsman rested.

"Please hurry, my good doctor. We both have ladies awaiting our return and neither of us shall disappoint tonight," Zorro suggested in a most braggadocios manner just before passing out.

Unhooking the satchel he had strung across his chest, Newton pulled out a burlap sack. "Dr. List gave me an entire arsenal of remedies and surgical supplies. I don't have the slightest clue what any of this does," he remarked as he lined up the contents of the bag along the ledge of the memorial.

The doctor surveyed the goods and noted, "That List character is sharp. It is all that I need and then some. Now, please, if I might have a little space to operate." The ghost gestured the quickly congregating crowd back. The gathered spirits followed the doctor's directive and moved away from the wounded apparitions. The physician first stood beside Zorro, who was still unconscious. The doctor examined his arm, studying the injury inflicted by the demon's sword. "He was lucky," Chamberlen said. "While this wound is likely horrifically painful, it's a clean cut that did not open up any major areas of concern. I just need to pack it and stitch him up to prevent ethereal leakage. He will be in a sling for a while but will be back to dancing with that blade in no time."

"And holding fair maidens!" exclaimed Zorro, suddenly coming back to himself.

Clearly relieved for the medical attention, the swordsman watched with concentration as the doctor ripped the remaining cloth from his sleeve to expose the wound on his arm. Chamberlen then took a few of the vials and jars from Newton's collection and muddled their contents. "Should help with the pain and provide a bit of numbing for you," he stated as he dabbed the paste onto the wound. Then, he threaded a needle, ready to stitch the fighter closed. "You probably want to look away for this part," the doctor encouraged. Like a clothing designer, Chamberlen pulled together the open seam in Zorro's arm and began stitching.

"Por Dios!' the patient exclaimed before passing out again.

When the doctor finished sewing closed the wound, he held out Zorro's arm and admired his work. "Perfect, though it's going to leave quite the mark."

"Ladies love scars." Although Zorro mumbled, it was still clear his energy and flirtatious attitude were beginning to return.

"Now, let me take a look at what the beast did to you." The doctor left Zorro and stood over Don Juan. "I must admit, this is my first tentacle wound."

Don Juan raised his torn pant leg over the large gash he sustained. "Looks more like a deep and terrible burn. I'm going to stir up a healing ointment to seal this once I've sewn you up." The medical professional paused for a moment.

"Newton, give me that flask of yours."

"What flask?" asked the scientist who was leaning against a nearby wall.

The doctor simply held out his hand, waving for Newton to hand it over to him.

"Oh, this flask?" Newton said, pushing himself off the stone, pulling the requested item out from his coat pocket, and walking it over to the doctor. "It is just a medicinal to keep my nerves at bay."

"At nearly 200 proof, I should think it would kill your nerves, but thank you, Isaac." Then, turning to the swordsman, the doctor continued. "Now, my good fellow, take a sip of this." Don Juan put the flask to his lips and screamed in agony as the doctor began to stitch his calf closed.

"No numbing potion for me?" asked Don Juan.

"That's what the flask was for," the doctor flatly stated as he continued to tend the wound. The Spaniard looked to Newton, who simply shrugged and stated, "I rarely feel anything while drinking it." Believing the ghost and needing relief, Don Juan gulped.

"My friend, might I try it?" Zorro had now taken an interest. Answering for Don Juan, Newton took his flask and handed it to the Mexican. As the doctor continued to sew, Zorro took a swallow. "Ay!" he exulted before passing out again.

"Novices," muttered Newton, catching the bottle before it fell.

Just as the doctor had finished applying a healing cream and bandage to Don Juan, Jane rushed through the door and into the vestibule. She ran towards the Spanish swordsman, physically and emotionally collapsing into his arms in utter despair. He embraced her while she wept. As her breathing slowed and as she calmed her tears, he lifted her chin. Looking into her eyes, Don Juan softly whispered, "He left us while full of love, a love he had never known before. You changed his world, Jane, and he knew it." A transient look of peace graced her face. She wiped her cheeks clean with a handkerchief Darwin had slipped into her hand.

"I hear that the entire abbey is planning a celebration for the capture of the tower," she softly noted to her friends. "I don't know that I shall attend. I have no feeling of joy or celebration."

"You should come, my dear. It will be a commemoration of heroic sacrifice by a legendary warrior. He would not want you alone, and I for one do not want you to face his loss in solitude either," responded Don Juan gently.

Olivier, walking forward from the crowd, placed his hand on Don Juan's back, acknowledging his words and announcing, "But for now, you all rest. I will stay with Jane. When you all are better able, we honor the life and death of Cyrano de Bergerac and revel with the two bravest and most skilled swordsmen the world shall ever know. Come. We have a place for you to recover privately." No other direction was needed; the ghosts supporting the apparitions again gathered up their comrades and began their trek through the abbey.

Olivier stood to watch them go and then turned to Jane. "My dear," he said simply as he held her hand and sat with her on a bench.

✦ ✦ ✦

Music, laughter, singing, and the clanking of glasses were heard throughout the terminal. The jubilant commotion was coming from a single establishment: "Spirits." The tavern was a popular place for lingering souls and offered a cozy, unpretentious setting for stories shared and memories recounted. Through the smoky hue that lingered in the establishment's air, pool tables, dart sets, and a jukebox could be seen. All the amenities gave deceased patrons the feeling that they had stepped back into their lives to a place where friends gathered and good times were had.

It had been several days, and tonight, the bar was lined shoulder to shoulder with ghosts and apparitions waiting to celebrate the work of the swordsmen. Word spread quickly through the abbey about the nature of the fight, the defeat of the demon, and the tragic death of a comrade. It was critical to all gathered that the evening's celebration honor de Bergerac's sacrifice and his place on the team of combatants who had disposed of the tower's evil. It was needed to heal the emotional loss of a friend and the type of memorial Cyrano would have loved.

As patrons waited, the bartenders concocted specialty drinks made in honor of the two remaining swordsmen and the one departed. The night's specials included *Masked Martinis* made with tequila as a tribute to Zorro, *Passion Fruit Daiquiris* as a salute to Don Juan, and *Cyrano Sours* mixed with a variety of aromatics that demanded the drinker take a full snort of its smell in the nose before quaffing the libation. Sounds of the ice hitting the metal shakers added percussion to the joyful singing of ghosts as tunes poured from the jukebox. "La Vie En Rose" was being piped through the bar, with spirits using their best French accents to belt out the ballad as they danced and clinked their glasses together in celebration. Servers donning black suits held elaborate silver trays and paraded through the crowd offering a host of hors d'oeuvres. From *Brie de Meaux* and tarts to escargot and goose liver pate, the delicious bites would have made the Frenchman proud.

The swordsmen pushed their way through the tavern's front doors, and as patrons recognized their arrival, the bar went from pure raucous to utter silence in an instant. Standing before a packed house, Zorro and Don Juan were unsure of what to do next. Slowly, claps arose from the crowd, and within seconds, all the gathered ghosts erupted with applause, whistles, and bursts of appreciation. As if rehearsed, music started again and in a heroes' welcome, "We are the Champions" filled the bar's loudspeakers while the crowd, understanding the good humor, began to laugh. The gathering of souls split down the middle, creating a pathway for the entourage of heroes who proceeded through the ghostly aisle, pausing every so often to shake hands, welcome an embrace, or do a quick pose for their newest admirers. Zorro abandoned his sling and started giving simultaneous "thumbs up" and "peace signs" for all those who had photo boxes. Thomas had shown him these gestures as a tradition for the pictures his fans now routinely requested with him. His smile almost glinted in the spotlights of the saloon. Don Juan refused to limp through the crowd and grabbed woman after woman who had lined up for a twirl at the hands of the Latin lover. With each kiss stolen by his partners, Don Juan seemed to grow in strength and verve.

The ghostly group made their way past the surging crowd. A maître d' directed them to a private room set aside with a table long enough to seat all the invited conspirators plus two. At the front of the room, portraits hung, one of Stephan Hawking and another of Cyrano de Bergerac. Darwin took the seat at the head of the table and was flanked by the two guests of honor. The other ghosts and apparitions took a place at the table, leaving empty only those seats designated for the fallen. Waiters immediately appeared and moved through the group pouring glasses full of Graveyard Grigio, an ethereal white wine favored for toasts at important post-funeral events.

The private room that had been so filled with boisterous noise calmed as Darwin picked up his glass and stood. Even the crowd outside in the greater bar sensed a silent moment was needed and quieted, seemingly of their own accord.

"Friends, colleagues, and honored guests," boomed Darwin's voice. "I shall not bore you with long discourse over what has happened or what has been accomplished."

"Hear, hear!" called Olivier, raising his glass.

Looking at the thespian with a laugh he only half tried to disguise, the biologist continued. "I know you all are keenly aware of what has come to be and at what cost. Even so, we must take pause to pay tribute to our fallen: Stephan Hawking, as brilliant as he was brave, and Cyrano de Bergerac; no purer or courageous spirit will ever grace this world," Darwin lifted his glass.

"One for the homies not here!" exalted Newton. He had been clearly enjoying his flask of medicinal and drawing from time previously spent with the rap artist, Tupac, who had made his way to the abbey on a ghost tour from the United States.

"Yes, Isaac," Darwin allowed. "To our friends, gone but never forgotten." The entire crowd raised their drinks in unison, drained the contents, and slammed them down on the table with a sound even the mortals of the abbey may have heard. Waiters appeared again and flutes that had been emptied were refilled. "I also think it fitting that we all take a moment to thank our two champions." Darwin again raised a toast to the gathering. "Never have I seen, nor do I think anyone shall ever see, a braver or cleverer bit of swordplay then was witnessed against our adversary. Killing the demon was a feat that changed history and so shall be remembered forever." Following a dramatic pause, he continued. "Ladies and gentlemen, I give to you Don Juan and Don Diego." Again, the collective toast was punctuated by the slamming of the glasses.

"Ah-ha" crowed Zorro in acknowledgment, while Don Juan stood and threw roses that appeared in his hand from seemingly nowhere to Glinda, Queen Anne, and Lady Arbella. Each of the women took their gift from the swordsman with pleasure and a feigned swoon. Before he took his seat, he produced one last rose and walked it to Jane. He placed the rose before her, bowed, and gently kissed her hand. Merlin took note of Don Juan's gesture, shrugged, and pulled an entire bouquet of flowers out of his sleeve. He turned and presented the arrangement to Glinda.

"Oh dear," flirted Glinda. She rolled her eyes and brushed off his attempt to seduce her.

"Just an old stage trick, my dear." Merlin joined with her in laughter.

"I'm not sure that you'd be able to handle me, Merlin, even with all the tricks in the books." She glowed, seemingly charmed by Merlin's attempt.

And so the night went. Despite the absence of Stephen and Cyrano, all of the ghosts present were ready to smile again. The small group that had so intimately experienced the loss and trauma of the last few weeks merged into the larger gathering of merrymakers and set down their concerns for the evening. Zorro had drawn a large circle of spectators around him while he reenacted the fight to the cheers of all. Don Juan sat with his own admirers and read from a book of poetry he had penned while recovering. Olivier and Newton clung together, drinking and singing loud songs out of key. Sir Laurence had somehow convinced Isaac to let him wear his powdered wig. Both seemed entirely amused by the arrangement. Shakespeare sat on a bar stool performing "slam poetry" to a small group who snapped their fingers in appreciation. Darwin and Raleigh had entered into an arm-wrestling contest refereed by Unk, much to the delight of Anne and Arbella. Sir Walter seemed to be winning, all the while puffing his pipe furiously. For her part, Jane sat with Dickens, sipped wine, and watched the throng of revilers. Charles sat quietly next to her, attentive to his companion's needs, but not entirely himself while doing so.

"They are all going to have headaches tomorrow," observed Jane, breaking the silence.

"Indeed," answered the author. "Except maybe Anne. She may not have a head at all."

Both laughed at the idea before feeling a pang of guilt at

finding humor in the misfortune of the kind queen.

"Charles?" asked Jane. "You don't seem quite yourself tonight. Are you troubled by something? Is there anything I can do for you?"

Dickens closed his eyes and thought for a moment. "There is nothing, Lady Jane," reflected the ghost. "Just feeling the night and my age, I suppose." He looked at his companion and offered a reassuring nod.

"If there is anything, you will share, won't you?" Jane pushed the point.

Dickens answered, picking his words carefully. "If there is anything, it won't be a secret, my dear." He laid his head back and closed his eyes yet again. "Can you hear Newton and Olivier singing?" he asked in jest.

"Yes," answered Jane. "They're awful."

So simply stated, neither ghost could contain their amusement and laughed out loud for the first time that night.

CHAPTER 28 | Brewed Awakenings

THE NEXT MORNING, the two swordsmen stumbled out of the bar into the abbey's terminal with pounding headaches and ringing in their ears. Zorro had taken off his signature mask and replaced it with a pair of mortal sunglasses he had found. Had the abbey been open for tourists at this early an hour, they would have seen the floating eyewear zigzag across the main chapel. Don Juan, still holding a glass of ethereal wine, beckoned his colleague on. "Come, my friend." The Spaniard drained his ethereal copper cup in a gulp and threw the empty vessel over his shoulder, letting it clatter back toward the drinking establishment.

While both staggered on, Zorro stopped at a just-opening newsstand and picked up a copy of *The Ghostly Gazette*. The headline story read, "The Swordsmen Celebrate and Mourn." Cyrano, Don Juan, and Zorro had posed for a picture the night before the duel, and now that photo served as a memorial for their bond and the sacrifice de Bergerac had made. Zorro flipped the page of the bestselling ethereal paper and found yet another story about the death of the beast. Don Juan, on the other hand, was less concerned about what *The Gazette's* reporters had portrayed and was more interested in what the mortal world knew of the last few days. Looking down into a discretely placed recycling bin, the swordsman found a single copy of *The London Times,* the city's biggest daily newspaper for the living. Inspecting the black and white print, Don Juan rubbed his eyes to ensure he was seeing things right. It was worth the necessary energy to lift the physical paper. Once in his hands, Don Juan quickly flipped through the first few pages before exclaiming, "Diego!" He was the only one who called Zorro by his simple given name. "I do not understand these English papers. Surely finding a demon's body slain on the streets of London would be front-page news. It is nowhere to be found. The entire paper is consumed with accounts of the king's swords being taken from the tower. That is certainly a story to tell, but it also is not the only story worthy of publication."

In a much calmer demeanor, Zorro, who suspected he knew what had occurred, looked over his sunglasses at his companion. "Juan, the police can't have the people of London knowing that a demon existed in the first place. It would cause utter fear and panic. It is clear, therefore, whoever found the body of that abomination quickly discarded it to guarantee no one else would find out about its death or their discovery."

"True. Yet, I would have liked the notoriety of being one of the elusive demon killers who slayed the beast," fantasized Don Juan. He then noted to his friend in mild lament. "They make films about you, so you have nothing to worry about. I exist only in books, my friend, and don't forget we exist solely because of mortal affections. The potential of being dubbed a true hero among our human admirers would solidify an eternity for my existence."

Zorro patted Don Juan on the back and said, "You don't need a headline. You will exist forever as mortals love you. As for being a hero, look at what we just did. We stopped evil in this world by killing the very creature that would have brought it into being. I don't need a newspaper to tell me how great our work was, and neither do you."

After taking a moment to acknowledge what was said, Don Juan rubbed his temples and then turned to Zorro. "I think I need coffee." The two made their way to Ghostly Grinds. From what they saw, they were not the only ones in need of a few stiff cups of joe this morning. Inside the shop, many of the ghosts they knew were gathered around a long table just in view of the window. Pulling up chairs, the swordsmen joined the morning coffee club.

When they had settled into their seats, Dr. List slid a small box down the table. "Take two of these. Figured both of you might need a little extra assistance this morning." He winked, while the others continued their ongoing conversation.

Dickens looked up from his journal where he had been scribbling thoughts. He carefully removed the tea bags from his mug before noting, "To be honest, I am a little embarrassed it took us so long to go after the demon. The key was nearly an impossible task." The author spoke to the table at large and then looked directly to the swordsmen. "You two were magnificent."

Sir Walter Raleigh was alternating puffs from his pipe with sips of his espresso. He glanced over his cup at Dickens and abruptly set it down on its saucer. "I cannot but agree. Still, remember, we also needed a weapon."

"Therefore, the additional accolades belong to Merlin for the creation of the demon killers," Dickens picked up on Raleigh's thought.

"Hear, hear!" regaled Unk, "To Merlin!" he raised his coffee and drank it completely down, with the rest of the group following him. Merlin, sitting quietly, nodded his thanks.

"Moreover, my good people, if you think about it, there is no way that the message the king gave when he died would have ever truly unveiled the location of the key. Edward and Rake were burdened with the inconceivable: to pursue something that they knew nothing about, not what it was, not where it was. I'm sure their father meant well, but the king sent those children on a wild goose chase for centuries." Dickens offered his thoughts while signaling a server for another cup of his choice of phantom brew.

Olivier put down his scone and defended the king. "I am quite sure the king would have preferred to stick around long enough to provide further clarity for his boys, but death has its own timeline, now doesn't it?" The actor looked from face to face and then added, "Even more, let's not forget the king was a victim of the demon and his infernal plans. He had to be careful in what he relayed."

"Without a doubt," Newton replied. "He didn't get to deliver the full message before his death. The man died whispering 'Pass them.' Pass them where? Pass them to the left, pass them to the right? Pass them..."

"'Pass *then*' you mean?" asked Carl. The recently deceased beefeater was casually sitting against the wall sipping his own coffee and listening to everything that was being discussed. "The ritual demands 'pass *then*' be said," the tower guard stated again with the sound of absolute certainty.

Distracted and noticeably perplexed, Dickens dropped his cup and it shattered across the floor. "That's not what the princes said that the king stated at all."

"'Pass them' is what he said. The princes have recounted that story to us more times than we can count," Unk retorted.

"I am not questioning their account," the beefeater was quick to reply. "They heard 'pass them,' but as someone who has dedicated their career to honor the history and ceremony of the tower, I can tell you, they heard wrong. The king probably said 'pass *then*.' It is part of the ritual of the keys."

"What does that even mean? 'Pass then?' That makes even less sense," Newton argued.

"Unless you know the tower. Then it makes perfect sense," Anne replied. She had heard that same dialog every night for nearly 500 years. And hearing it again in a new light, a connection struck her. "Could it be that simple?" she asked the group, not really expecting an answer.

"What is simple?" hollered Newton. "Can someone please

explain what you tower ghosts seem to already understand?"

"Certainly, Sir Isaac," the beefeater calmed. "It's part of our locking up tradition at the tower. Each night, at exactly 9:53 p.m., guards make their way to the tower sentry who queries, 'Halt, who comes there?' The Yeoman Warder responds, 'The Keys.'"

Newton was visibly frustrated. Raising his voice, he asked, "And you didn't think to tell us about this? Keys are literally on display every night, and you didn't think that was important information?"

"Calm down," the beefeater implored. "The key in the ceremony is a mortal reproduction that has been replaced in function with many physical keys. The key that would lock Acheron is in no way an earthly key."

"So then how is any of this relevant?" Dickens interjected.

"It is in the ending," answered the beefeater. "As the warder responds, 'The Keys,' the sentry, again, asks a question. 'Whose keys?' The response depends on the current monarch sitting on the throne, but regardless of whose name is said, the conclusion remains the same. As the royal's name is spoken, the guard announces, 'Pass *then*, all is well.'"

"That's when we hear the gates of the fortress close," Anne added.

"Precisely. Just like the ethereal gates to Acheron and Arcadia, this ritual mirrors the pledge the king took with the Templars so long ago. They entrusted His Royal Highness with the unimaginable responsibility of regulating the passage to hell. The unobtainable ethereal key we have been chasing is responsible for opening and closing The Binding in the exact same way the tower keys open and close the tower gates," concluded the beefeater.

Anne elaborated on her earlier epiphany. "What if what the king said was accurate?" The group looked further confused. "What if 'pass them' is indeed the message needed to retrieve the ethereal key, and the king knowingly placed the key in the warder's possession for safekeeping? 'Pass **then**' may signify the location and moment that the keys would be directly accessible to the princes or those of royal blood if only they provide the correct directive, 'Pass **them**.'"

It made plausible sense, but Unk was perplexed. "How is it that no one else in the tower dealt with this?"

"We knew the information, but the connection was not made, if, indeed, it is the right connection," Raleigh now cautiously interjected.

"Oh, it must be!" suggested Anne.

"Even more, had we seen the relationship, the key would still have been impossible to retrieve. Only kings or Templar descendants would be able to take responsibility for the key away from the guards. No one else would have power," Raleigh piped in. "And the princes themselves have no mortal voices to do so. Living beefeaters would not be able to hear the command."

"But we now have a way to let the princes be heard through the mouths of Templars!" exclaimed Dickens.

"For God's sake!" Newton called out. "I think we have it. And with the demon gone, the key is truly within reach."

"On the contrary," Darwin argued. "The demon may be gone, but evil is not. He has raised an army of dark spirits who know his goal. Even if they do not wish to unlock hell as the demon did, they will fight to prevent any good coming to the tower that might force their souls through back those gates for good. We will need a plan to make this attempt at the key."

"Another plan?" asked Zorro. "For God's sake, indeed!" the swordsman mumbled to himself while laying his head on the table in front of him. "I'm going to need another cup of coffee."

"Rest easy, my good man." Darwin assured, sliding a fresh cup of coffee to Zorro. "You and Don Juan need to recover. See what trouble you can get into with Merlin and Glinda. Others like you seem to have traveled to the abbey. Perhaps an Affirmation of Apparitions meeting is in order. We ghosts will handle this."

CHAPTER 29 | The Passing of the Key

IT WAS YET another effort of planned distraction, but with the help of their friends in the choir, the boys made it out of the abbey and into the tower for the ceremony. Thomas and William had positioned themselves amongst the crowd of observers waiting in anticipation for the ritual of the keys to begin. After shuttling the rest of the ethereal group into the tower, Rake and Edward were last to take possession of their now-familiar mortal vessels. All of the boys were nervous and distracted. William and Rake, in particular, seemed to be struggling with the moment. They had been isolated from the group since they had arrived. Thomas had tried to assure them, "No worries. This will be over before you know it."

"You are right, my brother," smiled William. "It will all be over soon."

Thomas looked at his brother with some concern. He really was not acting himself.

Alongside the boys stood the ghosts of the abbey, who had long anticipated this moment. They had all agreed with Darwin when he announced he'd be "damned" if he was going to miss the retrieval of the key.

Lady Arbella, however, was nowhere to be found. "Where is she?" Raleigh wondered. The ceremony was set to begin within minutes.

Suddenly, a young girl from the crowd screamed, "There! A ghost!" The entire group of onlookers spun in unison to see where the little girl was looking, and, sure enough, there stood the perfectly formed projection of Lady Arbella.

"It's The White Woman! Hurry, get the camera," hollered another man from the crowd. Sir Walter Raleigh rolled his eyes in amusement. It was in fact "The White Woman," and her appearance was in no way a coincidence or accident. In fact, she had exaggerated her dress, wearing more of a ball gown that looked worthy of an appearance on the grand staircase at a museum gala or with the sailing of the Titanic. Her hair was curled into an elegant updo and her arms and neck were dripping with ethereal jewels. She slowly sashayed across the path in front of the crowd, posing like a movie star on the red carpet. Every few steps, she would pause her walk to bend one leg back and with heel up, deliver a coquettish glance over her shoulder to tease a non-existent group of paparazzi. Still, every single onlooker with a camera was trying to capture this sighting of the famed tower ghost.

After her walk through the now excited crowd, she had returned to her more discrete form, invisible to mortal eyes to allow for its calming. Nonetheless, curious to know what the images taken looked like, she stepped behind some of the tourists who were scanning through the photos they had snapped of her arrival. To her chagrin, she was not in a single one. Instead, the best that appeared, if anything was captured at all, was a glowing orb or a small cloudy fraction of her outline. "What in the world? I put far too much work into my appearance tonight. In fact, it's the best I've ever looked," she said mostly to herself but also to any of the other spirits who were listening. Frustrated, she was determined to make it into a mortal photo. She snuck up behind yet another family, this one posing for a group picture. Exerting almost all that remained of her ethereal energy, she waited for the click of the camera before releasing her physical manifestation. This time, however, her efforts were amply rewarded. As the family reviewed their latest snapped image for quality, the mother screamed and nearly passed out. In between this mom and her son stood a fully visible and quite striking image of The White Woman. She was preening, blowing a kiss, and was the very image of a self-obsessed teenage girl at Halloween.

"Gads," said Darwin, looking over Arbella's shoulder.

"I could not have done better myself," added Newton, whose head popped up from behind Darwin also to look at the photo. He then puckered as if to prove it. Dickens shook his head at the duo and continued to watch the crowd.

"It only takes one good shot to leave a lasting impression," Arbella suggested. She was more than pleased with herself, yet she was utterly exhausted. Few understood the energy it took to manifest into a visible form as The White Woman did. She loved to tease guests by appearing and disappearing throughout the tower, but she had to be purposeful in her display. Once she showed herself, it would often take days to regain her strength to deliver a sighting again.

The excitement of The White Lady's appearance was silenced, when at exactly 9:53 p.m. the bells chimed, and the Chief Yeoman Warder began his slow and stylized walk from Byward Tower towards Traitors' Gate. He was dressed in a red, knee-length coat, wore black leather gloves and boots, and had on starch-straight black slacks as a statement of his discipline. On his head sat a flat-top black velvet Tudor hat with a brim surrounded by ribbons of red, white, and blue tied into immaculate bows. In one hand he held a lantern, and in the other hand, he gripped the royal keys.

Once at Traitors' Gate, the chief met a regiment of foot guards, who served as his escorts throughout the rest of the ceremony. The troupe was equally outfitted to their charge, dressed in elaborate red military coats, secured with white belts. Guns were slung over their left shoulders and tall black bearskin caps adorned their heads, held in place by an uncomfortable-looking strap that rested just below their mouths. One of the guards reached out to take the yeoman's lantern. From there, they all proceeded to the outer gate, where all on-duty paid homage and respect to the keys with a salute. The Chief Yeoman Warder then began the trek to lock gates at several locations throughout the fortress. After making these rounds, the guards proceeded through Water Lane and towards Wakefield Tower. A sentry kept watch and carefully observed the progression. He and the gathered crowd laid in wait within the eerie shadows and stillness of the Bloody Tower's archway. As the escorts approached with the chief warder, the pounding of boots and military cadence gave way to the noise of the spectators' excitement. The demonstration that all had come to see began as if the onlookers did not exist. Thomas and William, the princes inside, stood towards the front of the crowd watching, with the spirits of the abbey standing alongside them.

The guard at the gate called out in a booming voice, "Halt! Who comes there?"

In a confident and purposeful tone, the chief warder responded, "The Keys."

"Whose keys?" inquired the guard.

"Queen Elizabeth's keys," noted the Warder.

This was it. Thomas had been waiting for this very line. He released himself completely to Edward's control. Fully possessing his mortal vessel and without hesitation, the long-dead prince, who had become king with his father's murder, cried out, "Pass them!" Instantaneously, a powerful clap of thunder rattled the tower walls and the moon seemed to blink for a moment, darkening the site of the ritual. A white haze swirled up from the ground to engulf the escort of guards. This group of mortal men came to an impossibly slow crawl, still moving through their reality, though almost unperceptively to those looking in from the realm of the ethereal.

From the mortal body of the Chief Yeomen Warder stepped a hurried but kindly looking spirit. He, like his vessel, was dressed in military regalia, though it was a bit disheveled as though he had been sleeping in it. He continued to straighten his jacket and hold down his hat even as he did an about-face and stared into the crowd. "Say it, again," he commanded.

It worked. Thomas' voice and Edward's command had caught the attention of the spirit warder, and their efforts had a magical effect. Edward stepped out of Thomas' body and stood in front of the ethereal yeoman. Making eye contact with the ghost, Edward took a deep breath and repeated his command, "Pass them."

The spirit dropped to his knee, exclaiming, "Your highness. I have dutifully waited for centuries for this moment, consigned to silent possession and passing through the history of the chief warders since the death of your father." The guard's hat shifted suddenly, but he quickly caught it before it fell.

"Rise," instructed Edward, overlooking the ghost's embarrassment at being caught off guard in this long-awaited moment.

"It is an honor to serve you, my lord," proclaimed the yeoman. He reached into his pocket and retrieved an ethereal key. It exuded a blinding glow as if it, itself, had just awakened from a long slumber. As the ghost held the key out for Edward, he noted, "With this key comes great responsibility. God speed, my king." A large grin spread across the spirit's face. His work was done. Edward took the key from his hand, and the ghost disappeared back into formation, taking his place inside the chief warder. The magical spell that had filled the space evaporated as quickly as it had begun. The demonstration that had moved mere inches during the exchange regained its full momentum.

The summoning guard shook his head in confusion, and to gain clarity asked again, "Whose keys?"

"Queen Elizabeth's keys," responded the chief warder with more force and a hint of frustration that the guard was repeating lines and creating a disruption in the ceremony.

"Pass, then. All's well." The four guards walked towards the Bloody Tower archway, as the chief warder commanded them to present arms. Raising his hat from his head high into the air, he called out, "God preserve Queen Elizabeth." The other guards responded with a roaring "Amen."

The tower clock struck ten with a strongly gothic yet calming tone. The melody of the bells complemented the delicate sound of a bugle player performing "The Duty Drummer." With music accompanying his walk, the Chief Yeoman Warder began his march back to the Queen's House to hang up the keys. The guards were dismissed and at exactly 10:05 p.m., the tower staff beckoned the visitors towards the exit.

Lingering towards the back of the group of tourists, Thomas could not contain his excitement. "I can't believe this! We did it!" Holding the key in his hand, he looked with exuberance at the entire ghostly gathering. From inside, Edward truly felt like he had stepped into the role of king the moment the key was in their possession.

Sir Walter Raleigh held his pipe in his hand and slapped Darwin on the back with the other. The biologist vigorously shook Dickens' hand. Raleigh then grabbed Lady Arbella, spun her under his arm, and then gracefully dipped her before planting a kiss directly onto her pale lips. She giggled, pushed the English nobleman away, and ran towards Thomas. Shakespeare looked on at the gathering as an audience would enjoy the stage. Newton gazed at the place where Hawking fell and raised his flask and a toast to his friend.

Olivier walked up beside him. "He would have reveled in this victory, Isaac." The actor said it knowing what the mathematician was thinking.

"Indeed, he would have, Laurence." Newton acknowledged his company without looking in his direction.

A silence grew between them. "Might I have a taste from

your flask?" Olivier asked after a moment spent.

Sir Isaac passed it and said quietly, "To Stephen."

"To Stephen," Olivier repeated, taking a sip.

Lady Arbella had met Thomas, pinched his cheeks, and then wrapped him into her arms, bouncing the boy up and down in her embrace. Lady Jane and Queen Anne, each on one arm of Unk, were beaming as they approached the boys. The old soldier, for his part, was beaming at the opportunity to escort the two ghostly ladies into the midst of the gathering.

"Unk," commented Darwin, "It looks as if you are about to burst for your company!"

"Aye, Charles, so I am!" replied the military man.

"The capture of the key is a great achievement," pronounced the naturalist.

"Indeed, it is, my friend. But for me, there is more. With what little I remembered, my Lady Jane found me in the military records of the 'Battle of the Bulge.' I know who I am!" Unk practically laughed the last statement.

"Jane!" remarked Darwin. "I had no idea you had taken such a project on."

"The idea came to me on the visit to the King's Library. The records there are quite complete. It was nothing at all to locate him with our dear Unk's help."

"Well, sir," Darwin turned to the solider. "Out with it. Who am I addressing?" All the ghosts in the group had stopped their chatter and stood silently for the response.

"Sergeant Bartholomeus Cubbins, at your service." Unk immediately snapped to attention, delivering a salute to the group.

After a beat of quiet, Darwin raised his hand in a symbolic toast and announced, "Cheers to Sergeant Cubbins. Well met, sir!"

"Hear, hear!" called the rest of the ghosts.

Even in all of the commotion, William stood silent with Rake still inside. Only Jane took notice of the young boy's lack of emotion and excitement. "Good friends," she announced to the group, still observing William out of the corner of her eye. "While this is indeed a time of great joy, we can celebrate later. Let us return across The Binding. We must allow these boys to get out of the tower and to their school before they are noticed gone. Please, let us go."

"Jane is right," echoed Darwin. "We need to get back. Danger lingers here, and we must attend to our young wards. The demon's soldiers are still about from their day or will be waking into their night. We are lucky to have not yet been seen by them, and I do not trust their dispositions without the control of the demon. The key must be taken from here until we fully have control of it and the situation inside the tower." Dicken concurred.

"Charles and Charles, you can both be so dreary. If you two had stayed back at the abbey, we all could be dancing a jig right now!" roared Sir Walter Raleigh as he placed his pipe back into his mouth. Still, he followed the naturalist's directive and began moving toward the exit in a slight dancing motion. The others followed behind, making their way back across the courtyards and to the border of The Binding. For all, it was difficult to believe that the chaos of the last few months—not to mention the last several hundred years—had finally been resolved. The demon was dead, work to truly heal The Binding could be started, and the key was now in the possession of those in the abbey for safekeeping. The true significance and magnitude of the events that had just transpired were immense. They had all helped fulfill the promise and pledge that the English monarchy had given to the Templar Knights so long ago. In the face of it all, the group became silent.

"Here, Mister Darwin," Thomas said, holding the key out as he walked beside the ghost. "You should have this!"

"No, Thomas. You hold it for a bit longer," Darwin replied. "That key is a thing of magic, and I am uncertain of what may happen to it should it not be in the possession of a rightful heir. I want Merlin to look at it and see if there is any insight he can offer before anyone else touches it. The key was to be held by royalty and their operatives. Let us keep to that until we know it is safe to do otherwise."

Thomas nodded at Darwin as Edward added his own agreement from within. Then, looking toward his brother, who was alone and slightly outside of the group, he excused himself and proceeded to catch William to walk by his side.

The collective of spirits lingered just inside the exit to the tower wall. It was close to the boundary of The Binding but a bit obscured to mortal eyes. They would leave when the last family had left the fortress to minimize the chance of detection for the boys. Gone was some of their initial emotional boisterousness as Darwin's words about the tower's evil spirits really took hold. This was not yet a safe place. As they waited, they murmured quietly between themselves.

William, still isolated, gazed at the key hanging in Thomas' hand. "I can't believe it. It doesn't seem real," William said as he quietly approached his brother. He put out his hand and asked, "Can I hold it?"

Thomas paused for a moment. Mister Darwin had seemed concerned about letting others touch the key. "Though," he thought to himself, "Rake is royalty, and William is Templar. It should do no harm."

"Pass them," whispered William.

Before Thomas was even aware of what he was doing, he hesitantly handed his brother the key. Doing so, he looked at William. Immediately, he knew something was amiss. He was sure of it and instantly regretted turning the key over.

"At last, it is done," William muttered to himself in a low voice not his own nor Rake's, the ghost he held inside. Staring at the key, as some prized possession in the palm of his hand, William smiled in a manner so feral that his brother took a step back.

Jane gasped, seeing what had transpired, and rushed to

Darwin, who was standing with Raleigh and Unk. "Charles," she cried, breaking the relative silence of the group. "Something is wrong with William."

"Brother." It was Edwards' voice coming from Thomas. "What is wrong?" Controlling his mortal vessel, the elder prince used it to approach Rake in William's body. Thomas seemingly put his arm over William as Edward intended to console Rake. "A job well done, Rake. Father would be so proud," he affirmed.

Glancing back up at Thomas, William slipped his one arm around his brother's waist and quietly responded, "A job very well done, indeed." As the last word left his mouth, William used the arm he had around Thomas' waist to pull his brother closer to his body. His other hand pulled a jagged dagger out of his coat pocket, and he plunged it into Thomas' chest. Thomas' eyes grew large in confusion. Fear and helplessness flooded his face as he dropped to the ground, first, on his knees and then awkwardly straight back, his legs trapped beneath him. Thomas stared at the hilt and handle of the dagger that protruded from his shirt, now saturated with blood. A small pool of red was forming around him.

"What did you just do?" Thomas begged.

"I finished what you all started," answered William. He took his foot and placed it on Thomas' abdomen. He pushed the blade of the dagger deep into his brother's body and then pulled it out.

Edward escaped Thomas' mortal body and frantically ran to Lady Arbella, who froze, horrified by the trauma that played out before her. Jane went to Thomas and knelt beside him, trying with all her might to place ethereal pressure on the gaping wound in the mortal boy's chest. "No!" she screamed in panic and terror.

"Am I going to die?" Thomas looked up with tears in his eyes.

Darwin, Dickens, Raleigh, and Unk rushed towards

William, uncertain what to do but clearly aware of the diabolical grin painted across the mortal boy's face. They pulled up short while he stared at them in amusement, and Thomas struggled to breathe. A shout from another mortal turned William's head, the joy on his face fading. A yeoman, who apparently saw the two boys from a distance, was signaling for help.

Dangling the key, William turned his back to the ghosts and walked out the exit, away from the tower. His whistle seemed to serenade a stirring of evil. He paused only to discard Rake's ethereal body from the mortal boy. The young ghost immediately fell to the ground. William and the thing inside him, however, faded further and further away from the tower and into the darkness. All the while, the whistled tune he slowly blew continued to echo back through the shadows.

The ghosts moved away from Thomas' body as mortals began to cluster around the boy. Security personnel worked feverishly to revive him, and the arriving police immediately closed the doors to the tower, hoping to keep whoever committed the act inside.

"It was him. I am sure of it. Living with his stench for hundreds of years, a man doesn't forget." Raleigh was pacing and puffing furiously. "How could this have happened?"

Darwin was staring back into the tower along the route they had egressed. "I do not know. We both saw the work of the swordsmen. There was no doubt of the result."

"I will kill it myself, next we meet," Raleigh claimed. He was beyond anger.

Unk held Lady Jane as she sobbed, and the others looked to Darwin for direction.

"We are trapped here," stated the naturalist flatly.

"Worse," added Newton, walking up to Darwin's side. "We are found out, Charles. Look." The mathematician was pointing out to a courtyard at a group of evil spirits walking toward them. Their ethereal blades were already drawn.

Darwin hesitated only for a moment. "Walter? Anne? Arbella?" asked the erstwhile leader, turning back to the group. "You all survived here. Is there a place we can go?"

"There is," said Anne, "but they will follow if we cannot distract them."

In an instant, a yell filled the air. "Run," bellowed Unk as he charged into the courtyard and the oncoming dark force. He had no sword but struck the group with such ferocity and intent they stopped their approach, two falling in retreat. "Run!" he roared again before turning back to his foes.

Anne moved. "This way!" she implored. The group of abbey ghosts began to follow.

"We need to help him!" cried Olivier. "He moved only a step toward the courtyard before he felt Darwin's restraint. Unk let out another scream. A sword had found him.

"He has made his choice. Don't give up what he is giving us, Laurence. You must honor his decision." Darwin and Raleigh both yanked the actor in the direction of Anne. Yielding to the inevitable, he obeyed the shove of his friends. Newton also hesitated and then followed.

"I am Sergeant Bartholomeus Cubbins!" was the last shout they heard from the ghost before Unk passed to the beyond.

EPILOGUE

TWO CURATORS STOOD in front of the King's Swords in the tower's Crown Jewel Room. Since the break-in, the employees and guards had been on high alert. Attempting to restore the swords' presentation, the curators had been tasked with replacing the stolen plaques taken by the thieves during the raid. Abigail clung to the metal markers in one hand and her other held a host of screws.

Hugh began to attach the first of the three small signs. As he reached for another screw, he reflected, "I am still astounded the stolen swords were the replicas."

"Unbelievably fortunate. A blessing, in fact. It just doesn't make any sense. The only time we display the replicas is when the swords go in for their annual cleaning, and that's not for several more months" noted Abigail, as she watched Hugh attach the other plaques to their case. Trying to make further small talk, she added, "It was a relief to see Carol back at work today. I was worried sick about her after her attack."

"Did anyone ever figure out what happened to her?" inquired Hugh as he closed his tool kit.

"Not a clue. Carol doesn't even recall. She said she was finishing her usual evening rounds, and everything went to black." Abigail shook her head in disbelief before continuing. "When they found her, she was unconscious with no idea of why she passed out."

Hugh shuddered. "A real concern for her, I'd wager."

✦ ✦ ✦

Dickens sat alone in a room secreted in the back of the tower library. It was dark and quiet, with a thin stream of light shining from a burning candle onto a small collection of books. Utterly despondent, his tears and bouts of hopelessness were met with confusion and rage. He paced back and forth in a repetitive, self-soothing nature. Squinting his eyes, he stared at his desk and at the pages of his journal. He became fixated on the haphazardly scribbled notes he had made. "How could I have read this so wrong?" Dickens asked himself. "How did I so cavalierly dismiss Nostradamus' predictions that so clearly suggested the horror that just happened? I thought we were being so careful. I was so confident we were keeping the boys safe."

He flipped furiously through the pages, seeking three verses that burned in his mind. The first quatrain now leaped from the paper with a sense of urgency.

The moon is obscured in deep gloom, his brother becomes bright red in colour. The great one hidden for a long time in the shadows will hold the blade in the bloody wound.

Licking his thumb and forefinger, he continued to search for the next entry. He found it written at the top of a tattered, yellow page, midway through the notebook.

The ancient work will be finished, Evil ruin will fall upon the great one from the roof. Dead they will accuse an innocent one of the deed, The guilty one hidden in the copse in the drizzle.

As he turned to the last entry he had written, Dickens' heart sank to depths he had never known existed.

In the city of God there will be a great thunder
Two brothers torn apart by chaos while the fortress
*   endures.*
The great leader will succumb.
The third big war will begin when the big city is
*   burning.*

"How did I not see it; how did I not know?" Dickens muttered to himself. "I thought to protect the boys from everything but each other." In that moment, Dickens screamed in frustration, recognizing again the magnitude of the group's choices and mistakes. "God forgive us. We let him out. It has started."

✦ ✦ ✦

The photograph of Lady Arbella was evaluated and officially declared a hoax to the public. The forensics lab of the Baker Street Division knew otherwise. "Something is happening in the tower," the examiner told her supervisors privately. "Arbella has never been so bold as this. And there was also the incident with the boy." Her captain simply nodded his agreement and took the evidence file from the hands of the lab technician. He was confident his superiors would also want to see the information.

✦ ✦ ✦

In a small fishing village located on the northernmost coast of the Isle of Man, a community elder looked down into his augury bowl and gasped.

A young man rushed into the room and broke the silence of the day. "It is happening. We can wait no longer."

The old man looked up at the intruder and closed his eyes, hoping for one last moment of peace. As his eyes opened, he stated "Prepare the others."

✦ ✦ ✦

Famine, disease, war, and death.

✦ ✦ ✦

Thomas bolted up from where he lay and gasped.

APPENDIX | Main Characters, Historical Events, and Culture References

(page numbers indicate first appearance)

221-B, *pg. 154*: A nod to Sherlock Holmes, using the numbers of his address to replace the Baker Street Detectives' badge numbers in this story.

Albert Einstein, *pg. 91*: (1879–1955) A physicist and mathematician who developed the theory of relativity and gained fame for his mass-energy equivalence formula $E = mc^2$. He won the Nobel Prize in Physics in 1921.

Anne Boleyn, *pg. 209*: (1501–1536) Boleyn served as Queen of England from 1533 to 1536 as the wife of King Henry VIII. She was crowned in an elaborate celebration at Westminster Abbey on June 1, 1533. After she failed to give birth to a son, a would-be future king, Anne's marriage began to suffer. The public scrutiny against her also grew, as she was often blamed for her husband's tyranny, mocked as an impure queen, and considered worthless in her inability to produce an heir. Despite her husband's affair, Boleyn would later be charged with adultery, incest, and treason. Anne was sentenced to death and beheaded on Tower Green at the Tower of London.

Archbishop's Park, *pg. 148*: A public park that is located in Lambeth North, London, near the River Thames. The park offers sports fields, walking trails, and picnic areas.

Baker Street Detectives, *pg. 154*: The name given to the Scotland Yard Detective Bureau in the book responsible for investigating supernatural activity in England. Baker Street is where Sherlock Holmes resides.

Basilica of Our Lady Guadalupe, *pg. 249*: One of the most important symbols and pilgrimage site of the Roman Catholic Church, the Basilica of Our Lady Guadalupe is located in north Mexico City, Mexico.

Beefeater, *pg. 125*: These guards, also known as Yeoman Warders, are the protectors of the Tower of London. Historically, they were tasked with guarding prisoners and the British crown jewels. Now they mainly function as cultural attractions, tower tour guides at the tower, and as fixtures at royal engagements in England. There are twelve beefeaters.

Beyoncé (Beyoncé Giselle Knowles-Carter), *pg. 78*: An American singer, songwriter, and actress who rose to fame as the lead singer of the 1990s girl group Destiny's Child and now performs as a solo act.

Big Ben, *pg. 148*: The nickname associated with the iconic Great Bell, clock, and clock tower located at the north end of the Palace of Westminster in London.

Bloody Tower, *pg. 8*: One of 21 towers that comprise the Tower of London. Originally named Garden Tower, this location controlled the main river entrance of the fortress. The Bloody Tower is where many prisoners, including Sir Walter Raleigh, were held and the location where the two princes, Edward and Richard, were believed to have been murdered. The princes' ghosts are believed to haunt the tower.

Brass Mount Battery, *pg. 166*: An area of the Tower of London, located underneath Martin Tower near the northeast corner of the inner wall.

Buckingham Palace, *pg. 184*: One of the most iconic buildings in England, Buckingham Palace is located in the city of Westminster. It serves as the residence of Her Majesty the Queen and is one of the last remaining working royal palaces in the world. It serves as the site for celebration and mourning for the British people.

Byward Tower, *pg. 301*: Now used as the main entrance for visitors, Byward Tower sits at the southwest corner of the Tower of London next to the moat.

Caesars of Rome, *pg. 44*: A title given to the absolute leaders of the Roman Empire dating back to 27 BC.

Ceremony of the Keys, *pg. 96*: This ancient ceremony is performed each night at the Tower of London. It is the most well-known tradition at the Tower and is believed to be the oldest military ceremony in the world.

Chapel of St. Hubert, *pg. 168*: A gothic chapel located in Amboise, France, in which Leonardo DaVinci is buried.

Charles Darwin, *pg. 4*: (1809–1882) Darwin was a geologist, naturalist, and biologist who is known for the theory of evolution, now considered one of the foundational concepts in the scientific community. Darwin has been referred to as one of the most influential humans in history, earning an honorary burial at Westminster Abbey in the north aisle of the nave.

Charles Dickens, *pg. 3*: (1812–1870) Dickens was a social critic and English writer, often referred to as a literary genius and as the greatest novelist of the Victorian era. His classic works include *A Christmas Carol, A Tale of Two Cities, Bleak House, David Copperfield, Great Expectations, Little Dorrit, Nicholas Nickle-by, Oliver Twist,* and *The Pickwick Papers.* Charles Dickens was buried in Poets' Corner at Westminster Abbey.

Chief Yeomen Warder, *pg. 297*: The head of the Yeoman Body, responsible for ceremonial duties during events such as Constable Dues, Opening Ceremony, and the Ceremony of the Keys. The chief is also in charge of the 36 other Yeoman Warders.

Coronation Spoon, *pg. 195*: Considered the oldest object of the Crown Jewel collection, the coronation spoon is dated to the 1300s. Historically, the spoon is used during the anointing stage of the coronation ceremony for British royals. During the service, the spoon is filled with aromatic holy oil that is poured onto the monarch's head, chest, and hands.

Crown Jewel Room, *pg. 112*: The Jewel House is a vault located in the Waterloo Block at the Tower of London. It contains the British Crown Jewels, a collection of over 23,000 gemstones that adorn regalia, jewelry, and artifacts used in royal ceremonies and traditions.

Crusades, The, *pg. 46*: A number of holy wars fought between Christians and Muslims and started to gain control of places considered sacred by both groups. Eight major "Crusades" took place between 1096 and 1291. The wars were bloody conflicts carried out in the name of God.

Cyrano de Bergerac, *pg. 257*: (1619–1655) An author and a duelist, de Bergerac (full name: Savinien de Cyrano de Bergerac) is best remembered for the numerous fictional characterizations of the man. He inspired Edmond Rostand's drama *Cyrano de Bergerac*, which exaggerated his life. He is portrayed as a joyful and talented swordsman with an extremely large nose.

Don Diego de la Vega "Zorro," *pg. 254*: (c. 1919) Zorro is a fictional character that was created by Johnston McCulley. His character first debuted in McCulley's novel *The Curse of Capistrano*. He is usually depicted as a charming, masked hero, skilled as a swordsman and horseman. Zorro is the secret identity of Don Diego de la Vega and is commonly referred to as "The Spanish Fox."

Don Juan, *pg. 255*: (c. 1630) Don Juan is a fictional character portrayed often as a womanizer or seducer of women. He was first presented in Tirso de Molina's Spanish play, *El burlador de Sevilla y convidado de piedra* (The Trickster of Seville and the Stone Guest). Jane Austen was particularly fascinated by the character, noting "I have seen nobody on the stage who has been a more interesting character than that compound of cruelty and lust."

Dr. Hugo Chamberlen, *pg. 284*: (n.d.–1728) Chamberlen was a renowned medical doctor who spent his career working to protect people from fevers and treating babies born with various illnesses. A memorial statue was erected in Chamberlen's honor at the North Choir Aisle at Westminster Abbey.

Dungeon, *pg. 118*: Many people were held in small rooms within the Tower of London while they awaited trial and/or execution. These "dungeons" were designed to isolate the prisoner. One infamous cell which is commonly referred to as the "Dungeon of Rats" was located below water level and completely dark, and would draw in rats from the River Thames at high tide. These rats would proceed to feed on the prisoner while they waded out of the water.

Duty Drummer, The, *pg. 304*: Every night for the last 700 years, the Yeoman Warders have completed a ritual known as the Ceremony of the Keys at the Tower of London. As part of that ceremony, the Chief Yeoman Warder and his escort halt at the steps at the Bloody Tower and the officer in charge gives command to present arms. The Chief Yeoman Warder then raises his Tudor bonnet and pronounces "God preserve Queen Elizabeth." The rest of the guard answers "Amen" as the clock strikes 10 p.m., and The Duty Drummer then sounds "The Last Post" on his bugle.

Excalibur, *pg. 61*: A legendary sword most commonly associated with King Arthur and his rise to power. The reference is often a nod to Sir Thomas Malory's 1485 work, *Le Morte D'Arthur,* yet Excalibur was present in Geoffrey of Monmouth's 1136 book *History of the Kings of Britain* and in Chretien de Troyes' 1160 poem *Conte du Graal* and many other literary works.

Ghost Princes, *pg. 16*: The ghosts of the two princes, Edward V and Richard, Duke of York, are believed to haunt the Tower of London. The spirits of the young boys can be seen by spectators wearing their white night shirts and playing on the castle roof near the Bloody Tower. The sound of children's laughter filling the grounds and the castle halls have been reported.

Glinda The Good Witch, *pg. 62*: Glinda is a character from L. Frank Baum's novel *The Wonderful Wizard of Oz* where she is referred to as 'The Good Witch of the South.' In the 1939 film version of *The Wizard of Oz*, Billie Burke portrays Glinda, who on screen is known as 'The Good Witch of the North.' Her character has been portrayed throughout literary, cinematic, and theatrical adaptations, such as productions of *The Wiz* and *Wicked*.

Guy Fawkes, *pg. 218*: (1570–1606) A soldier, Fawkes is most notably associated with the attempted assassination of King James. Commonly referred to as the Gunpowder Plot, Fawkes and a group of conspirators planted and planned to detonate explosives under Parliament. His plan was foiled when a tip led to Fawkes and the gunpowder. He was tortured and later convicted for high treason. Drawn from the Tower of London to Old Palace Yard at Westminster, he was hanged and quartered as an example to other would-be traitors.

Hamlet Reference, *pg. 187*: Holding the skull and reciting lines is a nod to Shakespeare's play *Hamlet*. In Act 5, Scene 1, an iconic moment in theatrical history is played out, as the character Hamlet holds out a skull and exclaims, "Let me see. *(takes the skull)* Alas, poor Yorick! I knew him, Horatio, a fellow of infinite jest, of most excellent fancy. He hath borne me on his back a thousand times, and now, how abhorred in my imagination it is! My gorge rises at it."

Heathrow Airport, *pg. 185*: United Kingdom's premier international airport, located in London, England. It is also commonly referred to as London Heathrow.

Holmes Detective Agency, *pg. 28*: This agency is a reference to the character of Sherlock Holmes, a self-described consulting detective. Holmes and his assistant, Dr. Watson, investigate mysteries and crime by employing brilliant, if not fantastic, methods and deductions. Many of the investigations begin at his address of 221B Baker Street in London. The *Guinness Book of World Records* lists Sherlock Holmes as the most portrayed movie character in history.

Isle of Man, *pg. 7*: The Isle of Man is a self-governing British Crown dependency located in the Irish Sea between Great Britain and Ireland. The presiding King or Queen of England holds the title of Lord of Mann. The island has been occupied since before 6500 BC. In 1266, the Treaty of Perth made the island part of Scotland under the Treaty of Perth.

Jane Austen, *pg 35.*: (1817–1775) Austen was an English novelist who often based her books on women's dependence on marriage for social status and economic security. She's best known for her novels *Sense and Sensibility, Pride and Prejudice, Mansfield Park,* and *Emma*. Posthumously, many of her novels have since inspired other literary works and many film adaptations. Austen was buried at Winchester Cathedral and later immortalized with a plaque at Poets' Corner in Westminster Abbey.

Kensington Palace, *pg. 185*: Located in Kensington Gardens in the Royal Borough of Chelsea and Kensington in London, this palace is the birthplace of Queen Victoria and has served as a residence to young British royals for more than 300 years.

King Edward IV, *pg. 17*: (1442–1483) Edward served as King of England from 1461 to 1470, when he was overthrown and Henry VI took the throne. Less than a year later, in 1471, he regained his title and served again as king until his death in 1483. He left behind two sons, Edward and Richard, the oldest of which took the throne before being deemed illegitimate, at which point Richard III was named king and the two young princes went missing from the tower. His body was laid to rest at St. George's Chapel at Windsor.

King Henry VIII, *pg. 186*: (1491–1547) He served as the King of England from 1509-1547. He is often remembered for his six marriages, disagreements with the pope that led to his dissolvement of convents and monasteries, and for being "the father of the Royal Navy."

King's Diary, *pg. 228*: While many royals throughout history kept personal logs, journals and diaries, this reference is a fictional nod to such a historical relic.

King's Library, *pg. 199*: In the book, the King's Library is located at the Tower of London. This collection actually exists in the British Library and is considered one of the most important collection of books, pamphlets, and writings from the Age of Enlightenment.

King's Swords, *pg. 251*: Three swords used in the processional during the coronation ceremony at Westminster Abbey. The collection includes the Sword of Mercy (also known as Curtana), the Sword of Spiritual Justice, and the Sword of Temporal Justice. Now part of the Crown Jewels of England Collection, the swords reside at the Tower of London.

La Vie En Rose, *pg. 288*: The song that defined the career of French singer Edith Piaf. The song was written in 1945 and was released as a single in 1947.

Lady Arbella Stuart, *pg. 211*: (1575–1615) Often referred to as

"The White Woman," Stuart secretly married William Seymour without the permission of King James. The couple was imprisoned and planned their escape. Arbella escaped, dressed as a man, but was later recaptured and sent to the Tower of London where she refused to eat, fell ill, and died. She was buried at Westminster Abbey; her lead coffin placed directly on top of Mary, Queen of Scots' casket. Her ghost is said to stalk the Tower of London. Visitors report feeling chills, being tapped on the shoulder, or smelling her pungent perfume as they catch a glimpse of the elaborate white figure pass.

Laurence Olivier, *pg. 33*: (1907–1989) Olivier was an English actor and director. He was a staple on the British stage and starred in more than 50 films. He is often remembered for bringing Shakespearean roles to life. Three of the five films he directed in his career were dedicated to his love of Shakespeare, including *Henry V, Hamlet,* and *Richard III.* Often considered one of the greatest actors of his generation, his body now rests in front of Shakespeare's memorial at Westminster Abbey in the south transept.

Laws of Motion, *pg. 30*: Sir Isaac Newton founded three laws of motion. First, the law of inertia states that every object in a state of uniform motion will remain in that state of motion unless an external force acts on it. The second law focuses the rate of change in an object's velocity, defining it as proportional to force which equals mass times acceleration. Newton's third law details conservation of momentum, noting that for every action there is an equal and opposite reaction.

Leonardo DaVinci, *pg. 167*: (1452–1519) DaVinci is best known as one of the most prolific artists of all time, famously known for his works such as the *Mona Lisa, The Last Supper,* and *Vitruvian Man.* Perhaps DaVinci is lesser known for his significant contributions to diverse fields including architecture, science, engineering, and literature. He is believed to have sketched many modern-day inventions including the parachute, helicopter, and motor vehicle. Born Leonardo di ser Piero da. Buried in Chapel of Saint-Hubert in France.

London Times, The, *pg. 293*: Founded in 1785, *The Times* is a British national newspaper that is printed in London daily Monday to Saturday and supplemented by its sister paper, *The Sunday Times*.

M. Lisa, *pg. 168*: A play on Leonardo DaVinci's portrait, *The Mona Lisa*. This piece is often considered to be the most well-known and referenced work of art in the world.

Mad Hatter, *pg. 58*: A quirky, fictional character, first depicted in Lewis Carroll's *Alice's Adventures in Wonderland*. In the book, he is simply named 'The Hatter,' but is referred to as 'mad' by other characters in the book and in a chapter about a 'mad' tea party. The popularization of the name 'Mad Hatter' is believed to be attributed to the saying "mad as a hatter" which pre-dates Carroll's works.

Madame Tussauds, *pg. 77*: Tourist museum that houses life-size wax figurines of famous historical and fictional characters.

Martlets, *pg. 23*: A small bird of the swallow family that is often used in English heraldic art. The seal of Westminster Abbey contains five golden martlets.

Marylebone Rd, *pg. 82*: A London street most well-known for the presence of Madame Tussauds Wax Museum.

Memorial Gardens, *pg. 184*: These gardens were created in 1901 in an effort to pay homage to Queen Victoria, who had died earlier that year. Comprised of formal flowerbeds, the garden is laid out in a semicircle around the Queen Victoria Memorial monument.

Merlin the Magician, *pg. 55*: (c. 1136) Merlin is a legendary wizard first appearing in Geoffrey of Monmouth's *Historia Regum Britanniae.* His character is featured throughout medieval poetry and Arthurian legends and has been a significant part of various literary, film, and television works. He is often portrayed as a man born of a mortal woman and demon, thus inheriting supernatural powers and abilities. Merlin became a mentor and advisor to King Arthur, creating the enchanted and powerful sword 'Excalibur' for Arthur's use. Merlin is believed to have been bewitched or killed by the Lady of the Lake and buried in a magical forest.

Monument of King Edward IV, *pg. 186*: A monument of King Edward IV, in St George's Chapel at Windsor.

National Archives, *pg. 185*: The official publisher and archive for England, Wales, and the UK government. The archives house many historical and iconic national documents.

Nostradamus, *pg. 4*: (1503–1566) Born Michel de Nostradame, Nostradamus was a medical doctor who tended to plague patients throughout Europe. After a psychic awakening, he began to prophesize predictions of the future, which were published in his 1555 book, *Les Propheties.* Many believe he accurately predicted many historic tragedies including Hitler, John F. Kennedy's assassination, September 11th, and the atomic bomb.

Notre Dame (Notre-Dame de Paris), *pg. 250*: Located in Paris, France, the Catholic cathedral serves as a symbol of faith, French Gothic architecture, and culture.

Order of Assassins, The, *pg. 46*: Began in the mountains of Persia and Syria in about 1090, just before the first crusade. The name was bestowed on them by their enemies in Syria. The order became a threat by capturing and inhabiting several mountain fortresses throughout this region. Specialized tactics and psychological warfare were often used by the assassins to force their opponents, including Crusader leaders, to submit rather than seeking to fully eliminate them. Mentions of Assassins were preserved within European sources—such as the writings of Marco Polo—where they are depicted as trained killers.

Oz, *pg. 62*: A magical setting first depicted in L. Frank Baum's novel *The Wonderful Wizard of Oz*. In total, 14 full-length Oz books were written with him as author.

Parliament Square, *pg. 164*: A tourist attraction and square located in Westminster, London. The square is surrounded by many official buildings including the Palace of Westminster, Houses of Parliament, the Supreme Court, Westminster Abbey, and executive offices. The square contains multiple statues of statesmen and notable figures.

Poets' Corner, *pg. 36*: The name given to a section of the South Transept of Westminster Abbey where writers, playwrights, and poets have been commemorated and/or buried.

Prince Harry, The Duke of Sussex, *pg. 79*: (b. 1984) A member of the royal family, Harry is the son of Diana, Princess of Wales, and Charles, Prince of Wales. He is the younger brother to Prince William and is sixth in line of the succession to the British throne. Prince Harry was born Charles Albert David.

Prince William, The Duke of Cambridge, *pg. 79*: (b. 1982) A member of the royal family, William is the son of Diana, Princess of Wales, and Charles, Prince of Wales. He is the older brother to Prince Harry and is second in line of the succession to the British throne. Prince William was born William Arthur Philip Louis.

Princes in the Tower, The, *pg. 27*: Edward V (b. 1470) and Richard, Duke of York (b. 1473), were the sons of King Edward IV and Queen Elizabeth Woodville. The two boys were last seen in the summer of 1483. It is believed that they were murdered by their uncle, Richard III, who then became the successor to the throne. The skeletal remains of the two boys, estimated to be 10 and 13, were discovered beneath a stone staircase in the Tower of London in 1674 during tower repairs. Both princes were placed in urns and laid to rest in Lady Chapel at Westminster Abbey.

Queen Elizabeth Woodville, *pg. 113*: (c. 1437–1483) Wife to King Edward IV and mother to Edward V and Richard, Duke of York. She is buried beside King Edward IV at St. George's Chapel at Windsor Castle.

Queen Victoria Memorial, *pg. 185*: The memorial is located in front of Buckingham Palace and consists of the dominion gates, memorial gardens, and a monument in honor of the Queen who died in 1901. The monument is constructed of white marble and gold, is 25 meters high, and in addition to Victoria, there are statues that depict courage, victory, truth, charity, constancy, and motherhood.

Queen's Guards, *pg. 184*: Infantry and cavalry soldiers assigned to protect the official royal residences in the United Kingdom. When the ruling monarch is male, their title becomes the King's Guards. They are tourist attractions in their own right, as tourists come to take pictures of the guards with their stoic demeanor and elaborate dress. Guards are not allowed to smile, cannot be relieved from duty for bathroom breaks, and are instructed to fall like toy soldiers if they feel weak.

Queen's House, *pg. 304*: The half-timbered Queen's House was built in 1530 during the reign of King Henry VIII. The structure faces the Tower Green and was constructed in a very different style than the rest of the Tower of London. The quarters were probably built for Anne Boleyn, who was executed soon after their completion.

Ravenmaster, *pg. 12*: A prestigious position within the ranks of the Beefeaters and which is responsible for tending to the ravens at the Tower of London.

Ravens of the Tower, *pg. 11*: Legend has it that if the ravens were to leave the Tower of London, the monarchy and Britain would fall. The story suggests six ravens must be present as a staple at the tower to prevent this calamitous event. A raven graveyard exists to honor the birds who have served at the tower.

Red Telephone Booths, *pg. 179*: These once popular, functioning public telephone kiosks now serve as a British cultural and design icon worldwide.

Richard III, *pg. 17*: (1452–1485) Seized the throne from his nephew, Edward V, in 1483. Many historians believe he was one of the worst and wicked of kings. He died in the Battle of Bosworth Field, leaving Henry Tudor (Henry VII) to become king. Richard III is also known as Richard Plantagenet and Richard of Gloucester and was laid to rest at Leicester Cathedral.

Ripper, *pg. 154*: A reference to the unidentified serial killer known as Jack the Ripper who terrorized areas around Whitechapel district of London in 1888. The killer's methods were heinous and precise, leading many to believe he was likely a surgeon or a butcher by trade.

River Thames, *pg. 148*: This 215-mile river flows through southern England, passing through London. It is the longest river that exists entirely in England. Also known as 'The Isis.'

Royal Archives, *pg. 199*: Located at Windsor Castle, the Royal (or Queen's) Archives are a division of the Royal Household of the Sovereign of the United Kingdom. The collection contains documents that capture the most iconic and important moments in British History. The archives house collections ranging from personal and private correspondences of monarchs to national speeches and administrative records.

Royal Botanical Gardens, *pg. 185*: London's largest UNESCO World Heritage Site, this garden is home to the world's most diverse display of flowers and plants. Kew Palace, once a summer residence of King George III, is located on its grounds.

Santa Claus, *pg. 35*: Originating in Western Christian culture, Santa, also known as Kris Kringle, Father Christmas, and Saint Nicholas, is believed to bring presents to well-behaved children's homes on Christmas Eve.

Shaolin, *pg. 46*: The Shaolin Monastery is the most famous temple in China, renowned for its kung fu fighting Shaolin monks, the ultimate Buddhist warriors. The history of Shaolin begins about 1500 years ago, around 480 CE, when a wandering Buddhist teacher came to China from India. He was known as Fotuo. In 496, the Emperor of China gave Fotuo funds to establish a monastery. This temple was named Shaolin. The temple's fortunes rose with the ascension of the Tang Dynasty in 618. Shaolin monks famously fought for the Tang Emperors against opposing warlords. By the 1500s, the monks of Shaolin were famous for their staff-fighting skills. The monks also had learned caution, however, and empty-hand fighting began to displace weapons training—it was best not to seem too threatening to the throne.

Sir Isaac Newton, *pg. 25*: (1643–1727) Newton is considered one of the most influential scientists of all time, serving as a key figure in the scientific revolution. He is well known for formulating the laws of motion and the law of universal gravitation. He is also known for the development of the reflecting telescope. He is buried at Westminster Abbey in the nave in front of the choir screen, near a monument built to memorialize his legacy.

Sir Walter Raleigh, *pg. 210*: (1552–1618) Raleigh was an explorer who was instrumental in the colonization of North America, helping to settle Virginia and prepare the area for additional English settlements. After a secret marriage, imprisonment at the Tower of London, a second exploration, and a charge of treason, Raleigh was executed via a beheading at Old Palace Yard at Palace of Westminster. His final resting place is at St. Margaret's Church at Westminster Abbey. Raleigh is often remembered for popularizing tobacco in England. Many historians believe he was also a major author and contributor to Shakespeare's famous works.

Spiritual Justice, *pg. 252*: The obliquely pointed sword that is one of two swords of justice.

St. Edward's Oxford, *pg. 259*: Affectionately referred to as "Teddies," St. Edward's is a boarding school founded in 1863.

The school's alumni list includes many notable scholars and public figures, including Laurence Olivier.

St. George's Chapel, *pg. 162*: Roman Catholic church located in London. It is also known as The Metropolitan Cathedral Church of St. George.

Stephen Hawking, *pg. 25*: (1942–2018) Hawking was a professor of mathematics and a prolific physicist. He wrote the international bestselling book *A Brief History of Time.* Driven to become an eminent researcher and scholar, Hawking is remembered for his theory of black holes. In 1963, Hawking was diagnosed with amyotrophic lateral sclerosis (ALS), which eventually left him paralyzed. He continued to communicate with a speech-generating devices and to pursue his research until he succumbed to the illness 50 years after his diagnosis. Hawking is buried at Westminster Abbey in the nave between Isaac Newton and Charles Darwin.

Sword of Mercy, *pg. 252*: A blunt sword that signifies leniency and compassion, also referred to as Curtana. Accompanies the two swords of justice in the coronation ceremony.

Sympathy for the Devil, *pg. 178*: A Rolling Stones' song written by Mick Jagger and Keith Richards and released in 1968. It is featured as the opening track on their album *Beggars Banquet.*

Templars, *pg. 15*: The Knights Templar were a devout group of Christian soldiers who worked to protect European pilgrims visiting the Holy Land. The organization has fascinated historians and the public for centuries. Accounts of the Knights Templar and their financial resources, their military might, and their efforts on behalf of Christianity during the Crusades are an ongoing part of popular culture.

Temporal Justice, *pg. 252*: This sharply pointed sword signifies a monarch's judicial power, including the power over one's life and death. Once potentially the executioner's sword, the sword is now strictly ceremonial.

Three Ceremonial Swords, *pg. 252*: Three swords representing kingly values that are carried unsheathed and upwards during the British coronation ceremony; a practice dating back to 1189.

Tower Green, *pg. 216*: Located just south of the Chapel Royal at the Tower of London, Tower Green is a space where nobility were executed. Privacy was deemed a privilege, thus allowing the execution to be carried out away from spectators. Queen Anne Boleyn, Queen Catherine Howard, and Lady Jane Grey were all believed to have been killed here. Today, a memorial marks the location of the scaffold.

Tower of London, *pg. 8*: Officially Her Majesty's Royal Palace and Fortress of the Tower of London, this historic castle is located in London on the north bank of the River Thames. Construction began 1066 under the direction of William the Conqueror, and it has served as both a royal residence and an eventual prison. Today, the tower is primarily a tourist attraction, welcoming more than two million visitors through its gates each year.

Traitors' Gate, *pg. 301*: The Traitors' Gate is an entrance through which many prisoners were delivered to the Tower of London. The gate was commissioned by Edward I and provides a water entrance to the Tower and was designed to provide privacy for the royal family. The name Traitors' Gate came into use in 1543, when that moniker was used on Anton van den Wyngaerde's *Panorama of London*. Prisoners were brought by barge along the Thames, passing under London Bridge where the heads of recently executed prisoners were displayed on pikes. Notable prisoners such as Sir Thomas More entered the Tower by Traitors' Gate.

Tupac, *pg. 290*: (1971–1996) Born Lesane Parish Crooks, Tupac Amaru Shakur is referred to by many as one of the greatest rappers of all time. He performed under the stage names 2Pac and Makaveli. He was shot and killed in 1996 in Las Vegas, Nevada, USA. It is suspected that gang activity and/or a fellow rapper, Notorious B.I.G., were involved in the killing.

Unknown Soldier, The, *pg. 35*: In 1916, Reverend David Railton, an army chaplain, saw a grave marked with a rugged cross with the inscription 'An Unknown British Soldier.' He proposed that the unknown soldier be brought to Westminster Abbey to be buried amongst the kings in honor of the hundreds of thousands of soldiers who died on the battlefields in World War I. In 1920, the chaplain's vision came true as 'The Unknown Warrior' was laid to rest in the abbey at the west end of the nave.

Wakefield Tower, *pg. 302*: The Wakefield Tower is one of the 21 towers that compose the Tower of London. It was built by King Henry III between 1238–1272. The Great Hall of the Wakefield Tower is memorable as the scene of Queen Anne Boleyn's trial. Several murders took place in the Wakefield Tower, including those of King Henry VI and his notorious wife Margaret of Anjou.

Water Lane, *pg. 302*: The Water Lane runs east to west inside the Tower of London as part of Outer Ward. It was built during the Tower expansion in 1275–1875. Reclaimed from the river, the inner wall stood on the river's edge—hence the name

Water Lane. Historically, much of this area was occupied by workshops, offices, and the Royal Mint.

We Are the Champions, *pg. 289*: Considered one of the most recognizable rock songs, "We Are the Champions" was written by Freddie Mercury and recorded by the British rock band Queen. The song was first released in 1977 on their album *News of the World.*

Westminster Abbey, *pg. 3*: The abbey was founded in 960AD by Benedictine monks. Today it serves as a symbol of the Christian faith and offers daily services, tours, and special events. More than 3,300 famous historical/cultural people have been buried or commemorated at the abbey. Approximately 1.5 million tourists visit the abbey each year.

Westminster Abbey Choir School, *pg. 67*: Located in the Dean's Yard at Westminster Abbey, this boarding school for boys offers students, aged eight to thirteen, academic and musical education. It is the last remaining choir school in the United Kingdom that solely provides education for its choristers. The exclusive student body serves the abbey in the choir, performing daily services, concerts, and other special events.

Westminster Bridge, *pg. 148*: A bridge in London that crosses the River Thames and connects Westminster with Lambeth. The bridge is designed to accommodate auto and foot traffic.

William Shakespeare, *pg. 34*: (1564–1616) Shakespeare was a prolific actor, playwright, and author. He is often referred to as the 'Bard of Avon' and denoted as England's national poet. He is considered to be history's greatest thespian and author. His collection of works includes 39 plays, 154 sonnets, poems, and more. His plays have been performed more than any other playwright's and have been translated in every language. He is buried at the Church of the Holy Trinity, Stratford-upon-Avon, in the United Kingdom and a memorial statue was erected in his honor in Westminster Abbey's Poets' Corner.

Winchester Cathedral, *pg. 96*: Also known as the Church of England, Winchester Cathedral is located in Winchester, Hampshire. It is one of the largest cathedrals in Europe.

Windsor Castle/Palace, *pg. 162*: A royal residence at Windsor known for its architecture. It has been used by the reigning monarch and is Europe's longest-occupied palace. Within the castle walls sits St. George's Chapel.

ACKNOWLEDGEMENTS

WE ARE SO grateful for friends and family who reviewed and helped revise this story. Your belief in our vision and many insights were invaluable. Many thanks to the incredible team at Atmosphere Press for their guidance in bringing our ghosts to life. To those who read this book, thank you for allowing us to take you on this fantastical journey. We hope you enjoyed the ride.

ABOUT ATMOSPHERE PRESS

ATMOSPHERE PRESS IS an independent, full-service publisher for excellent books in all genres and for all audiences. Learn more about what we do at atmospherepress.com.

We encourage you to check out some of Atmosphere's latest releases, which are available at Amazon.com and via order from your local bookstore:

Twisted Silver Spoons, a novel by Karen M. Wicks

Queen of Crows, a novel by S.L. Wilton

The Summer Festival is Murder, a novel by Jill M. Lyon

The Past We Step Into, stories by Richard Scharine

The Museum of an Extinct Race, a novel by Jonathan Hale Rosen

Swimming with the Angels, a novel by Colin Kersey

Island of Dead Gods, a novel by Verena Mahlow

Cloakers, a novel by Alexandra Lapointe

Twins Daze, a novel by Jerry Petersen

Embargo on Hope, a novel by Justin Doyle

Abaddon Illusion, a novel by Lindsey Bakken

Blackland: A Utopian Novel, by Richard A. Jones

The Jesus Nut, a novel by John Prather

The Embers of Tradition, a novel by Chukwudum Okeke

Saints and Martyrs: A Novel, by Aaron Roe

When I Am Ashes, a novel by Amber Rose

Melancholy Vision: A Revolution Series Novel, by L.C. Hamilton

ABOUT THE AUTHORS

DR. ASHLEY WELLMAN has been a scholar specializing in crime since 2008. She has published dozens of academic articles, spoken at national and international conferences, and frequently serves as an expert commentator in the media. She turned to creative writing in 2018 to redefine her life and create magic for her daughter, Reagan. Ashley writes children's stories and is the curator and owner of aMUSEd Fine Art & Extraordinary Books in Eureka Springs, AR. She hopes her work will inspire others to find adventure and friendship in all places.

DR. PATRICK KINKADE has spent the last 30 years of his life working as a teacher and scholar. He is currently a professor of Criminal Justice at Texas Christian University. Pat is published in both academic and popular presses and has hosted television programming in the United States, Australia, and Great Britain. He looks forward to a rapidly approaching retirement to continue to travel, explore, and create memories with friends and family. He has a love for literary fiction and treasures his collection of children's books and fantasy novels almost as much as time spent with his three sons, Zac, Nic, and Max.

Made in the USA
Monee, IL
17 October 2023

44711423R00204